LISA HELEN GRAY

HAYDEN

A NEXT GENERATION CARTER BROTHER NOVEL
BOOK FOUR

HAYDEN

FAMILY TREE

(AGES ARE SUBJECTED TO CHANGE THROUGHOUT BOOKS)

Maverick & Teagan

- Faith engaged to Beau

-Lily

-Mark

-Aiden

Mason & Denny

-Hope

-Ciara

-Ashton

Malik & Harlow

-Maddison (Twin 1)

-Maddox (Twin 2)

-Trent

Max & Lake

-Landon (M) (Triplet 1)

-Hayden (F) (Triplet 2)

-Liam (M) (Triplet 3)

Myles & Kayla

-Charlotte

-Jacob

Evan (Denny's brother) & Kennedy

-Imogen

-Joshua

PROLOGUE

MEN!

Time and time again I've gone through the same crap with the opposite sex. Mostly with the men I've dated. I don't know why I bother. If I were more attracted to females, I'd be putting all my efforts there.

I'd probably get more orgasms too.

Russell, my current boyfriend of two months, is hit or miss. And not just in bed. He's good looking with a bit of roughness to him, just the way I like it, but he has his flaws. In fact, he has a lot of them. The only reason I've put up with the wanker this long is because I don't want to prove that my exes were right when they said I self-sabotage my relationships.

Maybe I do. Maybe I don't.

What I do know is that I'm not this person. I don't let anyone walk over me.

Tonight is New Year's Eve, and Russell and I were meant to be spending it together at a new club that opened in town. It's cold, and I'm wearing a black shimmery dress that drops just below the globes of my arse. It's girly, along with the underwear I spent a fortune on to give Russell a show later tonight; a last ditch-effort to save our relationship.

I'm glad I didn't let Hope talk me into wearing stilettos. Instead, I opted for my black ankle boots, giving me comfort and a rocking look.

Twenty minutes I waited outside the club, which was ten minutes longer than I would have given any other guy. This isn't the first time Russell has cancelled on me, but at least with all those other times, he had the decency to text or call. I haven't heard a peep from him tonight, so unless he's dying, I'm going to kill him.

Fuck trying to prove others wrong, and fuck Russell. No one treats me this way and gets away it.

With that revelation in mind, I head to the door, anger simmering inside of me.

My frozen finger hovers over the call button to his flat, ready to push his number, when a guy who looks to be in his mid-fifties pushes open the door. Smiling at me, his teeth rotten and yellow, he says in a gentle voice, "Go on in, out of the cold, little one."

I wink, sliding past him as he holds the door open. "It's the small ones you have to watch out for."

He laughs. "Yep. My wife would tear me a new one if I ever stepped out of line. She was small, but fierce."

"Happy New Year," I tell him, waving goodbye.

"Happy New Year," he calls after me.

The door shuts, blocking the cold breeze and no doubt saving my legs from turning blue. I make my way across the foyer and push the button to call the lift.

There's a buzz echoing from a light flickering down the hallway, yells and screams coming from adults and children in rooms above. I grimace when I hear doors being slammed and smell the foul odour surrounding the short entrance.

I'd never be able to live in a flat. The noise alone would make me commit murder. It just seems to echo, making the infuriating sounds so much worse.

When the doors open, I step into the lift and press the button for the sixth floor, before crossing my arms over my chest. The lift jolts as it ascends, and I wince, wishing I could have taken the stairs. But during my second visit to this charming building, I learned that they are far riskier. Crackheads sleep on the stairs, along with the homeless, trying to keep warm. Some are okay, but others need to learn when to leave another person alone.

Yet it was the bad odour that made me regret taking them. It's what I imagine a garbage dump smells like.

I scan the tiny space of the lift, cringing at the smell that is no doubt coming from the yellow liquid puddled in the corner. It's covered in graffiti, and even though it has a camera in the corner, my guess is, it doesn't work.

It's nothing like my brother Landon's old flat, which is upscale, warm and inviting. This place seems like it was built with no care and is now forgotten to those who are meant to keep up with the maintenance.

But here is all Russell can afford on the hours he gets at work.

And since he's the first guy I've dated that has a job and doesn't live with his parents, I don't mind where he lives. It isn't like I can take them home with me. I wouldn't put it past my dad to have cameras on the front and back door, ready to defend my 'innocence'. My dad would slaughter him and hum a tune whilst doing it.

Getting off on his floor, I head over to his door, not bothering to knock. He leaves it unlocked when he's home, so when the handle tilts down, my question of whether he's in or not is answered.

Anger sears through me and my pulse slams against my neck when the distinct sound of fucking echoes throughout the flat.

I can handle a lot of stuff when it comes to men. I can pay for my own food, open my own doors, buy my own shit and even pick them up if need be. I can even tolerate bad manners, to an extent. But the things I can't handle in *any* relationship are uncleanliness, lying, and fucking cheating.

Instead of leaving, I carry on down the hall and past the bedroom, where there's a distinct sound of skin slapping and loud moans coming from inside. I'm just about to pass the bathroom when I come to a skidding stop, pausing just outside the door when an idea hits me.

An evil grin spreads across my face as I step inside the small room. I was going to change his hair gel to glue, but I'm under a time limit and I've got no clue if he even has any glue. The toothbrush calls to me, so I grab it and scrub the grime from the toilet before dipping it into the stained yellow water, then wash the bits off that get stuck to it. The toilet was the one thing I made him clean before I even came over. I haven't been around for a week, so it's disgusting. I guess he wasn't planning on us coming back together tonight, even after I cancelled on my cousin's party.

Next, I head to the cupboard that holds the boiler. After years of watching my uncles fix stuff, I've learned how that stuff gets broken, especially with two triplet brothers. I turn the hot water tap off before completely breaking it, cringing when it makes a loud *clink*. I pause, waiting for any signs they heard me, but the sex marathon continues, fuelling my anger.

The girl he's fucking gets louder, and all I can do is grit my teeth and roll my eyes.

"Bitch, he ain't that good," I mutter, helping myself to some eggs, flour and tomato sauce. I grab the mop bucket, which is full of dirty water, and start making my concoction. Maddox had fun with this one as a kid, though he never used dirty water. Once it's all in there, I look through the cupboards, cringing when I find the stale bread. I throw that in there too before finding a few other items, including bolognaise sauce, brown sauce, and some kind of jelly—though when I open the sealed bag, I don't think that's what it is. I tilt my head into my shoulder, covering my nose as I try to get myself under control and stop gagging.

Looking around the small kitchen, the fridge catches my attention. I grin at hitting the jackpot and do a quick dance before yanking the door open.

Everything is for the taking, and it's gross as fuck.

Milk weeks past it's expiry date and a few tubs of already made foods fill the shelves. Perfect for what I have in mind. I quickly set on pouring it all into the bucket, turning when the foul odour gets stronger.

Breathing through my mouth, I lift the bucket and head out of the kitchen, my body locking when I see the string of underwear and clothes strewn across the room. I block it out, heading towards the sound of them fucking.

I lift my leg and kick open the bedroom door, before stepping inside. I try to veil the simmering anger, but it's no use. The second I step inside, the sight alone has fury thundering through me. He actually thought he would get away with this.

The globes of his pale arse bounce up and down like a jockey on coke. Whenever he got that excited with me, it diminished my arousal. It's a shame because he's a good-looking bloke and has the right goods down below. He just needs to learn how to use it. Which is why I always demanded to be on top. I could control his movements then.

The girl squeals, begging for more, and I cringe at the desperation. I guess she'll fake it till she makes it.

Neither have noticed me, or felt the anger swirling around the room, which gives me time to walk closer to the bed.

"Honey," I call out in a sickly-sweet voice.

Russell squeals, jumping away from the girl and turning to me, wide-eyed and open-mouthed. "Don't tell your family. It was an accident," he rushes out, holding his hands together in prayer.

I inwardly snort. Like it's my family he has to worry about right now. The one he should be worried about is standing right in front of him.

But again, he underestimates me and what I'm willing to put up with.

"Get out!" the girl squeals, failing to cover herself.

It takes me a few moments to realise where I know her from. She's the slag that moved in across the hallway a few weeks ago and had no problems flaunting her body.

I narrow my eyes on Russell. "No, falling down a set of stairs is an accident. Cheating is a choice."

"We can work this out," he pleads, sitting up, his floppy dick hanging low.

Yeah, I have too much self-preservation and dignity to ever fall for that crap.

"Happy New Year, you wanker," I sing, before throwing the concoction all over them both, exploding into laughter when something thick and brown runs down his forehead, over his nose, and into his mouth. His scream is cut off when he begins to choke on the mysterious substance.

I mentally clap myself on the back as the two try to scramble off the bed.

To further my revenge, I hold my phone up, snapping a picture. Luckily, the indecent parts are covered in either crap, soggy bread, or the blanket, so I won't need to black anything out.

Clicking on the Facebook app, I quickly find Russell's Facebook page and post the picture, with the caption, 'When you not only discover your ex cheating, but find out it's because he's into the sick stuff. Russell, I hope she can give you all your sick desires'. #WhenHeTakesCheatingToAnotherLevel #GladItWasn'tMeHeShatOn

Grinning, I put my phone back in my bag and turn to leave, but the bat resting next to the bedroom door calls to me.

Screams really.

And my dad always said never to let anyone take advantage of me. It would be wrong to not listen to him.

I shrug, ignoring my mum's inner voice telling me to calm down, and swing the bat over my shoulder. I pass Russell and Blondie, who are struggling to get untangled from the sheets.

Huh, they weren't that tangled before.

"My eyes burn!" he screams, swiping thick goo out of his eyes as he tries to get out of the bed.

"Your dick just poked me in the eye! Stop moving!"

"Fuck! What went up my arse?" he squeals, and the high pitch of it has me cringing.

And gagging. The smell is horrendous.

A huge sigh escapes me as I tune out the fighting going on behind me. Bringing the bat up higher, I swing it down, smashing the fifty-two-inch television in the centre, shattering the screen. His Xbox is next, and oddly, I feel more satisfied destroying the love of his life than I do throwing a bucket of random crap on him.

"Oh my God, did you just vomit on me?" he growls.

As I turn to leave, laughter spills out of me as I watch the girl struggling to hold it in before throwing up all over his crotch.

"Are you getting hard?" she screeches, pushing him away from her.

Stepping out of the room, I head for the front door, but her bag on the floor stops me. I look behind me to the bedroom, hearing them still yelling at each other.

She deserves it, Hayden. She slept with a guy she knew was taken.

With that thought, I bend down, searching through the suitcase she calls a bag.

"Gotcha," I cheer when my fingers clasp around the cold metal of a key, before dashing out the door.

I only wish I could be here when they realise they don't have hot water to wash all that crap off. And they won't be using hers for a while.

Still laughing, I make sure to shut the front door behind me. Whistling the Game of Thrones theme tune, I head over to the lift and press the button to go down.

Hopefully I'll still be able to make it to Faith's party.

A woman with two kids steps out of the lift, her eyes widening when she hears the expletives coming from Russell's flat.

I twist my lips as I pretend to wince. "It's shocking, isn't it?"

She nods, still open-mouthed as she ushers her kids away. The lift hums as it descends.

It's only then that I realise I'm not upset about him cheating. In fact, it gave me the perfect out. Because no matter how many men say it's girls who get emotional during a break up, I've only ever encountered men who do. They beg, get clingy, call you constantly, or threaten to sleep with your sister, one you don't even have. It's ridiculous. And if I hadn't caught him tonight, I can only imagine what he would have gone on to do.

I tried to make it work between us, yet that spark just wasn't there. I'm young, however I want more than meaningless encounters with the men I've dated. And then there's my overbearing dad to take into account. Russell was that dimpy at times, my dad's insults would have flown way over his head.

As I push through the doors leading outside, I lose the keys, throwing them in the bin just outside the door.

Cold licks at my face and bare skin and creeps under my clothes, causing me to shiver.

It's then that I hate myself for not bringing a jacket. I had hoped to spend the night inside a hot, sweaty club. Not outside where I could get frostbite.

Annoyance flares through me when my phone begins to ring and vibrate. If it's Russell calling to try and—

Seeing my dad's name flash across the screen, I groan. However, it's still better than listening to Russell cry.

If he's calling me about those damn mini muffins, I'm going to lose it. He can't prove it was me who ate them. And it's been a week. He really needs to get over it.

I answer. "Dad?"

"Hey, Hay," he greets.

"Har, har," I mutter, rolling my eyes.

"Hey, sweetie," Mum calls over the phone. I hear cars in the background, so they must have me on the car speaker.

"Hey, Mum."

"Um, I know you had plans with your friends tonight, but we need all the family tonight. Would they mind if you cancelled?"

"Um, yeah, I can. They won't mind at all," I tell her, my voice hard at the end when I think of Russell.

"What aren't you telling me, woman?" Dad screeches, and I wince, pulling the phone away from my ear.

"Nothing. Will you just drive, already?"

"Liar," he accuses. "Where do you want picking up from? I'm coming to get you," Dad explains, talking to me now.

I sigh, looking up at the block of flats, knowing I won't be able to talk my way out of it. "I'm not out with girlfriends."

"Where are you?" he asks, his voice calm, stern. It's his 'I mean business' voice.

I suck in my bottom lip. "I'm at the Duncan Fall flats. I was going out with my boyfriend."

"Boyfriend?" he explodes, and I roll my eyes at his dramatics.

"Not anymore," I rush out before he goes into one of his rants. All I bloody need is for him to give me a sex education lesson again. The first time was horrifying enough.

"Who is he?"

"That guy I said was trying to sell me a vacuum last week."

"That weird looking kid who was flirting with you?"

"Dad," I groan, wishing he'd drop it.

"What happened tonight, then?" he asks, his voice hard.

I smile, bouncing on the balls of my feet. "He cheated," I cheer.

"Um, why are you happy? I'm going to rip his balls off and feed them to the pigs."

I snort. "We don't have pigs, Jaxon does," I tell him, then cringe when I realise who I mentioned, so I rush on before he can go on yet another of his rants. "It's fine. I caught him and his new neighbour going at it, but before I went in, I made the Maddox Concoction and added a few of my own things. I'll send you the picture later. Don't worry, I got my revenge."

"That's my girl," he hoots, and I hear my mum groan.

"Thank you." I beam, even though he can't see me. "I just hope he doesn't call the police and sue for damages."

"If he knows what's good for him, he'll never speak of it again," Dad growls, and I hear a horn honking loudly in the background. "Fucking move! We don't have all year; it ends tonight."

"Max, calm down," Mum scolds.

"Fucking old drivers."

"She was in her twenties," Mum snaps.

"Guys," I call out, beginning to shiver. "Why are you coming to get me?"

"Jaxon is marrying Lily tonight," Dad explains, shocking me to my core.

"What?" I screech. "When, how—*what*?"

He laughs. "I'm not happy about it, but I love her and want her to be happy. We visited Jaxon tonight, got a few things straight."

"You mean you threatened him."

Dad sighs, exasperated. "I'm not a violent person, Hayden." He takes a deep breath when I snort. They nearly killed Jaxon when they overreacted. "Lily doesn't know and we need all the help we can get."

"All right."

I'm all for giving Lily a happily ever after. It was my dad, uncles and cousins who hadn't seen how in love the two were or how happy he made her.

"Oh, and I've done a timeline on who was in the house last week. It's only you who could have eaten those muffins."

"Dad!" I snap, pissed he brought it up. "You can't prove anything. Whoever ate them—and I'm not saying I did—clearly enjoyed them. They didn't save you one. You need to move on."

"I'll get you back for this if it was you. Don't think I've forgotten that it was you who ate the last of the pigs in blankets at Christmas."

"Dad, just hurry up. The new year starts in a few hours and it seems we have a wedding to plan."

"Kids. I told your mum, if we didn't wrap it—"

"Dad!" I screech, before ending the call.

―――――――――――――

I DISCRETELY WIPE away the tear that slips free. No fucking way am I showing these fuckers the wedding got to me. They'd never let me live it down. I could blame it on all the alcohol I'd consumed, but I'd be lying.

Seeing Lily find her happy, warms me. She's always been a kind soul, and just like the rest of our family, I treated her like she was made of glass. I regret that. Because maybe we held her back from finding her freedom. She's the strongest of us all. And Jaxon made us see that.

"You know what they say about weddings," Reid Hayes drawls, stepping in front of me and blocking my view.

This should be good.

I cock my eyebrow at him. "If it was a funeral, I'd say, you're next, because if you spout some cheesy line at me right now, it *will* be your funeral next."

He grins, flashing those pearly whites. "I think they only say 'you're next' to couples at weddings. But if you want to get busy—"

"The fact you said 'busy' puts me off," I interrupt, not even turning to look at him. Instead, I take in Faith's home and huge land. It's a beautiful four-bedroom house. A little outdated, but with the work they're putting into it, it will have the upgrades it needs to look perfect.

If it wasn't for the work they had put into her new practice for stray animals, it would already have been completed. I'm kind of jealous she has it. She's worked her arse off to get where she is. That said, I'm really glad I'm not the one who has to mow the grass every two weeks.

Everyone is still partying away, even though Lily and Jaxon left. I thought for sure once the ceremony was over, the Hayes family would have gone home, but their mum, mine, and Aunt Teagan are having an animated conversation near the gazebo, laughing and joking.

Reid interrupts my musings. I had forgotten he was even here. "You'll give in eventually. You can't resist my charm."

I size him up, slowly scanning his body, taking in his ripped jeans and black jacket that has been left open to reveal his black T-shirt, his abs tensing under the tight material. His body is lean yet muscular, his tanned skin covered in tattoos. But it's his eyes that draw you in. His smoky, dark green eyes hold intelligence, and no matter his mood, they always show his easy-going, light personality. They shine bright and are pure sex.

It's hypnotising.

I flick my top lip with the tip of my tongue, drawing his attention to my mouth. "You couldn't handle me, Hayes."

He smirks, raising his hand to tuck a piece of hair behind my ear. The touch is gentle, smooth, and I can't help but look more closely at him, giving him a second thought. "Something tells me you're too scared. You're worried *you* can't handle *me*."

With a flick of my hair, a flutter of my lashes, I step closer, straightening my back so my breasts jut out, brushing up against him. "Really? Or are you just hoping I don't say yes, so you don't make a fool of yourself?" I ask, keeping my voice low, seductive.

He gulps, gripping my sides, just under my boobs. His thumbs stroke lightly under the soft globes of my breasts. It feels good. Erotic. And I wish he'd go a little higher. "Why don't we find out," he rasps.

Through my peripheral vision, I make sure no one is looking. Seeing the coast is clear, I press closer, leaving no room between us.

My lashes flutter at the feel of his hardness against my stomach. He's big. He wasn't just bragging.

I have to bite my bottom lip to stop the moan from slipping free.

I tilt my head up, watching him for a moment, wondering if this is something I can really do. It's Reid Hayes, a guy who has driven me insane and made me lose my temper on more than one occasion. I'm surprised I haven't killed him yet.

On the other hand, I just got cheated on. I need this.

Fuck it!

He's hot, I'm hot, and the sexual tension has always been there, no matter how much he could repulse me at times.

I rapidly blink up at him, trying to keep my calm. "No one can know," I warn him.

He blinks in surprise, clearly not expecting me to agree. "That means you can't brag to your friends."

I snort. "Like that would happen."

"Where do you want to do this?" he whispers, caressing my breasts, his thumbs brushing over the hard peaks of my nipples.

I rise to the balls of my feet, swaying forward at the intimate touch.

I want more.

If he can get me this revved up with such a simple move, I want to know what else he can do.

I grab his hand, surprised to find it warm when it's so cold tonight. "I swear to God, if you've had these down your pants to keep them warm, I'm going to lose it," I grouch. "And I know a place."

He looks around, seeing what I'm seeing: everyone is distracted, all high on the night's celebrations.

I pull him towards the side of the main house and head for the outhouse, where Beau works when he's helping Faith out with the pet sanctuary. It's also out of sight from the party.

We stop outside the door and Reid pushes me against it, leaning down. "Don't get clingy. I'm only letting you have me once, baby."

Snorting, I grip his cock over his jeans, smirking when his mouth falls open and his eyes flash with fear. "Trust me, it won't be me turning clingy, Reid." I reach behind me, twisting the handle on the door and pushing it open. "And, Reid?"

"Yeah?" he croaks huskily.

"Never call me baby, not if you want to keep your dick."

His smirk spreads into a grin as he lifts me up off the ground. My legs wrap around his waist as he kicks the door shut behind us.

Tilting his head down, he presses his lips to mine, kissing me breathless. My fingers run over the stubble along his jaw as I deepen the kiss.

He slowly drops me down onto the counter—when something sharp digs into my arse.

"Fuck!" I squeal, trying to keep as silent as I can. Tears spring to my eyes as he lifts me back up, looking over my shoulder and down. He chuckles, swiping something off the table, which clangs to the floor. I look down, noticing nails all over the floor, and roll my eyes. I should have known nothing would be easy with Reid Hayes.

"You okay?" he asks, pretending to care.

I nod, pulling him towards me to continue what we were doing, trying to find that fire that normally ignites between us. So far, there's nothing, even though I was turned on outside.

Our teeth smash together and I groan, pulling away. "Jesus, Reid!"

"Sorry, I was going for hot and heavy."

I shake my head, pulling him back, this time slower. The kiss is good, amazing in fact, but it doesn't exactly make me see stars. There's no toe curling, no lust. Nothing like we have when we banter back and forth.

It's kind of disappointing.

I've thought about fucking Reid more than once, and I wanted to see if it would be as good as I imagined.

It's not.

He stops kissing me when he realises I'm not into it. Pulling back, his eyebrows drawn together, he tilts his head to the side. "What?"

"Um, this is awkward."

He rolls his eyes. "Maybe we've had too much to drink?"

"Maybe," I mutter, but I don't think it's that.

As hot as he is, I don't think I'm attracted to him in that way. And it's kind of a downer, since I really needed the release after tonight.

The door to the outhouse flies open, and when I look, my dad and mum are standing in the doorway, open-mouthed.

"Oh my God," I cry out, shoving Reid away before I straighten my dress, pushing it down my thighs. I jump off the side, giving my mum an appreciative glance when I see she's holding Dad back.

"Honey," Mum calls, tugging his arm back.

His face is red with anger, and he's glaring holes at Reid. "It's not free fucking rein on my daughter, dude. She's off limits. We might have let the whole Jaxon thing go, and yes, Landon is with your sister, but it ends there. You don't get to look at my daughter, touch her, or, or, or…" he waves his hand around, flustered.

Reid smirks. "Fuck her?"

Dad grits his teeth, taking a step forward, but me and Mum get between the two. I glare up at Reid. "Go! This was a mistake anyway. You're clearly all mouth."

I don't believe what I'm saying, but it will be good for Reid to have a knock to his ego, especially after pissing my dad off.

Astonished, his mouth drops open. "I'll have you know I'm the shit in bed."

"No, you're probably just shit," I tell him, rolling my eyes.

"Let's go, right here, right now. I'll prove you wrong," he rushes out, reaching for his belt buckle.

I smile, patting his head, glad the banter is back between us. I won't admit it, but I get thrills sparring with him. "It's okay. I'll keep it a secret."

My dad's boisterous laughter breaks us apart, and I turn to find him leaning against Mum. "Yep, we're good here, Lake."

"I can't take you anywhere," Mum groans, shaking her head at him.

"I'm not shit in bed!" Reid yells, throwing his hands up.

We all stop by the door and turn to look at him. I shrug, smiling. "Guess we'll never know."

ONE

MY JOB ISN'T SOMETHING I'M exactly proud of. In fact, I'd have more dignity stripping my clothes off than doing some of the degrading things I have to do.

But I have to do it.

It isn't necessarily the job title. I want to be on the radio after all. It's because it isn't me.

I don't do the whole mushy, girly crap. I'm a rock chick that listens to rap or rock—unless I'm drunk; then I'd rock to Taylor Swift if one of her songs came on.

I drink rum, swear like a sailor and don't give a fuck about speaking my mind.

The only reason I haven't quit is the anonymity, the pay, and the fact some of these girls really need someone to give it to them straight and not spout some bullshit they think they want to hear.

What I want to do is what I was promised I would work towards when I first started: a chance to report on real life issues going on in the world right now. I don't want to give advice about some arsehole who can't get his shit together.

I don't want to tell my family about my job. It isn't some huge secret like they assume. I just don't want to deal with the awkwardness that would happen when they become supportive and shit. And having them listening in while I give sex and relationship advice is something that will scar us all.

Mum thinks I work in a care home, since I work in the home Hope works at when they're understaffed. Dad is oblivious, probably telling himself I work in a church every time he goes to sleep at night. I've got no clue what the others think, but it's probably just as crazy as what my dad could come up with.

And to be honest, I like to keep them guessing.

Chrissy, our floor manager and one of our many producers who help run the different online forums and podcasts, walks into the staff room, shaking me from my thoughts. My gaze zeros in on the McDonalds coffee cup in her hand, and I wish I'd thought to stop off and get one on my way in.

I'm always jealous of how professional she looks when she comes into work. She makes the corporate style look fashionable and elegant. Her light blonde hair is tied low at her nape today and crowned with a thin black headband. She has on a white shirt with an open collar, showing off her silver necklaces that match her bracelets. Thrown over her blouse, she has on a loose black blazer, the sleeves crumpled to her elbows. And paired with her black suit trousers, she has on black pointed boots. I sigh, knowing I'll never look that professional. She might be thirty-five, but she looks twenty-five. She's smoking hot.

Tonight, I'm wearing ripped jeans and a black T-shirt with 'AC/DC' written in washed-out red. They look good with my new biker boots Dad got me after he lost a bet on who could drink the most shots on New Year. What he doesn't know is some of mine were water.

"Our new boss, Clayton Cross, starts tonight, and he wants to change things up," Chrissy greets.

Hope blossoms in my chest. "Really? Do you think he'll give me a new angle for the podcast?"

She bites her bottom lip, her face scrunching up. "I don't know. We get high ratings through your channel. He won't want to stop that."

I groan, stretching back into the softness of the red armchair. It's midnight and I'm tired, the past week catching up with me.

"Have you met him?"

She shakes her head. "No. Mr Cross had his lawyers deal with the takeover. None of the producers were involved. I didn't even get to say goodbye to Mr Cross Senior."

I snatch the coffee out of her hand, taking a gulp. "I thought for sure when Cross Senior left the company to his son that we'd be able to make some changes. Isn't his son meant to be young?"

She tilts her head. "I'm not sure. I think someone said he was in his late twenties. Don't quote me though."

There's a ruckus out in the hallway before Leana, one of our computer experts, comes barrelling inside, slamming the door shut behind her. Out of breath, she bends over, gripping her knees.

I'm on my feet in seconds, taking a step towards her. However, when she tilts her head up, cheeks flushed, I stop, crossing my arms over my chest and taking a step back.

I know that look.

It's the look she gets when she's done something… well, Leana.

"He's hot," she pants out, waving her hand at us.

I glance to Chrissy for answers, but she looks just as confused as me. She shrugs and we both turn to look down at Leana, waiting for her to catch her breath. She's always been nutty. I think sitting at the computer all day and night didn't help her form any social skills. She reminds me so much of my cousin Charlotte it's not even funny. Both girls are intelligent beyond belief, and neither have a filter when it comes to speaking their mind. It's verbal vomit and there's nothing they do to avoid it.

Leana's hilarious to work with, especially when she gets flustered over some of the questions she has to read on our online forum. Some of them can be downright dirty.

"Who?" I ask, interested. I've waited months for some eye candy to start working here. Ever since Abel left, there's been no one to ogle.

"Mr Cross," she screeches, before taking a deep breath. Her shoulders slump. "I think I made a fool out of myself."

I chuckle before even knowing what she's done, because I can guarantee it's comical. "What did you do?"

She glares at my amusement. "One, I'm not liking your tone. Two, it's nothing." She tilts her head up, looking to the ceiling.

"Tell us," Chrissy coaxes, hiding her amusement better than me.

Sighing, Leana snatches the coffee cup from me, taking a swig.

Chrissy groans. "I knew I should have called for all your orders before coming in."

I wave her off, staring Leana down. "Come on, spill."

"Bloody hell. Okay. I went to go greet our new boss, first impressions and all that. I took some coffee and muffins and forgot to knock on the door. I didn't think he'd be in yet since we were closed this morning. The main segment doesn't start for another hour. I wasn't prepared," she whisper-hisses, her face turning bright red again.

"What did you do?" I ask, holding back the laughter.

Her head downcast, she slides the tip of her foot back and forth along the carpet. "He spoke, and I was startled at how sexy he sounded. I looked up and I just froze, staring at this… this godlike man. I mean, *model* worthy man. I'm pretty sure he starred in one of my wet dreams," she rattles on, staring off into space.

"Do women have wet dreams?" Chrissy asks from the corner of her mouth.

I shrug. "I've woken up mid-orgasm, if that counts."

"Listen!" Leana yells, quickly looking towards the door like someone is going to burst in.

"Go on," I order, sitting down on the arm of the chair.

She tightens her ponytail, taking a deep breath. "So yeah, I was too shocked over his appearance, and then he yelled at me."

"He yelled at you?" I ask, standing up again. Job or no job, I'll put him in his place. Leana is one of the sweetest and kindest people I know. It kind of makes me sick. Still, no one has the right to yell at her.

"Yes!" She throws her hands up, still red as a beetroot. "I didn't know my left from my right, I was that out of it. I rushed over to introduce myself and give him his coffee and muffins, and I fell."

I cringe, seeing where this is going. Only Leana could do that.

"Are you okay?" Chrissy asks, unable to look at Leana head-on.

"Am I okay? I fell into his lap! Face first!" she screeches.

I press my lips together to keep myself from bursting into hysterics, but it's no use. Laughter spills out of me and I bend forward, clutching my stomach.

"Oh my Gosh," Chrissy murmurs, her laughter more dignified than mine. I'm pretty sure I've snorted twice.

"It's not funny! I went to apologise—while I was still in his lap. My mouth was around his *very* large appendage."

I fall back into the chair, laughing uproariously. "Leana, you have made my day."

"He's going to fire me, isn't he?" she asks, sounding so defeated I laugh harder.

I wipe at my eyes, straightening in the chair. "No, but you should be worried about Stewart."

Her eyes go round. "Oh my God, do you think he'll think I cheated on him?"

Getting up, I walk over. I rub her arm, still struggling to hold back my laughter. "Nope. You have nothing to worry about there."

"Do I pay you to stand around and talk?"

"Mr Cross," Leana squeaks.

My back is to the person with the warm, smoky voice that slides down my spine. My stomach swirls and my heart races. It's pure sex. Husky with a slight hint of a London accent.

I'm not into dirty talk during sex, but fuck me if I don't imagine him doing just that. Though knowing my luck, he's probably dog ugly.

I don't know what compels me to look at Chrissy first, but I do, gauging her reaction to the mystery voice. When the normally straight-laced, dignified woman openly gapes at the newcomer with desire written all over her, I know his looks will match that sexy voice of his.

I slowly spin around to address him, and I'm nearly knocked on my arse.

Damn, he's even hotter than his voice suggests.

His cat-like green eyes with flecks of gold stare back at me. They're sharp, yet narrow, giving him an immediate intensity about him.

Men in uniform have always been my kryptonite—well, that and tattoos.

But I think men in suits is my new favourite look.

His charcoal grey slacks fit him well, especially around the bulge area.

I lick my lips as I raise my gaze, letting it roam over what I hope are hard abs under the crisp, white shirt. His sleeves are rolled up to his elbows, leaving me breathless at the sight of his tattoos and thick veins.

God, even his red tie is bringing on dirty thoughts.

I clench my hand when I go to fan myself. I'm a goner.

His golden skin looks smooth, yet the five o'clock shadow and crooked nose, which must have been broken at least twice, gives him a rough appearance—in a ruggedly handsome kind of way. He wears it well, just like he does his tattoos, which decorate his arms and peek out from the collar of his shirt.

He's everything I want in a guy. The whole package. Not even the age difference bothers me, though he doesn't look that much older than me.

Fingers click in front of my face. I blink out of my haze and stare up at the sharp features of my boss. If I was a normal person, I'd be turning red with embarrassment right now over being caught checking my boss out.

But I'm not.

It isn't in my blood.

His lips pinch together as his eyes tighten, narrowed down on me. "Are you with us or would you like more time staring at me?" he snaps harshly.

And there goes my dream of him being the whole package.

I sigh, tilting my head. "You had to go and ruin it," I murmur, causing his eyebrows to crease.

I guess everyone has a flaw.

"Excuse me?"

I wave him off. "What were you saying?" I ask, ignoring his question. I might not enjoy my job as much as I would doing something else, but I still need it. It pays for my mortgage on the two-bed I recently bought off my uncle.

He looks to the other women in the room, an exasperated sigh escaping him. "Is this really Hayden Carter?"

I grit my teeth. I don't like being spoken about like I'm not even in the room. Chrissy must feel my anger because she runs a shaky hand down her outfit, glancing at me briefly before turning back to him. "Yes, sir."

"And do you wear that to work every day?" he asks, disdain colouring his tone as he critically scans over my attire.

I look down, wondering what he means. The rips might be a little indecent. I have one just below my arse, and at the right angle, you can see the soft globe of my butt. I thought it looked hot.

Maybe he's gay.

"What's wrong with my clothes?" I ask, feeling a small loss of confidence, which is rare for me.

His eyebrows scrunch together as he looks at me like I'm stupid. "It isn't very business-like. You work at a radio station, not in a bar. We have an image to uphold. And it's not appropriate. You are here to work, not flash your body."

Gritting my teeth, I stop myself from yelling at the guy about women's rights. It's my body and I can wear what I like.

Instead, I force a sweet smile, clasping my hands together so I don't reach out and punch him. "Have our contracts changed since we signed them?"

"Excuse me?"

"It's okay," I tell him snidely, yet keep my voice sweet. "You're new. But if you like, I can bring in my copy of my contract, which doesn't state what the dress code is. If I worked front of house or in an office, I'd probably wear what Chrissy is wearing. But, I do not. Therefore, I choose to wear whatever I'd like to wear."

"We'll discuss this later. Things will be changing around here."

"I bet," I mutter under my breath.

"Pardon?"

I give him a wide smile, flashing my teeth. "I said, I'm glad."

He forces a smile, the frown lines giving away the fact I'm annoying him. "I'm changing your segment."

I grin, bouncing on the balls of my feet.

And that… that is music to my ears.

He might have ruined his perfect exterior by being a pig, but hearing those words makes me want to kiss him.

I pump my fist into the air, giving a loud cheer. "Yes! I've been waiting for this day. I have some ideas of my own. I was hoping we could report on real life stories. We could still stream with the same name, so we wouldn't need extra marketing. I was hoping to report on the signs of domestic abuse, on how to get help. Or we could do the dangers of online dating," I ramble, completely blowing off the way his teeth grit together. "And then have a ten-minute news report at the end. We could even add it in to the Late-Night magazine."

"I'm sorry, but did my father leave his company to you or to me?"

"Excuse you?" I reply, clenching my hands into fists.

"No, excuse you," he bites out. "I've been in here all of ten minutes and have been objectified by you ogling me, spoken rudely to, caught my staff talking when they should be preparing to go on air, and now I've been told how to do my job. Who gave you the right?"

"You need to pull the broom out your arse," I snap, ignoring Chrissy and Leana's gasps. He may as well learn now that there's only so much I can take when it comes to being spoken down to. "I gave an idea, one I think the station could benefit from. If you had been here longer than a day, you would know we have calls, emails, and messages swarming through with women asking for help over ex-partners, partners, or over a friend who's dealing with abuse. We can't talk on the matter, even though I've taken a basic counselling course. We have a platform that is listened to by thousands and we use it to give advice on what any one of them could get from a friend or their mum." I take a deep breath, trying not to knee him in the balls. "And you might have it going on in the looks department, but the second you open that mouth, it's ruined, so you won't need to worry about me *objectifying* you."

For a moment, I swear I see his lips twitch, but when I blink, he's glaring back at me, his jaw set in a hard line.

"You can take this as your verbal warning. I won't have members of staff talking to me in that tone. I can replace you with anyone."

I step forward, getting in his space a little. "Well, you need to get used to it. I won't take shit from anyone. I'm polite, on time, and do my job to the best of my ability, even though there are days I hate it. I'm outspoken, and if that offends you, deal with it in your own time. I won't have you or anyone else speaking down to me. If you can't take it, don't dish it. And before you threaten my job, make sure you have someone else who can do it better than me. Your dad fired me twice because I spoke back to him when he was rude, and he hired me back each time, with a raise, because his ratings went down without me."

And it's true. His dad was the sweetest, but whenever he was in a bad mood, he was a right fucking wanker.

He runs a hand through his hair, the motion causing his white, crisp shirt to pull taut over his flexing biceps.

He watches me for a moment longer, seeing I'm clearly not going to back down. "I'm not my father, just remember that." He takes in a deep breath, not looking away. "Now, as you've wasted ten minutes of my time, I will get to it. We're making changes to the segment for the next eight weeks. With Valentine's Day coming up, this is the best time to do it."

My heart sinks, because if he's going to suggest what I think he's going to suggest, I'm going to be leaving here crying.

Pasting on a fake smile, I step away from him, leaning against the desk shoved against the wall. "And what is this change?"

"We are going to be doing a piece on online dating."

I groan. "No."

His wolfish smile gives me a mini orgasm. Jesus, he should come with a warning.

I can see it now: '*He can make your knickers melt right off you with one smile.*'

"Oh, yes. We've partnered up with Date Night to give people a virtual experience of online dating. And you, Miss Carter, will be testing out these dates for your segment."

I shake my head. "Nope. No way. My cousin was robbed and attacked by the person she met online. Just no. Have you even heard the horrors?" I screech, getting dramatic. It always works for my dad. "And since when did you become my pimp? Are you asking for a law suit or do you just live dangerously?"

Chrissy clears her throat. "I'll, um, leave you two to it. I'll go get us set up."

No one pays attention as she hurries out of the room with Leana, leaving Clayton Cross and I in a stare off.

"I very much like to live dangerously," he tells me, his voice low, demanding. It holds a promise, and all I can do is squeeze my legs together. I swallow, trying to appear unaffected. "Have you finished?"

"Did you want me to go on?" I snap back, aware he's taken a step closer.

His lips twitch and my heart swoons. He really should stop doing that around me.

"One, this is all completely legit. Date Night has partnered up with a series of businesses all over England to give people a safe environment in which they can go on a date."

I snort, looking at him like he's mad. "Are you kidding me? Have you been living under a rock or are you just naïve and stupid?"

"Careful. I'll be happy to give you a written warning," he threatens, a glint to his eyes.

I just bet he would. I shake away the dirty thoughts of him bending me over the desk and smacking my arse with a ruler.

I step forward, poking him lightly in the chest. "People can be whoever they want to be in this day and age. You won't even know a serial killer until they've stabbed you in the chest. Everyone is easily fooled by a pretty smile and witty charm. Hell, even people online can portray whoever they want. At home, they're probably miserable bastards who hate Christmas, and yet online, they *love* it."

"Christmas?" he asks, eyeing me like I'm one sandwich short of a picnic.

I roll my eyes. "I'm not doing it. It's dangerous, and I don't know about you, but I love my life."

"Look at it this way, you might find someone who likes your *bubbly personality*."

I raise my eyebrow at his tone. "Don't be sarcastic. It doesn't suit you. And how do you know I don't have a boyfriend who will be extremely jealous?"

Something I don't recognise flashes over his expression before he masks it.

"Do you?"

I think about lying for a second. I could even back the lie up and blackmail Reid into being my boyfriend. But putting up with him for six weeks would drive me to commit murder. He's still sore over New Year's and uses every chance he gets to make it right. Like that would happen. I had a moment of misplaced judgement.

"No, but it doesn't matter. I'm not doing it, not after what happened to my cousin." I pause, using the opportunity to sell one of my ideas. "Which would never have happened if people knew the dangers of online dating."

He places his palms on the table, leaning over a little. "I'm not going to pussyfoot around you. We've already signed the contract. It's happening with or without you. But my guess is, you don't want to lose this job, otherwise you would have left by now. If you don't do it, I'll have to find someone who will." He steps back before leaning against the table next to me.

I turn to flash my glare his way. "Are you serious? You can't fire me."

"I can and I will. My dad handed me this business to make it great again. Other areas of the station aren't doing as well as yours, but even your ratings have dropped since last year. We want to branch out, do something new."

"Then go with some of the ideas I've told you."

"You really want to talk about domestic abuse on a station called Love Loop Live?"

I sigh, leaning back against the wall. "Okay, you have me there." I look up at the clock on the wall, seeing the time. I need to go. "All I'm saying is, you need to listen to the calls we don't answer or have time to answer. We keep them logged, along with messages and emails in case we ever use them for our online article. You'll see what the listeners want."

"The online dating won't be the only thing to change," he tells me, getting up from the table and brushing off his trousers.

"What else?"

He grins, flashing his pearly whites. "It will no longer be a girl-only call in. Men will finally have a chance to voice their opinions and ask questions. I've heard your podcasts. You rip men to shreds. It's only fair they can defend themselves."

"Are you kidding me?" I growl.

"No, a little diversity goes a long way. I think having two streamers will bring in more listeners."

"What?" I practically yell. "It won't be my show anymore?"

"Nope, for forty minutes you'll be working alongside someone else."

"Who, because if it's Barry from upstairs, I quit."

His eyebrows draw together. "Nope, he got fired this morning."

I smile, giddy over the fact. I thought for sure that after we set his car on fire, he would leave the female employees alone. He didn't. I was getting ready to bring in my brothers, but I guess now I don't have to. "That's the best news I've heard all day."

"That's good, because you'll be working alongside me until we find a replacement."

The blood rushes from my face as I stare at him. I must not have heard him correctly. He can't be serious.

"You have to be kidding, right?"

He holds open the door for me. "No, so let's go launch our new segment."

I glare at him, calculating how much damage I'd have to cause for him to give the company back to his father.

"Have you not heard of the term, 'If it ain't broke, don't fix it?'"

He shakes his head at me. "Before you leave in the morning, we need to discuss your wardrobe and hair. Don't think I've forgotten."

I follow him, spitting and cursing all the way to our studio.

TWO

ANGER THUNDERS THROUGH ME as I glare over the mic at our new hot boss. Chrissy and our technical team must feel the tension brewing between us because they're staying away from me, whereas before, they didn't mind joking around and playing pranks on me before we went live.

I press the online button, leaning forward in my seat.

"This is Hayley and you're listening to Love Loop Live," I greet, smoothing my voice out. I still worry I'll fuck up and say my real name, especially now with Clayton here. I feel like the world is tipping off its axis. He's driving me crazy.

Hopefully, my listeners won't know I'm two seconds away from throwing my Ribena all over my new boss.

Clayton, sitting smugly back in his chair, arches an eyebrow at my name. I ignore him. There's no way I'm using my real name online. And I'd quit before he even thought about changing it.

"Tonight, we have something new in store for you. I'm sorry, ladies, but it looks like we're going to have to bring the men to the party," I explain, reading from the script Chrissy handed me. Reading the next line, I decide to go off track, giving Clayton a smug look across the table. "But don't worry, ladies. This is the moment many of you have been waiting for. Men will finally listen to what you have to say. Maybe now they can find the front door and not the back." I pause, putting on a pout as Clayton narrows his eyes on me. Sighing down the mic, I continue. "Or better yet, maybe they can find our G-spot and let us get some before they get theirs."

Surprising me, Clayton leans forward, turning on his mic. "Maybe it's not the man doing it wrong?"

"Are you saying women are?"

"No, but it takes two," he tells me, running his eyes over my breasts, his gaze heating.

Taken off guard, it takes me a minute to gain my composure. "For some, it only takes one," I quip. "But that's neither here nor there." I pause, my lips twitching a little. "So, why don't we start the show with listening to your worst or funniest sexual experiences. Call in or message."

Glancing over at Clayton, I become unnerved. I know the look he's giving me all too well. It's the look my brothers get when they're about to do something dumb and don't realise it until it's too late.

"While we wait, Hayley, what's your worst sexual experience?"

"Why don't you tell us yours?"

He grins, showcasing dimples, and I sigh, clenching my legs together. "Ladies first."

"I guess it would be the time I tried shower sex. Not only did the fucker get shampoo in my eyes, but he didn't have the strength to hold me against the wall. He ended up dropping me on my arse."

I arch an eyebrow at him, daring him to go on. I can tell by his slack jaw that he didn't think I'd answer. What he doesn't know is that wasn't even my worst. Reid was my latest disaster—well, kind of, since we never got to the fun part.

Clayton chuckles, the raspy sound causing me to shiver. "Did you at least get to orgasm that night?"

I keep my smoky, dark brown eyes on him when I lean forward to answer.

"Yes. I've got a wild imagination, so it didn't take long to get myself off when I got home."

His eyes widen at my declaration as he shifts in his seat, unable to meet my gaze. He clears his throat, opening and closing his mouth.

"Now, why don't you tell us about yours, Clayton? Oh, and, ladies, Clayton is my new boss, so make sure you give him a warm welcome. I'll post a picture for you all later."

I'm a giving person after all.

I shrug at his put out look, sliding my finger across the screen of my phone before opening the camera app and snapping a picture.

I quickly mail it to Leana, knowing she'll post it online for me.

He clears his throat once again, a pink tinge to his cheeks. "I guess it would be the time I got a blow job off my girlfriend when I was younger. Her parents were away for the weekend, so we stayed in and ordered pizza. Before we had finished eating, we started going at it. She had jalapeños on her pizza, and just when it started to get good, my dick began to burn. It was on fire. I pulled out quickly, just as she bent forward. I ended up poking her in the eye with my dick."

I can't help it, I laugh. His face is so adorable right now. All flushed and rosy. It's such a huge difference to the arsehole I first met.

Maybe having him on the show today is a way for me to change his mind about how to take the segment to the next level.

"Men!" I sigh, playing along. "They can never get the right hole."

"She's the one who nearly gave me a heart attack. My dick was on fire."

I chuckle, shaking my head. "Teaches you for not going down on her first."

His lips twitch into a smirk. "Oh, I went down on her before we started dinner, and she screamed the house down."

"Most women fake it," I tell him, bursting his bubble.

"Trust me, there was nothing fake about it."

"Probably not during oral sex, but I bet it didn't feel or sound the same when you had sex," I argue.

"When I fuck someone, I make sure they're taken care of first."

I take in a steady breath, clenching my thighs at hearing the word 'fuck' roll off his tongue. "You do know it's rare a woman will orgasm during sex? Seventy five percent of women never orgasm during sex, and ten to fifteen never orgasm at all, leaving only ten percent of women who actually orgasm. Most of the time it's brought on by either her finishing herself off when she's alone or during oral sex. They say it's nothing about the man, but believe me, I've been so close to orgasming during sex, but just before I finally get that release, the guy will do something to squash that libido. Or they just have no clue what they're doing."

"Then you've not been with the right man," he tells me, his gaze heated.

I scoff. "That's what they all say."

"When I'm fucking someone, I can guarantee you they aren't thinking about anything but how good it feels. It's not just about sticking your cock in a hole. It's touch, sight, and for some, whether they are in control or not. It's a fantasy. Everyone has one."

My entire body is burning, and I have to look away, unable to be under his scrutiny. The screen beside me shows we have a number of callers.

"Clayton talks the talk, but, ladies, how right is he? A poll will be up on our site soon to see how many of you orgasm during sex, how many of you haven't, and how many of you only orgasm by yourself or not at all."

"It's not talk if it's true," he tells me, not looking away.

I blink, trying to shake off this lustful haze. It's hard when all this sex talk with him is making me hornier than hell.

"Let's go to line one. Juliette is calling from Devon. Hello, Juliette."

"Hi."

"How are you tonight?" I ask.

"Okay-ish, it's why I'm calling. But first, I want to address the sexual tension going on between the two of you. Is he as hot as he sounds?"

I glare at Chrissy, who looks away with a smug smile. Before calls are put through to me, they're screened. She knew exactly what Juliette was going to ask.

"Hotter," Clayton announces, and I groan, rolling my eyes.

"Don't get too carried away; your attitude stinks," I tell him.

"Oh, the picture has just been posted. He *is* hot," she squeals dreamily, and I snort at his condescending smile.

"He's got really small feet," I snap, almost shouting. "And, girls, he wouldn't let me wear my ripped jeans, saying they were too revealing."

"No, I didn't," he argues, looking pissed. "And I don't have small feet."

I wink, leaning forward. "It's okay. Size doesn't matter." I chuckle when he grits his teeth. "And yes, you pretty much did. You should see what I'm wearing Friday. I'm going out after work and won't have time to go home and get dressed."

Friday's are my nights where I pre-record. My uncle is throwing my cousin an engagement/wedding/welcome home party. She gets back Thursday and I can't wait to see her. Jaxon had taken her on a last-minute honeymoon. But then again, their wedding was last minute.

I glance away when his smouldering gaze burns through me. "Did you have a question, Juliette?"

"Yes, I was wondering if you'd give me advice. My boyfriend and I are having trouble in the bedroom. Just when it's good and I'm getting close to orgasming, he does something that irritates me, or he shifts, and it puts me out of the mood. And I never get it back. He gets funny if I ever ask him to go down on me or when I tell him I haven't finished."

I give Clayton an 'I told you so' look before addressing Juliette.

"Girl, do you love him?"

"Yes, we've been together for three years."

"You've got more restraint than me," I tell her, trying my hardest not to give her advice that will upset her. But people call for my crazy. They call for my honesty, so I guess I should give her some. "Tell him straight. Tell him you want an orgasm too. And if he gets funny over you communicating your needs, he's a wanker. You don't need that negativity in your life, especially when you don't even get some for putting up with it."

"Or, maybe him hearing he didn't hit the mark in bed was a hit to his ego," Clayton adds.

"Maybe he should man up and start making things right. He has heard of Google, I'm guessing, so it's not like he has to ask a friend. He should want to experiment. She took a chance talking to him, he should do the fucking same."

His jaw clenches. "Or maybe she's in the seventy-five percent of women who can't orgasm during sex."

He's got me there. "But she admitted she was close. That's more than what most women get.

"Juliette, talk to him again, tell him you aren't satisfied and if he can't act like an adult, then he shouldn't even be having sex. Or tell him you'll find someone who will. If you don't want to break up with him, let him know he won't be getting an orgasm until yours is completed."

"Or you could try something new. Close your eyes when you're in bed tonight and think of your dirtiest fantasy. Everyone has one. Men and women. No matter how kinky it is or taboo, use it. Twist it in a way that will fit you and your man. Maybe then you'll have that push to be so turned on, you're crazed with lust and will finally orgasm," Clayton advises her, surprising me.

I have to wonder if his advice is from experience, and if it is, what does he fantasise about?

"Um, thank you," Juliette murmurs, clearly thinking it over.

I stare over his cut jaw, his firm lips, and wonder if he'll be willing to shut up for an hour while he plays in my fantasy.

Licking my bottom lip, I force myself to look away and read who the second caller is. "Thank you for calling in, Juliette. Don't forget to let us know on our forum how everything went." I pause, waiting for the green light to come on to reveal we've connected to our second caller. "Let's go to line two, where Frankie from Stoke is waiting. How are you tonight, Frankie?"

I hear a sniffle and sit up in my seat, preparing for the worst. We have rape victims and abused women call in, and from time to time, someone slips up and they're put through. It's not like we don't want to help, it's that we aren't allowed.

For a while I've been wondering if I should start my own blog. I might not be able to give professional advice, but I could give them an anonymous platform to talk to others and give my own advice.

"Not good," she answers, before blowing her nose.

"What's up, Frankie? Is everything okay?"

LISA HELEN GRAY   40

"No." The heavy breath of a sigh echoes down the line, and I can tell she's trying to compose herself. "I broke up with my boyfriend a few months ago because I saw a text from a girl on his phone. It ended badly, with a lot of arguing. We were together for a year. But I was cheated on repeatedly before by an ex, and I promised myself there was no way I was letting it happen to me again.

"I've been trying to date again for the past month, but they all keep cancelling or have left me waiting. Tonight was the seventh cancelation, and I found out why when I asked the guy who ditched me. We share mutual friends with my ex, and he told me my ex has been saying some things about me."

Hearing another girl cry over a loser gets my back up. "What did he say?"

"He's been telling everyone and anyone that I'm crap in bed, that I lie there like a sack of potatoes, and that I have a fishy fanny. Apparently, that was the reason we broke up, and the story of him texting other girls was just to cover up the fact I smell. He was trying to save me the embarrassment."

I roll my eyes. It's the oldest remark in the book.

When Clayton leans forward to the mic, I watch him curiously, surprised he would answer this kind of question.

If he fucks up and smarts off some bullshit about how the guy is just jealous and clearly still loves her, I will fuck him up. Because the guy isn't doing it so he has a chance to get her back. He's doing it because he's a fucking wanker. Plain and simple.

"Then it's good you broke up with him, Frankie. Men like that need something to prove. They want to feel powerful, manly, and the only way to put you down is to say something so demeaning. And the funny part is, none of his friends truly believe him. They know he's being a dickhead. I bet whilst you were together, he bragged about you to make them jealous. They're just saving face so they aren't taken the piss out of by the people who do believe it."

I stare at Clayton in disbelief. He got it spot on. But it was more than that. I not only heard the truth in his words, but I saw it too. He meant what he said.

The worry lines across his forehead show his concern too, his compassion for the stranger over the line.

He looks up, and for one single moment, everything around us fades away. For that one single moment, I see him.

Really see him.

A throat clearing snaps me out of it, and I do the only thing I can do at being caught.

I give him a dirty look.

I straighten in my chair, leaning forward a little. "Clayton's right. But I will add that he's an immature dickhead. And I hate to go there again, but we're back to orgasms. I bet every time you had sex, he got his while you didn't get yours. That doesn't mean you're crap in bed. He is."

"Yes, he always did," she sniffles.

"As for the fishy fanny comment, have *they smelled* their privates? And this doesn't go to just you, Frankie, this goes to all the girls. Men piss out of their dicks, and then the fuckers just shake the residue off. At least we have the common decency to wipe ourselves clean."

"We're kind of taught to," Clayton interrupts.

I gnash my teeth at him and he draws back, a line etched between his brows. "I've not finished. I haven't even gotten to the worst part of going down on a guy. One," I start, holding my index finger up, "pubic hair is not your friend. Most of you have more than women but you expect *us* to be the ones to go through excruciating pain to get *ours* wax. And two, if that isn't bad enough, *ball sweat*. Am I right, Frankie?"

She giggles over the line, making my lips pull into a small smile. "Yeah, it's not the best smell."

"I know. You'd think they'd make breathable joggers for them, let that fucker breathe."

"Hey, pubic hair isn't good for men either," Clayton interrupts, looking affronted.

I raise an eyebrow, crossing my arms over my chest. "Please, do tell before I get to the last part."

His lips twitch but a smile doesn't form, disappointing me. "You going to town on a knob isn't the same as us going to town on you. We're licking, sucking and what-have-you *on* your pubic area. I think that should give us a legitimate reason to want you to shave it down there. Personally, I'm not a fan of a girl being bald down there, but I do like them to keep it trimmed. Have you ever gotten a pubic hair stuck in your teeth?"

I cringe, nearly gagging. "Dude, it's not a competition. And going by your expression, you have. Now all I'm going to see or look for is pubic hair in your teeth."

Once again, he surprises me, throwing his head back and laughing. I pause my rant, watching as his face transforms into something more beautiful. He's hotter when he laughs. Lines appear in the creases by his eyes, and a promise of dimples appear in his cheeks. He's hot. Gorgeous.

And I badly want to forget he's a jerk and my boss—and fuck him.

Maybe.

Clearing my throat, I turn my attention back to Frankie and our listeners. "But to finish off what I was saying, they also don't have to taste cum. I don't give a shit what those romance books tell you, it tastes like shit. It's nasty."

Frankie tries to smother her laughter. "Thank you."

"What for? I haven't given you any advice."

"No, but instead of stressing and worrying over what they're all saying over social media, I can laugh about it. And I can finally see the silver lining and tell them where to go."

"Well damn," I mutter, sinking back in my chair. "I was going to advise you to tell them where to go. I'm proud. I'm all for revenge, so anything petty you can do, do it, though I will guarantee not retaliating will get to him more. It's like smiling at the person who loathes you. They hate it. But I can be bitch, so I can't talk for everyone."

"I will. Thank you, Hayley. This has really helped me."

"You're welcome. Let us know how it goes." I pause, waiting for Chrissy to end the call before addressing my listeners. "We're going to take a fifteen-minute break, but we have some banging tunes for you to listen to. So, go put the kettle on, make yourself a cuppa and just enjoy. We'll be back after the break to see what Kyle needs help with."

My eyes follow Clayton's movements as he slowly drops his headphones onto the desk, staring right at me.

"What?" I ask, forcing myself not to check whether I have something in my teeth.

"You're as good as my dad said."

Pride fills me. There are times when I don't enjoy doing these live chats, but I still dedicate and pride myself on doing the best I can.

"Thank you."

"You're welcome. But you really need to watch your mouth when addressing callers. No woman should swear like that."

I grit my teeth as I glare holes into him. "Fuck you."

THREE

IT FEELS LIKE A LIFETIME SINCE CLAYTON STARTED working at the station last Monday.

His new addition to the segment has added a lot more to our workload, and we're paying for it. Yesterday lasted longer than expected because of it, so today, I'm dragging after another long day pre-recording.

I used to love pre-recording on Fridays.

Fridays before we pre-recorded were boring and slow. I ended each segment hating the sound of my own voice.

Everyone was always busy, going out and getting pissed on the weekends. So it got awkward when we didn't get many callers.

When Mr Cross Senior came up with pre-recording the show and using callers from previous segments we couldn't get to, I thought it was great. We could still it like we were live as it's never edited.

Now, not so much.

With the new addition letting men call in added to the podcast, we have been overloaded with calls and messages.

It's crazy.

The website crashed on Tuesday because so many people were wanting to get in on the next podcast or voice their opinion. And Clayton wasn't even around for me to take it out on him. It was his idea to bring in the opposite sex, but he couldn't be bothered to be there to help deal with the extra load. If he doesn't hire someone else to help with the extra work soon, we're going to ruin a good thing. Because no one likes to be ignored and they'll eventually get tired of trying.

I want to throttle him.

And kiss him.

And then throttle him again.

But that's neither here nor there.

Wednesday, he was just as frustrating as Monday. I've got a lot of people in my life who know how to wind me up, but not in the same way Clayton does.

I've never met a man who makes me want to fuck him then kill him in the same breath.

And the worst part about it: he doesn't seem as affected by me as I am him. After our small moment on Monday, I couldn't stop thinking about him. It's been driving me nuts.

Wednesday, I wore my shortest denim skirt with thick black tights and paired it with my favourite black, ripped T-shirt. It was hot, giving a glimpse of my stomach and cleavage.

And the only reaction I had from him was one of annoyance.

Not lust.

Not desire.

Annoyance.

And I can't stand the fact that I cared.

I even made sure I looked hot as fuck tonight for Lily and Jaxon's party, but he isn't around to see it. It isn't just about getting a reaction to me as a person, I get a kick out of trying to blow his fuse. He's just so easy, and if the past few days have taught me anything, it's that he hates that he can't tell me what to wear.

Pulling my leather jacket tighter around me to at least try to cover some of my cleavage and ward off the cold air, I walk up the steps to Uncle Maverick's and Aunt Teagan's.

Fairy lights have been wrapped around their shrubs and over the archway that leads to their small porch.

Growing up, the only thing I hated about this house was that it wasn't on our street. Before Nan and Granddad died, they lived in the house next door to my aunt Harlow and Uncle Malik, and at the back of the garden was Mason and Aunt Denny's house. Down from them was our house, and just around the corner, still considered the same street, was Myles and Aunt Kayla's house. But Maverick and Teagan chose to move a few streets away.

Personally, I think it was because my dad drove him nuts, but no one will either confirm or deny it.

And now, slowly, we're all moving away. It's kind of depressing, even if we aren't far from one another.

Hearing a car door slam, I drop my hand from the front door handle and turn to see who it is. Maddox glares at his sister, Madison, who is giggling away. I take a step down the stairs, waiting for them to acknowledge my presence.

"Holy fuck! What happened to your eye?" I call out, taking a few more steps down when I see how nasty Maddox's eye looks.

He glares down at Madison, who laughs harder. "Nothing."

Knowing Madison will tell me, I look to her. "He snuck into Lily's house last night. Or tried to. Jaxon punched him, thinking he was someone breaking in."

"He knew it was fucking me. It was payback," Maddox grouches.

Her lips press together as she looks away, trying her hardest not to laugh. It's useless though, because moments later, she bursts into laughter once again.

I grin at Maddox, who seems so unhappy, he looks like a lost puppy. He's probably more bothered that he doesn't look as good with a black eye and swollen jaw than he is that Jaxon hit him. "What on earth drove you to do that?"

He throws his hands up before dropping them to his sides with a slap. "They took my fucking key. How else was I meant to get in?"

My lips twitch in amusement. "Not what I meant," I tell him. "She's married. You can't go sneaking in anymore. They want privacy."

He tilts his head, his brows furrowed. "What does that have to do with anything?"

"God, I worry how you made it this far in life. They have sex."

"Hayden!" he yells, covering his ears.

The front door behind me flies open and I glance over my shoulder to see Dad looking flustered. "What's—Woah, what happened to your eye?" Dad asks, grinning as he comes to stand by my side.

Maddox looks away, pretending to be interested in the old lady unloading her car, so I answer for him. "He snuck into Lily's and Jaxon hit him."

Dad snorts, crossing his arms over his chest. "I would have punched you too, but I'm an arsehole." He pauses, seeming to think about something for a second. "Then again, if it were me, he wouldn't have known I was there. I wouldn't have been punched," he brags.

Maddox glares. "Are you serious? They'd hear you from outside, old man. And he didn't sneak up on me. I was drunk, tired and hungry. You know what I'm like when I'm hungry."

Dad's stomach grumbles at the mention of food. "Yeah, but you're still an idiot for sneaking in their house. Didn't she take all our keys except Teagan's?"

Maddox pouts, throwing his arms out in a tantrum. "He's changing everything! She didn't care if I was there before or if I ate her food. Now he's there, he's all, 'Don't eat that, we need to go shopping'; 'You can't sleep here, we want the night to ourselves'; 'Maddox, you have your own house to play the Xbox in'. I just want some peace, ya know?"

I shake my head, then roll my eyes when my dad nods in agreement. "I hear ya. Maverick was the same. He would always be, 'This is my dinner'; 'Did you take the last pack of Jammie Dodgers?'. I mean, who can eat just one, am I right? And whenever we used to go and see the girls, he'd go on like he was the favourite," he rambles, then snorts. "I'm the favourite. Everyone fucking loves me."

I glance at Dad, seeing he's serious. "Dad, you do realise most of the population want to murder you."

He glares down at me. "No, they don't, and if this is about that old lady across the street, I don't want to hear it. I paid for that pizza. It was mine. And she needs to get over it."

"It was meant to be for her. She ordered it," I tell him, rolling my eyes.

"Like you can talk. Didn't you steal Aiden and Bailey's food not long ago?"

Fuming, I place my hands on my hips and turn to him. "Hey! That's not fair. I was doing them a favour. Sunday was poorly and the food was going cold. You know how Aiden is about wasting food." I take in a breath before continuing. "And wasn't it you who stole the cake Aunt Kayla made for Uncle Myles last year?"

"It was my birthday too," he snaps back.

"She made you your own," I yell.

"What on earth is going on?" Mum calls out, rubbing her arms up and down against the cold.

Dad presses his lips together, his eyes scrunching as he narrows them on me, warning me not to talk.

"Nothing, Mum, we were just talking about how Maddox shouldn't be sneaking into Lily's."

Mum looks over at Maddox in disappointment. "Maddox, sweetie, they're married. You can't keep doing that."

Pushing past us, he huffs, heading into the house as he mumbles how unfair everyone is being.

Mum looks at the closed door in concern. "Maybe we should get his dad to sort his neighbours out. They must still be making a lot of noise."

"He doesn't want to move," Madison replies. "He's been waiting on the council to do something. The last time he spoke to them, they said they would be installing something to prove they're making noise."

Dad, suddenly straightening, glances at Mum. "Did you leave the cupcakes out?"

She sighs, looking up to the sky. "Yes, Max, I did. I bought them for everyone, not just you."

"God dammit, woman, you know these kids eat us out of house and home."

Please give me strength to get through tonight.

LILY AND JAXON ARE yet to arrive. It's taking a toll on my uncle Maverick. He's finding it hard letting go of his girls, and with Faith's wedding coming up, it's showing. From as young as I can remember, my granddad told us how Maverick was the caregiver, the one who went above and beyond to help raise his brothers, even after Granddad was given custody and he no longer needed to put that pressure on himself. I wish there was something I could do to make it better for him.

His expression morphs into one he only gives us girls when Bailey hands over Sunday to him so she can clean up the mess she's made behind the sofa. He laughs at the mess the beautiful little girl has made of herself. It seems the mini Carter will take after her dad and love her food. She has icing, chocolate and ice cream smothered around her mouth and down her dress. I should feel an ounce of guilt—I saw what the little girl was up to—but I don't. Those cupcakes were the best.

My ringtone blares from my jacket pocket. Pulling it out, I groan, loudly, seeing 'Hot Jerk Boss' flashing across my screen.

"You okay?" Mum asks, her glittering blue eyes pinning me in place. "You've been acting weird all week. Is it that boy?"

Silencing the call, I place my hand on Mum's arm. "It's not about him, Mum. He was forgotten the minute I walked out of the flat. It's just work."

"Difficult customer?"

I laugh quietly as I bump my shoulder into hers. "No. I don't deal with customers as such."

"I wish you'd tell us. We're already proud of you, and we'll be proud no matter the profession."

"Even if I was a stripper?"

She flashes her megawatt smile at me, one that matches my own. "Even if," she tells me. "You could teach me some moves."

My phone starts again and I roll my eyes at the name I put Clayton under. "I should take this. They won't stop calling otherwise."

"Go on, we can continue after."

I give her a brief hug before walking out of the living room and past everyone talking amongst each other. I head upstairs, where it will be quiet and no one can overhear. Everyone, even the Hayes family, is downstairs, so they're all occupied.

Going up the stairs, my eyes run over the pictures hung on the wall, one's I've seen a thousand times. But the one at the end catches my attention. It's new. I'm not sure who took it but it's lovely, and not only because the girl pictured is angelically beautiful.

It's Lily and Jaxon on their wedding day. From what I remember, they had just finished giving their vows. Lily's expression is one of awe, but it's the love shining in her eyes for Jaxon that really moves me. It's the same strength of love I see in Jaxon's as he gazes down at Lily, her hands in his.

It's breath taking.

A lump forms in the back of my throat at the sight. I want love—who doesn't? But I've never gone out of my way to find it. I won't force the next guy I'm with to be my 'one'. It's either there or it isn't. I won't rush it. In fact, it's not something I've been overly ecstatic to find.

But seeing it captured in one frame… It makes me wonder if I'll ever get it. If I'll ever feel that level of emotion these two clearly share with one another. If I'll ever have what my parents have.

Holy fuck!

Would I find someone who would put up with my dad's crazy? Would I want someone who couldn't handle my dad's crazy?

The terrifying thought has me nearly tripping up a step. Gathering myself, I push open the door to Faith's old room and answer the phone when it begins to ring again.

"If someone doesn't answer, it usually means they're busy or asleep," I greet, my tone snappish.

His laugh is loud and unrestrained. "Do you always answer your phone so rudely?"

"Only to those I deem annoying."

"Maybe if you answered the phone, I wouldn't have had to keep ringing."

I sigh, exasperated. "Is there a reason you called so urgently?"

"Yes, a couple of reasons. I've got your new contract to sign."

"And I told you, I'm not signing it. There is nothing wrong with what I wear. Unless I turn up in my underwear, you can't tell me to change my appearance."

I wait for him to clear his throat. "We'll discuss it before next weekend."

"Why next weekend?"

"Because we're setting up your online dating account."

I groan, angry. "I told you, I want to keep my anonymity. If my family find me on that dating site, they will kill me. You've not met my dad, and trust me, you don't want the first time to be on bad terms. He will eat you for breakfast."

"We're using the name Hayley, so it shouldn't be a problem. All potential dates will be screened. It's an exclusive site. It's not like other dating sites where every Tom, Dick and Harry are on there just to get laid."

"I don't care if you're using the name Hayley. I could still be recognised. My family will find out, and then they'll find out it's for my job because they know there is no way on earth I'd ever choose to use one."

"This company is relying on you to come through, Hayden. We need this exposure."

"Date Night can kiss my arse."

"Hayden," he calls sternly.

An idea forms in my mind. "I'll do it on one condition."

"What is that?"

"You let me run a story on the recent break-ins. I've noticed a pattern—"

"I'm going to stop you right there. We aren't a newspaper. We're a podcast/radio station. And I'm not having you look into something that is becoming dangerous."

"Dangerous," I snort. "So, you're telling me you aren't allowing me to run the story because I'm a girl, but you're happy to let me go online dating with men I don't know and could attack me?"

"This is getting out of control. You're twisting my words. I'll see you Wednesday to get you an outfit."

Hearing that, I perk up. "Do I get to choose?"

"See you Wednesday, Hayden," he answers curtly.

I pull my phone away, cursing under my breath when I see he's ended the call. "Prick!"

"Even after hearing that, I still can't figure out what you do for a living," Reid announces, causing a small scream to escape my lips.

I turn around, finding him in the doorway. "Are you fucking crazy? I could have taken you out."

"What with, your phone?"

"How much did you hear?" I ask, knowing I divulged more than I have to my family during that phone call.

"Enough to know you were talking to your boss but not enough to know what you do," he replies, grinning at me.

I roll my eyes. "You do know it's rude to listen in on people's conversations."

He shrugs, not bothered. "I was coming out of the loo and heard you. Thought I'd come say hi."

It's my turn to grin. "You mean, to see if you could get in my knickers. Which is never going to happen. You had your chance."

"You wish. You look like you could do with a good fucking though."

"The fact you described it like that says it all," I murmur, stepping towards him so I can leave the room. He steps in my way, blocking the door.

"In all seriousness, don't let your boss push you into something you don't want to do. I can't say I have experience—we're our own bosses—but I do know neither I nor my brothers would ever treat an employee like that."

Speechless, it takes me a minute to gather my thoughts. This is a side I've never seen of the playboy and joker. "Um, thanks."

He smirks, back to his playful personality. "And as much as you'd enjoy me fucking you, I'd prefer to have you as a friend. I think two members of our family being involved is enough. And honestly, your dad makes me nervous. Did you see him holding that knife when I first arrived? He spent thirty minutes glaring at me."

I give him the once over before tilting my head and tapping my chin with the tip of my finger. "You're right." I shrug. "But Dad wasn't just glaring at you because of New Year. You took one of the cupcakes my mum handed to you. Word of warning: don't go near his food, especially something his wife has cooked. He will kill you."

His mouth gapes open. "Um, okaaay. And right about what?"

I use his distraction to walk past him, chuckling under my breath. He follows, cursing. "He wouldn't really kill me, would he? I'm too fucking hot to be killed. Women all around the world would mourn."

I snort, still not answering.

"Great. Fucking great," he murmurs. "I'm too fucking young to die."

FOUR

WHEN I WALK BACK INTO THE FRONT room, Dad is glowering at Aiden, who is now holding Sunday. It doesn't take more than a guess to know Aiden ate the rest of the cupcakes Sunday had earlier. The cupcakes Mum made.

The second Dad sees me enter the room, his gaze goes over my shoulder to Reid, who is still mumbling under his breath behind me. Every muscle in his body is tensed.

I inwardly groan as he marches over. "Look, I'm too good looking to go to prison, but I will happily do time if he doesn't leave you the fuck alone. And my wife's food."

"Holy fuck," I murmur, hoping he doesn't cause a scene this early into the party.

"Don't let your mother hear you swear. You know how she gets," he snaps, moving in closer and toning the volume down.

"She only does it to piss you off," I admit.

"So…?" he drawls, glancing at the back of Reid's head.

"So nothing, Dad. He was in the loo. I went to make a phone call and we happened to come downstairs at the same time. But you really should give him a break. You're more alike than you know."

He rears back like I've punched him, staring at me like he doesn't know who I am. "Take that back. I'm better looking than that fucker."

I twist my lips in amusement. "That's not what Mum said," I tell him nonchalantly.

"She said what?" he screeches, drawing attention from everyone around us.

"Lily and Jaxon are here," Charlotte squeals, running through the door, her thick, fiery red hair flowing behind her. "She looks so happy."

"This isn't over," Dad hisses, making my grin spread wider. "Now, where is that mother of yours."

Lily and Jaxon step through to the living area and cheers echo around the room. Lily jumps, reaching for Jaxon, before she realises what's going on, her mouth gaping open at the huge 'Congratulations' banner hanging above the large archway.

Uncle Maverick is the first one to reach her, lifting her up and swinging her around. "I've missed you, princess."

"I've missed you too, Dad," she murmurs, choked up.

He gently places her back down on the floor, leaning back to get a good look at her. "Hey, I thought you had a good time."

Tears brim the corners of her eyes, yet her smile is blinding. "I've just missed you all like crazy."

Her mum, Teagan, hugs her. "We Facetimed every day."

"It wasn't the same," Lily explains, ducking her head. "But we had such an amazing time, Mum. It was magical."

Resting her hand on her daughter's cheek, Teagan gives her a gentle smile. "I can't wait to hear all about it."

Lily nods, a pink flush rising in her cheeks as she cuddles back up to her husband, who happily wraps his arm around her as he chats with his brothers.

Charlotte steps up next, while I wait, not wanting to crowd her. "You look amazing. So radiant. Are you pregnant? I mean, it could happen. You've been married a while now and have probably been going at it like rabbits. I can't wait. I'm seeing someone. I think it could be serious," she rambles, and the tension in the room expands.

There's not a male Carter in the room not tense right now.

Myles opens his mouth to argue, but the women in the room look expectedly at him, warning him with their glares to shut up. He sighs, glancing at the floor, knowing he can't argue. He can't make the same mistake Maverick did when it came to Jaxon. They promised they'd never overreact again.

Reid steps up beside me. "I'm a little concerned for my brother's safety, but right now, I'm more concerned for the fucker crazy enough to take on Charlotte Carter."

"And what's wrong with Charlotte?" I grit out, my hand clenching into a fist.

He raises his eyebrows. "What's right with her would have been easier to answer. She's batshit looney. She's hot, don't get me wrong," he rambles, so lost in being an arsehole he doesn't notice me stepping forward until my fist meets his stomach.

"Any fucker would be lucky as hell to be with her."

"Okay, okay," he wheezes.

"She's got time to have babies," Maverick comments, not looking happy about Charlotte revealing personal details about the couple.

Charlotte shrugs. "I can't wait. I love babies."

"Yes, but you're happy to wait, right, baby?"

Aunt Kayla glares at her husband. "I'm happy to have grandkids running around when she's ready."

"Yeah, but not yet, right?" Myles wheezes, questioning Charlotte.

"Not yet. We're going on our first official date tomorrow. I need to get waxed and have my nails done."

"What?" Myles and Dad yell, causing everyone in the room to startle.

"Baby, you don't need to do anything like that," Myles warns her, looking so pale I'm worried he's going to faint.

Mum and Harlow are laughing, leaning against each other as Aunt Denny tries to smother hers but fails.

"Baby, I need to sit down. I do. I need to sit down," Dad tells Mum shakily. "She's going to be in so much pain," he whispers, and I gape at his overreaction.

He's put it on in the past, but never like this. He looks truly distraught.

"Dad, what would you know about the torture of waxing?"

Both Mum and Kayla bring their men a chair and Dad sits down, gulping. "I can't talk about it."

Uncle Myles nods in agreement, staring down at the floor. "I can still feel it."

"Me too, brother. Me too. And the smell... I still smell it."

Myles whimpers. "Our girls."

"The pain."

"Oh, stop being babies," Harlow snaps.

Dad glares, pointing his finger at her. "I nearly died!"

"I was traumatised," Uncle Myles cries out. "She can't do it. I'm not having my baby go through that."

Charlotte takes a step back, her eyes wide. "Sheesh, I can use a razor."

Dad's watery eyes meet mine. "And no babies. Or dating. Or waxing."

I roll my eyes. "Not all of us are wimps, Dad."

"Nobody cares that I suffered a traumatic experience that day. Laugh it up. One day it could be you," he warns, glaring at Maverick and Mason, who are also laughing.

My uncle Malik, as always, remains quiet, his face passive as he listens to Maddison talk to her mum.

"I'm lost. Did you get waxed? Like, on purpose?" Liam asks, watching Dad with disgust.

"Son, don't make me smack you. No one willingly gets waxed," he grits out, glaring at the mums.

Walking over to Lily, I lean in and give her a kiss on the cheek. "You look absolutely stunning, Lil. Marriage looks good on you."

"Thank you." She beams before looking adoringly up at her husband with so much love it hurts to witness.

"So, when *are* the babies coming?"

Jaxon stiffens slightly, glancing over my shoulder before looking down at Lily. "Why don't you give your mum her present?"

Lily nods, picking a bag up off the floor. "Good idea."

Once she's gone, Jaxon turns to me. "Are you trying to get me killed?"

I grin, crossing my arms over my chest. "I need a distraction."

His eyes narrow into slits. "So, you're using me?"

"Yep. My dad doesn't know Mum baked an extra box of cakes. I want them before he finds out."

"So you'd hurt Lily to get cake? I'll buy you a fucking cake."

It's my turn to glare at the handsome fucker. "No, they'd never hurt you again. And I'd never hurt Lily. They'd just give you a stern warning."

"You do realise Aiden has a kid? They can't say anything. And we're married."

I hold my hands up. "Don't try to understand their reasoning. They're Carters. They won't see it like that."

"Now I've got to spend our time here with your dad and uncles glaring at me."

"It could be worse," I tell him.

He scrubs a hand across his face. "You are all crazy. I don't know why I'm standing here arguing with you. Just don't do anything to hurt Lily."

"Wait," I call out when he goes to leave, curious about something. "You didn't answer about kids…"

The corners of his lips twitch. "I'm ready whenever Lily is. Having a son or daughter that takes after their mum will be a blessing."

"Really?" Lily asks, her voice low. She twists her fingers together in a nervous gesture. "Do you mean that?"

I watch as the hardened man's features soften. Jaxon pulls her into his arms, gazing down at her. "Of course I did. I'm already a lucky man where you're concerned. But having a child that follows their beautiful, kind, loving mother… I'd be blessed."

A flush rises up her neck, to her cheeks. "We can talk about it later."

I smile, leaving the happy couple to it.

Dad's sharp glare is still following my movements, so I head over to him, ready to get it over with. He should know by now that he can't control me.

"Dad, you're going to give yourself an aneurism. What is it?"

"Look, I know we said we wouldn't interfere when you guys found someone, but I'm not ready to be a granddad. Not yet. I just got over you three moving out. And you aren't allowed to date until you're twenty-eight. We agreed. Ask your mum. I made the promise when you were a baby, and you know I can't break my promises."

Seeing the rare seriousness coming from him, I walk over and hug him. "Dad, even if I was ready for kids—which I'm not—you wouldn't be losing us. You'd be gaining another person, one who will love you." I take a deep breath. "And just to add: not your promise to make."

His eyes are watery when he stares up at me. "I know, but they'd have Carter blood."

My nose crinkles at the statement. "Um, what does that have to do with anything?"

A tear slips down his cheek. "It means less food for me. I can't deal with that kind of loss. Feeding you three growing up nearly had me starving to death."

"Oh my God, Dad," I groan, glancing at Mum when she steps over.

"Is he giving you the speech about food, because I had to hear it all night whilst I was baking."

A cunning thought enters my mind, and I let my shoulders sag as a sniffle escapes me. I pretend to wipe a tear away, letting my eyes tear up.

"Baby, what's wrong?" Mum asks, glaring down at my dad.

"I just… I just thought Dad loved me," I sniffle, resting my head on Mum's shoulder.

Dad stands, reaching for my hand, and I pretend to flinch. "Hey, I do," he explains softly. "I didn't mean to upset you."

I fake sob, letting the tears fall. "But you won't love my baby. You'd be such a great granddad, but my kid won't know because you'll hate him or her."

"Max," Mum snaps.

"What? I didn't—I didn't mean that," he rushes out. "Baby, Hayden, I didn't mean it like that. I swear."

"But you did," I cry. "And you said we nearly killed you."

He forces out a laugh, gulping when Mum tenses. "I was joking, sweetheart. I tell you what, when you have babies in the very far future, I'll give them half my food."

Mum snorts. "Like that will happen. He ate my last chocolate bar when I was pregnant with you, claiming he had my food cravings."

"I did," he snaps, but then softens his voice when he turns to me. "I'm going to love my grandkids no matter what. Why don't I go to the car and get you your favourite cupcake?"

"We brought them all in," Mum tells him.

Shuffling on his feet, he glances at the floor. "I may have left a few in the car."

"Max, go get them. Now."

"Are we good?"

I shrug, looking away. "Depends. Hearing I'm your favourite always helps."

"You're my favourite," he claims, pulling me into his arms. "I'm sorry for upsetting you. Your mum not letting me eat any cupcakes last night has made me irritable. But then she happily went and shared my yummy goods with the others." He puffs out a breath. "And the more mouths we have to feed, the more I lose."

"It's okay, Dad. I understand," I tell him, sniffling.

"As for dating, I'm your dad. It's going to take time to get used to, but I do promise to try my hardest not to kill them. It's just hard for a dad to see his daughter growing up."

He leans down, kissing my forehead, before he walks out to get those cupcakes. He's going to be looking for a long time, because I ate them on the way in.

"You're a mean girl," Mum scolds. "But I love it."

I laugh, leaning into her. "He deserved it. At least now he'll be nicer when he realises I ate the cupcakes and am about to find the extra stash you brought in."

"Liam ate them already," she tells me gently.

I twist around to glare at Liam. That traitorous bastard didn't even share. "I'm going to kill him for not sharing."

"I'm sure the chocolate fudge cake Harlow baked is still in there somewhere. But Denny also did pulled pork and stuffing, so don't go stuffing your face," Mum warns, but then runs her gaze over me. "Never mind. You're going to do it anyway. I'll go tell Teagan to unlock the kitchen."

I glance away quickly, but it's too late. She sees the guilt on my face. "What did you do?"

I look around, making sure no one can hear. "Don't tell anyone, but Landon saw Charlotte take a cake in when she arrived."

"Oh," Mum drawls, understanding. "Did you get it?"

I glare at her. "Yes, after Teagan locked the door. She didn't see the cake she brought in."

"And you didn't touch the food?" she questions.

"Who ate my cupcakes?" Dad roars, walking into the room. "Who? I mean it—*who?*"

I give Mum a sheepish smile. "I may have helped myself to the tray of pigs in blankets. But Landon did help."

"They were the only ones we had," Mum hisses. "They sold out at the shop."

"I don't know what to tell you. They were delicious," I tell her, before rushing off.

"I mean it. I'm not having it. They were my cupcakes!"

Landon sidles up beside me, Paisley at his side. "Did you grass?"

I narrow my eyes. "No, I didn't, but there's something you should know."

"What?" he asks, his gaze watchful, wary.

I lean in closer when Madison and Maddox begin glaring at us. "Liam ate the spare cupcakes."

"Without us?" he asks, his tone deadly.

"Yep."

"You guys are really scary when it comes to food," Paisley comments, grimacing when I glare at her.

Landon shrugs. "I'm not going to defend my sweet tooth. We all have issues. This is our family's."

"And Liam knows the rules. We always share with one or the other, but we never, and I mean ever, share with Maddox and Madison."

"Maddox is the worst. Madison isn't as stingy with food as him," Landon comments.

"Are you serious?" Paisley asks, eyes wide at Landon. "You ate a large breakfast and a McDonalds before we arrived."

I snicker. "She's rethinking being with you."

He pushes me lightly, glaring, before pulling Paisley tighter against him. "I'm going to see Liam."

I turn to face the others in the room, ignoring Maddox and Madison's glares. Dad is arguing with Malik over food, and although Malik looks bored, inside, he's probably planning Dad's murder.

Lily is cuddled up with Jaxon on the sofa.

Faith is sitting on Beau's lap, her dogs by her feet.

And then there's me.

I want more.

Need more.

I'm a Carter, so I'm willing to fight to get it.

Whatever that 'more' is.

FIVE

A YAWN ESCAPES ME AS MY EYES begin to droop at the sound of rain pattering across the window.

Yesterday, I took a shift at the home Hope works at, and instead of finishing at five in the evening, I worked till four this morning.

One of the live-in residents who was admitted that night was struggling with the new adjustment.

Okay, struggling was putting it mildly. The woman was a bitch and didn't want to be there. I could understand why her grandkids were eager to get rid of her. She caused a fucking riot, and war broke out between other residents on her floor.

And let me tell you, old people aren't as weak as they portray.

I shouldn't have been surprised to find out the new resident was related to Lily's next-door neighbour, Blanche.

Lily has a good sense when it comes to reading people, but somehow, the witch, Blanche, has put a spell on her. She's blind when it comes to Blanche. Lily can't see her for who she is.

Satan.

That old bat threw what she thought was a cup of juice down my back when I was trying to stop Edna from ripping out Betty's dentures. It wasn't.

It was urine.

I wanted to commit Blanche after that incident. The only time she's ever nice is when her grandkids are around.

Maybe no one will find it suspicious if she suddenly dies. I mean, she's old, and old people die all the time.

Right?

"Are you even listening to me?" Clayton snaps, bringing his fork sharply down on his plate.

Pulled back to the present, I push my thoughts of murdering Blanche aside. I remember why I'm here and pay attention.

Clayton looks stressed, and I know he's working hard to get the station back on track.

Still, that's no excuse for being rude, especially when he could have waited until tonight at work to talk to me. I could have gone out myself and got my damn outfit.

"Not even a little. You ramble a lot," I tell him as I reach over, stabbing my fork in a piece of his steak before shoving it in my mouth. If I can't have sleep, at least I can have food.

"This is a business meeting," he snaps, slapping my hand lightly away when I go for more. "You need to pay attention."

"Hey! If you aren't going to eat it, I will."

"If I knew I wouldn't get a word out of you whilst you ate the restaurant out of supplies, I would have just met you in the office," he growls, running his fingers through his thick hair.

I glower at him, chewing quickly and swallowing. "Are you saying I'm fat?"

Mid-sip of his water, he begins to choke. "No, but you've eaten all your spaghetti bolognaise, your two side orders of garlic pizza bread and a bowl of onion rings, and all the extras you had. And don't get me started on the amount of cheese you put on your bolognaise."

I slowly set my fork on the table, unable to look away. "I'm good with you being there, sitting close by. I'm good with the restaurant you've booked instead of that ridiculous spa day. I'm happy with all the security measures in place, and the time. I'll be polite, but still be myself. I'm good with the timeline you've given me to review the date, and the process of it all. What I'm *not* good with, is you sitting across from me, judging me for what I've eaten. I didn't get a chance to eat last night because I was working till gone four this morning at my second job. I didn't get a chance to eat breakfast because I got up late due to very little sleep and then had to rush to meet you," I lie, knowing full well I pigged out last night and this morning on my way here.

I sniffle, glancing down at the table. "I don't like to be judged about my weight."

Surprising me, a hand slides across the table and over mine. I look up from the hand, locking gazes with him. My heart stops.

Growing up with two boisterous brothers and a family of nut cases, I had to be loud, strong. I couldn't let anything get to me. It never meant I wasn't loved, and it didn't mean the other women in my family were weak. It was because I was Max Carter's daughter. And if someone could live through his overbearing behaviour, they could live through anything. And I did. And no one ever apologised if they said anything offensive to me. They knew I could take it, and I could. And if any relative actually upset me, I knew they'd regret it immediately. And not just because I would flip out on them. But because they love me and would never want to truly hurt me.

But until now, I never knew what it meant for someone other than family to care. It gives me pause. A strong pause. And the rapid beat of my heart doesn't make it any better. I want to melt into a puddle, which isn't me. It's so damn confusing. I have to remind myself he's my boss.

And a massive jerk.

With slumped shoulders and straight mouth, he looks ashamed of himself.

And if I was anyone else seeing that inkling of guilt, I would confess or scream 'joke'. But I'm not just anyone. And I kind of get a kick out of making people feel uncomfortable.

"That came across wrong, and I'm truly sorry if I implied otherwise. Would it make you feel better if I let you order whatever dessert you want?"

I snub my nose at him, wiping under my eyes. I dragged him to the shopping centre thirty minutes from home and made sure I chose the most expensive restaurant.

"It would be a start."

"I said I'm sorry," he tells me, his voice gentle, caring. I turn to face him, lost in the orbs of his green eyes. "What would make it better?"

I finish taking a sip of my drink and stare at him straight on. "For starters, you can let me pick my outfit."

"Of course, of course," he says, briefly looking away.

When he turns back, I smile wide and grab another piece of his steak. "Great."

His lips tighten, his eyes narrowing into slits. "You just played me, didn't you?"

I finish chewing before singing, "Like a violin."

He crosses his arms, resting them against the table, a slow grin spreading across his face. "I was letting you choose your outfit anyway."

I gasp, hurt someone actually got one over on me. "You weren't?"

He shrugs. "I might criticize your clothes for work, but I would never have forced you to wear something you weren't comfortable in."

"That's not what it seemed like the first day I met you. Do you know how uncomfortable a suit is? And how ridiculous I feel wearing one?"

"I bet you don't look ridiculous in one," he says, his eyes widening a touch, like he hadn't meant to say it.

I inwardly groan when I automatically wink at him. "I didn't say I'd *look* ridiculous. I'd look fucking hot. I'd just feel it. I don't mind toning down what I wear, but I'm not changing who I am."

He doesn't speak for a moment, seeming to think it over. He gives a sharp nod. "I can deal with that."

"Good. Now, is there anything else you need to go through, or can we order that dessert you promised?"

He grins, shaking his head. "Go ahead, just don't bankrupt me."

I extend my middle finger towards him. "Now you're asking for it."

––––––––––––––––––

"How come you took over the company?" I ask Clayton, shoving my hands into my coat pockets. The wind blows around us, the air frigid and freezing now the rain has passed.

He gives me a second glance before deciding to answer. "Dad isn't well. He's been trying for over a year to keep the station going, but he's not getting better and the workload is getting higher."

"I didn't know he was sick. He'll be okay though, right?"

He ducks his head, tucking his chin under the black scarf wrapped around his neck. "No. He was diagnosed with cancer five years ago and survived, but last year he went for a check up and it's back, stronger and faster. He doesn't have long. He's been grooming me for a while to take over the business, but he got taken in a few weeks ago, moving the process up. He'll be moved tomorrow to a live-in care home."

Well, shit. I kind of liked the old guy. We come to a stop in the middle of the paved walkway surrounded by shops.

Reaching over, I rub his arm soothingly. His attention turns to my hand before coming back to me. "I'm really sorry about your dad. He's a good guy. A hard arse. But… not everyone can be perfect like me."

A small laugh slips free as he fixes his gaze on me in wonder. "You should have been me growing up. You think he was hard on you… he was harder on us. But he loved us. And we love him. It's going to be hard." He gulps, unable to meet my gaze.

"Is that why you fucked up my podcast and then disappeared after two segments?"

He chuckles, turning back. "I'll be doing it every week. The statement was published yesterday. If I want to keep on top of things, I can't be sitting in on every one of your segments."

Tilting my head to the side, I mull it over. "You should give Chrissy and Morgan from the 2nd floor more work. Chrissy has wanted more responsibility in the company. And if you ask me, her diploma is wasted on that place without more work."

"And Morgan?"

I shrug. "He sits around drinking tea for ninety-two percent of his work day. He needs to earn his wages."

"Okay, I'll look into it and move some stuff around."

I lightly shove him in the shoulder. "I'm not just a pretty face." I pause, narrowing my eyes. "But this doesn't mean you can spend more time pissing me off in my studio."

Laughing, he gestures for me to go ahead. "Noted. Now, which of these shops would you like to go in and how long does it, um, take you to pick an outfit?"

I want to kick the fucker in the shin, but because he just told me his dad is dying, I can't. I can't play him up. He already looks pale, probably imagining the amount of time he's got to sit inside a shop.

Before I can even take a breath, two people ahead catch my eye, and I panic. My breathing speeds up as I turn, shoving Clayton away from me. He was meant to go inside the shop, but when he begins to fall, I want to cry. I walk off when he hits the beautician stand, knocking a display of gift boxes all over the floor.

Crap!

I speed-walk faster and paste on a smile when Charlotte and Aunt Kayla wave.

"Hayden," Charlotte calls out.

If it had been any other female in my family, I'd be good, but Charlotte doesn't know how to keep a secret, or be subtle.

And I don't need my dad being… well, being him.

Aunt Kayla looks like she's trying not to laugh, and I know she saw me push Clayton. But there's no way I'm addressing it, not now. Not ever.

"What the hell, Hayden?" Clayton yells, just as Charlotte and Kayla reach me.

I groan, glancing up to the sky.

"Hi Charlotte, Aunt Kayla," I greet, pretending not to have heard Clayton.

"You just knocked me over," he snaps, walking up beside me.

"Do you know him?" Charlotte asks, staring in awe at the man beside me.

"He's homeless. I'm feeding him."

"He doesn't look homeless to me," Aunt Kayla announces, waggling her eyebrows at me.

I scrunch my nose up, glaring at her. "He is," I snap.

"Homeless?" he asks, anger from the push gone and replaced with confusion.

Charlotte claps her hands in excitement. "You aren't Satan like the others call you, you're an angel. I'm so proud of you."

Clayton chuckles beside me, so I shove my elbow in his stomach.

"Thank—Wait, they call me fucking Satan?"

"Why am I not surprised," Clayton mumbles.

Charlotte's forehead creases, and her lips form a pout. "Yes, all the time. Though it's mostly the men in our family. Your dad was telling mine about you finding his sweet stash this morning."

That is it.

"How dare he accuse me. Did you know?" I ask, looking at my aunt.

She tries to hide her smile but it's useless. "I tuned them out, but there was something about a lock box and code."

He can't prove it was me. He can't. And I'm offended he's even accused me. I'm fed up of getting the blame, even if I did do it.

"And video," Charlotte adds, pushing strands of her fiery red hair out of her face.

"Video?" I gulp, feeling the blood drain from my face.

Well, that explains the twenty-three missed calls when I woke up.

"Yeah, he said he had video evidence."

"Oh God," I groan. "I'm so screwed."

Clayton clears his throat, bringing everyone's attention to him. Charlotte smiles, reaching for her pocket and pulling out a five-pound note. "Do you need more food? Not that you look like you're starving. Oh God, that was rude. I mean, you just seem to be in good shape."

I burst out laughing, causing her to stop her rambling. He gently puts his hand up, declining the money. "I'm not homeless."

I can feel his accusing gaze on me.

Charlotte looks from him to me before taking a step back. "He's not another creeper, is he?" she whispers-yells.

"Yes," I tell her.

"No," Clayton yells. "I'm—"

"He's helping with Faith's hen party," I blurt out, turning to glare at him. When he opens his mouth, I elbow him in his side again. "Aren't you?"

"Um, yes?" he questions, and I roll my eyes.

His expression is comical right now, looking at me like I'm crazy.

"You found somewhere for the hen and stag party?"

"The stag party?" I ask Aunt Kayla, clearing my head. No one mentioned the stag party to me.

"Yes, she wants a joint one now. Beau's friends might not make it down in time, so she said to do it as a family and friends thing, somewhere they can go at the same time."

Stuck on the spot, I stare at Clayton with wide eyes. "Um, Clayton had some ideas, didn't you?"

His mouth opens and closes, his face a little pale. "Um, Mingles."

"Mingles?" Kayla questions, her forehead creasing.

"Yes, it's um… it's a club?"

I face him once again, glaring. "Are you asking or telling us?" I snap. A bloody club. It's a hen and stag party, not a Friday night. We could have just done this ourselves. "What kind of planner are you?"

He holds his index finger up to Kayla and Charlotte, before gripping my arm and pulling me away for a second.

"Why are you acting like I'm actually a party planner? I'm not," he grits out, smiling at Charlotte and Kayla, who are watching expectantly.

Grimacing, I shrug. "Sorry. I forgot and got carried away. But what in the hell is Mingles?"

He throws his hands up. "I don't know," he yells, before wincing. He looks over his shoulder again for a second before stepping closer, leaning down to whisper, "It's a new place Date Night wants us to check out. It doesn't have the seal of approval from their company board, so they like to get feedback before any checks are done."

"So what is it? It sounds like a strip club."

He glances back over his shoulder. "I'm not sure. Don't forget, I'm not a bloody party organiser. Just go with it. You can always change the destination after."

"Every year we all go away together, or try to, and once in a blue moon, someone fucks up. Usually one of the lads. If you fuck this up for me, you can kiss your job goodbye. Because I will bury you," I warn him, before turning to Kayla and Charlotte with a bright smile. "It's going to be fantastic, guys."

"Yes, you'll love it. It has everything. A friend of mine owns Cabin Lakes. I can get him to rent you some cabins for a cheap price. If he has any spare."

I turn to glare at him. What happened to changing the destination? Now they're going to hear the cheap price and want to go.

Charlotte looks up from her phone. "Does it have men stuff?"

Rubbing the back of his neck, Clayton nods. "I know Dean had a mud track put in on the new field he purchased. It's meant to be really popular with the locals and tourists."

"So, um, we should get going. Let's make sure it's everything Faith and Beau are looking for before we say anything. We should keep looking."

"Faith said yes," Charlotte announces, ruining any hope I had to change this. "It's in two weeks. She asked if you could book places for everyone, including Jaxon and four extra rooms for any last-minute arrivals. There are a few who still aren't sure if they can make it."

"Me?" I squeak, feeling my breathing speed up. I don't have the patience for this shit. And if it's crap, it's me who will get the blame. "Why me? Shouldn't we keep looking?"

"Yes, you. Lily is trying to calm her down, so she can't. She's getting stressed, so she just wants it booked now."

Kayla's expression softens into a sad smile. "She's missing her grandparents."

Guilt hits me like a truck. "Well crap, of course I will."

Her glove-covered hand reaches out, patting my arm. "You're a good girl."

"Thanks," I tell her, deflated.

I flick my gaze to Clayton beside me, thinking of ways to pay him back for this.

Charlotte steps forward, hugging him. "You've saved the day. Thank you."

He looks at me, his eyebrows furrowed and his jaw clenched. He doesn't hug her back, looking so tense I want to laugh.

"It was all Hayden," he tells her, gently pushing her away.

She turns her smile to me. "I can't believe you said he was homeless, silly. I know you wanted it to be a surprise, but you could have told me. If me and Scott get married, you can organise mine."

Kayla, looking panicked, watches her daughter for any signs of joking. I know she won't say anything about it being too soon for that kind of talk. Not yet anyway.

"I'm amazing, I know," I rush out. "Well, we'd best be going. Loads of organising and all that."

"Have… fun," Kayla comments, her eyes twinkling.

"I'll get Hayden to send me your email address to finalise everything. If I have time, I'll send you a thank you cake," Charlotte tells Clayton.

He smiles smugly, like he's won the jackpot. "Thank you."

"Maybe—"

"That's so sweet of you," I tell Charlotte, interrupting Kayla. I grin over the perfect revenge.

We exchange goodbyes, and once they're gone, I turn to Clayton, narrowing my eyes on him. "You," I snap, pointing my finger at him, "can buy me some new shoes too."

SIX

STEPPING INTO THE POURING rain, I race across the car park to Nightingale Care Home, which is part-owned and run by Tracey, my boss. My fingers ache from trying to keep the umbrella from blowing away.

Stepping under the alcove of the front entrance, I shake the droplets of rain off the umbrella before putting it down. I let out a sigh of relief, grateful I made it, even if I am soaking wet.

The car park is surprisingly empty, due to the unrelenting rain. It rains a lot—it is England—but this is just maddening. It felt like shards of glass hitting my skin it was coming down that hard. The wind isn't any better. Rubbish litters the roads and pavements from where it's blown bins over, leaving destruction everywhere. The news had reported on the radio, saying trees had fallen, blocking roads.

If Tracey didn't desperately need me here, I wouldn't have risked driving into work at all. But some of her nurses and careers had called in to say they couldn't make it, either due to blocked roads or from floods.

Wanting to get out of the cold, I reach for the door, but my phone ringing in my pocket has me stepping back to see who it is. Sliding it out of my pocket, my heart races at the name flashing across the screen. Rob is a colleague of Beau's at the station. I met him at Beau and Faith's engagement party last year. He's ten years older than me but is still a good-looking guy. And although we didn't hit it off romantically, we did get on as friends.

Before the night had ended, he had offered to help if I ever pursued my dream of reporting. I didn't get a degree in English to waste it on love advice.

So, when I asked him for information on the increase in burglaries in the area, he was happy to stick to his word and keep me informed. I want to do an article or a segment on ways to prevent your home from getting broken into; cheap and efficient ways to get security, and what to do if you ever find yourself in the position of being in the house while it's being burglarised. People imagine what they'd do if there was an incident, like your house getting broken into, a fire, or your child being snatched, and you can plan as much as you'd like, yet nothing can prepare you for the real thing. I want to give people advice on how to pull yourself out of that panic, the frozen state, and then give them steps on what to do next.

"Rob, what you got for me?"

He grunts, making me smile. "Hello to you too."

"Sorry, hi. Now, what you got?"

He laughs through the line. "You really are something."

"Amazing, I know. Now…"

The heavy sigh doesn't bode well. A sinking feeling hits me and I rest against the wall, bracing myself. This isn't going to be good.

"You need to find another story."

"What? Why?"

"Just trust me."

"No. I need this. If my boss is going to take me seriously, I have to bring him something he can't say no to, something exclusive."

"It's getting dangerous, Hayden. The reporter, Christina, who was following leads on the story before you, was attacked last night. She was found up Rock

Lane an hour away from where she was taken. She died from internal bleeding in the early hours of this morning."

"Oh God," I breathe out, shocked. "Wait, you were leaking leads before giving them to me?"

"What? No—well, kind of. We have certain information we can release to the public. I just gave her a few extra tips or updates. She was looking into a lady who gave a statement during the Sutherland break in. I did keep some stuff back, but she's a friend of a friend."

"Oh, right."

"Leave it alone now and let us deal with it. I've met your family. I don't want them gunning for me. Your dad kind of scares me."

No! I can't give up. I don't want to get into politics when our papers are already bleeding with political bullshit or rambling about what some celebrity had for breakfast. I want something different, something readers want to read about. I want to give something they can relate to. I need this story.

"Wait, what was she looking into? Maybe they aren't connected to one another."

"Hayden." I can hear the pity in his heavy sigh. "They're connected. She received letters telling her to keep her nose out."

"And that was the only story she was following?" I ask, my brain working overtime, trying to figure out what is bothering me.

"No, there's a couple more, but—"

"So, they might not even be connected. Tell me what you have so I can decide," I order, my voice pleading. "And send me details of the reporter. If you want to keep me safe, you won't force me to look for answers."

"I'll email you what we have, but I'm warning you not to do this."

"Look, earlier I thought this was just some guys looking to make quick money 'cause they can't be bothered to get a job. But it's not, is it?"

"No," he tells me, sounding resigned in the way his voice lowers. "There's a new gang near town that we've been looking into. At first, they didn't seem to cause trouble. They kept to themselves. But now, evidence keeps leading us back to them and they keep changing their location."

"Break-ins?" I ask disbelievingly.

"Yes. We think it's the way for new recruits to join. A way to pledge their loyalty. Their crimes are escalating, like a simple break-in isn't enough now. They need to do something more to prove they're better than the last guy who joined. It's becoming violent, and every time we get close, they move to another hideout. They're always one step ahead of us."

"Did you not get evidence from Christina's murder?"

My brain is working overtime, trying to compartmentalise the information and scenarios so I can ask the right questions.

"No, nothing. Whoever is leading this gang knows exactly what they are doing."

"Hmmm," I mumble, more to myself than to him. "That doesn't add up though. Not to me. Gangs aren't masterminds. They're clever, ruthless, dangerous and illusive, but they aren't masterminds. I can't see them murdering someone and knowing how to cover it up."

There's something they're missing.

"I'm sorry?"

Ignoring him, I continue, wanting to get more facts. "What about her notes?"

"We've got officers looking for them, but so far, we've had no luck locating them."

"Or they aren't there," I muse. "What aren't you telling me about her?"

The phone rustles, and I picture him rubbing a hand across his jaw. "She messaged me a few days ago saying she had another note, but she wasn't stopping. She believed it was a scare tactic, that they wouldn't show themselves. I warned her against it. She felt like she was onto something, but wouldn't reveal what. Then yesterday, she text to say she was thirty minutes out, that she had enough evidence for arrests, and that she needed to grab something from the office. She never made it here. When she didn't come after an hour, we had the team go out and look. There were signs of a struggle but she was found out of town."

"It's not your fault," I tell him, hearing the guilt pouring through his words.

"Isn't it? I told my boss what she was doing over a month ago, when we found out it might be connected to a gang. I told him she needed to stop looking into it. He agreed and had a word with her. She wouldn't listen to him either. When the first letter arrived, we had the night shift do drive-bys."

"Then she should have listened to your advice. It isn't your fault."

"Does this mean you'll leave it alone?"

"Maybe. I don't know," I admit, and before he can complain, I continue. "I promise to keep you up to date with what I'm doing. I promise I won't go asking questions or snooping where I shouldn't. I'll keep it research only. Although, I would like a chance to speak to her boss or co-workers or whoever she went to when she had breakthroughs."

"Alright, but I'm begging you here, Hay. I don't want you snooping. Promise me," he pleads. "If I find out you've gone asking questions and put your name on their radar, I'll arrest your arse myself."

"What for?" I snap.

"You stole a twenty out of your brother's wallet at the engagement party."

I roll my eyes. "He owed it to me."

"It didn't seem that way when he got angry."

"That wasn't at me," I remind him, thinking of Liam's expression when he saw the last of his money gone.

"No, when he figured out it was you, there was a lot of hair pulling."

I laugh, fond of the memory. Liam cried for an hour over his bald spot.

"Jesus, okay, I promise."

"Thank you."

"You sound surprised," I say grouchily.

"I've met you and your family. You love drama."

Damn Beau for painting us Carter's as crazies. We're a well-respected and normal family.

"I'm not stupid. Plus, I think the reporter already had the whole thing figured out, and I'm assuming it's bigger than the break-ins."

"If you say so."

"I know so. Call it intuition. She had something big; big enough that she was taking it to the police first and not her paper."

"You should have become a cop," he muses.

I laugh. "And deal with dickheads all day? No thanks. I would end up arrested. I have two brothers and a lot of cousins to deal with already," I tell him, scrunching my nose up at his suggestion. "Look, I need to go. I'm outside work and really need to go in."

"I'll let you go then, and I'll get this sent over."

"Thanks for doing me a solid."

"You're welcome."

We say goodbye before ending the call. Once the phone is safely back in my pocket, I jump up and down, waving my hands around. "I'm going to rock this story and become a news reporter," I hoot, wiggling my arse side to side.

"Good heavens, Hayden, get inside," Tracey yells, causing me to scream. I catch my breath and see the way she's watching me. Most likely wondering how my crazy arse ended up working for her. "Are you going to come into work or not?"

I nod, stepping forward. "Sorry, I'm coming."

———————————

THE PUNGENT SMELL of lavender on the fresh linen is pleasant. Lavender is a smell that never took my fancy before my grandparents passed away. Now, I favour it. It reminds me so much of Gran, of the love she spoiled us with.

It smells like home.

Grabbing a pillowcase off the brown suede chair, I begin to finish making the bed. We have a new live-in patient being transferred from the hospital and I need to get the room set up for his arrival.

The sound of someone approaching has me glancing to the door. Amelia waddles in, head down, her prodigious stomach leading the way.

"Evening, Amelia."

She covers her stomach in a protective gesture, jerking in fright.

"Holy sugar," she squeals, gasping for breath.

Holding my hands up, I panic. "Please don't go into labour."

She laughs, but it's forced. The strain on her expression gives it away. She's scared out of her mind. I can see it in the way her gaze darts around the room, and the way her body shakes.

"It's okay. I just didn't see you in here. And I won't. I'm not due for another two months."

Amelia is one of the many nurses who work here that I like. She's stunning. Her dark hazel eyes are mixed with a deep forest green. They almost glow, the colour is that intense. They're warm and sparkle with mirth, but every so often they grow dim, haunted and lost. It worries me, and I wish she'd open up. But the one thing I've come to know about the mysterious woman is she doesn't talk about her past. Or the father of her unborn child and the young little girl she brought with her when she and her mum came to visit her aunt.

Her rich black hair falls just below her shoulders when she has it down. Today, she has it in two French braids twisted to the nape of her neck.

And although she's seven months pregnant, I can tell she still holds her slim figure.

"Phew."

"Sorry I overreacted. I, um, I really didn't think anyone was in here."

"Is everything okay?" I ask, noticing she seems more distracted than normal.

Sometimes, patients who need life care don't make it from the hospital.

She shakes her head, seeming to get her thoughts together. She's in that place where she doesn't seem here, in the present.

She pastes on a bright smile, nodding. "Yes, everything is fine. I'm in my own head. I came in to check the room was ready because the movers are here. It reminded me I still need to find somewhere to live."

"I'll ask my uncle. He owns his own letting agency. I'm sure he can hook you up."

"Thank you." She smiles, running a hand down her tunic. "Just let me know. In the meantime, our new patient, Mr Cross, has arrived."

Mr Cross. It couldn't be. No, she couldn't mean…

"Here is your room, Mr Cross," Tracey declares, smiling at her niece, Amelia, as she steps inside.

I gawk at my former boss, sitting in a wheelchair, his leg raised and in a cast. He's aged ten years since the last time I saw him. His skin looks withered and old. He has oxygen tubes up his nose and black bags under his eyes. I've never seen him look so… well, so old.

"Hayden?"

I groan at the sound of the voice I've come to love and loathe. Shock pours out in his tone with that one word. He's acting like I'm a stalker, and if Mr Cross wasn't a patient, I would play the part as payback.

Oh God, this isn't happening.

Wearing a navy-blue jumper and black trousers, he looks casual. Well, casual for him. He still looks like he ironed his boxers. I'm so used to seeing him in his suits that it's a little unnerving. I thought for sure the day he didn't wear a suit, I'd find him unattractive.

I was wrong.

If anything, he looks hotter. It's kind of unfair. My casual wear consists of my 'Nightmare Before Christmas' pyjamas that have Dorito stains on them.

"Mr Cross," I greet, staring at the gorgeous man invading my dreams.

Senior Cross draws back suddenly, his expression crumpling with despair. "Please tell me you didn't fire the one person keeping that station going," he fumes. "What did I tell you?" He aims the frustration my way. "He will pay you triple to come back."

"Mr Cross—" I start.

"Dad," Clayton begins.

"Don't you 'Dad' me, son," he fires back. "And, Hayden, I'm no longer your boss. Call me Weston."

I gulp. It's like I'm back in his office and he's telling me off for punching Harry in the stomach when I thought he was groping me. He wasn't. He went to shake my hand. However, I didn't know that at the time.

I shake the thoughts away. "Weston, what I'm trying to—"

"Hire her back, son."

"Jesus, Dad, I've not fired her," he practically yells.

Weston's expression is adorable. He isn't sure if we're telling the truth or not. "Then why is she here, son?"

"This is your second job?" Clayton asks, breaking the silence that follows after his dad's question. He scans the room for a moment before his lips twitch in amusement, like he can't believe it.

"Yes. Is it so hard to believe I dedicate my time to helping old people? They deserve to be treated with respect in their last moments on Earth," I tell him sharply, before grimacing, turning to Weston. "Sorry."

He smiles. "Don't be."

Both Tracey and Amelia snort. Frustrated, I glare at them. "I do."

White frizzy hair is the first thing I see when Sally barges into the room, her face bright red. "You!" she yells. "You stole my treats again."

Sally is another witch on the floor who complains about everything. I wouldn't be surprised if they've formed their own group.

Condemning expressions fixate on me, and I groan, unable to meet their gazes.

I'm going to make sure only channel two works on her TV when everyone has left later.

The movers give her a wide berth as they begin to place boxes in the room, and the orderlies get Mr Cross settled in his bed.

"No, Sally, I didn't." And I really didn't.

This time.

Furious, she goes to charge for me, but Tracey blocks her. "I want her fired!"

"Sally, she said she didn't—"

"She did. Betty saw her leave my room."

I snort. She's the other witch. Why they let them share a floor, I don't know. I call it the crazy hall. "Betty probably has them."

I tune out Tracey trying to calm the old woman down when Clayton comes to stand beside me, giving the men room to bring in the boxes. I tense, keeping still. I'm worried that if he gets any closer, I'll start to rub myself against him. He smells so good. Like cinnamon and spice.

He leans down, his breath blowing across my ear. "Why am I not surprised you rob from sweet little ladies," he comments, failing to keep the amusement out of his tone.

"Sweet my arse," I snap. He steps away, and I tilt my head, meeting his gaze. "And I didn't—this time anyway."

"Yes, you did," Sally screams. "You stole my fruit gums the last time. If I hadn't been so tired from the medication, I would have whooped your arse and got you fired then. You take Bernie's and others too."

Snorting, my lids lower into slits. "I helped you. You have dentures, Sally. There was no way you would have been able to chew them." I take a deep breath, not wanting to yell. "And I replaced them with marshmallows."

She sniffs, turning away. "I don't even like marshmallows."

"You ate the whole bag just fine. Don't lie."

"Sally, why don't we get you settled back into your room and I'll get you an apple out of the office," Amelia orders softly.

"I don't like apples, but fine," she grouches, before turning her hatred towards me. "This isn't over."

Once they leave the room, I feel all eyes on me.

"Really?" Clayton comments.

God, this man.

"You aren't my boss here, so don't make me punch you."

"Violent too," he taunts, raising his eyebrows.

That is it.

"I don't steal their treats—Well, I do, but only because I don't want to hear them moaning the next day because they've lost a tooth, that their sugar is too high, or that their IBS is flaring up."

"Well aren't you the giver."

"Jesus, you're an arsehole outside of work too."

"You work together?" Hope asks, stepping into the room with a clipboard tucked to her chest.

I'm still staring up at Clayton when my eyes widen in disbelief.

Why!

Why, after years of the best kept secret in my family, does Clayton walk in and ruin it after five minutes.

He's purposely turning my world upside down.

SEVEN

MY FUTURE FLASHES BEFORE MY EYES. All I can picture or hear is my dad's reaction. He will go on and on about how my job sent him into early retirement, and how it traumatised him for life.

Oh God.

My family will come to me for advice and I'll have to listen to them.

I'll be dead within a month.

I have to get out of this.

"What?" My laugh sounds foreign, forced, even to my own ears. "He's not my boss. He's a—"

A hand covering my mouth mutes the excuse I was just about to come up with.

"Oh no you don't," Clayton barks. "I don't know what preposterous excuse you were about to come up with, but I want no involvement this time."

I shove his hand off my mouth and take a step back, affronted—even if he is right. "I wasn't—" at the reprimanding expression, I sigh, my shoulders sagging. "Okay, I was."

"Um, what is going on?" Hope asks, her voice soft, concerned.

Facing her, I can't help but take in her white blonde hair, smooth pale skin and sharp green eyes. She is the spit of her mother and just as beautiful. What has taken me some time to get used to is seeing her in the blue tunic. I'm proud of how far she has come, and the uniform is a reminder of what she had accomplished. Before she got her nursing degree, she wore a white tunic like mine.

She's watching, waiting for answers, and I can't lie to her. She's one of my best friends.

"You cannot tell anyone, including Ciara and Ashton. I mean it," I warn her.

"Oh my God, do you really work as a spy for the government?" she whispers, rushing further into the room.

That's actually pretty cool. Why have I never thought of that?

"I d—"

"She works for me at a radio/podcast station, giving love and sex advice to women," Clayton interrupts, pointedly watching me.

At a quick glance, I thought Hope was processing it, but looking closer, her shoulders are shaking. I jump when she bursts into laughter.

She takes us both in before laughing even harder. And it continues. And continues.

Punching Clayton lightly in the arm, I release my fury on him. "You've broken her."

"No, I didn't," he fires back. "You should have been honest with her."

"Why would you tell her?" I yell, throwing my hands up. I'm trying so hard not to strangle him. Even drunk out of my mind I've not let it slip about what I do for a living. That I know of anyway. And in one moment he may as well have had my whole family in and told them.

"Why would you not?" he asks, stepping away when I slap him again. "Will you stop slapping me."

I grit my teeth. "If I wanted them to know about my occupation, I would have told them myself. Now my life is over. Over, Clayton!"

"Now you're just being dramatic. Stop acting so crazy."

"Crazy?" I grit out, taking a step towards him. He has the sense to take one back, his body tensing. "You've not seen crazy. My family is crazy. And you've just set them upon me. My dad is going to be insufferable for months, acting like I'm the one who traumatised him when we all know he brings it on himself. I'm going to be the person they come to for advice."

I step back, taking a deep breath.

"Um…"

I step forward, poking him in the chest. 'And do not act all snotty with me either. You did something I asked you not to do."

"Oh my gosh, he's serious," Hope interrupts, her voice low, disbelieving.

That's when I notice the entire room is silent. Uncomfortably so.

"You can't tell anyone," I warn her, desperation leaking into my voice.

"But you give people advice on relationships?" she asks for clarification.

"Yes," I whine, wishing she would forget what she heard.

Her nose scrunches up. "Is that wise?"

Why did she have to say it like she was worried for me, or rather, for other people? "What do you mean by that?"

Nervously, she fiddles with her hair, twirling it around her finger. "Well, when you gave Maddox advice about the girl who wouldn't stop stalking him, he slept with her sister. Who ended up being married, need I remind you. He nearly got arrested for defending himself."

I roll my eyes. "I told him to do something that puts her off him. Not like it would be hard with all his faults. I didn't know he would sleep with her sister."

"And that time you told Madison—"

"I didn't know all the facts," I rush out, my voice rising. "How was I meant to know the guy had a twitch? She said he was winking at her a lot."

"You told her to make a grand gesture, and not only did she fall on her face when she wore the heels you made her wear, but he was gay."

"Maybe we should look—" Clayton starts.

I point my index finger in his face. "Shut it."

"I'm just saying that maybe—"

"You've said enough," I growl, before pleading with Hope, hoping to reach her soft heart. "Will you please keep this between us?"

A cunning expression flashes across her face. "What's in it for me?"

"Are you serious? We're family. Isn't that enough?"

"Deadly," she declares. "I had to do your chores for a week when you covered for me over the whole Harry thing."

I laugh, remembering the time I caught her kissing a boy. Her dad was walking around the corner, and to keep quiet, I made her take my chores.

"Fine," I tell her, thinking of something she might want. I groan at the thought, but I know it's something she'd come up with anyway. "I'll give Maddox a key so he can sleep at mine and not bother you."

She grins in triumph, pumping her fist into the air. "Deal."

"Who is Maddox?" Clayton asks, and for a moment, he sounds angry, but I blink, believing I imagined it.

Laughing erupts around the room, and I freeze, forgetting for a moment that we aren't alone.

A woman stands beside the bed, her tall, willowy frame elegant in her white blouse and black trousers. She screams sophistication.

Her thick, light brown hair is pulled back tight into a bobble at the back of her neck. She's beautiful.

And from the familiar facial features, I'm guessing this is Clayton's sister.

She watches on in amusement, a twinkle in her eye.

"What?" I check my teeth, making sure nothing is stuck there.

"Told you she was great," Weston gloats.

I bounce on the balls of my feet. "Awe, you said I was great?" Pride fills me, but then something nags at me. "Wait, why am I great?"

"Nothing," his daughter replies, her lips still twitching. "I'm Mia, Clayton's sister."

"Hayden," I mumble when she shares a moment with her brother, leaving me out of the silent communication going on.

"No, Mia, just no," he affirms.

"Am I missing something?"

"Just ignore Mia. She thinks she's clever."

"Um, okay," I drawl out.

"I'm sorry to interrupt, but I need Clayton and Mia to come with me to sign in their father and fill in the paperwork. We can also go over the care plan while we settle Mr Cross in," Tracey announces.

"Lead the way," Clayton replies.

"Dad, we'll be back as soon as we've filled everything out."

"Go, I'll be fine," he promises.

She leans down, kissing him on the cheek before following Clayton and Tracey out.

"You really give advice?" Hope asks once they're gone.

"Yes, now drop it."

"I just can't picture it."

"Don't you have other stuff to do?"

"Yes, I'm going. See you at dinner," she informs me, dropping Weston's chart in the slot at the end of the bed.

Once she's gone, I look at the boxes stacked in the corner. The rooms here are a good size compared to other care homes. One half is basically set up like a hospital room, only a little homier. It has a bed that reclines, a sink, two chairs and a few cabinets. And the access to the bathroom is in the corner. On the other side, it has two comfy recliners, a bookshelf, a wardrobe, chest of drawers, and a T.V. unit that can be wheeled around the room. There are also a few shelves and wall hooks for personal effects and pictures.

However, even with the large space, it doesn't seem big enough to unpack what's in those boxes.

"So, I'd ask you what you're in for, but I already know. What I don't know is what you've done to your leg. You didn't try to do the Floss again, did you?"

He laughs. "I've missed your smart mouth, young lady."

"I knew you liked me."

"I fell while going to the loo. Fractured two bones."

I scrunch my nose up. "If anyone asks, you were riding a motorcycle around town. Sounds cooler."

His face gets some colour back. "I like that reason better."

"Me too, but, Weston, is that a reason to be here though? You could afford a nurse."

He pats the side of the bed, so I walk over and sit down on the edge, near his good leg.

"I'm old and I'm dying."

"Morbid," I comment, yet a sadness hits me. He's a good person, was a good boss. He doesn't deserve this.

His chuckle turns into a wheezing cough, so I lean over, pulling the tray with water on towards me. I hand him the glass, giving him a moment to gather himself.

"I didn't… I didn't want to be at home. They watched my wife, their mother, die there. I don't want them to go through that again. I don't want them changing their routines to look after an old man. Clayton, he was always going to take over, but his career was taking off, then the…" He closes his eyes, his face scrunched up like a memory is causing him physical pain. I want to ask more about Clayton, but I can tell now isn't the time. "He wasn't ready. And Mia, she just got partner at the accountancy firm she works at. She has a husband. I can't ask them to put their lives on hold for me. I'll be gone soon, and they will need their work to fall back on, especially Clayton."

I squeeze his knee, finding it hard not to become emotional. What he's doing is selfless. Even in his last moments, he is looking out for his children.

"That is very brave of you. But, Weston, they want to be there for you."

"And they can. But at least with me here they won't be worrying all the time that I'm alone. They won't need to drop anything or come to my aid if a nurse calls in sick."

"But—"

He reaches out, placing his cold hand over mine. "Stop, Hayden. I'm fine with my decision. I've not taken a holiday in ten years. I'm going to act like this is one."

"Okay, okay," I give in. "But, dude, what is with all the boxes?"

"They packed up my room at home. Anything sentimental was important to me, so they boxed it up. I need them close," he tells me, but there's more in his voice. There are treasures in those boxes that he wants to see before he goes. And I can understand that. My nan was ill before she passed, but she died peacefully in my grandfather's arms. When we found them, it was devasting but beautiful at the same time. If I could choose the way I would leave this world, it would be exactly how they did, in my sleep. I want to leave this world in the arms of someone I love and surrounded by family.

Weston is a ticking time bomb. He could go any minute, and he wants to spend it surrounded by the things he loves. The people he loves. And to know that everything will be okay when he leaves.

I can't fault him for that.

"Why don't I start getting you settled in while we wait for Clayton and Mia to come?"

"Go for it, but they won't mind doing it."

I check no one is at the door before telling him, "Between you and me, I'd rather clean toilets than go to the next room on the list. The woman staying there has a thing for hitting and spitting at me. And while we're on the subject, stay away from room two-zero-two and her guest."

"Why?" he asks, his lips twitching as he takes deep, steady breaths.

"Because Satan created them to be thorns in the world. I'm worried they'll take you with them. Don't let them corrupt you."

He chuckles, wheezing a little. "You, Hayden Carter, scared of two old women."

A deflated sigh escapes me. "No, I'm worried I'll kill them."

He laughs, slapping his thigh. "I'm so glad I'll have you here on the days you work."

I smile, giving him another glass of water. "It's because of my personality, right?"

"Something like that." He clears his throat before continuing. "How is it, working with my Clayton?"

Taken off guard, I dig my nails into the palms of my hands. I can't give him the answer he needs right now. Or wants to hear. Telling him that you want to kill his son, yet imagine fucking said son on his desk, isn't exactly something you should admit to a dying man.

"What?" he asks, clearly clicking on to the fact I don't want to answer.

"You do not want to ask that while you are high on meds."

"When did you start stopping yourself from speaking your mind? And what do my meds have to do with it?"

It's my turn to grin. "Because when I hand you your arse, I want you to remember. Now, get some rest and I'll get this room looking homier. When Clayton and Mia come back, they can let me know if they want anything moved."

"I won't argue. I am feeling a little drowsy," he admits, ducking his head. It must be hard for a hardworking, independent man to rely on the care of others.

"Get some sleep," I whisper, waiting until his eyes close to move.

Reaching for the first box, a thought hits me like a ton of bricks, and I groan. Not only will I be working at the station alongside Clayton or going on dates with him watching close by, but I'll have to see him here too.

I'm so fucking screwed.

EIGHT

THE AIR IS BELOW FREEZING TONIGHT as I step out of the car. I'm glad Hope had a coat that went with my red, form-fitting dress. All I had were leather jackets, nothing that went with the type of restaurant I'm at. The black wool coat falls to my knees and is buttoned up to my chest. It has a belt that goes around it, but instead of tying it around me, I decided to tie it at the back, not wanting that feeling of being restricted.

The restaurant is located next to a beautiful lake. Rivers has been open a few months, and the lavish steak house has nothing but good reviews online. I'm excited to try some yummy goodness off their menu.

Outside, it has a patio area with tables, sheltered by the wooden pavilion gazebo. If the food turns out to be good, I'd definitely like to come back to see this in a summer setting.

Stepping inside, the warmth engulfs me. The place is fancy, maybe a little too fancy, which is probably why I didn't hear about it opening until Clayton mentioned where I'd be attending my first date.

It's one of the many restaurants on a list of things to do with Date Night. It's the first phase of their programme. The second, if you choose to see your date again, is an activity date. They have nature walks to rock climbing to choose from. The third phase is an away date, though you have the option to continue with phase one or two until you are ready.

"Hayden?" Clayton calls, sounding unsure. I turn around and lose my breath. He's wearing a navy-blue suit with a burgundy tie, a sliver clip in the middle.

I can only ogle the fine specimen in front of me.

He is ridiculously hot.

Why did he have to be an ass?

And my boss?

It takes me a moment to notice he's checking me out too. I had undone my coat stepping inside, so he has full view of my tits and how hot I look in my dress. It clings in all the right places.

What surprises me is how suddenly his posture changes. He shakes his head, like he's clearing his mind, before he straightens. Jaw clenched, he glares down at me.

"Great, you're here. We now only have forty-five minutes to go over the plans for tonight."

Maybe he wasn't checking me out.

"I'm ten minutes late. I had to go back home to change my shoes. I couldn't drive in them."

"You mean the two-hundred-pound a pair shoes? That you *had* to have?"

I grin, finding satisfaction in his pouting. "Yes. Now, are we going to keep wasting time or go sit down?"

He opens his mouth to argue but decides against it.

"Come on," he orders, heading over to the podium.

I take the time to look around. There's a lot of beige, golds and soft tones decorating the restaurant. The dim lighting is what gives it warmth. What gives it colour is the green. There are lots of tiny shrubs with twinkle lights wrapped around them. I like it. It makes the place stand out against all the other restaurants who copy each other by having pictures of landscapes or old-fashioned ornaments decorating the place.

"Welcome to Rivers, Mr Cross. Tonight, you are in the Dove suite. If you'd like to follow me, I'll get you seated," the waitress explains, her perky ponytail swishing side to side with her energetic movements.

We follow her into the main room, just off the entrance. The main dining room is modern and inviting. Candlelight flickers from the tables, which are decorated with beautiful candle holders, gold swirls flickering in all directions.

When we step into the next room, I can't help the small shot of anxiety that tries but fails to creep up my spine. It's there, lingering on the surface, for reasons unknown. I'm a confident person in all aspects of my life, but this feeling is foreign. It's as if the room is screaming at me to get out, that I don't belong. And I don't. I have a foul mouth, don't care who I smart off to, and love hamburgers for dinner.

Once the thought enters my mind, I snort to myself. I'm Hayden Carter: I belong where I want to belong, other people be damned. And who cares if I stand out against other diners who are thick with jewels and sparkly dresses or expensive suits.

We head towards the back of the room, where four extremely large bay windows are, giving us the beautiful view of the lake. They've decorated the trees with fairy lights, and the reflection bouncing off the still water is mesmerizing.

But what takes my breath away is the ivy running up the walls and along the ceiling, white flowers blossoming out of the green.

Someone took great lengths to give this place character and charm, and they succeeded. It's bewitching.

With the twinkle lights weaving in and out of the ivy, it gives the room an intimate charge. It isn't just sexual, it's something else; something I can't quite grasp the understanding of.

"Are you coming?" Clayton asks, before having to clear his throat.

I pull my gaze away from the ceiling to find his heated gaze on mine. I get lost in his eyes, and for a minute, I forget we aren't here together on a date. For one split second, I forget he's my boss and take a step forward, wanting to pull him towards me and wrap my arms around his neck.

The realisation hits me and I pause, rubbing my chest, drawing his attention to my tits. My heart is racing, and although the crazy part of my brain wants to launch myself at him and make him forget his name, the other part, the part I inherited from my mum, has my feet firmly glued to the floor.

"Mr Cross, your table," the young woman announces, her tone showcasing how uncomfortable our stare off is.

"Yes, um, sorry," he replies, walking over and pulling the chair out for me. It's right by the window, giving me a beautiful view of the lake. I arch my eyebrow at his kind gesture. "I can be a gentleman, Hayden."

"I didn't say anything," I muse, finding it hard to cool my libido.

"Let me take your coat," he offers, stepping up behind me.

Well, isn't he full of surprises.

His fingertips brush the collar of my coat. He's not even that close, but I swear I can feel his body heat. All I want to do is step back and lean into his embrace.

Somehow, the small gesture feels sexual, like a game of foreplay. The light brush of his fingertips run along my neck, causing a fire to burn in my veins.

The back of my dress is quite low. It was the one thing he didn't get a glimpse of when we went shopping. I love it. It gives it personality and makes me feel more like me, rather than some fake Barbie playing dress up. That and I knew it would drive him crazy.

The second the toned skin on my back is revealed, there's a change in the room. He pauses his slow, torturous movements, leaving the coat down by my elbows, and takes a sharp intake of breath. The sound has my pulse spiking.

"My coat," I remind him, my voice low and breathless as I glance over my shoulder.

Desire oozes from him as he snaps out of it. "Um, yes." He reaches back for the coat, gently sliding it the rest of the way before handing it to the waitress. I take my seat, smiling when he pushes my chair in.

"Can I take your drink order? I'll have a waitress bring them over for you."

"Do you have Bowmore Darkest?"

"We do."

"I'll have one, please, and my friend will have an orange juice."

"Right away," she tells him, before leaving us alone.

I curl my lip. "I must have missed me telling you what I wanted to drink."

He lets out a tiresome sigh. "Let's not argue. I knew you'd be driving, so you weren't going to be drinking alcohol. You litter the offices with Ribena cartons, so I knew you liked sweet drinks. From experience, I can't see them having your choice of drink on the menu, so to save time and the embarrassment of going through the drink's menu, I ordered for you."

Well shit, how could I argue with that? I should be stunned that he noticed my addiction to Ribena, but all I heard was that I littered.

"Okay then," I reply stubbornly, needing the last word.

"Let's get on with this, shall we."

"Let's."

"As you know, we have screened all applicants Date Night matched you with. It was down to three."

"Did you Eenie, Meenie, Miney, Mo it?"

"Did we what?"

"Never mind. Continue," I tell him, waving off his confusion.

"As for the date as a whole, you'll introduce yourselves and go from there. Do what you would do normally. From Chrissy's notes, you'll be pleased with who we picked."

He doesn't seem pleased.

"What is his name?"

He slides his finger across the screen of the tablet he pulls out of his pocket, his forehead creasing with frown lines. "I'm not sure. It doesn't look like Chrissy sent over the documents stating his name."

"Tell me about him. I'm guessing he's read my file, so it's only fair."

He clears his throat. "He owns a successful business, and has recently shared his duties with another member of his staff so he isn't working the long hours anymore.

"Family is important to him, which is what you put on your questionnaire. He spends a lot of time with them so his match will need to be okay with a big family. Some of his answers pretty much match yours," he comments, his lips twisted like he's tasted something sour.

"He donates his time to looking after animals. It's even noted here that there was a photo uploaded with him holding a piglet.

"He's also big on sporting activities," he tells me, finishing off reading from the list.

"Sounds awesome," I reply bitterly. Because as much as I love the stuff I do with my family when we take our trips, I'm not really someone who would describe running as a hobby or fun. I wish people would call it for what it is. Torture.

He places the tablet onto the table before crossing his arms, leaning against the white linen tablecloth. "Now that is done, why don't you explain to me why you told my father I said you dressed like a slut?"

A boisterous laugh slips free, drawing attention from the other diners. "You basically wrote in the contract that clothing worn couldn't reveal too much skin and to make sure it was appropriate for work."

"I did no such thing," he snaps, yet keeps his tone low so others won't overhear.

"You did, but that wasn't why I exaggerated."

He scans my face, waiting for an answer, but I remain quiet. "I've got nothing. I don't get you sometimes," he groans, throwing his hands up. "Why on earth would you say that to him? Now he thinks he has to worry that I'm being unprofessional." He gives the waitress a curt nod when she sets our drinks down.

I thank her before answering. "Because you knew I was coming back for those truffles and cream cakes when I got a break. Your dad gave them to me, not you."

"I was hungry," he defends, but he's forgetting who I am. I can detect a lie a mile away.

"Really? Then why did your sister tell me you took the rest home with you?"

"Damn Mia and her big mouth."

I glare. I was looking forward to those damn truffles, since Sally made sure all the residents knew to hide their treat supplies. "Spill."

"I forgot."

"Try again."

"All right, I wanted to get a reaction out of you, but only because you told that nurse I was gay."

"She was flirting with you."

His mouth opens, then closes, before he thinks on what to say. "And? Does that bother you?"

I roll my eyes. "I was doing you a favour if you must know. She's been broody ever since Miss Wilma's granddaughter brought her baby in a few months ago. She's been wanting someone to get her pregnant. I've heard her talking on the phone."

The blood drains from his face. I know she gave him her number. Whether he kept it or not, I don't know.

"Really?"

No and yes. She does want a baby, but I reacted so harshly because I didn't like her flirting with him. I don't particularly like her full stop. She has a way of making others who work with her feel small, especially Amelia, who is new. I made her shift a nightmare that night, not only because of Clayton, but because she called Amelia fat.

"Yes, she's been going on about it for months. She even admitted to having unprotected sex with her ex-boyfriend."

Shock rolls off him and it takes him a few minutes to grasp the position he nearly let himself be in.

"Thank you. I'm sorry I took your truffles."

I tilt my head up, pretending to be fascinated with the décor before turning back to him. "Thank me by not bringing up the dress code again."

"I told you I threw the contract out. It was you who brought it up to my father."

"It also means you can't keep bringing it up every chance you get when you see what I'm wearing."

He narrows his eyes on me. "You are a very conniving woman, Hayden Carter."

I grin, pleased with the compliment. "Thank you."

He shakes his head disbelievingly. "I'll drop it if you do."

"Awesome," I tell him, going quiet for a few minutes as I take a sip of juice. "How will this work? I mean, are you going to sit with us, or do you have a table for yourself somewhere? If you do, it's going to look like you've been stood up."

His lips twitch. "You don't need to worry about me. I'll be right over there," he tells me, pointing to the table behind him, a row over. "And I have a date."

I begin to feel queasy at the news.

"What? Who? And how are you meant to watch out for my safety if you're paying attention to your date?" I hiss out, failing to keep my voice down.

"Wow, calm down. She's one of the women who work for Date Night. It's not only women who can multitask, you know."

I watch him sceptically. "Now you're just being rude. If I'm kidnapped because you are thinking about fucking the woman in front of you, be quick to get your will and funeral arrangements sorted."

"Now you're being dramatic again." He smirks. "Are you going to haunt me from the other side? I'm touched you'd care."

"Please don't take my warning for concern. And you'll pray I was haunting you by the time my dad is done with you." He mutters something under his breath that I don't quite hear. "Speak up, I didn't hear you."

"I said, you make your dad out to be crazy."

That wasn't what he said, but I drop it, sitting up in my chair. "Oh, he is, but not in the way you're thinking. Yes, if his only daughter was killed, he'd smile while he skinned you alive, but that's not all I meant. My dad has a way of driving people to the brink of their own crazy. You'll beg for death if he ever sets his sights on you."

"Have you ever dated?"

Startled by the question, I nod. "Yes."

"I'm surprised, if you warn them about your dad."

I grin, leaning a little on the table. "Oh, if I'm in a relationship, the bloke doesn't need to worry about my dad if he does something wrong. I have my own brand of crazy."

He looks unfazed. "That I can believe, but, Hayden, I don't have to worry about your dad. I'm taking this seriously, and if at any point you feel uncomfortable, I will be there in a flash."

"Good, because I'd hate to embarrass you by causing a scene in this exquisite restaurant."

He grins, holding his glass to his lips before pausing, then holding it out to me. "Take this. I'll drive you home in your car and have a taxi pick me up from your house."

Not one to say no, I take the drink from his hand, smelling the contents. "Thanks."

He smirks, and I know he's waiting for me to put it down and ask for a girly drink. I take a sip, watching his pupils dilate with admiration.

It's strong and bitter, but I don't let it show, swallowing the harsh liquid down my throat.

"Oh, and, Hayden, I don't embarrass easily. I can handle your crazy."

I squeeze my thighs together, unable to pull my gaze away from him as I slowly lower the glass to the table.

"I bet," I whisper huskily.

NINE

I CAN'T BELIEVE I'M DOING THIS. Everything that had happened with Faith is running through my mind. Am I putting myself in danger? Is this my end? Carter's have a way of getting themselves into trouble. Granted, they all ended up with their soul mates, but me, I don't even have a potential love interest. This isn't a novel or a movie.

I could be in the presence of a serial killer tonight, and I'd die without meeting him. Or maybe I've already met him and run him off with my charming personality.

The whole process of it all is a scary thing. I can look after myself, but it doesn't mean I go looking for trouble because of it.

Then there's the question of whether I'll like him or not. Will Clayton make me sit through a three-course meal, pretending to enjoy his company?

My stomach is in knots from the nerves. Nerves of meeting a creeper. Nerves of meeting someone I might actually like. That doomed feeling won't leave my stomach.

A laugh slips free at how crazy I sound, even to myself. It's a date, not a drama series on what not to do in the presence of a serial killer. If someone could hear my thoughts right now, they'd probably commit me.

Clayton watches me with a raised eyebrow. He's probably wondering how he got stuck with the mentally unstable co-worker right now.

"If something happens, he'll die first," I mutter.

"What?" he mouths.

I press my lips together when I realise I said it out loud, and shrug. His attention is pulled away when a tall, leggy blonde approaches his table. He stands to greet her, smiling like a cat who got the cream as he bends down to kiss her cheek.

Could he be any more cheesy?

He really needs to ring in for advice, because kissing her on the first date is leading her on. What if he doesn't like her by the end of it or she doesn't like him? It will be uncomfortable for both of them.

She's probably sat there picturing him on their wedding day. Poor soul.

Running her hand up and down his arm, she tilts her head back, laughing at whatever he whispered. She's laughing like the guy is actually hilarious. I instantly dislike her. Clearly, she's fake, because he wouldn't know a joke if it bit him on the arse.

Her outfit screams desperation. It's short, but not short enough to be slutty, and she's showing more cleavage than me. I bet he doesn't give *her* the riot act on how to dress appropriately.

A throat clearing in front of me has me nearly tipping out of my chair.

My eyes nearly pop out of their sockets when they land on Reid Hayes smugly sitting in the chair in front of me. His crisp, dark purple shirt is unbuttoned at the top, the colour looking good on him. He's styled his hair and smells divine. He's dressed for a date, so what I don't understand is why he's sitting in front of me.

I scan the room for any signs of my date, not wanting Reid to scare him away, before addressing the matter in front of me.

"Reid, you can't be here."

"Why?" He smirks, leaning back in his chair like he belongs.

"Why are you smirking? Go away, Reid, I'm meeting someone."

"I can't do that."

My God, he's infuriating.

He turns up everywhere lately, it seems. Landon and Lily have a lot to answer for, bringing this muppet into our lives.

Our waitress from earlier steps up to the table. "Can I get you a drink, sir?"

"He's not staying," I tell her sharply, glaring at Reid.

"Oh, I'm—"

"I'll have whatever beer you have on tap, babe," he orders, winking at her.

My phone on the table lights up with a text.

CLAYTON: You could at least pretend to enjoy your date being there. Be nice.

I glance up from my phone and stare at Reid, the realisation dawning on me.

No.

This cannot be happening.

Why couldn't I get the serial killer?

"No," I drag out, my stomach bottoming out.

He grins. "Now she's getting it."

"You cannot be serious," I snap.

"Believe it, baby."

"They said you were a successful business owner who just gave up some responsibility to free up their time," I remind him dryly.

His grin only gets bigger at my discomfort, and he shrugs. "I do own a percentage of Hayes' Removals. We just hired a receptionist to take on some of the workload. I'm pretty sure Wyatt wants to fuck her."

"I don't care, Reid," I snap. "And the part where you said you donate your time to animals?"

"I do. I help my mum out on the farm. The piglets were a cute addition to the form."

Well, isn't he clever. I can't even say he lied, because all he did was twist the truth to come across differently.

"And the sporting actives? Because I'm pretty sure checking yourself out in the mirror at the gym doesn't count."

He waits for the waitress to place his drink on the table before leaning forward to answer.

"I didn't think writing 'I like to fuck a lot' in the answer box was appropriate."

I roll my eyes. "You're a pig." I laugh anyway. I laugh at his answer, at how devious he was, and at just being in this situation. Only I could find myself on a blind date and have it end up being with Reid.

My phone lights up again, and I pick it up, reading the message.

CLAYTON: Do you want me to cancel the date?

I quickly look over to his table, and although his date's back is to me, I can tell she's talking away by the movements of her shoulders and the way her hands flap about.

HAYDEN: Are you even listening to your date?

He grins as he reads my message.

CLAYTON: I think I've met someone who talks as much as you, and I thought that was impossible. But to answer your question, I'm paying attention. I can multitask, remember?

HAYDEN: Prick!

"I'm hurt you're finding your phone more interesting than me. I'm a fucking catch, baby."

I place my phone on the table, staring into his eyes.

"Reid, let me be clear. I find paint drying more interesting than you. This isn't a real date." I take a deep breath, ignoring his pout. "And how did you even know about this? Why are you even here?"

He chuckles. "That night I found you upstairs at your uncle's? I caught bits of the conversation and pieced it all together. For the most part anyway. I wasn't sure we would match, so I guessed what you would put."

Yeah, and pigs fly. "For some reason, I don't believe you."

Laughing, he shakes his head. "I used to fuck one of the members of staff who works for Date Night. I got her to match us as a favour for someone in the family."

"I'm not your family."

"Close enough. And I knew you didn't want to do this. I'm bored, so I thought, why not?"

When his gaze hardens over my shoulder, I turn in my chair. An older man is dining with a girl closer to our age than his.

"You got a thing for the redhead?"

He looks confused for a moment before what I asked registers. "No, the bloke is someone we have an interest in. We thought he'd left this area and moved on. Clearly he hasn't."

"You want to go confront him?" I ask hopefully.

Chuckling, he downs his drink. "No, there's a time and a place for men like him. Here isn't one of them."

"Witnesses?" I muse.

"Yeah."

I sigh. "I have no idea how we're meant to review this date. It's not real now it's you here. It's just having lunch with a friend."

"Why did you say 'friend' like you tasted something sour?"

"Let's not get into it," I warn him, smiling sweetly when Clayton looks over.

"Well, why not treat this like an ordinary date," he tells me, running his finger along my forearm on the table. "You can use me however you like."

I run my finger around the stem of my glass, fluttering my lashes at him when I see Clayton watching us, his lips set in a firm line.

"And just how would you like me to use you?"

Reid, forever the charmer, smirks. "I can think of a few things."

I laugh, pulling back. "Honestly, as shocked as I am that you're here, I'm kind of glad. I've been dreading this whole thing from the moment I was informed."

"What is it that you do? Because everything I could come up with as to why you're being paid to go on dates all end up with me being thrown into your brother's trunk and dumped in the middle of nowhere."

I clip him around the ear. "Thanks, arsehole. And they did that two times. You make it sound like their hobby."

"Sorry," he grimaces, rubbing his ear. "From what I heard, they enjoy it."

My family do like making the men I date work for it. But to be fair, the last guy they did it to was to save him from my dad. The arsehole read my message wrong and met me at my house.

I hold my finger up, indicating I need a minute when my phone lights up once again with a message from Clayton.

CLAYTON: We should just pull the plug on this. We can figure something out with Date Night after.

CLAYTON: Did you just hit him? Want me to come over?

HAYDEN: I'm fine. And no, he had a bug on his ear.

CLAYTON: I'm going to cancel this whole thing.

HAYDEN: I'm good. Unless your date isn't up to par?

CLAYTON: This isn't about my date.

HAYDEN: Well, don't do it on my account. I'm okay.

CLAYTON: Fine!

HAYDEN: FINE!

I take in a calming breath. "Sorry, it's my boss checking in."

"The guy with the hot date behind us?"

I look at the woman in question. I guess she's pretty. In a snotty way. "Yeah, and she's not hot."

"Um, yes she is. If I didn't want to play you up so badly, I'd go chat her up in the car park. She looks like the type who wouldn't mind being fucked in a car."

"Well, good for you, but she's not his type."

Reid snorts. "She's everyone's type."

I scrunch my nose up, still watching her. "Why is she laughing? The guy doesn't even know what a joke is."

"Holy fuck, you like him."

I want to wipe the smug smile from his face. "What? That's absurd."

He laughs, earning annoyed glances from other diners. "Then why do you keep staring at him and judging his date? You sound jealous. And let's not forget, you've paid more attention to what he's doing than what I am."

"Shut up. You've got no idea what you're talking about. He's my boss."

"What is it that you do? Because I'm seriously fucking enjoying this. Hayden Carter, rattled by her boss."

I smile sweetly so Clayton doesn't know I'm about to kick this guy in the nuts. "Don't forget, I know where you sleep, Reid." I take a deep breath. "And I work at a station doing a podcast. At the minute, we're doing a segment on Date Night."

His expression drops, before a look of disbelief crosses his face. "That's it? That's what you do?"

"Yes," I hiss. "And I'd appreciate it if you didn't tell anyone else."

He holds his hands up. "I wasn't planning to." I arch my eyebrow. "Okay, if it was more exciting, then yeah, I was going to brag to your brother that I know and he doesn't."

I snort. "It's Landon. He probably already knows. Not much gets past him."

"Don't I know it," he mutters.

The waitress steps up to our table with a tray of food, and I look at Reid questioningly. He shrugs, seeming as stumped as me. "Here are your starters."

"We've not ordered anything," I tell her apologetically.

She smiles away my concern. "It was pre-ordered by Mr Cross," she explains, putting a bowl and a plate of bread in front of Reid. "For you, sir: pea and mint soup. For you: Cornish crab on toasted crumpet. Please let me know if there is anything else you need."

She leaves, and all I can do is stare at the disaster in front of me, whimpering. "I want a menu with real food on it."

"I think your boss hates you," Reid mutters.

"Why do you think that?"

"Because mine looks like a bowl of vomit and yours… I don't even have words. I can tell you that doesn't look like crab, more like skinned balls."

I swallow the bile in my throat at the picture he just painted. Because believe it or not, it does look like a ball sack. Skinned.

I whimper again when my stomach rumbles. "Why would people pay a fortune for this?"

"Where's the steak?" Reid complains, stirring the spoon in the bowl.

I glare over at Clayton, who is happily sipping on what I assume is soup.

HAYDEN: Do you know what fucking century we live in?

CLAYTON: Yes, of course.

HAYDEN: Then who the hell gave you permission to order for me? I can order my own damn food. A rat wouldn't eat this.

CLAYTON: Funny. Cassandra is fully enjoying her starter.

HAYDEN: Cassandra can choke on it.

Not one to let food go to waste, unless Charlotte had a hand in making it, I grab my fork, praying it doesn't taste as bad as it looks. Or for the kitchen to suddenly set on fire and get me out of this whole ordeal. Because if they all come out looking like this, I'll be grabbing something from a drive-through on the way home.

TEN

THE RESTAURANT HAS PICKED UP SOMEWHAT since we first arrived, yet the atmosphere stays calm and relaxed.

The waitress leaves after dropping off a sticky toffee pudding for me and a chocolate, chestnut truffle cake for Reid. I'm not complaining. It's the most appetising part of the menu. It even smells delicious, and I can't help but eye it as I lick my lips.

"Is it just me or are they really stingy with the portions?" Reid comments, pouting down at his dessert.

Chuckling, I nod in agreement. There isn't enough here to satisfy a toddler.

"If this place didn't cost a fortune, I would think they were rationing the food."

Reid's remark goes unheard when, from the corner of my eye, Clayton stands with his date and leads her over to the hostess desk, where the waitress hands over her coat.

He's seriously going to leave with her? She's really his type? All she's done is laugh and basically throw herself at him. Who acts like that on the first date? She could at least pretend to act normal.

"That fucker is leaving me," I grit out, slamming my fork down once they leave the restaurant together, his arm around her waist.

Reid scans the room, probably looking for the guy who has been giving him problems. "Who?"

"My boss," I tell him, kicking him under the table when he continues to glare over my shoulder.

Reid shrugs, going back to his pudding. "The dude is probably fucking her in his car."

"He didn't drive," I snap. "And give me that."

He pulls his plate out of reach, covering it with his arm. "No! I shared all my dinner with you. Sod off. I'm fucking starving."

"You fed bits to me to try." I pout, fluttering my lashes. "Just one bite?"

"No. I only did that 'cause I could feel the jealousy rolling off your boss. I'm surprised there isn't a knife in my back."

True. Not about the jealously, but about Clayton not looking happy the few times I caught him looking over. I'm not convinced it was jealously, like Reid, who spent the entire dinner feeding me bits off his fork, lightly touching my hand or running his finger along my arm.

"You're an arsehole."

He grins like it's a huge achievement. "Thanks."

Picking my phone up, I go to text Lily, to ask her to pick me up, knowing she doesn't gossip, but Reid snatches it off me.

"Don't go texting him. You aren't desperate. Don't start now."

"He was my ride home, and since he left, I need someone to drive me home. I was going to text Lily."

"She and Jaxon have gone ice skating tonight," he informs me, and I groan. "And isn't your car outside?"

"Yes, but I've had a drink."

His eyebrows scrunch together. "Did you drink drive here, because I've only seen you have one. One won't hurt."

"I don't like drink driving," I tell him.

He laughs at my expense. "That's not drink driving."

"I don't care what the limit is, I just don't like doing it. Although I have eaten." My thoughts drift off, wondering if the restaurant's stingy portions were enough to soak up the drink I had.

"Jesus," he mutters, shaking his head. "I've had two and I'm fine. I'll drive you home."

I roll my eyes. "Yes, because that makes a lick of difference."

"Come on, I'll take you home," he offers, trying to blackmail me by waving his fork with a chunk of truffle cake on in my face.

I would have said yes without the offer of food, but he doesn't need to know that. I lean forward, lips parted, ready to taste the yummy goodness, when my chair is pulled away from the table.

I look over my shoulder. "What the…" Clayton's powerful frame looms over us, and he does not look best pleased. "I thought you left with your *date*."

"We need to leave," he informs me shortly.

"I've not finished with my date."

"Oh, your date's over."

My jaw drops at the audacity. This is how I pictured my dad reacting, though there would be more hand movements and crazy rants.

"No, it's not, mate," Reid pipes in, and I send him a warning glance to shut up.

"I'm not your mate," he bites back before glaring down at me. "Come, Hayden. I've already asked the waitress to get your coat."

"Go back to your date," I snap, trying to shove my chair back under the table, but he doesn't budge or loosen his grip. "What is your problem?"

"There's an emergency at work and Chrissy needs you."

"Me? What could she possibly have done that would need her to call me?"

I'm stumped. The last time I tried to help Chrissy, I messed up her filing system and she went nuts. It took her weeks to put it back. It wasn't my first fuck up, either, which is why I never get called if someone needs a helping hand in the office.

"I'll explain in the car."

Anger rolls off him as he continues to glare at Reid, unable to look at me. If he thinks he can blag a blagger, he's wrong. Right now, he's full of shit. He reeks of it. And unless he explains himself, I'm not going anywhere.

"Well, unless you can tell me what is so important, I'm staying and finishing my date."

I manage to push my chair forward and silently gesture for Reid to give me the cake he promised.

He cocks an eyebrow, his lips twisting together in amusement as he holds a bite out to me. I moan around the fork, sensually sliding my lips off the prongs. It tastes better than the sticky pudding, that's for sure.

"That's it," Clayton snaps, pulling my chair back out again. "You're embarrassing yourself."

It's like a bucket of ice water has been thrown over me. His words cut deep, cooling me to the core.

I straighten in my chair, my focus solely on Reid as I try to make sense of the emotions trying to push through the anger. I'm hurt, embarrassed, but mostly, I'm fucking pissed.

Reid winks, crossing his arms over his chest as he kicks back, acting like he's sitting in front of a game.

"Excuse me," I whisper, deadly and stern, as I throw my serviette onto the table and stand.

"This is over. We aren't doing this anymore. We can find another way to help with Date Night."

Slowly, I face him, feeling my blood boil as it shoots through my veins. "I didn't want to do this in the first place. I practically begged you not to. But I did. For your company. And yet, I'm the one being an embarrassment? I'm not the one who is making a scene."

"Surprising," Reid mutters.

I glare at him. "Shut up."

"Why are you still here?" Clayton snaps, before addressing me. "You were right. I shouldn't have made you do this. But really, this guy? He hasn't even defended you."

"If she were anyone else, I'd have punched you already for being a dickhead, but you've got enough on your hands with her right now. You just made a huge mistake," Reid tells him, pushing up from his chair. "I'm going, but call me if you need me."

"She won't," Clayton snaps.

Reid stares him down before shaking his head in pity.

"I'll see you soon, Hayden. Unless you'd like a lift home?"

I go to take him up on the offer, wanting to get away from this situation. I mean, how dare he speak to me like this. I've done nothing but my job here.

"I've got her," Clayton assures him harshly.

Reid ignores him, pointedly waiting for me to answer.

"Let me get my coat."

Clayton grasps my arms, not tight, yet he's not being gentle either. "Hayden, please."

I close my eyes at the desperation in his voice. I want to knee him in the balls, but something in the way he pleads… it calls to me. Something tells me it's something he doesn't do often.

I don't look away from Reid, searching his face like he's got an answer for me. But he does nothing but wait, not giving me anything.

I'm torn.

"Hayden, please, let me drive you home."

I decide to stay, only to give him hell and to get answers.

"I'm fine. You can go, Reid." I don't wait for him to leave before turning to Clayton and poking him in the chest. "This might be a work thing, but I'm not on the clock right now. And even if I was, it gives you no right to speak to me that way, you prick. I'll wait outside for you," I snap, spinning on my heels.

The waitress from earlier stands near the podium, trying her hardest to avoid eye contact. She probably heard the entire thing.

As I get closer, I notice the flush to her cheeks and snort to myself. Reid clearly chatted her up on his way out.

"Enjoy the rest of your evening," she comments, her voice quivering.

"Yeah," I reply snidely, curling my lip. "I'm sure I will."

I snatch my coat, my temper flaring the more I replay Clayton's words and actions in my head.

The bitter cold wind slaps my face as I storm into the dimly lit car park. My heel catches on some ice and my heart races.

"Fuck," I hiss as I try to catch my balance—and fail.

Warm hands engulf me in a firm grip. "I got you."

Once I'm steady, I push Clayton away. "I'm so pissed at you. Livid. What gave you the right?"

"He was all over you."

"It was a date," I yell. "One you set up."

Disgust pours off him. "He was feeding you, touching you like he had a right. It was a first date. And you were lapping it up."

"What I do or don't do isn't your concern. I wasn't embarrassing myself."

"No, he was embarrassing you," he replies sharply. "He got the waitresses number when you went to the ladies room."

"Like I give a shit. It's Reid. He would flirt with his own grandma."

"You know him?"

"Yes, which is why we were so comfortable with each other."

Something flashes upon his face, and he rubs the back of his neck. "My God, I don't understand you at all."

A pain hits my chest. "Yeah, welcome to my club, you arsehole."

He reaches for me, the fight leaving his body. "Hayden…"

I slap his hand away. "No, Clayton. You overstepped tonight and made me look like a fool."

"The guy is a player."

"Like you and your date could talk. You were all over each other. And her laugh… my God, could she be any more fake?"

I lift my hand, ready to poke him in the chest, but this time he's quick, grabbing my wrist and pulling me towards him. I lose my balance, falling against him and landing with my hands on his chest.

The wind around us stills, the buzz from one of the streetlamps quietens, and in the mist of the dark night, there's us.

Just us.

An unforeseeable force pushes us together and sparks shoot between us, searching for a current.

Uncontrolled desire stares back at me, and before I can react, his hands are running along my jaw and up into my hair. He tilts my head up as he leans down—and presses his lips to mine.

My body loosens as I run my hands up his arms, marvelling over his physique, before resting them on his shoulders.

His kiss isn't innocent. He isn't teasing. It's hot and passionate, like he's dreamed of this moment his whole life.

He's showing me without words how he feels. So I show him back, pouring my everything into the moment.

I run my hands over his shoulders, down to his chest, feeling the rapid beat of his heart thump against my palm.

Pulling away, he rests his forehead against mine, breathing heavily.

"I'm sorry," he rasps, his voice wavering.

"Sorry?" I ask, still burning from that kiss.

The sigh he lets slip is full of regret. "I'm your boss. This can't happen."

It's like being doused with ice cold water for the second time tonight. With my hand still on his chest, I push him away.

His lips form a word, but a car door slamming nearby stops him from speaking.

We both turn to find Reid stepping out of his pick-up, a grin on his face as he zips up his jeans. His hair is tousled, his cheeks flushed. If I hadn't just been rejected after sharing the best kiss of my life, I would yell something dirty, happy he got some.

What shocks me is Cassandra stepping out behind him, wiping her mouth before smoothing her dress out.

At least tonight worked out for someone.

I snort, glaring at Clayton. "You can find your own way home."

I unlock my car, getting inside and quickly locking it again. It takes him a moment to pull his gaze away from Reid and Cassandra and take notice.

His knuckles tap on the glass, yet I ignore him, unable to face him as I slip out of my shoes and slide into my Uggs.

"Hayden," he calls, his voice getting louder. "Hayden, wait."

I start my car, giving him a chance to move. My expression must express just how I'm feeling right now, because he steps back, getting out of the way.

The last thing I see before driving out of the car park is his head bowed as he runs a hand through his hair.

If I wasn't so confused by the hurt and pain running through my chest, I would have reversed into him. It's what I would have done had he been anyone else.

I hate that I don't know what makes him different. Why I feel different when I'm around him. And as hard as I've tried not to, I like him. Not in a way where he has potential. He's the real deal. That kiss was everything my parents had warned me about.

"You'll know he's the one by the kiss, Hayden. It will be like your first kiss, even if you've been kissed before. Time will stop, you'll get this intense flutter in your stomach, and it will hurt to pull away. He'll be the only one to steal your breath with a kiss and make you see stars. Someone whose kisses are like that… he's the one," my mum had told me as a teenager. Her wisdom had stayed with me, and I knew I'd never settle for anyone without that kiss.

My dad, however, had another kind of wisdom to pass down.

"If someone kisses you like that, you should at least be thirty. Otherwise, knee the fucker in the balls and run. Run like you've never run before."

I should have gone with my dad's advice.

If I had, I wouldn't be driving on dark, windy roads with angry tears pouring down my cheeks.

ELEVEN

GEARS 5 IS PAUSED ON THE TELEVISION as I get comfortable on the sofa, a new tub of cookie dough ice cream in hand.

It's definitely needed after the phone call I had with Christina's boss. He was an arrogant prick, more bothered that someone else was going to jump on the headline story before him. So far, they could only speculate and ask for any witnesses to come forward, which doesn't exactly sell papers.

I have one more lead, but to pursue it, I need Liam to get me into the files Rob was unwilling to share with me.

The past twenty-four hours couldn't have gone more wrong. It's like the universe is against me.

After leaving the restaurant last night, I hit a drive-through and stewed on my anger. The touch and memory of our kiss was embedded in my head; it played over and over until I got to bed and fell asleep. Not even the best kiss I'd ever had could keep me from sleep. Nothing could.

He has fully managed to screw with my head, and that isn't an easy feat. I'm made of steel.

I kept replaying our moment, giving alterative endings. I went from him pulling me into his arms and whispering how much he wanted to take me home, to hitting him with my car as I pulled out of the car park.

I'm never at a loss for words. I have comebacks for everything. Which is why I spent the morning sulking, angry I didn't have anything to say to him. I'm not fond of this feeling. I'm giving myself until two to pout, and then I'm going to pull on my big girl pants and move on.

I have two weeks off after this week, and I plan on spending it by getting my shit together.

And drunk.

With Faith's hen/stag party coming up, there will be plenty of alcohol involved to soothe my wounded pride.

My mobile vibrates on the coffee table, pulling my attention away from my thoughts. Reluctantly, I place my ice cream on the table before picking up my phone.

"Hey, Liam."

"Hey, trouble."

"Did you find what we needed?"

Laughter slips through the phone. "Not even your dad was this demanding, and he could win awards for being a diva."

"Let's not rehash the old times," I tease, knowing he loves me.

"Old times," he mutters. "I'm not old."

"You know I love you really."

"Which is why I'm doing this, kid. I got into the paper's records and they're telling the truth. There are no records of the story she was working on. But her computer was wiped clean. Whoever cleaned it knew what they were doing because I couldn't find a trace anywhere."

"I was certain there was something there. Her boss has been avoiding my calls all week, and today he couldn't get me off the phone quick enough."

"You can be difficult," he tells me hesitantly.

I beam at the praise. "Thank you." It wasn't how I interpreted our phone call, however. "What about the witness Rob mentioned?"

"Are you positive they got a statement?"

"Yes. He said there was nothing they could use though."

"He saw this statement?"

What is he getting at?

"I didn't ask. I only assumed he had. He said a colleague went to take it. Why?"

"Because it doesn't exist, Hayden."

That can't be right.

"How is that even possible? They have a name."

"I've looked through their entire system, not just that case file."

"Isn't that illegal?"

"Technically, yes, but I helped improve their computer security. I'd say that gives me rights."

I roll my eyes. "Of course it does."

"I dug deeper on the name you gave me in case something stood out as weird. I got nothing. I do have an address. I'll email it to you."

"Thanks, but what about this statement?"

"Not sure, kid," he tells me, but I detect the lie rolling off his tongue. "The system hasn't been hacked. That would have come up when I did a system check."

"So, whoever changed it had access." I mull that over, none of the scenarios good. However, it still doesn't give me a link as to how that's connected to Christina's murder and the break-ins.

"I'm not sure. I don't know what was in the statement to say whether it was worthless information or if someone thought it was important to remove. Either way, it shouldn't have been removed from their file. It should be on their system, even if the statement was removed. The only way this exists at the moment is by word of mouth."

"I'll think on it, see what I can come up with. I'll keep it from Rob for the time being. Because if it has gone or been misplaced, it will put him in a difficult situation." I take in a steady breath. "I'll go see the witness and hopefully get some answers."

"Hayden, maybe you should drop this or get Beau to look into it. He's new there and won't have problems looking into what happened."

"I don't want to get Beau involved for that reason. He's made a home here. I don't want to get him fired. Then he'd have to work away somewhere."

His heavy sigh sounds conflicted. "Just don't do this alone, for heaven's sake. I don't want your dad to revoke my Godfather status."

"Didn't he already do that when you gave us those sour Haribo's?"

He sniffs. "He didn't mean it. He knew he deserved it after getting me drunk and putting me in that rubber dinghy on the river. I woke up to two swans going at it and no idea where the fuck I was."

A burst of laughter slips free before I pull myself together. "I won't go alone, I promise."

"Take Landon. No one will think to fuck with you then."

As much as I trust my brother to take care of me, I couldn't put him in that position.

Ever since the moment I felt him die, I've worried constantly about him. I could survive the pain of losing anyone, no matter how it hurt or what they meant to me, but if I ever lost one of my brothers, I would die inside. They're a part of me in a way no one else could or ever would be. We're triplets.

"I'll see if he's free," I lie.

"Okay, I need to get going, so I'll speak to you later."

"All right. Love you, Uncle Liam."

"Love you too, kid."

After ending the call, I take stock of the ice cream tubs and junk food wrappers littering my table.

I'm pathetic.

It's enough to get me off my arse and to my feet. I don't mope. I don't dwell. And this story isn't going to write itself.

I know exactly who can go with me, since they were meant to be coming over here at two.

SLAMMING MY CAR door shut, I then lock my car, hating that I have to leave the warmth of my car heater.

We always park outside Lily's house when we visit Charlotte. Her driveway is down a small lane between Lily's and the library Charlotte owns on the corner. It's a small cul-de-sac of some kind hidden behind the houses and other buildings next to the library.

Since Charlotte only has room for one car, we all park here and use Lily's garden to get there. It saves us having to walk down her shitty lane that has potholes and mud puddles when it rains, and from getting stung by the overgrown stingers to the side.

Blanche slams the lid on her bin down when she notices me.

"Why are you here?" she yells, her voice like nails on a chalkboard.

"Why are you? Aren't you past your expiry date?"

A gruff growl escapes her. "You are the spawn of Satan."

I shudder. "If it wouldn't offend my beauty, I'd say that made you my mother."

"I'm going to get you banned from coming here."

I shrug, knowing it will never happen. "Try."

"Is everything okay?" Lily's soft, musical voice asks.

She steps outside, wrapped in a long beige wool coat and a matching set of brown gloves and a hat. Jaxon steps out behind her, shutting the door with a smirk on his lips when he's sees who I'm talking to.

Prick.

I sigh. "Blanche was trying to get me to set her up with someone."

Lily smiles, her entire face lit up with happiness. "That is so amazing."

"She's lying. Stay away, evil child," Blanche growls, slamming her door shut behind her.

"Were you coming to see me? Lily asks, chewing her lower lip. "We were on our way out."

The guilt on her face has me reassuring her quickly. "I'm just going to see Charlotte, but I will catch up with you when you're free."

She lets go of her lip, visibly relaxing. "I'd really love that."

"I'll catch you both later."

"Wait, who are you setting Blanche up with?"

My gaze flicks from Lily to Jaxon, who looks smug as fuck.

"Jaxon's granddad."

I leave him with his mouth hanging open and race up the garden to the small gate Maverick installed a little while ago to make it easier for us to come back and forth.

Letting myself in, I hear sobbing and head towards the sound. What's she got herself into now? As I pass a set of shelves in her hallway, I see a flicker of movement and duck in time to miss her cat taking a swipe at me.

The thing hisses, so I hiss back, baring my teeth. "Don't make me lock you outside," I warn it, before stepping into the front room.

The scene before me doesn't surprise me. Charlotte has always been nutty—it's why she's my favourite. But what does surprise me is the gruesome scene on the television.

"You got scared to tears again?"

Jumping, Charlotte spills her bowl of popcorn. "Oh, Hayden, it's so sad."

I glance at the television to check I'm seeing this right.

I am.

My brows draw together. "What is?"

"He was bullied by the kids at his school and his parents always made fun of him. That one," she says, pointing to a brown-haired chick with an axe, "just taunted him about it and then killed him."

"Isn't he the killer?" I ask, motioning to the creepy looking thing on the screen as I sit down, grabbing a handful of popcorn.

"Yes."

"Then why are you crying?"

She bursts into tears again as the credits begin to roll. "It was so sad. He only wanted to be loved."

"Well, okay then," I mutter, before realising she's alone. "I thought you were spending the morning with Scott?"

She's suddenly interested in flicking through Netflix. "We should find a movie."

"What happened?" I ask, leaving no room for argument.

She shifts on the sofa, facing me. "I upset him. He thinks he likes me more than I like him."

"And if he did like you more than you liked him, what's the problem?"

I hate this Scott already, and I've not even met him. They just met. They should be getting to know one another, not having a competition on who cares for whom more.

"I really like him. I do. But I think I'm doing it wrong."

Please don't let this be about sex.

"Doing what wrong?"

"Being a girlfriend. I keep messing up." Her bottom lip begins to tremble.

"Does he tell you that?" I ask softly, hiding the need to yell about the piece of shit.

I can sense the lie before she even opens her mouth. Her gaze diverts to the side and she twists her fingers together in her lap.

"No. No, nothing like that."

"Charlotte," I warn.

"What do you want to watch?"

Sighing, I let her think I'm dropping it. I'm not. I'm going to give this Scott a real Carter greeting and let Landon know to do the same.

He's going to feel like shit once he finds out. He loves Charlotte. They've been close our whole lives. I think his hero complex was drawn to her bubbly personality and naivety.

With Paisley now in his life, he's not been around as much, and it's starting to show. I don't want some toss pot thinking he can take advantage of her. She's family. No one fucks with my family.

"Why don't we watch Grey's Anatomy until it's time to go out?" I offer, giving her a small smile.

"Out where?" she asks, visibly relaxing.

"I'll explain later." She's definitely holding back, but until she's ready to talk, there's no use in trying to push her. "What episode should we watch?"

"Ooh, we could watch the episode where Izzy gets married."

I roll my eyes. "Or the one where McDreamy dies."

She twists her lips. "That's not really a cheerful episode."

"Really? You just sat here crying over a serial killer. Horror movies aren't meant to make you cry."

She mulls over my words before shrugging. "All right, as long as you skip to the part where she tells people he's dead."

"After we watch the car scene."

"Deal."

TWELVE

"**Y**OU ARE SO KIND TO DO THIS, HAY," Charlotte comments as I follow the directions on the sat nav.

"I know. I love to give," I murmur, my thoughts on the tea hamper I put together. I'm hoping it isn't too much. It didn't feel right turning up empty handed though. And the residents at Nightingale care home swear by the tea.

"Tell me again how you found out she witnessed a break-in and was shaken up. You didn't answer earlier."

For good reason. I hate lying. Sure, sometimes it's fun to mess with people by overemphasizing or stretching out the truth, but outright lying to Charlotte seemed wrong. But sometimes, it was a necessity, like now. It's not because she could find out what I do for a living but because I know she would worry, and when Charlotte worries, she bakes and gets chatty. It never ends well. For anyone. Especially if she's really stressed and screams at you to try her cake. You eat that cake because, although it's rare she ever loses her temper, when she does she's a completely different person. But then they do say redheads have a hot temper.

Knowing it's the only way to save my stomach from being pumped again, I answer, "Her dad is a resident at the care home. I went to take him lunch and he asked me to check in on her, said he knew she was lying about being okay over the phone."

"You should show the others this side of you. They wouldn't call you a witch. You're so kind and always helping others."

"They just hate that they aren't me," I tell her, knowing it was Aiden and Mark who called me a witch. They're still sore that I got out of paying for our tab when I caused a fight between them and another group of lads.

"You're right. I've always wished I was more like you," she tells me, glancing down at her phone.

We come to a stop at a red light, so I turn to her, waiting until she meets my gaze to answer. "Don't ever be anything but you. You are special in a way other people wish they were. Never Change."

Her eyes dilate, filling with tears. "I won't," she promises, before I go back to paying attention to the road.

"We're here," I tell her a few minutes later. I slow down to read the house numbers.

When Rita's, the witness's house, comes into view, I pull into the nearest parking space.

I pull out my phone, scrolling through my emails. "I just need to double check something."

I want to make sure I have everything right, so I don't go up there and fuck up. After all, I'm going to pretend to be the granddaughter of the woman who was hurt when she had her house broken into.

According to the information I have, she never moved back in, which gives me a chance to pass this off.

"Are we going in?" Charlotte asks.

Or not.

"Um, Charlotte, would you mind if I just make sure it's okay for us to be here first? I don't want to overwhelm her."

Or have my cover blown.

"Of course, just wave me over when you're ready," she tells me absently, typing away on her phone.

I go to ask her if it's Scott but think better of it. If she gets upset when we've run him off, I don't want her to think it was because I didn't like him.

The guys can take the fall.

"Okay."

I leave her texting and head over to the house, one door away from where we've parked, and up a small path.

I rap on the door with my knuckles before standing back and waiting for someone to answer.

I hear movement before a loud crash echoes through the house. Seconds later, the door opens and a woman in her mid-twenties stands on the threshold. Her cheeks are flushed with a pink tinge, and although there aren't any tears in her sparkling blue eyes, I can simply tell she's been crying by how swollen and bloodshot they are.

"I'm sorry, I can see this isn't a good time. I can come back," I tell her, sensing a deep, grieving loss. It's the same look many of us wore when our grandparents died.

Dread fills my stomach and I want to reach out and hold her, tell her everything will be okay. She folds her arms across her stomach, vulnerability pouring from her.

"It's okay," she rushes out when I step away to leave. "What can I help you with?"

The only reason I answer, and the only reason I stay, is because this girl might be fragile, but she's screaming for a distraction.

"I'm Hayden Carter. I'm looking for Rita Jones," I tell her, cringing when my thoughts are confirmed.

Her face pales, her bottom lip trembling. "She—she passed away last week."

Fucking hell.

Sucking in a lungful of air, I move a step forward, taking her by surprise when I hold her hand, giving it a gentle squeeze. "I didn't know. I'm truly sorry for your loss."

"Thank you. Did you know my nan?"

"I—I, um." I pause to gather my nerves. I can't lie to this woman. She's already going through enough. She deserves my honesty. "I didn't personally, no. I'm friends with someone who is looking into the murder of the reporter that came to ask Rita some questions about the break-in."

I badly want to ask how her nan died, but the timing seems morbid. It can't be a coincidence that two people connected to the break-ins have died.

"I read about that in the paper. Do you think the two are connected?"

"They aren't sure. I'm just backtracking her footsteps before the murder," I partially lie.

"I'm sorry."

"I know this is a lot to ask, but could me and my cousin," I begin, pointing to my car, "come in? I'd like to ask some questions about the night of the break-in."

Her eyebrows scrunch together. "I don't understand. My nan already gave the police a statement."

"I know. I'm just wondering what she saw that night that made Christina come here to ask questions."

She looks back into the house, before nodding. "There's not a lot I can really tell you. But yes, you can both come in."

I stop myself from jumping with glee when I remember she's lost someone.

"I'll just go get my cousin."

"All right. Let yourself in, I just want to go sweep some glass up. I'm Beth, by the way."

I give her a nod before walking back down the path, waving Charlotte over.

She gets out, grabbing the hamper from the backseat. I wait for her to shut the door before locking the car.

"Everything okay?" she asks, reading my face.

"Rita passed away last week. Her granddaughter is there."

Tears brim the edge of her eyelids. "That poor girl. She must be really hurting. It still hurts when I think of Nan and Granddad. And I bet they didn't want to risk telling her dad in case he took a turn for the worse."

I pull her in for a side hug, careful not to knock into the tea hamper. Losing Nan and Granddad had been hard on all of us. They were the heart of the family and we all truly felt their loss.

"They went together and weren't in pain," I remind her, knowing it was the only saving grace of their death. They weren't alone. It doesn't change how much we miss them, or how hard it was to move through our grief, but it does help. "And let's not mention the dad in case it brings up more bad memories."

"Let's see if there's anything we can do to help. She's probably going through one of the hardest parts of losing someone."

I look up at the two-storey bricked house, sighing. Charlotte's right. When we cleaned out Nan and Granddad's, it was tougher than the funeral in some ways. It truly felt like a goodbye. None of us wanted to give or throw away anything that belonged to the two most important people in our lives. It felt like we were erasing them. It wasn't odds and ends, it was their life. Where we grew up. The only saving grace during that whole ordeal was we knew we wouldn't have to watch someone else live there.

"Come on," I tell her, leading her up to the door and letting us in.

"I've put the kettle on," Beth announces, stepping into the hallway.

I look around the small hallway with stairs leading up. The beige walls have lighter marks where pictures used to hang. The green patterned carpet is lighter where furniture used to be. I look at Beth once again, seeing nothing but sadness.

I feel guilty for being here, for intruding on such an emotional and dreadful time.

"We got your nan this, but, um, we didn't know…" Charlotte trails off.

"Is that earl tea?"

Charlotte beams. "There's lavender in there too."

"My favourite," she tells us, before she loses her smile. "My nan's too."

"I'm Charlotte," she greets. "Did you want me to put this in the kitchen? It's kind of heavy."

"Oh God, I'm sorry. Where are my manners? Come in. The kitchen is through there."

Beth leads us through a set of glass doors with dark wooden frames and into a living room.

"Why don't I make us all one," Charlotte offers when she sees the state of the living room. "You should sit down for five minutes."

"Thank you. It's just through that door," she explains, pointing to the far left. She surveys the mess and winces. "Let me clear some of this up so you can sit down."

"I'll help," I tell her, helping her transfer some of her nan's belongings to the floor in a neat pile.

"How did your nan die, if you don't mind me asking?"

She sits down on the wicca chair as I take a seat on the brown two-seater.

"I don't mind at all. It's still a shock, if I'm honest. They ruled it as a heart attack. I think getting herself worked up over the break-in caused it. I live an hour away and was on my way over when her care assistant called to tell me she had passed."

"I'm really sorry for your loss," I tell her sincerely. "What did you mean, she was getting herself worked up?"

She runs a hand over her jogging bottoms. "There's something you need to understand about my nan; she hadn't been well for a while. She hasn't been with it lately. For months we've had a call-out care assistant check in on her. She's been forgetful, suffering with mild insomnia, and hallucinating at times. When we spoke the week of her death, she feared she was being watched and would rant about them knowing she saw something and were trying to shut her up."

"Saw?"

"The break-in. She saw who did it."

"You didn't believe her?"

"I'm honestly not sure. It didn't seem like her usual ramblings or conspiracies to me. She was genuinely scared for her life. She changed a lot after she gave those statements; more lucid and less scatty. In a way, I worried she would leave a stove on. Instead, she just seemed quiet, distracted and withdrawn."

"Did she witness them breaking in or running out?"

"Nan said she saw a young male lurking around outside when she came down to make a cup of tea. She couldn't remember what compelled her to look outside. She was going to call the police, but her mind got distracted and she must have forgotten. She went back up to bed when she heard cars pulling into the street and saw the flashing lights. She said she went to the window that looks out onto the alley and part of the street to take a nosey. She said the young man from earlier was there with another man. They were arguing and the young man had blood on his cheek."

"Do you have a record of who took the statement?"

"I wasn't here for them. The break-in happened early hours of the morning and I didn't get here until ten. By then, they had already taken notes of what she saw. To be honest, I don't think they took her seriously, from what she told me. I think she kept getting the events of the night muddled and was changing her footsteps of what lead up to what she saw. The only thing that didn't change was what she witnessed."

"What about the second statement?"

"She didn't really want to talk about it to me. It was actually Joyce, her carer, who mentioned there was a second one. She didn't like the vibe she got from the officer or my nan's behaviour after he left. She seemed skittish and withdrawn."

This is the information. This is what Christina had been looking into.

I don't want to scare Beth, but I can't leave without asking. "Are you sure it was a police officer?"

"I asked the same thing. Joyce said he was in full uniform."

"What company does Joyce work for? Do you know if Christina asked for her details?"

"I only got the end of the conversation between the two, so not that I know of. She did speak like the officer and the guy from the alley were the same person, but like I said, I missed half of what was said. From what I read, though, they didn't catch who broke in, so that can't be true."

She really has no clue. I need proof, but if I were to guess, it was an officer in that alley, and that it was the guy who attacked Mrs Sutherland. It makes sense as to why Rita's statement went missing. I just need proof of his involvement. He could be protecting a family member.

"Here you go," Charlotte announces, walking into the room and passing us each a mug of tea.

"Thank you," Beth tells her, before looking at me. "Do you think it was the same person? Was she right and someone scared my nan that bad it caused her to have a heart attack?"

I glance at Charlotte, who's distracted by the piles of pictures. "I really can't answer that, but I know someone who can find out the answer. You can trust him too. He's marrying my cousin and completely trustworthy."

"Please," she pleads, tears slipping free. "I just need answers, but a part of me is wondering if that's to satisfy my own failings. I should have tried harder to find a job closer to her."

"You can't take on that guilt. I'll do what I can. I promise."

"Thank you."

"Would you like us to stay and help you? We know from experience how hard this is and it seems your nan was a hoarder like ours. You shouldn't be doing this alone," Charlotte offers, giving her a gentle smile.

"You don't need to do that," Beth informs us, her expression crumbling.

"She's right, you shouldn't be doing this alone."

She nods, wiping away her tears. "Thank you. It's been Nan and I for so long. I did try to reach out to friends, but they're all busy with work."

My phone begins to ring, and I groan at the inappropriate timing.

"Give me two minutes and I'll gladly help you. I just need to answer this."

I quickly rush to answer, getting up from the chair and heading outside as Charlotte begins to chat to her.

"Hello?"

"We'll talk about you ignoring me all night after you tell me why you are calling the local paper and hounding them about a reporter that was killed," Clayton grits out.

I should put the phone down and pretend my battery died. But I don't. I hate that my stomach swirls at the sound of his voice.

"None of your business."

"Well, you see, it is. You work for me, and looking into dangerous stories is not part of your job description," he bites out, his voice harder.

"What I do in my spare time is none of your concern."

"This is about the break-ins, isn't it? I told you not to look into that story, Hayden. It's dangerous. A woman was kidnapped and killed. What are you thinking, risking your life for a story we won't even publish?"

My back straightens, and I grit my teeth to the point my jaw hurts.

"Who said it was for your company?"

"What else would it be for?" he snaps.

"For my blog."

"Your blog?"

"Yes."

"You have a blog?" he asks, not sounding convinced.

"I will. I have my cousin's girlfriend building me a website."

I don't, but I will. It's something I want to do and no man or job will stop me.

"This is absurd. Do you have any idea of the danger you're putting yourself in? You'll stop looking into this right away, Hayden, or so help me God, I will—"

"You'll do nothing because you don't own me," I tell him, raising my voice a little. I'm fuming. I don't get mad, I get even, so Clayton getting a rise out of me only makes me madder.

"Hayden, I'm not kidding with you right now. This isn't your job. Your job is to give advice and answer questions, not risk your life doing a cop's work. Put an end to this. I'm not having you bring bad press to this company because you were idiotic. And I won't have you using my company's name to open doors for people to feed this hobby you have."

Yet again, he proves what a prick he is. How dare he squelch my dreams like they mean nothing. How dare he categorise it as a hobby.

"Now we've got that cleared up, we need to talk about last night," he tells me, his voice lowering.

"Clayton?"

"Yes."

"Respectfully, fuck off. I'm the kind of person who will put you in my boot and help the police look for your body. Don't piss me off."

I end the call, silencing it when it begins to ring again.

Charlotte steps out, glancing behind her before speaking, lowering her voice. "I can totally understand why they didn't tell Rita's dad now. He's ancient. Mrs Jones was eighty-five when she passed."

I need a drink.

THIRTEEN

Avoiding Clayton had gone successfully all week, up until this point. Now, the man is sat opposite me, waiting rather impatiently while I quickly answer another call. Trying to ignore him is impossible. If he sighs one more time he's going to get a microphone shoved down his throat. And he's looking at me like I just keyed his car. If anyone has a right to be pissed here, it's me, not him.

I guess after ignoring his calls and dodging him at work, he's finally reached his limit and feels like he has the right to be pissed.

It doesn't change anything.

I don't need him to sit me down and tell me all the reasons why he shouldn't have kissed me. If he does, I'll give him a list of ways in which I'll get revenge.

He's waiting for me to finish up, but that isn't happening as I press for another call.

"Hello, Russ, what can we help you with today?" I ask, focusing on the sheet in front of me and not Clayton, who has begun to twirl his fist in a circle, silently telling me to wind this up.

Completely ignoring him, I continue doing my job, not caring that I've gone over ten minutes already. I'm kind of hoping that if I take long enough, he'll get bored and leave.

"Yeah. A while back, a crazy girlfriend went psycho on me because I wasn't into her sick and twisted kinks. I love her, I do, but I can't get past it. We've tried having basic sex, but she doesn't get turned on, not like she does when her, um, kinks are involved. What can I do to stop it?"

There are not many times where I can say that I've frozen, but right now, all I can do is gape at the microphone, at the sound of his voice, before glaring up at Clayton, placing all the blame on him. If I hadn't been so off my game in his presence, I would have picked up on who the caller was.

"Hello?" Russell calls, but I can't form a word, let alone a sentence.

Eyebrows drawn together, Clayton then gives a small shake of his head, silently asking me what's wrong.

"Have you tried to get into her kinks, Russ?" Clayton answers when it becomes apparent that I'm not going to.

"It's wrong, man. How do I get her to stop liking it?"

"You can't get her to stop liking it. Everyone has their kinks. Some people fantasise about being in control, being submissive, or enjoy the adrenaline of being caught. There is never just one. Have you tried to talk to her and ask her what it is about it that turns her on? Maybe you can meet her halfway."

"There's no talking to her. I've tried. I'm the only one who will even touch her because of it. The girl is crazy."

Snapping out of it, I run everything he said through my mind. I can't tell if he's the woman in this scenario, and I'm the crazy part, or if he's actually met a girl with this fetish. From the way I left him on New Year, I'm guessing it's the first.

I'm not sure if he knows this is my show, but either way, I'm not letting this go.

"What is this kink?" I ask, deepening my voice a little, causing frowns from Chrissy and Clayton. "It could help give you answers."

"She, um, she likes a golden shower and other stuff deposited on her?"

"Is that a question?"

"Yes. No. Can you help make it stop or not?" he barks out.

"I'm not sure. It seems to me this is a form of dominance. Do you like being submissive?"

"What? I'm dominant. No bitch is going to tell me what to do."

My lips twitch. "So, really this isn't about a girl but about you. Do you like people taking a piss on you?"

"What kind of show is this?" he rages, genuinely offended.

The only thing that stops me from laughing is Clayton. I don't want to get fired, not when I'm meant to be neutral. I can give my attitude and blunt advice, but to laugh or make fun of someone's experience is frowned upon.

"Answer me," I reply harshly.

"Okay. Okay. So, my crazy ex threw some kind of concoction on me, and ever since, I like the feel of crap smothered all over me." I'm both disgusted and amused.

"And why did your ex throw it on you?" I ask, waiting for his bullshit excuse.

"Do I know you?"

"No, Russ, you really don't." And he never did.

"She's batshit crazy. Has a real problem taking instruction, if you get my meaning?"

My teeth grind together. "Or maybe she did it for another reason."

"No. Her entire family are nuts. I had her dad come by and shove my head down the loo, all because I broke it off with her and she didn't like it. She couldn't handle losing me. I get it a lot, but she's a new brand of crazy."

Why do people keep calling me crazy?

And his bullshit story about my dad is ludicrous. He doesn't even know who he is or which flat it was… God, who am I kidding. He's Max Carter.

"You mean you cheated on her?"

I grab my phone, quickly typing out a text to my dad.

HAYDEN: Did you pay Russell a visit, by any chance?

"We weren't exclusive."

"Or maybe you didn't like that she got one over on you."

"Why don't we calm down," Clayton interrupts, shaking his head in disapproval at me.

DAD: Did that pussy say I was there?

"Must be her time of the month," Russ tries to joke.

"Or maybe I'm just done with people who don't take this channel seriously."

"Are you sure we don't know each other?"

HAYDEN: Did you at least make sure no one saw you? You could lose your job if he decides to go to the police, Dad.

DAD: Kind of insulted you think I'm an idiot. I raised you better, girl.

I roll my eyes. "I'm sure."

"Russ, I'd find a substance that's not going to gross you out. Try chocolate syrup or honey," Clayton tells him. "That's it for tonight. Dream will be here to take your calls next week."

"You," he growls, when the red 'off air' button comes on.

"I need to go; my dad needs me." I get up, ready to make my break for it, when two arms sweep me off my feet and I'm thrown over his shoulder. "Put me down! This is misconduct."

"Take it up with the boss," he snidely remarks. "We need to talk."

———————————————

"YOU DIDN'T NEED to carry me off like a lunatic," I snap, slamming the car door.

"You wouldn't listen," he fires back, his green eyes seething. "You've ignored me all week."

Of course I have.

I survey where we are, my stomach grumbling at all the different aromas coming from the restaurants. He'd brought me to the one place I would never run from. Blueborn food court. The place is gigantic, filled with different restaurants supplying a range of food.

"You could have just mentioned food," I grumble under my breath, stomping up the entrance steps to Boo's.

It's my favourite place to get a burger. They have all kinds of amazing foods, but their burgers are their signature seller.

"Two please," Clayton declares to the waitress.

She picks up two menus before leading us through the busy restaurant to a booth opposite the bar.

Since I'm in a mood, I don't argue when Clayton orders our drinks, instead taking my jacket off before taking a seat.

"What was that back at work?" he asks, undoing his suit jacket as he takes a seat.

This is what he wants to talk about? Really?

"You don't want to know."

"I really do," he tells me, but from the tone of his voice, I'd say he really doesn't. He begins to shift in his seat, opening and closing his mouth a few times before finally asking, "Are you really into that stuff?"

I burst out laughing. He clearly had selective hearing and only heard the worst parts of the conversation once he realised I knew who it was.

"Yes. Yes, I really am."

He gapes, leaning forward on the table as he runs a hand over his jaw. "I mean, I assumed you knew the man, but I've been wrong before when trying to read you. I was just guessing he was an ex," he rambles, paling somewhat.

I throw the salt shaker at him, hitting him in the chest. "Do I look like someone who enjoys being pissed on?"

"Oh my God," the waitress blurts out, jerking to a stop next to our table, our drinks sloshing over the edge of the glasses. She slowly puts them down. "I'm sorry. I'll come back to take your order."

I lightly reach for her wrist, stopping her, ignoring the flinch. "No need. I'll have your double whopper bacon burger and chips, a side order of onion rings and garlic bread, and two sides of those cheese melt things."

"Okay, got it. I'll get someone to bring over two share plates," she tells me, scribbling fast on her notepad.

"Um, no," I bite out, wondering where she gets off on thinking I'd share my food. I clear my throat when she noticeably pales once again. "He just wants a burger and chips."

She scurries off and I slowly turn to Clayton, my jaw clenching before I lean over for the pepper shaker and throw it at him.

"Stop throwing shit at me, Hayden."

"She thinks I enjoy being pissed on."

A squeak from beside me has me closing my eyes briefly, wondering what I did in a past life to deserve this. My shoulders sag when I find the same waitress beside us.

"Um… do you, um—would you like the house burger sauce?"

"Yes, please, on both," Clayton replies, sounding amused.

That prick.

I smile sweetly, reaching over to grab his hand, taking him by surprise. "Now, let's talk about you wanting a golden shower."

The waitress rushes off, apologising to someone on her way, but I'm too busy gloating at Clayton. Well, I am, until I hear it—

"You will do no such thing," Dad roars.

I groan, sliding out of the booth and blocking Dad's path when he goes for Clayton.

Why is this happening today?

"Move, Hayden, I'm going to fuck up this sick twat."

"Maybe 'fuck' isn't the correct term to use, Max," Mum advises, and I glare at her for making it worse.

"Dad, stop," I cry out, pushing him back. "It's not what you think."

His stern gaze hits me, making me take a step back. It's the same look he gave me when I snuck out late so I could go hang out with my mates.

"How is him," he bites out, pointing to Clayton as the veins in his temples pulse, "wanting you to… to *urinate*, me getting the wrong idea?"

"Because I said it to embarrass him in front of the waitress," I tell him calmly, before glancing at my mum, who looks hot in her new outfit. "Looking hot, mummaliscious."

"Oh," Dad mutters, still glaring at Clayton.

"Thanks, baby. Your dad decided to treat me tonight, so I thought I'd make an effort."

Dad, only just registering what was said, pulls his gaze away from Clayton. "What? I always treat you, woman. Just this morning I did that thing with my—"

"Dad," I yell, covering my ears. "Shut up."

"Sorry for the misunderstanding. I'm Clayton Cross. It's nice to finally meet you. Hayden talks about you a lot," Clayton says, placing one hand on my hip while holding the other out for my dad to shake. Heat from his touch warms me, and my stomach flutters as I involuntarily lean back into his embrace.

Behind Dad's back, Mum smirks, waggling her eyebrows and giving me a thumbs up to cement her approval.

Dad, however, reminds me of someone who has woken up after sleep walking and has no idea where they are as his gaze flickers from Clayton's outstretched hand, up to his face.

"Of course it's fucking nice to meet me," he snaps, before glaring down at where Clayton's hand is resting on my hip. "Now, tell me what the hell you're doing with my daughter. My only daughter."

"Dad, you know the rules," I remind him.

He sniffs, turning away. "I know the rules, Hayden. But nowhere does it state that I can't ask questions regarding my daughter."

"You have rules?" Clayton asks, his interest piqued.

"Who are you again?" Dad snaps.

"Max, why don't we sit down and order food before last orders are called and leave Hayden to it."

"No."

She sighs, telling the waitress to give them another minute.

"I'm—" Clayton starts, but I spin, forcing him to sit down.

"Going to shut up and sit down," I grit out, giving him a pointed look.

"I'm not doing this again," he hisses. "The other day, you told that woman I was a male escort."

I wave him off. "She's a noscy neighbour of my cousin. She'd blab." Blanche probably wouldn't, but I didn't want to take any chances.

"Hayden," he growls.

I sigh, turning to my dad. "We're on a date. I'm still deciding whether to go on another with him. He's obsessed, and so in love with me. I kind of feel sorry for him."

"Hay—"

"Of course he is," Dad states, confused as to why he wouldn't be. "You're a Carter."

"That's not—"

"Shh,' I tell Clayton, pressing my finger across his lips. "I'm a hard person to get over, I know."

"Max," Mum calls. "They're going to give away our table."

The waitress, along with another, takes that moment to bring our food. I sit back down, getting out of the way, licking my lips at the sight of all the food.

Dad's stomach growls. "The cheesy goodness," he moans. "I want lots of those."

My waitress steps back, looking at Dad with an apologetic smile. "Actually, sir, these were our last batch for the day."

"What?" Dad screeches, placing a hand on his chest as he struggles to breathe.

Clayton goes to stand, but I grab his wrist, slightly shaking my head.

"Mum," I call, not needing to say any more as I grab the salt and pepper from Clayton's side.

"Come on, babe, we can see if they have those curly fries you love."

"With the cheese topping?" he asks, sniffing, letting her pull him away.

"Yeah, babe," she tells him, before glancing over her shoulder at me. "Enjoy your date, baby."

"I will, Mum."

Once they're safely out of earshot and across the room, I turn to an open-mouthed Clayton. I grin, clasping my hands together. "Well, that went *really* well."

"He…" he whispers, pointing to where Dad once stood.

"Is the best, I know. And sadly, you won't be seeing each other again."

"I'm sure we will at the stag/ hen party," he tells me distractedly as he pours vinegar over his chips.

I pause mid-chew before quickly swallowing. "Excuse me, could you repeat that?"

He finishes cutting his burger in half before answering. "Sorry, I assumed you were aware I was attending. We need to go check out Mingles, anyway."

No.

No, no, no.

"We can do that another time. Any time that isn't my cousin's hen party."

"Yeah, we could, but this saves taking more time away from the office."

"But wouldn't it be great if we did," I tell him forcefully.

"Plus, Charlotte kindly sent me an invitation via email," Clayton continues, ignoring me.

"No."

He sighs, placing his burger down. "Yes, Hayden. It will give us more time to talk about what transpired last week."

"You mean when you sabotaged my date, kissed me and then regretted it?" I snap, shoving a few chips into my mouth.

"That's not—"

"I can't talk about this with you right now."

I give him a tight smile when I see Dad looking over, probably trying to read our lips to see what's going on, but from where his gaze is aimed, he might just be sour over my cheesy bites.

I pick one up, inwardly laughing when his gaze follows, and pop it into my mouth. His expression hardens before he turns to Mum, beginning one of his rants.

From the corner of my eye, I notice Clayton go for one. I slap his hand away, narrowing my eyes. "Don't touch my cheesy bites. If you wanted some, you should have ordered your own."

"You didn't give me a chance," he argues, pouting.

I roll my eyes, throwing a scrunched-up napkin at him. "You're grown man. Don't use that excuse."

"Five days with you is going to be a nightmare, isn't it?"

"You'll never know, because I'm telling Charlotte you aren't going. I'll make up an excuse."

"Why? I'm going to be there regardless. It will only confuse her when she sees us together."

"Then I quit."

"You're under contract remember."

Fucking wanker.

FOURTEEN

"I REALLY DON'T WANT TO TALK about this. I want you to leave. It's for your own safety," I stress.

"Careful, I might start to think you actually like me," Clayton teases.

I don't understand why he is so set on coming with us. He only really knows me. Okay, I don't really care that he doesn't know anyone. I'm more bothered about the fact I have to spend five days with a man who I'm highly attracted to but who only sees me as an employee.

And then there's the drinking. I tend to get horny when I've had a few.

Or I end up doing something ridiculous, with no recollection as to why the next day.

"I'd like to keep your employees in work. With you dead, the company will go bust and all those people will lose their jobs," I lie.

"Your father seemed nice enough to me, so the rest of your family will be a breeze." He pulls into a free space before shutting off the car. "Now, about that kiss."

I throw the rest of my stale muffin that I grabbed from the staff room at the care home at him. Clayton arranged to pick me up there after my shift and even turned up early so he could sit with his dad.

He snatches the muffin mid-air, his reflexes getting quicker, before leaning across the parking brake and getting close. "If there weren't so many people around, I would bend you over the backseat and spank your arse. I'm getting fed up of you throwing shit at me."

Suddenly, I'm hyperaware of how close he is. I'm not sure if it's his proximity or the scent of his spicy cologne that has my pulse quickening and wetness seeping between my legs.

I shift in my seat, badly trying to soothe the deep ache between my legs. It's been a long time since I had sex and my vagina is feeling the effects.

Trying not to take a look at the backseat to see if it's big enough is useless. I'm a shameless hussy and have no bones about admitting it.

The need to have him becomes stronger when I calculate the backseat is indeed big enough. Big enough to bend me over and fuck me so hard the car rocks.

"Hayden," Clayton rasps, and I tilt my head to the side, bringing our faces closer together. His pupils dilate, watching me, reading me.

My dirty thoughts flash behind his eyes, and I inwardly moan.

I startle at the touch of his hand on my knee before he slowly slides it up over my thigh. My lips part, silently pleading with him to go higher.

A strangled, "Wha—" spills through my lips when he reaches up, cupping my cheek.

Tapping on the window has us pulling apart, Clayton groaning in disappointment as he presses down on his pants. I follow his movement, noticing the bulge.

I glare at Charlotte and Madison, who are standing outside the car, waving.

"Fuck!" I groan.

I know they've done me a favour. I didn't want to go through him rejecting me, not when he had my body on overdrive. It's one thing to desire the man beside me, but it's another to be seriously turned on by him. I've never once felt both towards a male, not even one I've been with. It's only been one or the other, even if most people confuse the two.

But right now, I'm going through both, and Charlotte and Madison have just cock-blocked me.

Clayton slowly waves back, before turning to me with a smug smile. "Looks like you can't get your way."

"You are a dick," I snap, pushing the door open and getting out.

Clayton follows, and as he pushes his door shut, Charlotte jumps him, wrapping her arms around his neck. I rush around to their side before she kills him.

"You made it," she squeals. "Hayden said you were going to Africa to entertain the children."

"She said that, did she?"

Charlotte's eyebrows bunch together as she slowly nods. "Um, didn't I just say she said that?"

"Um," Clayton drawls out, turning to me for help.

"Were you two kissing?" she asks, grinning.

"No, he had something in his teeth," I rush out.

"Hayden's lying. *She* had something in *her* teeth," Clayton argues, smirking at me.

Charlotte nods like it's completely reasonable. "That happens a lot when she eats popcorn."

"Why don't we go and get our bags and put them on the coach?" I declare, heading for the boot and pulling my case out.

"We're just waiting on Beau and Faith. The vet managing her sanctuary was running late but they're on the way," Madison explains.

I grin. "I bet."

We head across the terminal to the coach pick up. The wind howls, lifting my suitcase off the floor, and I struggle to keep a hold of it. Clayton grabs it off me as he throws his bag over his shoulder.

"Cheers."

"You're welcome."

We unload our luggage to the driver, who puts them under the bus, before walking towards the back where everyone is gathered.

Everyone goes silent when we approach, and I shift protectively in front of Clayton. "What are you all staring at?" I demand, noticing how quickly Liam walks over to Landon, whispering to him.

If they do something, I'm going to kill them. Liam is already in my bad books for putting one of my dates in his boot and driving him to the middle of nowhere. He was hot and he fucking ruined what could have been a good time and multiple orgasms.

"Um, who's the suit?" Maddox asks, munching on a burger.

I turn to give Clayton a once over, sighing at his black wool coat and dark jeans. He might scream 'privileged', but he's not. He's worked damn hard for what he has and it's not his fault he makes everything he wears look good, even when he has on his gym gear that flashes how much of his body is covered in tattoos. I got a front row seat to all that glory when he went to visit his dad at the home. And as much as I never thought I'd admit this, he still presses my buttons. I just need him to relax and let the real him out to play. So far, he's more concerned with not disappointing his dad. It puts him on edge. And until he gets over it and realises he's doing a good job, he'll seem too uptight to the others. I've seen flashes of the real him, and I like them.

"It's Clayton," Charlotte answers, before turning to him, her lips twisted. "I'm still unsure of his profession though. His email header didn't mention party planner."

"Does Dad know?" Liam asks, trying to appear intimidating, but the shirt with a picture of Beau's face on the front just makes him look weird. In fact, taking a look around, all the boys have one on.

"Were we meant to get a T-shirt?" I whisper to Madison.

"No. Apparently one of his mates couldn't get down so he sent these."

"Is Landon wearing one?" I muse.

"No. Apparently the dog chewed it."

"Don't ignore me," Liam growls.

Lily steps up, giving Clayton a small wave. "Hi, I'm Lily."

Clayton's expression softens, his lips pulling into a gentle smile. "I'm Clayton Cross."

"I'm Jaxon, Lily's husband," Jaxon grits out, pulling Lily into his arms.

I roll my eyes, glancing around. "Let's forgo the introductions. There are too many of you fuckers for him to remember."

"Is he too slow to remember?" Maddox asks, not looking up from his phone.

"Fuck. You." I sigh at the girls. They're acting creepy. "Stop staring at him."

"He's so…" Imogen whispers, in a daze.

"I hear you," Ciara murmurs, agreeing.

"Hey, guys…" Faith greets as she walks over, holding hands with Beau, before stumbling to a stop. "Who are you?"

"Her date," Landon grits out, earning a smack to his chest.

Faith's eyes widen, and she slowly turns from Clayton to me. "I didn't know he was male. Charlotte just said a friend." She winces, taking another look before Beau tilts her head away. "Does your dad know?"

"That's what I've been asking," Liam grouches.

"About Clayton?" I ask, still avoiding the question.

"Yes, I met her father the other night at dinner."

"Does Dad know *he's* coming?" Liam tilts his head towards Clayton.

"No." I narrow my eyes on him, silently telling him to shut up.

Charlotte clears her throat. "Um, actually he does. He came to dinner at Mum and Dad's last night and Clayton came up in conversation. When they told me what he looked like, I said it sounded like Clayton and that he was meant to be coming today but the African kids needed him so he couldn't. I got the impression your dad didn't believe me though."

Everyone stops what they're doing, until Maddox nearly falls off the table as he drops his fries. "Oh shit! We need to go."

"Why?" Madison asks, pinching his drink he left on the table.

He grabs his things off the table as Landon starts lifting up Paisley's bags, Liam helping.

My eyes widen when it hits me. I grasp Clayton's wrist in a firm grip. "We need to go."

"What? Why?" he asks, pulling his wrist back.

"Because you've scrambled my mind and I can't fucking think properly with you around. And now we are screwed," I scream in a panic.

I'm so off my game. It should have been the first thing I prevented when he revealed he was coming at dinner. You can't take any chances in my family.

We all begin to walk, heading to the coach, when five cars pull in, honking. We all pause, cursing.

I'm pretty sure I hear Liam whimper.

"Beau, you better have cop friends where we're going," Liam prays.

"Why?" Beau asks, glancing over his shoulder.

"Because he's going to get us fucking arrested again," Maddox growls, bumping into Clayton. "Way to go, arsehole."

"You want to hope we aren't near a train station," Imogen states, patting Clayton on the back before standing in line with the others, watching our parents pull into a parking spot.

"Or that he has glue," Faith adds, wincing as she glances down at his crotch area.

"I'll check Dad's bag when he's distracted," I murmur, wondering how my life got to this point. I'm always on top, the one who pranks people or fucks with them. I'm not the one who's in messy situations—unless you count the time I decided I wanted to knock on Buckingham Palace's door at two in the morning.

"And your mum's," Hope reminds me.

"Or that the town gets quarantined again. It could ruin the whole week," Charlotte adds.

"What?" Clayton asks, bug-eyed.

"It's okay," I assure him, patting his chest. "It was actually Charlotte who had the town quarantined when we were younger."

"Again, what?"

"I did not," she states, pouting. "It was definitely Uncle Max."

I shake my head. "No, it was you. Dad had the caravan park evacuated because they thought a mental patient was on the loose. You poisoned everyone at the cake fair competition."

"They couldn't prove that was me," Charlotte states, looking utterly dejected.

"Only because they couldn't identify the substance or link it to your ingredients. None of us were ill," Imogen argues.

Charlotte beams. "Exactly, and you were all fine."

Everyone finds interest in their shoes or the sky, not wanting to hurt her feelings by admitting we never ate any of it.

"Yeah, true," I answer, forcing a smile.

"Do you need to go to the loo before we go? You look a little in pain."

"I'm fine," I assure her, walking off to the front of the huddle, waiting for our parents to reach us.

They all walk towards us in a line, Teagan pushing Sunday with bags over the pushchair's handle, Uncle Maverick beside her, who is also loaded down with bags. Myles is next to him, carrying a few bags, with Aunt Kayla next him. Mason and Denny are next to them, cuddling together as she talks to Harlow, who has her arm wrapped around Malik. Beside them, Dad strolls, sliding sunglasses up his nose, even though it's windy out. Don't even get me started on the shorts. Mum walks beside him, rolling her eyes. Dad grins after saying something to Uncle Malik, earning a punch to the arm. I wince when Dad trips, falling over his own feet.

"Oh God," I groan.

"Who exactly are you guys?" Clayton asks, fear evident.

If he wants to survive this week, he'll have to find a way to mask that fear. My family will feed off it.

Me, along with all the others, stare up at him, pulling his attention away from the huddle walking towards us.

"We're the Carter's," we say at once, minus the few that aren't.

"And you're fucked," Maddox laughs, throwing a Skittle into the air and catching it in his mouth—before choking.

FIFTEEN

WHEN THE PARENTS REACH US, FAITH is the first to step forward, hugging both her mum and dad. "What are you guys doing here?" As one, they all look to Dad, unhappy, whereas Dad tilts his head up, pretending they aren't all pissed at him.

"Not that I'm complaining," Aiden coos as he sweeps up an excited Sunday into his arms. She can barely move in her all-in-one snow coat. It's adorable, especially when she starts chanting, "da', da'".

"Yeah, I thought because Maverick and Teagan couldn't come, since they were watching over Sunday, none of you were coming," I state, giving Dad a pointed look when he finally turns my way, glaring over my shoulder.

"I knew it," he grits out, pointing at Clayton. "Didn't I tell you he would be here? Didn't I?"

"And I told you she is a grown adult," Mum reminds him, directing a forced smile my way.

Sucking in a breath, he stares at Mum with wide eyes. "She's our only daughter. Do you not care at all that he's going to try and sex her up or impregnate her?"

"Please never use that word again," I complain.

Mum, in all fairness, is just as crazy as my dad at times. I think after years of being together, she started projecting some of his mannerisms. Still, my mum is all about girl power, so when she opens her mouth to argue, I want to pump my fist in the air and hoot.

"Max, you need to drop this. When the boys were fifteen and you suspected they were being intimate, you sat them down and gave them a list of ways to please a woman."

"You didn't?" Maverick groans, running a hand through his hair.

"No… I also gave them tips on how to get a woman," Dad tells him, shaking his head in disbelief before grimacing at Liam and Landon. "Sorry, boys, you had the looks—you follow after me—but you didn't have the Carter game."

Liam grunts, rolling his eyes. "Cheers, Dad."

"You're welcome," Dad replies, looking like he actually did them a favour when he puffs his chest out.

"But…" Mum continues, raising her eyebrow. "Once a year, after Hayden started her menstruation when she was eleven, you sat her down and gave her reasons why she shouldn't have sex."

"With disturbing diagrams," I point out, shuddering.

"They got my point across."

"You told me in medical terms what STI's would do."

"I have them with me in case you needed to look at them again."

"Mum," I whine, praying he's joking.

Mum pinches the bridge of her nose. "Max, leave her alone."

He throws his hands up in a fit before slapping them down on his sides. "Does no one else care he's here, or that my daughter, *my only daughter*, could get pregnant, or worse, get heartbroken?" he yells.

"Sir," Clayton starts.

Dad holds his hand up, palm out. "Do not try to seduce me," he tells him, his voice deepening like it does when you don't take a breath.

"Max, if anyone can look after themselves, it's Hayden. She was raised in your home. Now that you've dragged us all here, let's go," Maverick starts, but is interrupted by Maddox.

"How *did* he get you here?"

Uncle Malik's eyes narrow dangerously on Dad, his jaw clenching. "He told me Hayden was worried about Madison meeting a guy she knew nothing about."

Myles, looking dejected as his shoulders slump, says, "He called me, pissed off. He said he had a heart attack thinking Hayden bought tickets to a sex club using the family emergency fund but felt better when she explained it was Charlotte who borrowed the card."

"Fucking wanker asked me what the ceremony he heard my girls were talking about was for, even said something about a test being positive," Mason bites out, glancing down at his shoes.

We all turn to Maverick, waiting for him to answer. He shrugs. "I helped raise him. The minute he told me Beau was planning on taking Faith away to get married, I knew he was lying. I told him to shut the fuck up."

"So why are you here?" Malik bites out.

Smug, Maverick shrugs. "To make sure he doesn't get my kids arrested again. Aiden has Sunday to look after."

"Traitor," Dad grumbles. "None of you care about what I'm going through."

"You are such a drama queen," I declare. "Now that you all know he fucked you over good and proper, you can go."

"Why?" Dad asks, narrowing his eyes on me. "What are you hiding?"

"Nothing, I—"

"Good, then you won't mind us tagging along," he declares, unloading his bags onto the back of the coach.

"Dad," I argue, following him over.

"It's fine. We can have some father, daughter time."

I spin around, walking over to Clayton and punching him in the arm. "This is all your fault. If I spend the night in a cell again, I'm going to kill you."

"Mine? What did I do?"

I storm off, hearing him follow behind me as I get onto the coach, passing the others. I take a seat in the middle, and when I get in, Clayton lightly pushes me over to the window seat, blocking my escape.

Dad ushers Mum up the aisle, giving her no choice but to take a seat next to us on the opposite side.

"I don't know how this is my fault," Clayton sulks as we push our carry-ons under the seat in front of us.

I tilt my head to the side, trying to find my phone in my bag, and whisper, "This week is going to end badly."

"I'm sorry," he whispers back as we both sit up.

"Son, you don't have to worry about Sunday. Just enjoy your time away. We've found places to take her. They have a messy and soft play," Maverick assures Aiden as they stop at the seats in front of us. Paisley gets the side Dad and Mum are on, but Aiden begins to fix Sunday's car seat.

"Yes, there's an amazing bookstore not far from Cabin Lakes. Looking online at the pictures, I can understand the great reviews. The place is truly beautiful. Sunday is going to love it," Teagan adds.

"It's not that. I'm kind of relieved. I just don't want to drink around her," Aiden admits, tickling Sunday before taking her from his dad.

"He really didn't want to leave her," Bailey explains, sticking her tongue out at Sunday.

"You won't be. We will have Sunday in our cabin," Maverick explains before taking the seat in front of them.

"I have beer for anyone who wants one," Maddox calls out from behind my seat.

Shit! I completely forgot about bringing drink.

Nina, Faith's best friend, yells from the front, "I've got cans of Malibu and coke, gin and lemonade, gin and tonic, and JD and coke. Oh, and mini bottles of wine."

"Me too," Hope yells, holding up the mini bottle of wine, already starting.

I groan as I get up, turning around on my knees to Maddox, holding out my hand and taking a can off him. "I'm not drinking girly shit."

"I got you rum and Doctor Pepper, Hayden," Charlotte calls from the front.

"Never mind," I mutter to Maddox, grinning. I pass the can to Clayton, not caring if he wants it or not. "Pass 'em here."

A few moments later, she heads up the aisle with a bottle of rum and a bottle of Doctor Pepper. "Here you go."

"There's only one?" I pout.

"No, there's another," she confirms, smiling.

I sag into my seat. "Thank God."

"Your dad is still staring," Clayton whispers as I pour my drink into my flask.

"Dad, stop staring," I order, concentrating on not spilling any of my precious drink when the coach pulls off.

"Whatever," he grumbles. "Aiden, you got any food in the changing bag?"

"I told you not to eat all the snacks on the way over," Mum reminds him.

"I'm a nervous eater," he argues.

"Sorry, I didn't bring any, but now you mention it, I am pretty hungry."

"Who doesn't bring snacks on a road trip?" Dad snaps, rubbing his stomach.

"You," I mutter, grabbing one of the sandwiches I bought at the garage when my stomach grumbles at the mention of food.

"You aren't going to share with your old man?"

"No," I mumble around a mouthful of food.

"We always had snacks in the changing bags," Dad complains, folding his arms across his chest.

"Yes, because when it came to feeding the triplets, it was one spoon for them and two for you, which ended up with me having to feed them again. It was easier to keep you stacked."

"I'm going to die of starvation," he complains. "Does anyone have any food?"

"I've got some cupcakes and muffins. They were meant to be sponge, but they look kind of green," Charlotte announces, sounding confused.

"Never mind."

"I've got this," Clayton offers, holding a breakfast bar out to Dad.

"Stop trying to seduce me into letting you corrupt my daughter," Dad growls as he snatches the bar out of Clayton's hand.

Clayton sighs. "Sir, we aren't dating."

I slap his arm. "Stop urging him on."

"Why? What's wrong with my daughter?" Dad asks, insulted.

"Oh my God," I breathe out, right before gulping down half my drink.

"Apart from the fact she's cunning, argumentative and is always pinching my food?" Clayton teases, yet no one laughs. He clears his throat. "Um, nothing."

"Those seem like good traits to have," Dad comments.

"That's the nicest thing you've ever said about me," I beam.

"Wait, you think you can have the cake and eat it too?"

"Isn't that what you do with cake?" Clayton asks, rubbing his palm down his leg.

I groan. "Please stop, Dad."

"No, I'm not having him think he can get the milk for free. You deserve more. Haven't you heard: if you like it, put a ring on it."

"That is not how it goes, Dad."

"She does," Clayton states, and I stop, staring up at him. He not only sounds serious, but he looks it too as he remains eye contact with my dad. "But we aren't dating."

"Then why are you here?" Dad asks, his voice going high.

Poor Clayton turns to me for assistance, but I'm a bitch and just shrug. It's not like I didn't warn him.

"Charlotte kindly invited me."

"You're cheating on my daughter?" Dad screams, going to get up. But Mum pulls him down. "Boys, get him!"

"Dad, we aren't dogs," Landon yells from the back.

"I'm not cheating," Clayton panics, wide-eyed. I tap his thigh, gesturing for him to get up and move out. "Don't leave me."

I roll my eyes, pushing him over to the seat I vacated. "Sit down."

"Like that will stop me," Dad muses.

My stomach bottoms out when Uncle Myles, the calmer one of my dad and uncles, heads up the aisle towards us, not looking happy at all.

He places his elbows on the seat in front before leaning over and holding out a hand to Clayton.

Clayton, after doing a double take, slowly reaches over to shake it, wincing at the grip.

"I'm Charlotte's father, Myles. She's never mentioned you before."

Clayton pulls his hand away, flexing his fingers, and I notice his hand, in places, go from white back to pink.

"Would you both stop bullying him?" I grouch.

"Not if I find out he's been sleeping with you and my daughter."

"We've not had sex," Charlotte calls out, earning groans from the others. "I'm still a virgin at the moment, although I am hoping Scott and I will take the next step soon. I'm doing research on—"

"Okay, we get it," Myles practically screeches. I watched him go from relaxed at the start of her statement to tense. It's amusing.

"All right."

Myles gives Clayton a sheepish smile, shrugging. "Sorry about the hand. I don't know my own strength sometimes." He leaves, calling out to Aunt Kayla, "Talk to our daughter, Kayla."

"I can—" Dad begins.

"No!" my uncles yell.

I feel Dad's stare on the side of my face. "Dad, just spit it out."

"I have the right to know why he's with you. Are you in trouble? 'Cause I heard there's a lake at the cabins we can dump his body in."

"Hey," Clayton snaps. "I'm right here."

Dad's lips twist into a snarl. "Is there any need to keep reminding me?"

"Dad," I call in a warning tone. "There will be no touching Clayton."

"That goes for you too," he grumbles.

"I'm not a bad person," Clayton argues, turning to me. "Hayden, tell him!"

"Don't tell my daughter what to do."

"Max, switch seats," Mum demands.

"No, not until we find out what he's up to."

"Max," Maverick warns.

Dad crosses his arms over his chest like a scolded child. "I'm not shutting up until they start talking. Don't make me force him."

"I've told you we aren't dating," Clayton declares.

"Why did you sound like that is a good thing?" Dad barks.

"Hayden," Clayton calls, pleading.

I throw my hands up before dropping them on my lap. "Oh my God, he's my boss. There. Are you happy now?"

"You're sleeping with your boss?" Maddox asks, before laughing.

"Oh my God, no," I groan—not that I haven't wished or imagined it.

"Hey, what's wrong with me?" Clayton asks, sounding put out.

I give him a dry look, raising my eyebrow. "Are you serious right now?"

He shrugs. "You made it sound like it would be disastrous."

"You really did," Dad adds, leaning over. He gets that smug smile on his face when he's right about something, and I don't like it.

"I'm confused, sweetie. Why would you bring your boss?"

Down the aisle, I notice everyone is peeking around their seats or over them, listening in.

"Because we're doing a piece on where to go for dates for my podcast," I admit, leaving out the online dating part.

Clayton sags back into his seat. "Thank you, God. I'm not going to die."

"Your work is podcasts?" Mum asks, smiling with excitement. "I'm so proud of you."

"Actually, it's a radio/online podcast, and she's one of our highest-ranking presenters," Clayton informs them, and I'm struck by how proud he sounds.

"Aren't you going to tell her you're proud?" Mum grits out, smacking Dad on the arm.

He rolls his eyes, sitting back in his seat. "Of course I'm proud. I sent her flowers and a five-hundred-pound gift card."

"You knew?" Mum screeches.

"I got that the first day of working as a presenter. I thought it was from my boss."

He looks at us and those being nosey. "I'm your father; of course I knew. Didn't any of you?"

"No, I thought she was stripping or worked as one of those dress-up characters," Mum admits, shrugging.

"We really should still take those lessons," I remind her.

Dad smirks at Mum, and I inwardly gag. "You really should."

"How come I didn't know?" Aiden pipes in when a few others nod, indicating they knew.

"I only found out the other week," Hope calls from the front.

"We're your parents. You can't hide anything from us," Dad adds.

"Really?" Charlotte squeaks, glancing at her dad.

"Not now, Charlotte," Kayla soothes, pulling Myles down in his seat when he begins to turn red.

"Did you and Liam know, Landon?" I ask, glancing up the aisle.

The 'duh' look he gives me has me rolling my eyes.

"Yeah, of course we did. We put a track me app on your phone when you started sneaking out at night and followed you."

"Besides, you were shit at being sly," Liam adds, snorting.

"Fuck off," I bark, turning back around.

"So, you don't work for the MI5?" Charlotte asks, pouting.

"Nope."

"Cool."

"Does this mean you'll stop planning my murder?" Clayton asks, filled with hope.

"No. I don't trust your intentions towards my daughter."

"Would free vouchers to an all-you-can-eat Chinese help?"

Dad sniffs, and although he thinks he's playing it off, he slips up and licks his lips. "It might."

"I guess that's all I can hope for," Clayton states, relaxing.

I wait for Mum to distract Dad with questions before leaning in a little to Clayton, keeping my voice low. "Don't let his friendly behaviour fool you. He might not physically harm you, but you'll wish that he had once he's finished fucking with you."

"I'll be fine," Clayton assures me, his lips twitching.

I shake my head in pity. "Famous last words," I mutter, downing the rest of my drink.

SIXTEEN

THE CUSHION I FELL ASLEEP ON stiffens under me, bringing me out of my sleep. When said cushion begins to vibrate, I stir awake, yet keep my eyes shut when I hear whispering.

The last thing I remember is getting back on the coach after stopping for food at a rest stop. I finished my rum and must have passed out not long after, which isn't surprising since I'd worked a double shift at the care home. What I don't remember is wrapping myself around Clayton. My head is resting on his chest, my arm wrapped around his stomach, and my leg thrown over his.

"Please stop staring at me like you're contemplating how to hide my body," Clayton pleads, and I just know he's talking to my dad.

"You like my daughter," Dad states rather than questions.

I sometimes wonder how he survived his brothers with his bluntness.

"Honestly?"

"I'd break your legs if you ever lied when it came to my daughter," Dad promises, sounding cheerful at the idea it might happen.

I'm about to put my acting skills to the test and stir awake so I can intervene before my dad forces Clayton's bank details, national security number and a list of his past relationships from him.

"She's hard not to like. She's such a contradiction to herself. I've never met anyone like her. She doesn't come across as feisty and blunt to cover up who she really is; she *is* feisty and blunt. It's the caring and kindness part of herself that she hides from others. She plays everything off.

"We were shopping once and walked past a homeless man. I couldn't look. It hurts too much to see someone in need and at their lowest. I didn't think Hayden took notice. It kind of struck me, since she's female and they tend to notice everything."

"This story is depressing and all but is there a point to it?" Dad chides, acting aloof. He would never admit he helps too, in every way he can. My mum was once a runaway living on the streets. It was how she met my dad. Ever since, he's done everything to give back.

"Yes. My company donates to homeless organisations monthly and has done for years. Yet, just as we walked past and I heard this guy cough, I couldn't just carry on. When I checked my wallet for money, it was empty. I felt bad. I know I can't help them all, but it struck me that I couldn't help the man.

"Anyway, we walked into this shop and Hayden shoves some clothes at me and says she needs to run back outside, that she dropped something. She didn't know I watched as she walked a couple of shops down to give this guy some money. And she never said anything when she came back in or when I questioned her about whether she found what she was looking for.

"Someone like that is rare. She didn't want praise for giving, or recognition. She just wanted to give without making a big deal about it. It surprised me. So yeah, it's hard not to like her."

"Of course you do. Who doesn't? She's my daughter. But that wasn't the kind of 'like' I was asking about, and you know it."

Because I'm his daughter. Pfft, it's because I'm fucking awesome.

"Respectfully, it's none of your business. It's between me and Hayden."

Ohh, those are fighting words.

"Well, *respectfully*, if you hurt my girl in any way, you'll find yourself put into a human blender or in another country and arrested for a crime you didn't commit. I'll make sure you spend years being Bubba's bitch."

Aw, that's so sweet. I knew I was his favourite.

"That's, um, very descriptive," Clayton claims.

"I hate misunderstandings," Dad confirms. "So, do you understand?"

"I'm not going to hurt her."

I hear Dad shuffling about. "I'm glad we cleared that up," he explains. "Hayden, you can open your eyes now. It's safe."

"She's awake?" Clayton asks, stiffening beneath me.

"Way to give me up, Dad." I curse, prying myself off Clayton and stretching the stiffness out of my back. I blink away the dim lighting. "Where is everyone?"

"They're getting keys, but by the looks of it, something is happening," Clayton comments, looking out the window.

He's right. Everyone has congregated outside a large building that I'm assuming is the reception, although parts look like a home. They seem to be arguing, fingers pointing and all.

"We really should go check in," Clayton reminds me.

Uncle Maverick steps onto the bus, making his way towards us. "There aren't enough cabins. Even if we share, there's still two people who we can't fit in."

"That's okay," Clayton begins. "I booked my own cabin, so Hayden can take the spare room."

Dad trips on his way down the aisle, falling on his face. "Fuck!" he curses, before getting up and facing us. "I don't think so."

"Is that okay with you?" Maverick asks, ignoring Dad, who curses again.

"With not sharing with the others? Fuck yes."

"What? No! You can bunk with your mum. Me and Clayton can bunk and get to know each other."

"You aren't sharing his bed, Dad. Don't get excited. He has a spare room."

"Like he wouldn't try to sleep with me," he argues, puffing his chest out. "I'm prime meat."

"You'll be mince meat if you don't shut it," I grumble.

"I heard Lake telling Teagan she was looking forward to hot tub sex," Maverick announces. "I didn't think you'd pass that up." His lips twist into a smile, and he ducks his head to hide it.

I gag. "Gross."

Dad, however, perks up. "Really?"

"Yeah." Maverick nods.

Dad takes a step to leave but then stops, spinning back to us, pointing at Clayton and narrowing his eyes. "Remember what I said," he warns him, before pointing to me. "And you remember our religion; no sex before marriage."

"We aren't religious," I remind him dryly.

He throws his hands up before flopping them down at his sides. "Will you just do as you're told for once?"

He storms down the coach, waiting for Maverick to turn. Me and Clayton grab our bags as I chuckle under my breath.

"I'd apologise for his behaviour, but I'd only keep doing it," I admit, shrugging.

He laughs, putting a hand on my back and giving me a gentle push down the aisle. "He's fine. He's just looking out for his daughter."

The wind howls when I step outside, and I pull my jacket tighter around me.

We pull the bags from the coach and begin to walk to the others, when Clayton stops me halfway. "Let me go check in and make sure everything is good. I'll come back out with the keys." I nod, reaching for his bag, but he shakes his head. "I got it."

I watch him leave before grabbing the handle of my suitcase and walking over to the others.

"Hayden," Dad calls, and I turn to see him approaching, leaving Maverick with a resigned expression.

If I were to guess, I'd say he just tried reasoning with my dad, which is hard to do for anyone, even Mum at times.

"Dad, I don't want to listen to you tell me why sex is bad before marriage, that I'll get pregnant and eat all your food."

"But you would. Your mum hid food from me when she was pregnant," he argues, pouting. "But that isn't what I wanted to talk to you about."

"And this isn't about stealing your order at the service station?" I ask, running the toe of my shoe along the gravel.

"That was you?" he cries out, looking cheated.

I yawn, rubbing my eyes. "Dad, you said you wanted to talk. I'm really, really tired."

"Yeah, I do, sorry," he tells me, rubbing his hand over my arm. "I know I can be full on. I'm just looking out for you."

"Dad, was that meant to be an apology? Because it sucked."

His eyebrows crease together. "But I'm not sorry."

"Of course not," I mutter, rolling my eyes.

"I'm just trying to be a good dad." The guilt and despair shining back at me has my shoulders sagging.

"You're the best dad. I couldn't ask for a better one. A saner one, yeah, but not better. Just… please go easy on him."

"I can't make that promise, but I'll try."

I let out a relieved sigh, knowing that's the best I'm going to get. "Thank you."

He glances over his shoulder to where Maverick is standing with Teagan, Lily and Jaxon, before turning back to me, lowering his voice a little. "And you know the boys aren't my favourite, right? You are."

I chuckle, knowing Maverick used that to make Dad feel bad.

"Of course I am."

His shoulders sag and his body relaxes as a goofy smile spreads across his face. He pulls me into his arms, kissing my forehead. "Just be careful. He's too polite."

I roll my eyes. "Yes, because he's going to hurt me with compliments."

"I'm telling you, it's dodgy, baby girl."

"If he was a scared bloke, you would call him a pansy who wasn't strong enough to fit in, and if he was rude, you would have kicked him off the coach in the middle of nowhere."

Dad snorts. "Give me some credit. I would have punched him first."

I grin. "True."

"I just want what's best for you."

"You're forgetting one major thing, Dad."

"What's that?"

"We aren't dating and never have."

"Yet," he grumbles, before straightening. "Here he comes. Act normal."

"Normal?" I grumble.

"We were just talking about how you were both going to stay in your own rooms and keep a few feet apart at all times."

I blink up at him. "Normal, Dad. Very normal."

"I thought so too."

"Whatever."

"I'm going to talk dirty to your mum," he announces, winking in Mum's direction.

I groan, smacking my forehead. "Jesus Christ, Dad. Stop trying to put me off sex for life."

He laughs, pulling me into his arms. "Love you, baby girl."

"Love you too," I grumble, lightly pushing him away.

He forms a V with his fingers to convey he's watching Clayton. "Don't fuck up."

Clayton gives him a sharp nod, watching him leave before turning to me and holding up a set of keys.

"Please tell me we have a hot tub," I plead.

"Yes, and a view of the lake."

I clap my hands, squealing with excitement, causing him to grin. "Let's go say goodbye and find out when we're all meeting up."

"Lead the way," he offers, grabbing my case.

We head over to the others, where a few are sulking. "What's going on?"

"A few singles have to share a cabin with couples," Hope explains.

"Ahh," I breathe, understanding. It's one of the reasons I didn't want to share. There's nothing worse than hearing a relative having sex. "Who is Lily bunking with?"

"Faith and Beau. Maddox is pissed off because he wanted to spend some time with Lily."

"Is that why he's glaring at Jaxon?"

Hope laughs. "No, he's glaring because Jaxon volunteered him to bunk with Liam and share with Aiden and Bailey."

"Oh God, they're going to get us kicked off site."

"I'm going to pretend we aren't with them."

"Is it really that bad?" Clayton asks, his breath brushing across my ear.

"Not really," Hope answers, then looks thoughtful. "Unless you count the time they got us kicked out of the hotel and there weren't any rooms anywhere else, so we had to sleep on the beach for the night."

"Bloody hell."

He's got that right. I didn't forgive Liam for a week after that one. Sand is not your friend.

"Where and when are we meeting up in the morning?" I call out, wanting to get out of the cold and to the cabin so I can check out the hot tub.

"Nine. There's a building near the entrance that serves breakfast," Faith announces.

"Are you not coming for a drink?" Charlotte asks, glancing up from her phone.

"No, I'm heading back. I'll catch you all later."

We leave after saying goodbye, following the map that was given to Clayton at reception.

SEVENTEEN

DUE TO THE DIM LIGHTING, I've not been able to take in much of the area, yet I can still see the beauty in what I have viewed. Whoever takes care of the presentation of the cabins, does it with love. They've put dedication into detail, into making each one look loved and cared for.

I feel terrible over how they've let us stay. Something is bound to get broken. I don't want their work to be ruined.

From the introduction Clayton gave me after we left the others, Cabin Lakes is family run and some of the cabins are long-term rentals.

I can see why. Not only is the scenery—from what I've managed to glimpse—stunning, but each cabin is warm and inviting.

Each end of the cabin has hanging baskets, ready for when the flowers bloom. Under the window is a flower bed, a wooden bench underneath. On each side of the door are two lanterns, the electrical candles flickering to replicate a real flame.

There's even a small wooden locker next to the door to place muddy boots and umbrellas.

"How did you find this place?" I ask as we continue along the path.

"My granddad was friends with theirs. We would come during the winter most years. When the lake is frozen or snow is on the ground here, it's spectacular."

"I can believe it. This place is incredible," I gush.

"It really is. That cabin," he continues, pointing to a two-storey brightly-lit home, "is Lola and Dean's home. They used the plot of land to build on when her parents' cabin was destroyed during Storm Ellen. He used parts of it in the house to give her some of it back. It was one of the last things she had left of them."

That's beautiful.

"As much as I love this place so far, I don't think I could live here."

Clayton doesn't seem convinced. "Really? Why? This is one of the most beautiful places in England."

"Exactly," I affirm. "Living here, unless it held sentimental value, would become ordinary. You wouldn't see the beauty like someone who was visiting for the first time."

"Huh?"

I sigh, stopping outside our cabin, and turn to him. "Why do you go on holiday?"

"To get away, relax, explore."

I nod, agreeing. "And for a change of scenery. People who live near the beach won't pay to go to another one that's the same. They won't see the beauty, enjoy the smell of salt in the air, or delight in being a tourist. They won't see the little things because they live with it. I couldn't live like that. I love that feeling you get when you experience something for the first time, when you taste something, or that rush you get. I can't imagine not having it. Although," I add, taking a look around at the paved walkway and sun-powered streetlamps, "I couldn't imagine there being anywhere as nice as this in England."

When he doesn't say anything for a moment, I glance up at him. His pupils dilate, his lips parting as he tilts his head to the side. I can't help but feel his surprise at my words, like he's seeing me for the first time or is taken off guard by the fact I'm capable of being evocative.

No one has ever looked at me this way. Usually when I speak, people roll their eyes or snort, thinking I'm joking.

I duck my head, uncomfortable with the emotions coursing through my body.

He clears his throat. "I get it. Sometimes, people take this world for granted, always sure it will be as it's always been. But it won't. Nothing lasts forever. I admire your perspective."

I get his point, yet… "Way to be morbid. But I get your point."

He laughs, pushing the key into the door as my phone rings. "Let's get inside so you can answer that."

"Thank you," I tell him, before answering the call. "Hey, Uncle Liam, is everything okay?"

"Take the master," Clayton whispers, pointing to the door on the left of the small hallway.

I nod, pulling my case down the hall and into the room.

"Are you busy?"

"Nope." I heave, dropping my case onto my bed, along with my backpack.

"I got you the contact details for Joyce. She was transferred to Liverpool."

"Convenient," I murmur, though I'm glad she's safe.

"That's not all. After our last call, I couldn't stop thinking about the missing statement and the cop we can't account for that visited the house and was seen in the alley. If we can figure out who that is, we can find out who has been giving the gang a heads up. You're not going to like this, but the case, the reporter, and maybe the alley cop, all have one thing in common."

Dread fills my stomach because I know where this is going. "Rob."

"I know it's not what you want to hear, but yes. He must be the leak in the department, and my guess is, he went and threatened Rita Jones, which caused her to have a heart attack." He lets out a heavy sigh, sounding exhausted. "You need to talk to Beau, get him up to speed."

I pace back and forth along the knitted red and brown rug. "I don't believe it."

"Hayden, all of this is leading back to him. I've searched through all the databases to see who has logged on to access the online files and his log in is used frequently."

"Because he's one of the lead officers on this case, Liam. What about paper files? Anyone could get their hands on them."

"It's because he's lead officer that I believe he's our guy. He's in a position where he's informed of what is happening and has the means to alter evidence."

I pinch the bridge of my nose, letting out a breath. "I've gotten to know him. I've spoken to him at great lengths about this case. He's genuinely upset about Christina. He wants her murderer caught and I think he's still struggling on whether it's for justice or vengeance," I explain. "I can hear how much of a toll this case is taking on him each time something else happens. The other day, a woman was raped and beaten. What's next? Another murder? Rob isn't the kind of person to cover up heinous crimes. I won't believe it until I get proof."

"Okay, say he is innocent, someone is still informing the gang. They have a dozen or so officers who are on file because they were the ones first on scene. There are three superior's, which include Rob, Colin Fisher and their boss, Jamie Walker."

"So all we need to do is break the list down," I murmur.

"Yes, but it's hard to do when we don't know who this gang is. We can't link any of them to that gang until we know who we're looking for."

I sit down on the edge of the bed when an idea forms in my head. Tucking my phone between my ear and shoulder, I pull my laptop out of my bag and start it up. "I'm going to speak to Beau as soon as I get chance because I think I have an idea. I'll need a week or so to put it together."

"Hayden, I think once you've told Beau, you should walk away."

"No! I have a plan. A good one," I declare, typing the names in my notes app.

"No, Hayden, you aren't listening. You need to stop this. Don't make me tell your dad."

I inhale sharply. "You wouldn't!"

"I would. I need you to take this seriously."

"And I am," I argue. "I have a plan."

"I don't care."

"You don't even know what it is," I growl.

"Probably something that will most likely have your dad getting arrested for murdering me."

I snort. "Like he would get caught," I boast.

"Jesus Christ."

"Just listen to my plan first. If I get all the potential suspects in the same room at their station and announce I've found a witness who claims she saw who murdered Christina, but who will only talk to me because she feels watched, the cop involved will panic, worry the witness will reveal who the guy running this thing is. He can't have anyone finding out he's been tipping them off. I can make up some crap and say I've made sure to get word out that I'm meeting her at location A, but really, I'll be meeting her at location B. So while the police will be watching location A for the gang to show up, the person involved is going to go to location B, where he thinks the witness actually is. And I think the cop will be that person. If I make up some story that can convince the potential suspects to keep this on the downlow, the cop involved will know he can't tip the gang off, nor risk the gang being caught or they'll reveal his identity. It will prove there's a cop working for them. He'll have no choice but to go himself."

"But there isn't a witness," Liam states.

"For a bright person, you can be slow. I won't actually be meeting anyone. It's a farce, remember? No one but the cops will know what is happening. So whoever is involved with the break-ins will turn up at location B in the hope to shut this witness up. I'm willing to put money on it."

"That's great and all, but how are you going to arrest a trained cop?"

He really is meant to be the smart one, but sometimes I wonder. "Do I look stupid to you?" I utter dryly. "I'll get Beau to stake out that location."

"Woah, okay, that's actually a pretty solid plan. What about Joyce, the carer?"

I think about it for a moment, before coming to a decision. "I think it's best we don't draw attention to her until after we figure out who we are dealing with. It could put her in danger. If she isn't already."

"Smart," he states. "Speak to Beau and keep me informed on the plan. I'll go with him and set up recording equipment. If our hunch is correct and one or more are involved, we will need more than our word."

I shut my laptop, smiling proudly. "I will. I might actually pull this off. My boss will have to give me space for a news report after this."

"You've done well, kid. And we need a reporter who reports facts, not hearsay or headlines that are just for money."

"We really do," I agree. No one can trust what is written anymore. One day, there's going to be something the world needs to hear, to be warned about, but the public will just pass it off as another lie, another article written to gain sales.

I pull myself back to the present. "Thank you for all your help, Uncle Liam."

"Any time. Stay safe."

"I will. Speak to you soon."

I end the call, dropping my phone onto the bed, smiling. It might seem inappropriate, but I've dreamed of this moment for so long. I've worked hard to get here, yet each story I took to Weston kept getting rejected because they weren't interesting enough or it wasn't new because someone else beat me to it. With this, I will have all the facts first.

However, I'm not here to work. I'm here to get drunk, relax and have fun.

For the first time since entering the room, I take a look around, and I'm impressed. The bed is a king with a dark wooden frame, swirled grooves on the headboard. It's beautiful. The furniture matches the bedframe, all dark wood with the same patterned grooves, and from the feel of the exquisite work, it's made from real oak. There are a few landscape canvases on the walls, and one that I think is the lake here at Cabin Lakes.

Moving around the room, the hamper on the dressing table with a large, round mirror above, draws my attention. Inside are slippers, facial packs, eye masks and a few other bits and bobs.

I'm impressed. They really went out of their way to make people feel special.

What would make me feel special right now is outside, and I can't wait to enjoy the hot tub.

Sliding my case across the bed, I unzip it and pull out my dressing gown and swimsuit. After stripping down, I slide the swimming costume on before walking over to the mirror, checking myself out.

I love this costume. It's one of my favourites. The black nylon fits snug to my body, and the bust area pushes my boobs together. I tie the straps across them into a knot, which makes them look bigger than they are. Turning, I check out my rear, loving how the globes of my arse look.

The cut-out sides are my favourite, though inconvenient when sunbathing. But I look hot nonetheless.

After pulling my hair into a bun and wrapping my dressing gown around me, I head out the door to double check the tub is on.

I come to a stumbling stop at the sight of a shirtless Clayton.

Bloody hell.

He doesn't just have full sleeve tattoos. On his right shoulder, his tattoo spreads down his back and around his ribs. It weaves perfectly over his muscular back. I can't see the art or script woven into the tribal pattern, but I want to.

Desperately.

I lick my lips when he turns, giving me a full view of his chest and abs. I've seen my fair share of abs, but never ones more defined than his. He isn't even tensing, yet I can see every dent, every dip. It looks natural, not like a few of the ones I've seen that look steroid injected.

I can only imagine what it would be like to have him under me, running my hands over his chest and down his body, watching it tense beneath me, his muscles bulging.

I squeeze my thighs together, still running my gaze over him.

A throat clearing startles me, and I snap my head up, meeting Clayton's unwavering gaze.

His lips twitch. "Can I help you?"

"Um, yeah, you really can," I tell him, my clit pulsing.

"How?" he asks, his voice husky as he stands straighter.

I shake my head, clearing all the dirty things I want to do to him from my mind. "Is the hot tub on?"

"Yes. I saw it when I checked everything out."

I grin. "Great."

Finally glancing at something other than his magnificent body, I note he's changed out of his jeans and into a pair of grey cotton jogging bottoms.

Fucking hell, he makes everything remind me of sex, because now I'm wondering if he's wearing boxers under them, and acknowledging how easy it would be to pull them down and fuck him until he forgets his name.

"Are you going somewhere?"

"Yeah, I'm just going for a run. Dean said they have a trail that's lit up near the entrance."

"But you're away," I remind him, my eyebrows pinching together.

He smirks, running his gaze over my body, making me feel naked.

I wish.

"You really don't like exercise, do you?"

Well duh, I'm not a masochist. "Not even a little. The only time I run is if someone is chasing me or I'm chasing one of my relatives."

He pulls a black hoody over his head, laughing, and I inwardly sigh, my jaw dropping at the sight of his muscles flexing.

"I shouldn't be long. There's beer in the fridge."

"Is there food?" I ask, turning towards the kitchen area briefly.

"All stocked. I took the initiative to get all the cabins stocked for our stay."

I sag against the side of the doorframe, smiling at his thoughtfulness, when a thought occurs to me and I stand up straighter.

Paisley.

Landon is probably freaking out and Googling the nearest shop to make sure she has plenty of food to eat.

"If that worried expression has anything to do with Paisley, she's fine. I made sure they have a range of foods for her. I emailed Charlotte in case someone had any allergies and she explained Paisley is diabetic."

"Thank God. I didn't want to deal with my brother tomorrow if that wasn't the case," I lie. "He's overprotective."

"Looks like he isn't the only one."

I roll my eyes behind his back when he leaves, heading towards the kitchen. "Before you go, do you know where the towels are?"

"There are some in a cupboard beside the sliding doors that lead onto the patio. I think they're for the hot tub because there's a towel dressing gown."

I run my hand over the fleece of my own dressing gown, relieved it won't be getting wet. "Thank you."

I head over, pulling open the cupboard, and grin when I run a hand over the beige cotton and find it warm.

When I turn around, he's grabbing his iPod out of his bag on the counter and a bottle of water out of the fridge.

I drop my dressing gown to the floor before turning to grab the gown off the hanger.

The crinkling of plastic has me turning back around.

"Fuck!" Clayton rasps, staring open-jawed at my swim-clad body. Water spills out of the bottle he's squeezed tight.

I walk over, putting more sway in my hips, and press myself against him, watching him swallow. I lean around him, grabbing an apple out of the bowl before standing before him, taking a bite out of the fruit.

"Have a good run," I tell him, before stepping away, hearing a groan behind me.

I tilt my head up a little, grinning.

He might not want to want me, but he does.

By the end of this week, I'll make sure he wants me so bad he regrets pulling away from me.

Or at least admit that he wants me.

EIGHTEEN

CLAYTON AND I TREK UP THE path to the café the next morning. It rained through the night, yet the promise of more is in the grey clouds above. The wind picks up, stirring strands of hair in my face. I brush them off.

Clayton takes the lead when we reach the door, grasping the handle. However, instead of pulling it open, he pauses, turning slightly towards me.

"Don't leave me alone today. I'm man enough to admit that I'm worried your father will kill me in the process of trying to scare me away."

Laughing, I pat his shoulder. "If you want to win my dad over, either supply him with unlimited food or play him at his own game. He respects nothing more than someone who can give as good as they get."

"So, you're telling me that if I accidently kill him, you'll still like me?"

"Who said I like you?" I drawl, and he arches his eyebrows in reply. I roll my eyes, exhaling. "You're underestimating my dad. You'll never be able to get one up on him."

He shoots me a roguish smirk, winking. "And you're underestimating my ability to get what I want."

"What do you want?" I mumble.

However, he ignores me, pulling open the door to the café, different aromas hitting my senses.

"You'll see," he taunts.

The noise in the café is deafening when I stomp inside after him. "Clayton, what do you mean?"

"Your dad and mum are here," he announces from the corner of his mouth.

He's right. In fact, I think we're the last to arrive. Our entire group has congregated to the left of the room, taking up a majority of tables.

We traipse over to Mum and Dad, and I lean down, kissing Mum's cheek before reaching over to Dad, giving him a one-arm hug.

"Morning," I greet.

"Morning, baby."

"I need food," Dad whines, dropping his head down on the table.

Laughter spills out of me as we move over to the next table, where Jaxon and Lily are cuddled together. Seeing them sitting alone is surprising to say the least. I would have thought someone would have jumped at the chance.

I search the room for Maddox as Clayton and I take a seat, finding him sulking into his coffee cup, every so often peeking in our direction.

I'd never admit it, but I do feel sorry for him to an extent. But still, I'm kind of fed up of him being pathetic. It needs to end.

I set my icy gaze on Jaxon, waiting for him to take notice before saying, "You should let him spend some time with her."

"What?" Clayton asks, glancing up from the menu.

I ignore him, continuing to stare blankly at Jaxon. He exhales, dropping his mug on the table. "He's infuriating."

"So are you, buttercup. I guess you have it in common."

"What's going on?" Lily asks, biting her bottom lip.

I roll my eyes when Jaxon doesn't answer. "It's Maddox. He's really missing you. I think he feels pushed out."

"Hayden," Jaxon growls.

I stick my tongue out, shrugging.

"I told you he was upset when he left before dinner the other night."

"He wasn't. He really wanted to go," Jaxon lies.

Lily glances over her shoulder, her lip trembling. "I miss him too. I didn't mean to hurt his feelings."

"Why don't you do something tomorrow? We've all got the morning free until we go Go-Karting."

I wave Maddox over. He nearly tips his coffee all over Liam's lap in his haste to get up.

"Everything okay?" he asks, pulling out the chair from the next table over—the one Mark was about to sit down on—and dragging it over to ours.

"Take a seat," Jaxon grumbles, shifting his phone and cup away to leave room for Maddox's.

"Lily wanted to ask you something," I declare.

"Yes, I did. I know we've not spent much time together in the past couple of months, and that's no one's fault but my own. I'm really sorry."

Maddox's jaw clenches as his gaze flickers to Jaxon. "We've been busy, that's not your fault."

Lily visibly relaxes, and her smile lights up her entire face. "Would you like to hang out tomorrow, before we go Go-Karting?"

"Just us?" he asks, his eyebrows arching.

Lily sucks in her bottom lip, blinking up at Jaxon.

"I can hang out with Hayden and her new boyfriend," he assures her, smug.

"We're busy," I grit out, trying to keep my tone smooth. "But you should use the time to get to know your in-laws."

Lily bounces in her seat, linking her arm through Jaxon's. "That's actually perfect. Mum and Dad would love it too. She's always telling him to get to know you better. Tomorrow, they're taking Sunday to messy play."

Instead of listening to him try to dig himself out of the hole he's dug, I lean back on two legs of my chair before reaching around and tapping Faith on the shoulder.

"What's the plan for today?"

Her chair scrapes along the tiled floor, and I cringe at the grating sound. "We're booked into the spa today. It's a part of this facility but on another plot of land. The guy on the desk said it would take ten minutes to walk there," she explains before taking a breath. "Did you bring your swimming costume, like I asked?"

"Yeah, but I've got to tell you, I was worried for a minute that you wanted us to go swimming in the lake. I'd have done it, like, for you, but I really didn't want to freeze my tits off."

She lets out a mirthful laugh. "God no. It's quiet here due to the cold season, so one of the owners said we could have the private pool they have for private parties. We've got champagne and health snacks waiting for us when we arrive."

"Yummy," I mutter dryly.

"Shut up," she chuckles. "They've got a sauna, hot tub and gym there. After lunch, we've got treatments for those who pre-booked. Then a make-up artist and hairdresser are coming to do our hair and make-up ready for our cocktail making and our night out."

"Can't I go with the lads?"

"We're separating?" Clayton sputters.

"Dude, cut the cord," Maddox jibes.

I roll my eyes at him before nudging Faith. "No, you can't. Even Mum and Sunday are coming. They have a kids pool, but they've said we're welcome to bring her into the private pool."

"All right," I sulk, dropping my chair to all fours.

"What am I meant to be doing?" Clayton asks, sounding nervous.

"You came," I remind him. "Don't blame me for this. But for your information, you'll be spending the day off-road mud karting."

His expression lights up as he grins at me. "I guess I could bear to be apart for that."

I snort at his attempt to be funny. "I bet."

"That is so sweet," Lily gushes. "I never want to be apart from Jaxon either."

Jaxon gazes softly down at Lily, pulling her into his arms before addressing

Clayton. "Just make sure you wear your seat belt. They're going to kill you. I'm talking from experience, mate."

Maddox slams his fists down on the table, causing everything to shake. "We said we were sorry for that. You didn't die, so you really need to get over it."

"Over you guys nearly beating me to death? Of course I'm over it." Jaxon stops when Lily tenses, squeezing her tighter. "Sorry, princess."

"He wasn't joking?" Clayton sputters, drilling holes into the side of my head.

I grimace, shrugging. "What's the worst that could happen?"

Already a sense I'll be choking on those words later, haunts me.

SUNDAY GIVES A joyous laugh that echoes around the enclosed room. Her little legs kick in the water mercilessly as she slaps her hands down, splashing me and Mum.

When it was evident Sunday wasn't impressed with the pool we occupied, me and Mum decided to bring her to the kids pool, giving Aunt Teagan time alone with her daughter and Bailey, to have a break. Although she isn't Sunday's biological mum, she loves and cares for her like she's her own. She couldn't sit by and relax and pretend she wasn't there.

Sunday loves it here though, especially the slides.

"She really does look cute in her swimming costume," I admit, laughing when Sunday splashes me again, giving me a toothy smile.

"I think splashing us has become a game to her, but let's cut the small talk. Stop avoiding the talk you know I want. Tell me about Clayton."

I avoid making eye contact with Mum and instead find fascination in twirling Sunday in her float, causing her to laugh. "There's nothing to tell."

"I find that hard to believe. He's hot, you're hot, and there's some serious chemistry between you. I watched him on the coach with you. He knew when you needed something before you did. No one is that in tune with someone if there isn't something there."

Sunday expresses her displeasure when I stop twirling her, gripping the float and crying out, "Da, da, da."

Resuming the twirling at a slower pace, I turn to Mum. "That's all we have in common, Mum. Don't get excited. He's a majority owner of a successful business while I work for a little over minimum wage. For him. He dresses to impress whilst I'd live in my PJ's if I could. And the worst: can you believe he doesn't like gaming? He's never even played Call of Duty."

Mum chuckles half-heartedly, a smile teasing the corner of her lips. "Has anyone ever told you opposites attract? Me and your father couldn't have been any more different when we were younger."

"Yes, but you fit in a way that all the edges meet. You put up with his outrageous behaviour."

"Exactly, we couldn't be more opposite. But we built a life together where we grew, where we, like you said, fit. As your dad would say, he's the bacon to my egg, salt to my pepper."

My heart stutters as I slouch. "He doesn't like me like that."

She scoffs. "I don't believe that for a second. I didn't raise a stupid girl, Hayden. I raised a clever and strong one."

"Thanks, Mum," I mutter dryly. "But it's you who's wrong this time. He kissed me, then regretted it, saying it shouldn't have happened."

"You like him," Mum states without caution. "You'd have moved on by now if you didn't."

I chuckle at how right she is. "I was going to, but then I got a glimpse of him at work and I couldn't help it. I wanted him again. There's just something that draws me to him."

"You like him more than just wanting to do the naughty with him."

"Yeah, okay," I tell her, rolling my eyes.

"Yes, you do. You wouldn't have let him come with you on a *family* trip if you didn't."

"Have you not stopped to consider whether I brought him because I didn't like him?" When she continues to stare, I sigh, my brows scrunching together. "I tried to stop him."

"You are your father's daughter. If you had tried, he wouldn't be here, and we both know it. He'd be locked in or tied up somewhere."

"If that's a dig about the time Dad got locked in the cellar, I'm offended. Someone else put the bolt across and blocked it with a tumble dryer. Just because I didn't want him to come to the school dance, doesn't mean it was me," I lie, inwardly smiling at the fond memory. He's never gone back down there.

Mum struggles to hide her disbelief. "You're strong-minded, Hayden. You resemble your father in a lot of ways, which is why I know you'll be stubborn about Clayton. Don't hold it against him, or at least give him a chance to explain why he pulled away. He's a man, so the reason is probably ridiculous."

"It's because he's my boss."

"See, ridiculous," she points out.

"You're amazing, Mum. Have I told you that lately?"

Laughing, she pulls Sunday towards her. "So are you, my girl."

The door to the pool swings open and Imogen strolls in, waving a phone in her hand.

"Your phone hasn't stopped ringing or receiving messages for the past ten minutes. They're all from 'Hot Jerk Boss'."

"Oh cra—crazy," I rush out, forcing a smile towards Sunday, grateful I didn't slip up. "I need to go. Tell Faith I'll be back in time to shower and get my hair and make-up done."

"I am going to kill your dad," she claims, before leaning down to kiss Sunday. "That's right, Sunday, Aunt Lake is going to kill your uncle Max."

"I'm coming. I don't think I'm a zen person," Imogen announces.

I laugh, tugging her hand after pulling myself up and out of the pool.

"Let's go smash some shit."

"It's mud karting, not bumper cars," Mum yells after us.

"I'll call a taxi while you get changed," Imogen offers.

"This is going to be awesome."

NINETEEN

IMOGEN FALLS IN STEP BESIDE ME as we march over to the buggy bay, helmets in hand. We had rented one after the quickest safety course in a dummy kart ever. Personally, I think the guy just wanted us to get our family under control or get them to leave. He was sweating, stuttering his words and stumbling all over the place in a rush to get us on the track.

"Why did it have to rain?" Imogen complains, blowing into her hands.

I reach into the blue overalls I'm wearing, grab the pair of gloves I found earlier and hand them over to her.

A man in his late twenties, wearing an orange jumpsuit, spots us, venom pouring from his eyes.

I pull my green knitted beanie further down my head as I lean in to Imogen. "Why is he staring at us like we just killed his mum?"

He throws his hands up when we draw closer. "Please don't tell me they sent two fucking girls to sort these hooligans out?"

I cut him a sharp gaze, my lip curling. "Yeah. You know the saying, 'Never get a man to do a woman's job'."

"I don't think that's said right," Imogen helpfully interjects.

"Just sort them out. There's only three of us on duty due to the season, and the guy out with your group is missing. We can't reach him on the radio."

I tilt my head to the sky, sighing before locking gazes with Imogen. "Dad."

"Max," she agrees, giving a sharp nod.

Wanting this over with, I reach my hand out, palm up, impatiently tapping my foot against the tarmac. "Keys."

He shoots me a furious glance as he slaps the keys in the palm of my hand.

"Your buggy kart is number nine."

He storms off, and with one shared look from Imogen, I grin, swinging the keys around my finger. "Let's do this."

The buggy kart looks nothing like more than red scrap metal. I just hope it doesn't run like it too.

After pulling the helmet over my head, I lower myself into the bucket seat, Imogen following on the passenger side.

"This is awesome," Imogen yells, yet I can barely hear her through my helmet.

I double check my straps before turning the engine on. It roars to life, vibrating to the point I begin to shake.

"Whoohoo," I holler, pressing my foot down on the accelerator.

We both slam back into the seats, the tyres screeching as we fly off the track and onto the dirt road.

Imogen tilts her head up, throwing her hands up in the air, and screams.

I don't blame her. If I wasn't worried the wheels might spin out of control, I'd let go myself. This has to be the most exhilarating thing I've ever done, and coming from a family that is dominated by men, that is saying something.

Scenery flies past us in a blur, the wind whipping around us, howling. I laugh as mud splatters from the tyres, covering the buggy and our overalls.

I've never been happier.

I shift the wheel to the left as I spot the sign the guy from the front desk told us was the beginning of the track Dad and the rest were on. I just hope we catch up to them before they get someone killed. There is no way they'd act like mad men if we were on the track. None of them would take the chance of putting us at risk. They might be hazardous when it comes to every other aspect of their lives, but when it comes to the females in their lives, they are careful, protective.

A pothole in the dirt track causes us to bounce in our seat, and I nearly lose control of the wheel.

Imogen yells something I can't hear, so I lean in, keeping my gaze on the road.

When I still can't hear what she's saying, she points to the distance. Up ahead, a buggy kart is facing forward down a ditch, shrubs covering the front of the cage. There's another buggy not far up, still on the path.

Shit!

We skid to a stop behind the buggy at the top of the bank. In seconds, I have my straps undone and my helmet ripped off, dropping it onto my seat as I get out.

I reach the top, coming to a stop and placing my hands on my head. "What the hell?"

A head pops up from the car. "Hayden? Hayden, is that you?" Clayton yells.

I exhale, dropping my arms to my sides as I take another step down the bank, slipping when my feet hit the mud slide.

"Shit," I curse as I nearly topple over. I steady myself, walking around to the driver's side, my jaw dropping at the sight of Clayton tied up to the steering wheel. He stops trying to loosen the knot with his teeth and lifts his head up.

I step back when he levels me with a furious glare, his lips tight.

I can feel his temper flaring, so when he opens his mouth to most likely yell at me, I step forward, holding my hands up in surrender.

"I'd like to take this opportunity to point out that you wanted to come. I warned you, more than once, so really, you only have yourself to blame for this predicament."

"Most people would rush to help the person stranded and tied to a vehicle," he points out, his tone coated in annoyance.

I shrug as an idea occurs to me, and I pull out my phone, absently answering him. "I'm not most people."

He snorts. "No shit. Your dad needs locking up. He—Hey, what are you doing?"

I stick my tongue out, concentrating on getting the right angle. "I need proof. The guys at the office will get a kick out of this."

"Holy shit, are you hurt?" Imogen asks, skidding to a stop next to me, her eyes wide.

Clayton stares blankly at me. "No. My pride, however, is crushed between the bumper and the bush. But thank you for being the only person to care."

"How did you text me if you're tied to the wheel, and why isn't anyone helping?" I ask, scanning the area. I don't even hear the sound of an engine close by.

"Well," he drawls, a bite to his tone. "After your father ran me off the road for the tenth time, I tried calling for help. The bloke on road with us pulled up to help. That's his kart. Your dad came back and snatched him so he couldn't help. I tried calling and texting you to sort him out, but he doubled back and tried to pinch that too."

I bend down to help with the knots, wondering how he kept still long enough for my dad to do this. There's more than one knot.

His phone poking out of his overalls catches my eye. "He didn't get your phone though. It's there."

"I panicked and blurted out about my dad. I'm next of kin, and if something happens, it's me they'll call."

My shoulders drop with a light sigh. "I didn't think of that. He would have taken it had you not said. He was just playing around though," I lie, finally getting the knots undone.

I stand up, stepping back as he pulls himself out, flexing his fingers. "I need to get him back for this."

"Of course you do. Most people react the same," Imogen tells him, chuckling.

"Maybe that's not the best idea," I explain slowly, grimacing.

"She's so right," Imogen states. "Everyone gets drawn into the Carter shenanigans. It's like a calling. However, it never ends well for anyone other than a Carter. Many men have tried, my friend."

"You aren't helping," I mutter, yet I can't help but nod in agreement as I point to her. "What she said."

He holds Imogen's gaze for a second, taking in her words, before turning to me, giving me a pointed gaze. "You told me that to get him to ease up or respect me, I need to play him at his own game. I'm going to do that. Two can play this game."

"You don't like games," I remind him.

"This one I do. And I'm going to fucking crush it. I'm not going to be your boss, the guy who needs to run a successful business, or a son who doesn't want to let his dying father down. Right now, I'm Clayton Cross, and I'm going to forget about all my responsibilities and be me. I'll get payback." He storms off, heading towards the dirt track.

"So… basically, you're going to pull the stick out of your arse?"

"You'll see. I'll show him," he yells back, glancing over his shoulder. His feet slip out from under him and he lands in the dirt.

Laughter spills out of me as I step over to him, bending down to pat his back. "Yes, you'll definitely show him."

He rolls over to his side, staring blankly up at me. "Hayden?"

"Uh huh," I mumble as I reach for my phone in my pocket.

A squeal escapes me when he grabs my wrist, pulling me down next to him. Dirt cakes my mouth, and I gag, spitting out the dry, foul-tasting texture.

He did not just do that.

"You wanker!" I breathe out, my temples thumping. I reach in front of me, digging my fingers into the dirt, and grip a clump of slush.

I'm about to show him what payback looks like when the sound of footsteps splashing through puddles reaches us.

We tilt our heads up to the top of the bank, where a lad in his early twenties comes to a halt. He bends at the waist, his face red as he gasps for breath.

"T-thank God you're okay. He took me by surprise, mate. He's lost the plot, I swear. And he has my keys."

Clayton crawls forward before pushing himself up. I follow, trying hard to get as much dirt off my face as possible, but it feels like I'm making it worse.

"I can't get my kart out. Something has lodged its way around the wheel. I was trying to tell you before he took you."

"I'll call it in. You guys are our only group today, so Stevens will come pull it out for you," he explains, as another kart pulls up behind ours.

Clayton grabs his helmet off his seat before following me up the bank to meet Jaxon.

Jaxon takes in the kart as he pulls his helmet off, running a hand over his tousled hair, making it messier.

"Fuck, man. I'm sorry I couldn't stop to help. Maddox was up my arse."

"Up your arse, huh? Did you enjoy it?" I tease, my lips twitching.

His hands briefly clench. "Remind me why I've not killed you yet."

I hold up my finger. "One, because I'd bury you before you even touched me, and two, Lily loves me," I smart.

"We have a bigger problem to deal with right now," Clayton interrupts, stepping past me. "I'm going to get him back. You in, Jaxon?"

"Hey, that's ours," I yell when he jumps into the driver's seat of our kart. I race after him, sliding into the passenger side.

He passes me my helmet and I hold Imogen's out to her, grimacing when I'm reminded of our predicament. "Go jump in Jaxon's."

She rolls her eyes, snatching the helmet. "They always have all the fun."

She's not wrong.

When the engines roar to life, her eyes widen slightly before she jogs off, getting into the kart behind us.

"Wait! You can't leave me here," the guy working yells, his face ashen.

My back slams against the seat as he peels off, the wind and rain whipping around us.

I tilt my head to the side, watching his powerful frame maneuverer the kart with ease and practice. Each corner we take, his body moves with the kart. From years of seeing my uncle Malik race, I know a born rider when I see one. At some point, Clayton knew how to ride and excelled at it. It's information I'm going to store for later.

Five minutes later, I'm slapping Clayton's hand away. Each time we've hit a bump in the road, he's placed his arm across my chest, pushing me back into my seat.

A clearing comes up ahead. It's the widest part of the track we've been on. Maddox and my dad are struggling to push a kart out of a mud puddle, which is the better condition of the two karts. The other one with a black frame is on its side, half stuck a bush of shrubs.

Thinking Clayton will slow down when we reach them, I'm surprised when he doesn't and instead presses his foot flat to the floor. I grin, pulling my phone out of my pocket and praising myself for getting a waterproof case.

I hit record as Dad lifts his head, smiling, but when his gaze lands on the mad man next to me, his smile drops. He stiffens, planting his feet apart, right up until the realisation hits him that Clayton isn't stopping. He flinches, turning to the side at the waist to avoid us.

It's too late. Clayton spins the wheel the second we reach them and breaks, causing dirt and puddles to splash into the air, hitting Dad head to toe. I glance behind us, still holding my camera out, as Dad stands there, unmoving for a moment, before all hell breaks loose. His body begins to shake as he yells out at us, punching the air and kicking at the ground.

Laughter spills out of me when Maddox, still bent at the knee behind the kart, turns his head—just in time for Jaxon to make the same manoeuvre, hitting them both again. This time, Dad slips, falling on his arse.

The last thing I see is Jaxon spinning off, following the track instead of coming back on himself like Clayton has.

We come to a stop off track, into a secluded area hidden by bushes. He slides up his visor, grinning like a mad fool, his cheeks flushed.

"Did you see his face?" he yells, squeezing my hand.

I lift my visor up, my smile causing my jaw to ache. "I caught it all on camera," I explain, waving my phone at him. "Let's do it again and then make this track our bitch."

"I didn't get all of that, but I think we should do it again. To be certain we hit him."

I give him a thumbs up, tilting my head back and laughing uproariously.

Clayton pulls out of our hiding spot before lining the car up and revving the engine.

His foot slams down on the accelerator, causing us to jerk back. When the guys come into view, I struggle to breathe at the sight before us. They remind me of the time we took them ice-skating and they struggled to hold each other up.

Dad glances up at the sound of the engine, his jaw dropping. He pushes Maddox in front, as a shield. However, Clayton guns past them, causing mud to spray like a wave all over them.

Looking around the back of my seat, I get to witness Maddox lose his footing, landing flat on his face, Dad toppling over him.

We lose sight of them as we take the corner, and as I face forward, the wheels spin at the same time the steering wheel locks.

Clayton's head jerks briefly towards me, panic flashing in his eyes. His fingers grip the wheel, fighting to turn it as he pushes down on the brake.

He notices the bank the second after I do. It's steeper than the one we just left, and instead of a shrub, we are heading right for a tree.

I can hear him yelling over the noise, yet can't understand his words as I lean over to help, grabbing the wheel and yanking as hard as I can. It's no use, we're going to roll down that bank and hit the tree. There's nothing we can do to stop it.

We're seconds from the bank when Clayton gives up on the wheel and startles me by swinging himself around, his body partially covering mine.

I press myself into his shoulder as he grips me, shielding my head. A scream escapes as we begin to pick up speed, my stomach rolling as the kart spins in its descent down the hill.

I grip the metal cage with one hand, the other clutching Clayton, holding on for dear life. My knuckles ache, along with body.

My heart thumps against my rib cage, as well as rings in my ears, when we shoot forward before being yanked bank in our seats as the kart comes to a sudden stop.

Clayton slowly pries himself off me as I dazedly blink, scanning my surroundings.

We had hit the tree from the rear end. The bank looks a lot steeper from this angle than it did approaching it.

I recoil when Clayton reaches for my helmet, unclipping it and sliding it off my head.

"Are you okay?" he rushes out, guilt ridden as he tilts my head side to side, checking for injuries.

I swat him away gently. "I'm fine, but what the hell happened?" I ask, unclipping my harness.

Reading my mind, he gets out, coming around to my side and helping me out.

"It was my fault. I was driving like a dickhead. The steering wheel locked and the engine cut out. I'm so fucking sorry, Hayden."

"Don't be. I don't think that's because of your driving," I tell him honestly, watching the engine steam as the rain hits it.

From the corner of my eye, I watch Clayton stumble forward. I brace myself as he grabs me, pulling me into his arms and squeezing. Relief pours out of his hold, yet his body remains tense, on edge. "I'm so fucking glad you're okay."

He pulls back, yet keeps close, anguish shining back at me.

I reach up, wiping back a strand of hair sticking out next to his temple, before meeting his gaze. My mouth dries as I suck in a breath.

"You protected me."

He runs a hand over his forehead. "Why do you seem surprised?"

My lips twitch. "Because you've been planning my death since day one."

He steps forward, his expression void of anything as he cups my cheek. I briefly close my eyes, not wanting this moment to end.

"Your death isn't what I've been planning to do to you since day one, Hayden," he admits, his voice hoarse as he leans in further.

"Don't kiss me unless you mean it. This place looks great for hiding your body."

He tilts his chin down, frowning. "I meant it the first time."

"I sense a *but…*"

"*But*, I'm your boss."

I step back, giving a sharp nod as I swallow the lump in my throat, even though a part of me wants to knee him in the balls. "I get it. You don't want to be seen with the 'help', so to speak."

He rears back, his body locking. "Not at all. I'm worried others will make it difficult for you at work if they think I'm favouring you because we're together." His lips twist. "Do you really think so little of me?"

He swings around, heading back up the hill before I have a chance to answer. I blink back my confusion as his words finally settle in, my heart racing.

"Wait!"

"No. I am done with today, with it all, Hayden."

Running up behind him, I grab onto his overalls, pulling him back. I gasp when he loses his footing, taking me with him as we fall to the ground.

We roll apart and he leans up on his hands, glaring down at me as I lie on my back, in the mud, on the hill. "What was that for?"

I lean up on my elbows. "If you had stopped, I wouldn't have had to take drastic measures."

"God, you're infuriating."

"It's not nice to talk about God like that," I reflect, the comeback flowing easily.

"You aren't even religious," he reminds me.

"We're going off track," I snap. "Do I look like someone who cares what people think of her?"

His eyebrows draw together. "No."

"No," I confirm with a nod. "So why would you think that I'd care what they thought at work? They don't even have to know."

His pupils dilate as he looms over me, shaking his head. "I'm still your boss, and if you hadn't noticed, we argue *now*. I don't want a relationship argument ruining our work atmosphere or vice versa."

A chuckle slips free as disappointment sets in. "And I didn't think you were scared to go after what you wanted. I don't play these games."

He grabs the back of my neck, lifting my head towards him, stopping when my lips are a breath away. Hot air mingles between us as my pulse races. "I'm not, and I'll show you just how much I'm not."

The touch of his lips has mine parting and my eyes closing, already anticipating how good it will be.

His tongue flicks my upper lip as the sound of an engine skidding to a stop above us breaks us apart.

I groan, falling onto my back and looking up the hill. "Fucking hell."

The guy called Stevens, who gave us the keys to our kart, rips himself out of the harness, coming to stand at the top of the hill.

"Are you fucking out of your mind? I told you to take number nine, not six."

"Hey, don't talk to her like that," Clayton snaps.

"It does say nine," I yell, getting up, not bothering to wipe the dirt away.

He points to the kart, his nostrils flaring. "It's a fucking six."

Taking a look, the number attached to the top, on a metal board, says nine, but the number sprayed on the side, says six.

I grimace, shrugging. "Sorry?"

"Sorry? Sorry! It's under repair for engine troubles. You could have gotten yourself killed," he yells, throwing his hands up. "Do none of you listen?"

"Oh no," I mutter as the sound of Dad's maniacal laughter entwines with the roar of an engine.

I open my mouth to warn Stevens but think better of it. He could use it as a learning experience. Instead, I pull Clayton away from the bank.

Everything happens quickly. Dad speeds towards Stevens, and the minute he notices, he reacts, jerking back. He loses his footing, clearly not taking in how close he is to the hill, and falls, his arms flailing as he tries to save himself from embarrassment.

I tilt my head up to Clayton. "It's time to leave."

"Huh?"

"Just trust me," I tell him. "Nothing good will come from this moment on. It's better to get out while we can."

"Alright," he answers, grinning at me as he grips my hand. "Let's rob his kart and get back to the entrance."

Laughing, I nod. "You can buy me dinner for saving you."

"Of course I will," he mutters.

TWENTY

A COLD BREEZE PICKS UP MY HAIR, blowing strands across my face. I'm glad now that I chose to have my hair wavy with a few plaits hidden throughout.

I can only be grateful it isn't raining. I don't want my thigh-high, suede boots getting ruined. Between my short, ripped, black skirt and the boots, I'm only revealing a small part of my thigh, so the cold isn't touching me just yet.

I pull my jacket tighter across my body, covering my Guns n Roses T-shirt.

I've never felt so good with my choice of outfit. With a few bangles and a choker necklace, it feels complete.

The team Faith had hired were the best of the best. They had done wonders on us ladies. My make-up is flawless. After describing my outfit in detail to the make-up artist, she perfected my desired look, giving me smoky eye make-up, a shimmer to my cheeks and ruby red lips. I made sure to write down everything she used, though I don't think I'll get it to look as good as this. I'll probably end up looking like a racoon.

There's a bounce in my step as I meet up with the others waiting outside Mingles.

The guys are already waiting for us, and as the last two taxi's pull in with the rest of the group, I'd say we're the last to arrive.

The tension leaves my body when Clayton steps through the crowd. After deeming it safe, I had left him with the guys earlier so I could get back to the girls. It didn't stop me worrying somewhat. It wasn't that I doubted Clayton, especially after today, but I know my family. It doesn't matter how strong you are, they can and will break you without using violence.

My lips pull up into a smile as I lift my hand, waving when he finally spots me. He stops in his tracks, nearly tripping over his feet, unable to peel his gaze away. He scans my body, starting low and building his way up, taking his time.

A low, pleasant hum warms my blood at his appraisal. After earlier, my hormones are all over the place, and right now, I don't trust myself not to jump him. I saw a different side to him today, and it only made me want him more. It's like a hunger.

"Nothing going on, my arse," Dad mutters over my shoulder.

I glance behind me, arching my eyebrow. Before he can say anything else, Mum pulls him away.

"How did the rest of your day go?" I ask Clayton as he draws closer.

He makes a sound at the back of his throat. "I'm alive, so there's that."

"But?" I tease, knowing there is always a but when it comes to him

He gives me a lopsided grin. "You know me so well."

"So?"

"I'm hungry," he moans. "I could eat a cow right now.

"Did you not go with the rest of them to the restaurant? You were invited," I remind him, worried he didn't.

"Yes, Hayden, I did. Your dad is worse than you when it comes to food. How the hell does he stay in shape?"

"High metabolism and good genes," I immediately answer, used to being asked the question. "What did he do?"

"Apart from scar me for life? You don't want to know. It's safe to say we won't be allowed back during our time here."

Which is what I was afraid would happen after this morning's incident.

"We're all here," Charlotte announces, stepping up beside me.

We begin to head over to the entrance, when everyone suddenly stops, nearly causing me to walk into my aunt Denny.

"What the fuck is this place?" Mason growls, turning and sending an accusing gaze towards Clayton.

I take a peep around him to the entrance, my jaw dropping. Men and women exit and enter the large building, kitted out in black leather, collars and chains.

"Holy crap!" I whisper.

"What the fuck have you got my daughter into, Cross?" Dad snaps, his tone going high-pitched towards the end.

Clayton takes a step back as nearly everyone forms a group in front of us, aiming their angry glances at him.

He holds his hands up. "Don't blame me for this."

"You booked it," I point out. "Why on earth would you bring us here?"

He sighs heavily, his eyebrows pinched together. "For the last time, I'm not an actual party planner."

"You suck at it," I admit, nodding.

"Why would you pretend to be one?" Dad accuses.

"Max," Mum soothes.

"Ask your daughter."

I shrug impishly. "Sorry?"

"Hey," Faith interrupts softly. "We really appreciate everything you've done by doing this, but I really don't want to go in there. You don't mind, do you?"

"My girls aren't stepping foot in there either," Mason snaps.

The large bouncer manning the door steps up to the side of our group. "If you guys aren't going in, I'm going to need you to move back and away from the doors."

"What is going on in there?" Charlotte asks, her gaze shifting to the door.

"It's BDSM night. They're doing role play this week and selling sex toys," he answers, running his gaze over Charlotte, licking his lips.

"Really?" Charlotte and I ask, both glancing back at the entrance.

"No!" Dad yells. "Over my dead body."

Charlotte pouts. "But—"

"No, Charlotte," Myles declares, red-faced.

The bouncer takes another look around our large group. "Barbra's, around the corner, is having a drag night. Karaoke."

"Yes." Faith grins. "I love drag."

"I love karaoke," Maddox announces, causing us all to groan.

He might love karaoke, but karaoke doesn't love him. A dog is more in tune than him.

"Barbra's it is," Beau yells, taking Faith's hand.

"Have a good night," the bouncer announces, heading back to the entrance.

MY UPPER BODY sways to the beat of the music, my hips wiggling in my seat. Mingles had me interested for a second, but I'm glad this is where we ended up. Men in drag are the best.

When we first arrived, they had a drag queen called Luna doing stand-up. We hadn't even been seated before we were laughing.

It must be a regular night here because pictures of them are mounting the walls, along with advertisements of what else is happening in the week.

"Whoohoo," I howl when another tray of shots is placed on our table. I reach for mine, then shoot it back, the dark liquid burning my throat.

"Your dad and uncles are up to something," Clayton yells as he leans in, his cologne reaching my senses.

Twisting my head to their table, I note that he's right. Dad, after monopolising time with a red-headed drag queen, questioning her with random crap, finally sits down with Malik, Mason and Myles, not letting anyone sit next to them. I'd noticed not long ago that he kept looking over, but until now, I didn't see his cunning expression.

The minute they spot me watching, they glance away so quickly I'll be surprised if they don't have whiplash. Uncle Malik, however, seems bored, his attention on Aunt Harlow.

I sigh, sitting back in my seat. "You'll be fine. After they nearly killed Jaxon, they promised they wouldn't overreact again."

"That really does not make me feel better."

"Next up for tonight, we have a hot totty, Clayton Cross," Cindy, the stage diva, announces.

Liquid sprays across the table as Clayton chokes on his drink.

"Really?" Maddox mutters, wiping the alcohol off his arm.

Clayton turns to me with wide eyes. "Please tell me I didn't hear my name."

I grin, because this I have to see. "You really did."

"Did you do this?"

"Nope," I admit, turning my head to Dad's table, where he's laughing it up with the others. "You really can't back out. They're counting on that. Live a little."

He turns away from their table and focusses on me, his lips pulling into a smirk. "Then you won't mind doing it with me."

"I'm not drunk enough," I yell, grabbing a shot off the table and downing it when he pulls me up.

We reach the stage, where Cindy greets us. "Hey, sugar. Hey, hot pie," she drawls, running her gaze over Clayton. I can't blame her. Tonight, he's skipped his black slacks and gone for dark, navy-blue jeans and a white shirt with light blue stripes on, his sleeves rolled up to his elbows. Brown shoes and a brown belt to go with it.

He looks good enough to eat and smells even better.

"Hey," I greet, giving her a small wave.

"Do you still want to sing 'It's Raining Men'?" Cindy asks, her voice scratchy.

"God no," I mutter, shuddering. "Do you have 'Islands in the Stream'?"

"Dolly Parton? You're a girl after my own heart, darlin'," she gushes, pressing her padded chest into my arms as she hugs me.

I twirl a strand of her hair around my finger, grinning. "This is Dolly all over."

She winks, her long, glittered lashes fluttering. "Maybe later we could sing 'Jolene' or, my favourite, '9 to 5'."

I push away, smiling. "You're on."

Clayton rubs his hands down his jeans before reaching for the mic.

"Why this song?" he whispers as we walk onto the stage, to where the screen sits, facing us.

"It has a lot of intro," I explain on a whisper, beaming out at the crowd.

He chuckles under his breath as the song begins to play. "Baby when I met…" he sings, shocking me to my core when it turns out he's pretty good.

I shake my head, grinning like a fool when our duet comes. "You do something to me…"

His lips spread into a wide smile as he arches his eyebrows. I'm not one to brag, but I'm pretty fucking good.

The female members and a few male members of our group stand, cheering and singing along with us. I sway side to side, bumping my hip with Clayton's when he slips up.

A laugh breaks from his chest during the middle of the song. He gazes down at me, wrapping an arm around me as he continues to sing.

I'm so caught up in his crooked smile that I don't realise I've stopped singing. Joy and happiness radiate from him, and I'm unable to turn away.

I startle when someone slips up behind me. Everything hits me at once. The sound of cheers, the light intro music playing, and Cindy standing between us.

"Singing like that, this couple will go far," she shouts into the microphone.

"They aren't a couple," Dad yells. "Fake news."

The crowd laugh, and I snigger at his crestfallen expression. I take a bow before standing, raising my arms in the air. "Thank you for coming. I'm here all week."

"Not so fast, short stuff. We need you for the next game," Cindy reveals.

"What?" I ask, forcing a laugh.

"We have a hen and stag party in attendance. Can the bride-to-be and groom come to the stage," she declares, before scanning the crowd. "You two love birds swallowing each other's faces… yeah, you, come on up. And you two hotties."

Aiden and Bailey slowly push up from their seats, reluctantly making their way to the stage, along with Beau and Faith and, to my horror, Mum and Dad.

"Oh God," I groan, standing closer to Clayton.

Another drag queen steps out from behind the curtain, carrying four balloons.

"Please tell me they're to throw in the air and not for what I think they're for."

"Bucker up, buttercup, we're doing this. My dad has his 'I'm going to win' face on."

"Seriously? You want to do this because of your dad?"

"We're a competitive family," I argue.

"First couple to get the balloon from their waists to their mouths, without popping it or touching it with their hands, will win a bottle of champagne."

"Prepare to lose, spawn of mine."

"Bet you fifty quid I win."

"You are on. Get that fifty ready. I'll be cashing in."

I roll my eyes, yet it's Mum I address and not Dad. "You're going to need his favourite pudding to pacify him after he loses."

Dad snorts. "Pudding is a euphemism for sex."

"Really," I snap. "I'm already piling up things to talk to my therapist about when I get one. You had to add to it?"

"Ignore him. He's lying."

I scoff because her deep blush says differently.

"Get ready," Cindy yells.

Clayton puts the balloon between us, before lightly placing his hands on my sides, just below my boob area. He clears his throat, jerking them away and placing them lower down.

My fingers twitch as I fight to keep them at my sides.

"Steady."

Clayton takes in a deep breath, his pupils dilating as I press a little closer.

"Go!"

It's a rush of movement as everyone begins. Bending at the knees, we thrust and wiggle our hips and stomach, trying to move the balloon higher, yet we only manage to get it lower.

"Stop moving and let me do all the work," I snap.

Clayton freezes. "I hope you aren't this demanding in bed."

"You say that like you're going to find out," I heave out, bending lower and pushing the balloon up with my boobs.

"I-I just—oh my God, what are you doing?"

"Shut up and keep still," I growl, ignoring my breast brushing over his dick.

"Stop bossing me around," he orders hoarsely.

"It's my competitive side—sorry." I grimace, reaching his chest.

I duck my head, using my chin to get it higher, before reaching my target.

A horn blares as Cindy announces, "We have a winner."

The balloon pops and our mouths smash together. Heat rises in my chest as Clayton grabs me around the waist, stopping me from falling.

It could be the drink, the adrenaline, or maybe it's just the chemistry constantly simmering between us, but I kiss him. My tongue flicks his bottom lip as my lips enclose around his.

His fingers dig into my sides, and as I'm about to deepen the kiss, my surroundings slap back into place at the sound of my dad's voice.

"No, we're going to do this," Dad yells.

"Babe, it's over," Mum explains, amusement in her voice.

Slowly, I pull away from Clayton, blinking away the lust coursing through my system.

"I-I—"

"They aren't even a couple. They should be disqualified," he argues.

"Didn't look that way to me, sugar," Cindy mutters.

Pulling my gaze away from Clayton, I turn to the others, laughing at Dad's sour expression. "You are such a sore loser. Pay up." I hold my hand out, tapping my foot on the wooden floor.

He reaches into his back pocket, pulling two twenties and a tenner out before slapping them down in the palm of my hand. "This isn't over."

TWENTY-ONE

THERE'S STILL A BIT OF A BITE TO the wind as we step out of Chicken Palace, in the middle of town, on the other side of where Cabin Lakes is located.

A group of us who were hungry let the others get in the remaining taxi. It's one in the morning and most pubs or clubs are closing, so taxis are limited.

So, me, Clayton, Dad, Charlotte, Malik, Maddox, Mark and Hope all decided to grab something to eat and walk the rest of the way. Luckily, we don't have much further to walk, though with the way Mark's swaying, it could take double the time. He had taken part in the roulette shot game with Beau, winning a free drink at the end. Beau was worse off when we left him passed out in the taxi with Faith and a few others.

"This is so good," Clayton mumbles around a mouthful of food.

I chuckle as I wipe a bit of mayonnaise off his lip. "I can tell."

"Can we go to the library now?" Charlotte asks, hopeful.

"You can do whatever the fuck you want, princess," Dad tells her, digging into his family bucket.

"Maybe tomorrow," Malik offers, glaring at Dad as he struggles to keep Mark upright.

"I want to go swimming," I declare, turning to Clayton. "We should totally go swimming."

"You can go to bed," Dad orders, narrowing his eyes. "You never listen to me. Charlotte listens to me."

I roll my eyes. "And I'm not going to start now."

"Who took my bed?" Mark stammers, closing his eyes as he rests his head on Malik.

Dad points a southern fried chicken drumstick at Clayton. "You've corrupted my daughter."

"If anyone was corrupted in this scenario, it was me. Have you met your daughter? No one tells her what to do," Clayton replies, more relaxed than I've ever seen him.

I beam at the praise. "Thank you."

"Ooh, look at that fighting talk," Maddox teases, stepping close to Dad. "He's making out you don't know your own daughter."

Dad snorts. "Pfft, like he could beat me."

"I dunno, Max, I think you're losing your touch," Maddox taunts, smirking at me. "Did you see him all over her on the stage?"

"What?" Dad screeches, going for Clayton.

Malik lets go of Mark, who falls against a lamp post, to stop Dad, placing a hand on his chest. "Eat your food."

Dad steps back, ripping into another drumstick, his gaze still on Clayton.

"I think we should go on a nature walk," Charlotte blurts out. "We could look for bears."

"Where's the bear?" Mark slurs, rubbing the lamp post.

"We don't have bears," I remind her, before turning to Maddox, narrowing my eyes. "And stop trying to cause a fight because you're still sulking over what happened earlier. He got you back for running him off the road, fair and square. Live with it."

"Aww, does he need a girl to stick up for him?" Dad sings, wiggling his chicken in the air.

"I really did you both good. Your faces," Clayton muses, laughing abruptly at the image he's probably painted in his mind.

"They were hilarious," I agree, noticing a cop car pull up just ahead, followed by two officers getting out.

"Look at him laughing at you," Maddox whispers next to Dad's ear.

"Stop trying to goad him, son," Malik orders, slapping him upside his head.

"Child abuse!" Maddox yells, acting like Malik gave him a blow to the head. He steps back, and before anyone can warn him, the backs of his legs hit a small bench and he flies back, his arms flailing as he tries to keep his balance.

I flinch when he falls onto his back, rolling into a water fountain. Water splatters over the side and all over Mark, who is now resting near the bin.

"I don't want a shower," Mark whines, swatting thin air.

I lean in to Hope, whispering, "Did you get any of this on camera?"

"I've been recording since your dad started going off again."

The two cops come to a stop in front of us. "We've had some complaints about a disturbance. Have you guys been in the area long?"

"No, we've just grabbed food and are on our way home," Hope replies, grimacing when Malik accidently drops Maddox back into the fountain.

"Sir, we're going to need you to come out of the fountain," the taller of the two officers orders.

"I'm trying to get him out." Malik heaves, grabbing Maddox's hand.

"You need to arrest him," Dad suddenly shouts, pointing at Clayton. "Not them two misfits. He's been trying to get in my daughter's pants. She's not even eighteen."

"Sir, have you been drinking?" the smaller officer asks, bracing his feet apart, his hand resting on his belt.

"Legal age limit is sixteen, Dad," I point out before forcing my eyes to well up. "I can't believe you forgot my age. You never forget Liam or Landon's, and we're triplets."

Dad shoots Clayton a venomous look before he throws a drumstick at him. "Now look what you did. You made her cry."

I place my hand over my mouth as the drumstick bounces off the bridge of Clayton's nose and lands on his box of food, which knocks it out of his hand.

He whips his head up, skewering Dad with an unflinching look before turning to the police. "That's assault. I'd like him arrested."

I clutch my stomach, laughing at Dad's crestfallen expression. "Oh God, this is funny."

And hot. In fact, whenever Clayton takes charge, it makes me hot. Unless it's me he's trying to boss around.

"I can't believe you pushed me," Maddox yells, shoving Malik away.

"Stop it," Malik warns, pushing Maddox back lightly.

"Fuck!" I whisper, stepping back as I watch the horror play out in front of us.

Maddox knocks into Mark, who in turn knocks into the officer, both falling to the floor.

"All right, we're taking you in," the smaller officer announces, reaching for Dad.

"No. This is what he wanted. Don't you see that?" Dad yells, running from the police.

"This is not going to end well," Hope mutters.

"I think Mark is going to be sick," Clayton claims.

I wince as the cop finishes lifting Mark to his feet, only to be covered in vomit. The cop tilts his head up, taking a breath before turning Mark and cuffing him.

The one chasing Dad around the fountain calls in for help while the other tries to detain Maddox.

"What did I do?" Maddox yells.

"We should go," I grumble, taking another step back.

"Are you going to leave them to get arrested?" Clayton asks, his jaw dropping.

I arch an eyebrow at him. "I didn't survive my childhood by standing by. Trust me, they'll take us in, and I don't know about you, but I don't want to spend the night in a cell."

"And they've not been arrested. They'll just keep them overnight," Hope explains. "Although Mark is going to have a cleaning bill in the morning."

"Does this mean we can go the library?" Charlotte asks, grinning ear to ear.

"Let's go see what's at the cabin."

"Hey, you can't leave us," Dad yells, struggling to get up from the floor where the cop has him pinned down, but his attention is pulled away to his box of food that's close by. He reaches over with his free hand, grabbing a drumstick.

"I knew you'd get us arrested," Maddox growls, glaring at Dad.

"Bye. See you in the morning," I yell, before taking Clayton's hand and running in the direction that leads back to the cabins.

"I'M TIRED," CHARLOTTE grumbles. "But I really wanted to go on a bear hunt. There's so much land here."

"We don't have bears," Hope explains, holding her close.

"We have wild cats. We could go find some of them." She yawns, gazing at Hope.

"We'll see you tomorrow morning," I comment, grimacing at the pain in my feet from all the walking.

"Night, guys," they croak, reaching the door to their cabin.

"My feet are killing me," I moan, gripping Clayton's arm.

"Jump on my back," he offers, stepping in front of me and bending down. When I don't move, he straightens, facing me. "What?"

"Have you seen my skirt? I'd be flashing my arse to every Tom, Dick and Harry. I have a great arse, but that doesn't mean I want everyone to see it."

Laughing, he steps forward, pulling his jacket off. "Jump up front. I'll cover your great arse with my coat."

I grin, placing my arms around his neck and heaving myself up, before wrapping my legs around his waist. The cold hits my bare arse as my skirt rides up to my waist. "I knew you liked me."

He groans as he holds his coat over my arse. Clearing his throat, he says, "Do I need to worry your dad is going to kill me tomorrow?"

"He'll be too sore over you getting him arrested. Malik, on the other hand, is going to be pissed. But not to worry, we've messaged Mum and Aunt Harlow to get them in the morning."

He shifts me up higher on his body, his hand dropping the jacket a little, causing his hand to slip onto my bare arse. "Sorry," he croaks.

My clit pulses as it rubs across his abdomen. I bite my lip, concerned that when I get down, he'll see how turned on I am.

I run my finger along his temple, unable to look away. "Have I ever told you how beautiful your eyes are?"

Every neuron fires, every skin cell tingles, and the hairs on the back on my neck stand on end as electricity passes between us.

His lips part as his lids lower, pooling with desire. "Hayden," he whispers hoarsely.

"Clayton," I murmur, clenching my thighs around him.

"Fuck it!" he growls, marching us off the path and to the side of a building, into the shadows where we can't be seen.

"Clay—"

His lips mesh with mine, his tongue teasing mine as he presses me against the wall, his jacket forgotten.

He places a possessive hand on my cheek, tilting my chin up to deepen the kiss, before pulling away and kissing along my jaw and across my neck.

"I shouldn't be doing this," he whispers, dousing some of my arousal. "I'm your boss."

"No one has to know. What happens here can stay here," I partially lie. I might be able to say the words but meaning them is something else entirely. For the first time since I started being intimate with men, I'm unsure how to separate my feelings.

"As soon as we leave, it has to stop," he breathes out, peppering kisses along my neck as I undo his belt, ignoring the sting of the buckle catching on the inside of my thigh.

"Here?" he asks, inhaling sharply.

"I want you. Call this an appetiser."

I feel him reach around before hearing a rustle. He leans back, keeping me pinned to the wall by his lower half as he pulls a condom out of his wallet, then drops the wallet on the floor.

"Maybe we should go back to the cabin before someone hears or sees us," I murmur, even though my body thinks differently as I undo the button on his jeans and unzip him. "Or not."

I can't keep my lips off him, flicking my tongue against his as he struggles to get the condom on.

Cold fingers slide up the inside of my thigh and into my thong, his fingers slipping between my legs.

I moan into his mouth, tightening, trapping his fingers inside of me. I can feel how wet I am, how turned on I am.

Unable to resist any longer, I bite his bottom lip, sucking it into my mouth. "Fuck me!"

In a rush of movements, he slides his fingers out of me, moving his hands around to my arse as I reach between us, pumping his dick once, twice, before lining it up at my entrance.

The beat of my heart echoes in my ears as I scan our surroundings, wondering if anyone has spotted us or can hear us.

He slips inside of me with one rough thrust, covering my mouth with his when I moan in pleasure. He's big, and the sensation has me closing my eyes as spasms shoot through my body.

"Quiet," he warns. "You don't want anyone to catch me fucking you, do you?"

"Right now, I wouldn't care," I groan. "Do that again."

He thrusts deep inside me again, twisting his hips in a way that hits the spot, causing my stomach to tighten.

He fucks me possessively, his hand sliding up the inside of my top, reaching under my bra to catch my nipple between his thumb and forefinger, tugging and twisting to the point I feel it to my core.

"Harder!" I breathe against his lips, clutching his shoulders and neck with all my strength as I lift my hips, slamming myself back down on him. My heels dig in to arse, feeling it clench with each thrust.

My body is heated, no longer cold from the night air as I tilt my head back, moaning.

"Fuck, you're beautiful," he rasps, running his hand up my neck to my jaw, gripping it tightly as he leans back, thrusting harder.

My arse scrapes against the wall, no doubt breaking skin, but I don't care. I'm close. Really close.

I reach between us, rubbing two fingers over my clit in a swirling motion, panting heavily.

Clayton looks down between us, his eyes darkening as he watches. "I'm not going to last if you keep doing that." He groans when I clench around him. "Fuck!"

"Harder. I'm so close."

He grips my hips, pulling me down so hard I cry out, no longer able to mask the noise as my orgasm hits me.

I squeeze my eyes shut, seeing colours as every nerve ending alights.

"Oh God," he moans, his movements jerking as he chases his own release, panting heavily.

He looks up, his cheeks filled with colour as he skims his lips over mine. "Are you ready to get back for the main?"

I chuckle, still heavy with lust. "And dessert."

It has never been that good before. I've had quick, and I've had fast, but never in a combination where it exploded between us like that. It could have been the weeks of built up tension, or the risk of being caught, but never have I felt passion explode like that before.

And I can't wait to find out if it was a fluke.

TWENTY-TWO

MY ALARM RINGS IN MY EARS, the sound pounding against my skull as it pulls me out of my slumber.

I groan, slamming my hand down on my phone and dragging it in front of me. I slide my finger across the 'dismiss' button, shutting off the sound. Instantly, the pounding quietens down.

My body aches in all the right places, deliciously so. I can't remember a time when I've ever woken up to this feeling, yet the image of his tongue sliding over my belly, across my thighs and in other sensitive places, has me wanting more.

After another round of fantastic sex, we got a bottle of vodka out of the freezer and hit the hot tub, but it wasn't long until we were going at it again. We couldn't keep our hands off each other, even though our bodies were sore, and we were both spent.

Each time he or I moved through the rest of the night, it started all over again. We started the night off wild and ended it slow, but that fire still burned between us.

"I guess this means it's time to get up to go meet the others for breakfast," Clayton rasps, rolling over to face me. His jaw drops as he moves back a little. "Holy shit!"

I touch my face at his wide eyes. "What? Do I have something on my face?"

Chuckling, he leans forward, pressing a kiss to my lips. "You look like you just auditioned for the part of Batman."

"No," I moan, rolling over a little to reach for my phone. I pull up the front facing camera, and groan. "Maybe I won't be doing the smoky eye look again."

Black eyeshadow and glitter particles are smudged across and down my face. I look like a vigilante.

"You still look sexy," he murmurs, pulling me against his naked body.

My lashes flutter up at him. "What happened to it being a one-time thing because of work?"

He gives a one shoulder shrug, his brows knitting together. "I don't know. What about for our time here?"

I sigh, pushing away slightly. "I need you to be honest with me right now. Are you using work as an excuse because you have commitment issues, or because you don't want anything more than a fuck? Or are you genuinely worried they'll treat me differently at work? Because I'll be honest with you, I'd have fucked you anyway. I just don't want to be played. I'd rather be on the same page." I sigh, running a hand over the blanket. "I normally have a good read on people, but you kind of fry my brain."

He watches me for a moment, not speaking, and I pull away, ready to get out. I guess I have my answer.

"Wait," he pleads, pulling me back.

His lips brush against mine, causing flutters to erupt in my stomach. "Why?"

He inhales, his lips turning down. "My father worked with my mum, once upon a time. They met the day he took over the company for his dad and were married within a year. They clashed at work, having different ideas or opinions. It drove a wedge between them, and they nearly split because of it. Dad loved her so much he was going to give it all up for her and hand over the business to his brother. Mum didn't want him to and decided to find a job elsewhere to save their marriage. Shortly after, she fell pregnant with me and decided to dedicate her time to being a full-time mum. It saved their marriage.

"He's drilled it into me not to get involved with anyone at work. It's his number one rule. I already feel like I'm letting him down," he explains, ducking his head. "And I really don't want anyone mistreating you at work because of me, Hayden. It happened to Mum, and Dad said it took a lot out of her."

"So, it's not because of me?" I confirm.

"God no. I want you, have from the minute I rolled up into the office and you were wearing those ripped jeans that showed a lot of flesh and your AC/DC T-shirt."

"I love that T-shirt," I admit.

He chuckles, running a hand over my waist. "I'm not the guy who gives bullshit excuses to women to get them into bed. I'm just looking out for you."

"Your dad though... I don't think he feels that way anymore. I got the impression he wanted me to date you. He's not real subtle when it comes to hinting at it. But he's your dad; he could have been doing it to wind me up."

"He does love messing with people. I'm sorry if this hurts you, but I can't let him down. He's done enough for me in past. I wouldn't have survived without him. I couldn't bear it if he died, only to be left knowing I had disappointed him."

"I would talk to him before you worry yourself sick. Don't take this the wrong way, but I think you're stressing yourself out for no reason, and not just about this but with the station. I've seen you with your dad. There's nothing you could do that would disappoint him. Unless you supported Man United."

"I can live with this stay here at Cabin Lakes. I'm a big girl."

He exhales, squeezing my hip. "You're right. I'm sorry."

"Can I ask you something?"

"We have thirty to forty minutes left until we have to meet the others and you want to spend it talking?" he drawls, running his hand over my thigh and up to my arse.

My gaze is drawn to his lips briefly, before returning to his eyes. "Oh, we can do *that* in the shower after. I wanted to know what you did before taking over your father's business, and if whatever it was is what caused the scars on your leg and knee?"

He goes limp, his expression sagging. I feel like I've just opened an old wound.

"After university, I took a year out to travel. On my way back home, I stopped off at a racetrack not far from here. I loved racing as a kid and competed a few times. There, a team approached me and asked if I'd be interested in racing. So I did. I wasn't ready to commit to the station, so I did the training, the hours of work, and nearly won all the amateur races."

"But?" I ask, my stomach sinking.

He forces a chuckle. "But… I was a race away from being entered to partake in the Moto Grand Prix. I had just hit a bend when the guy I was up against, who was also in the running for being picked, clipped the back of my wheel. Our bikes spun, flinging us both off. I dislocated my knee, which caused nerve damage. My wrist needed surgery and pinning into place.

"Although I could still ride after months of physical therapy, I'd never have gotten to that level again. Health and safety restricted me too. That, and it hurt to ride for long periods of time. So the year before last, I decided to finish the training I needed to start working with Dad. I've been doing stuff behind the scenes for just under a year now."

"You miss riding," I surmise.

He watches me for a moment, stewing on his thoughts. "Yes and no. I loved riding, don't get me wrong, but it was never my end game. I knew I couldn't do it for the rest of my life. Taking over for my father is what I've always wanted to do." He inhales, shaking his head slightly. "It was hard to let go of that part of my life, but I did. I was lucky to survive that accident. It could have been a lot worse."

"What about the other guy?" I ask gently.

"He was paralysed from the neck down."

"Fucking hell."

His expression lights, the corner of his lips pulling up slightly. "You know, you're the first person I've told who hasn't reacted with 'I'm sorry'."

I push my head back a little, my eyebrows scrunching together. "Why would I be sorry? I didn't do anything. Plus, if it hadn't happened, we wouldn't have met, and you wouldn't have had the best sex of your life last night."

"Best sex of my life, huh?" he asks, smirking.

"Don't act like it wasn't," I tell him, running my finger down his magnificent chest. He tenses beneath me.

"How about you remind me in the shower?" he orders, rolling over me and jumping out of the bed. I squeal when he pulls me up, throwing me over his shoulder.

"I would have gone willingly," I yell through laughter.

"YOU SMELL OF SEX," I mutter as we head up to the café.

Laughing, he says, "Because I can wash that away."

"Well, it would have been had you not jumped me while I was pulling my knickers up."

"I couldn't help it. You looked fucking hot, rolling them up your legs," he admits, shrugging.

"I miss the days when you were rude and bossy," I grumble, pulling open the door. "God, I'm starving."

I'm not just hungry, I'm tired, and me without food is like a smoker without fags. Combine the two and I'm a volcano ready to explode.

"Hey, guys," I greet, waving.

"Mum is pissed. She left with Aunt Harlow to get the others from the police station this morning," Liam greets, snickering. "She didn't get your message until this morning."

I hadn't noticed they weren't here until now. In fact, I'd completely forgotten all about last night's adventures.

"They aren't back yet?"

"No, but Harlow texted to say they were on their way back. What happened last night?" Uncle Maverick asks.

I glance at Clayton, who looks panicked. I don't blame him. Maverick is a scary dude. He makes it a point to intimidate people. My uncle Malik, however, many underestimate, because he's quiet.

"I'll go order our breakfast."

Chicken!

"Didn't Charlotte or Hope fill you in?" I ask, noting that Charlotte is passed out, her head resting on her arm on the table.

"No."

"Well, um, there were two cops and you know how Dad is. One thing led to another. I tried to stop it, I swear," I tell him.

"And they didn't arrest you?" Landon asks, seeing right through my lie.

My grin stretches across my face as I take a seat at Uncle Maverick's table. "Nope, we left."

"You left?" Liam asks, leaning between Maverick and Teagan, laughing.

I shrug, sticking my tongue out at Sunday, who is sitting in a highchair. "Dad would have done the same. It's like I said, I did all I could."

"I feel sick," Faith moans, looking worse for wear as she falls against Beau, who doesn't seem much better.

The door opens, the wind causing it to smack against the wall. Mum and Harlow storm inside.

"Ut oh," I mumble, ducking my head.

Dad, Mark, Malik and Maddox dawdle behind at a slower pace, all looking like they've been through the wars.

Mum sits down at the empty table beside me, puffing out a breath. "I cannot believe your father."

"What did he do, other than the obvious?" Landon asks.

"Apart from manage to run up a food bill at a police station?" she growls, shaking her head. "He wound up a group of other guys being processed, and all hell broke loose. It seemed the ones who got hurt weren't happy, and as we were leaving, your dad pulled one of his stunts and had them all arrested again after he caused another brawl."

"Did he?" Maverick bites out, glaring at Dad, who is still making his way over.

"Apparently it gets boring on desk duty, so he had them playing hot potato and watching YouTube videos while they tried to find a single room for him. Everyone they put him in a room with ended up losing it."

"You okay, son?" Maverick asks Mark when he plops down in the chair over by Mum.

Mark lifts his head, his bloodshot eyes landing on his dad. "Yeah. I don't know how or why we were arrested. Everything is still a blur. They put me in a cell on my own, so I passed out almost immediately."

"Tell him the rest," Dad orders, grinning as he takes the seat to the right of me.

Mark glares over at Dad. "Fuck off."

"What happened?" Aunt Teagan asks, biting her lip.

Dad laughs as he steals Maverick's coffee, taking a sip. "He woke up naked, and it wasn't exactly a warm floor we were on, if you know what I mean. Bright spark there stripped off his clothes and woke up to a female officer."

"Was she hot?" Liam asks.

"She was old," Mark snaps, placing his head on the table when everyone begins to laugh at his discomfort.

Clayton places the plates on the table before pulling out the chair next to me, taking a seat.

The smell of the full English has my stomach rumbling, so I waste no time in picking my fork up.

Dad pulls my plate away before my fork can reach the sausage, blocking the meal with his arm. He digs in, stabbing his fork into the sausage I was eyeing.

"Dad!"

"You owe me. Don't think I forgot that you left your own father to be taken away. After everything I've done for you. I let you shit in my favourite hat."

"I was three months old," I snap. "I can't believe you're going to let your only daughter starve."

"Why do you smell weird?" he asks, sniffing my hair.

I swat him away. "It's called being fresh, unlike you, who smells like a brewery."

"Have mine. I'll go get another," Clayton rushes out, pushing back his chair.

Dad sniffs the air, tilting his head up. "Did someone speak?"

"Max," Mum chides.

I snort. "Dad, stop acting like you wouldn't have done the same. I only did what you taught me to do."

"She has you there," Mum scolds. "You're old enough to know better."

"Why are you all blaming me? Malik was the reason we got arrested this time. I'm innocent."

"You were the cause of it, dickhead," Malik grits out.

"And," Dad drawls out, turning to me, "I would have had the genius idea to record it. Not so smart now, are you, short stuff."

I smirk after swallowing a piece of bacon. "Ah, but I *am* a genius. Hope got the whole thing."

Chairs scrape across the tiled floor as they get up to see the footage Hope has saved on her phone.

"Guys, me and Faith cancelled today. We've rearranged it for tomorrow. No one is in any fit state to get behind a wheel today."

Everyone sighs with relief, clearly not looking forward to being tossed around on a Go-Kart.

Since Dad is occupied eating and talking to Mum, I lean in to Clayton, whispering, "Want to try hot tub sex?"

He grins against his mug. "After we try kitchen counter sex. I saw some chocolate I'd love to try," he tells me, his eyes heating.

My pulse spikes at the promise, and I squeeze my thighs together. "It would be a shame for it to go to waste."

"What are you two whispering about?" Dad snaps.

"Nothing," Clayton and I squeak.

TWENTY-THREE

I**T'S OUR LAST NIGHT HERE**, and it's bittersweet. I don't want our time here to end, or to go back to a reality where I don't get to sleep next to him every night.

I've only slept over at two guys' houses before, and both were more out of convenience than actually wanting to be there. And with both, it was a struggle to fall and stay asleep.

With Clayton, neither were a problem—not that we did much sleeping.

Tonight, however, has felt… different. Our large group had split up to have a chilled night, and although others had made plans, Clayton and I decided to stay in by ourselves. He surprised me by cooking us dinner, and even more so when he didn't make a move to rip my clothes off. Instead, we sat and talked about anything and everything.

It felt like a line had been crossed, and the simple 'no strings' had gone out the window. And although I'm more than open to having a relationship with him, I won't beg. I won't force or manipulate him into having one, like so many in my situation do. Though it's hard to keep myself firmly on my side of the line, I respect his choice, even if it is a stupid one.

It isn't just his behaviour that's changed, but the intimacy too. Earlier, I had been washing up, when Clayton stepped up behind me, pulling my back against his chest as he nibbled on my neck. I felt closer to him in that moment than I did when we had sex. Which is why his actions are confusing me.

Now I'm in bed, wearing my Ninja Turtles pyjamas, making notes on my report—or trying to, at least.

After a night of amazing sex, I woke up exhausted yet inspired. An idea occurred to me, and yet I'm torn on which direction I want to go with the article. It could go one or both ways. I want to write an article revealing the truth of what happened, but I also want to write the entire story, so the public gets more of a grasp on what happened, from the very first sighting of the gang. When people read it, I want them to truly feel what each victim has gone through, from the first to the last. And there will be a last.

I'll make sure of it.

I only need one of them to talk, and if a cop is involved, and it's he who falls into my trap, he's going to sing like a canary. There is no way he won't plead for a deal in exchange for giving up the others in the gang.

All criminals do. Because what sets them apart from everyone else is that they're out for themselves.

When I get home, I want to get some quotes from victims, get their side before I continue writing it. When people read it, I don't want them doubting my evidence, which is what most people do now because of the 'fake news' constantly being published.

I mean, how do they expect people to take the truth seriously if they continue to publish fake articles?

The door creaks, alerting me to Clayton's presence. I quickly change the screen to the Love Loop Live website before smiling up at Clayton.

"You made me hot chocolate," I gush, taking the steaming mug from him. "Marshmallows!"

"I ran over to Dean and Lola's to stock up. I knew how much you wanted one."

I did. The machine at the café was broken this morning and I was gutted. I need the substance to wake me up. "Thank you."

"You working?" he asks, sitting on the edge of the bed next to me, staring at the screen.

My attention drifts to the foamy marshmallows, so he doesn't see the lie. "I like to read posts, answer some if I can. It gives me more time when I come in to go over our segment."

My mind drifts to Beau. I had hoped to speak to him before now, but he's always been busy, or my interfering, lovable dad was watching me. He might come across dumb to some people, but for those who know him, we're well advised on his intelligence. He would know something was up the minute I pulled Beau aside.

"You okay? You seemed to have spaced out."

I place my mug on the side before facing him. "Yeah, but I, um, need to pop out a minute. I just remembered there's something I need to talk to Beau about."

"Give me a minute and I'll come with you," he offers, getting off the bed.

I jump out, unable to look at him. "That's okay. I won't be long."

"Okay," he drawls, sitting back on the bed and leaning against the pillows. "Before you run off, there's something I've been meaning to ask you."

I stop reaching for my trainers and sit on the end of the bed, giving him my attention.

"If it's about the jelly in the fridge, I didn't know you were saving it," I tell him, biting my lip.

"What? Wait, that was you? I thought your dad ate it yesterday when he came to see how you were, even though it was obvious he only came to do a room check."

"I did warn you that would happen," I remind him. He didn't believe me when I told him he couldn't leave his clothes in my room because my dad would do a surprise visit at some point. He only has himself to blame. "But by your reaction, that wasn't what you wanted to talk to me about."

"No, it isn't. I've got another few days before they need me back in the office. I was wondering, if you didn't have any other plans, if you'd accompany me to the Butterfly Village."

"Isn't that one of the places on the list we were given by Date Night?" I ask, forcing myself not to frown. I don't know why I held hope that he was asking me out. Of course it's for work.

"It is, but there's a Comic Con the day after that I thought you'd like. The itinerary that Date Night has in place isn't something we need to do. But we do need it to finish this segment."

It takes me a moment to realise he's serious. I squeal, jumping across the bed and landing on top of him. He falls back, laughing.

"Are you for real?"

"I'm taking that as a yes, you do want to go."

"Dude, I've not been to one since I was thirteen years old and my dad got us kicked out for taking the virtual game seriously."

His smile is wide as he pushes my hair away from my face. "Well, I made some calls and got us two tickets."

I can't believe he's done this. It's the sweetest thing ever. I hadn't even known he paid attention to me. Most of the time he looks like he wants to strangle me. But when I was rambling at work a few weeks ago about how unfair it was that I couldn't get tickets, he was paying attention.

"Wait, isn't that the day after Valentine's Day?"

"Yes, is that okay?"

"You're the one with issues, not me," I tell him, shrugging. "And it's not like I have anything better planned."

"Thanks," he mutters dryly.

I'm still grinning like a fool, excited about going. "I do need to type up the online piece the night before, so it does work out perfectly."

"I sent Chrissy my notes about Mingles. She emailed Date Night to cancel that review and recommended Barbra's instead."

"That's actually a pretty good idea. I've written up my thoughts on the dating site, but since Reid tripped the system, it's not really an accurate review."

"It's mostly on the destinations anyway. Chrissy has handled the review on the site itself as she's the one inputting all your information and using the app. We had hoped to visit more destinations before Valentine's Day, but I guess with short notice, they can't complain."

"I think it helps that I've been to some of the places on the list, so I can give my honest opinion on them. I also conducted another list of places that I personally recommend and gave them to Leana, ready to post out on Valentine's Day."

"Their ad is up on our website, and we've had a lot of interaction from people asking for cheaper or closer alternatives. It got me thinking about people already in a relationship. I wanted to see how you felt about running a segment on how to keep the spark alive, maybe recommend places they can go for one on one time."

I can't help but gape in astonishment. "I'm flattered you would even run it by me, so don't get pissed when I say this—respectfully, of course—but you really haven't had a relationship if you think advising couples to go on holiday will spice up their love life. If they're already having problems, it's going to end them. Moving homes, weddings, christenings or a new-born all test the best of relationships. But holidays bring on a whole new level of stress. It's been known to break couples who think time away will do them good. Their routine is out the window, so all they are left with is each other. It will drive one to commit murder."

"Surely not," he argues.

I shrug, running my hand over his chest. "Not everyone, but most couples. My mum nearly killed my dad when he left the passports at home. He had one job, and he failed. My mum was stressed, worrying that she hadn't packed everything we needed."

His nose scrunches up. "You can't really use your dad as an example. Your mum is a saint."

I sigh because he's right. My mum wants to kill him on a daily basis. She just loves him more. "You're right. Maybe you could recommend holidays to those new to a relationship and research ways to help improve those with issues in their relationship."

"So, you're okay with that?"

"Why are you asking? You haven't cared enough to ask before. In fact, you've pretty much demanded everything from me," I remind him, not liking the sinking feeling in my gut. "You said you didn't want other people treating me differently, but here you are, doing just that."

He runs a hand through his hair, grimacing. "I'm not going to lie, after putting a stop to your story, I felt bad."

I inwardly flinch at the deceit, glancing away. "But…"

"*But*, despite what you may think, I'm not always a prick. That night I first met you was the anniversary of my mother's death. My dad was refusing any further treatment and Leana had just spilled coffee down my shirt and fallen head first in my lap. Then I walked in and was immediately drawn to your arse. When I found out you were Hayden, Dad's words about not dating staff hit me, and I got angry."

I force myself not to snort at the memory of what Leana had done. His reaction makes more sense now that I've gotten to know him.

"Oh," I mumble.

"Yes, oh."

"In my defence, I didn't know that."

"I know, and it's not really an excuse. And it certainly doesn't mean I won't be a dickhead in the future."

"Noted," I reply, chuckling. "I really want to kiss you right now, but I really do need to go see Beau."

He smirks, wiggling his eyebrows. "Hurry back."

I roll my eyes, pulling myself up. "You're insatiable."

———————————

AFTER RAPPING MY knuckles on the door to Faith and Beau's cabin, I take a step back, rubbing my hands together and blowing between them.

Faith answers the door, smiling when she spots me. "Hey, Hayden, have you come to watch a movie with us?"

When she pulls the door open a little wider, I notice Mum, my aunts, and half of my cousins. I don't know of a way I can ask for Beau without raising suspicion.

Unless…

"Is Beau around?" I whisper, ducking my head.

She closes the door a little after stepping outside. "Is everything okay?"

"Yeah, I'm good, but Clayton isn't. He doesn't want me to, um, talk about it with any of my relatives. You know how men are. I would talk to Jaxon about it, but he'd piss me off in two seconds."

"Oh no, what's happened?"

I point to my crotch. "He's, um, experiencing something down there and doesn't feel comfortable asking Beau or Jaxon himself."

"Ah, I understand." She winces, her expression scrunching up in pity. "Beau is on the back deck with Dad."

"Thank you. I'll head round. Tell the others I was asking what time we were leaving and that I'll see them in the morning."

"Okay, I hope Clayton feels better soon."

I nod, giving her a short wave as I make my way around the side of the cabin, to the back.

Maverick and Beau are chatting about the boxing when I reach the bottom of the deck steps.

Uncle Maverick is the first to spot me. "Hey, short stuff, you looking for your mum? She's inside."

I wave him off as I make my way up the steps. "No, I'm actually here to see Beau. I need to talk to him privately."

I don't like the scrutinizing gaze he's sending my way. "Why?" I cross my fingers behind my back, my lips parting as I inhale, ready to answer. "And before you think you can fool me, I know that look. It's the same look your father gets before he makes up some wild bullshit story or tries to con his way out of shit."

I slump down into the deck chair, pouting. "What I'm saying is confidential,

Uncle Maverick. I can't let you jeopardize what's happening because you can't keep it to yourself. People's lives are at stake."

He sits up straighter at the seriousness in my voice. I don't have time to mess around. This is my last chance to talk to Beau before we get back.

"What's going on, Hayden?" Beau asks, also leaning forward in his seat, his forearms resting on his thighs.

I arch my eyebrow at Uncle Maverick, waiting for him to agree not to repeat anything. "I won't tell anyone anything. I can call it even with your dad for getting Mark arrested. If you're at risk, though, I will intervene."

I don't know how Beau is going to react, and until this very moment, I hadn't even thought about it, nor remembered that Rob is his friend.

I inhale, preparing myself for the worst but hoping for the best as I launch into everything I know and assume about the gang and break-ins.

When I'm finished, he's pale, sagging back into his chair.

"And this plan… you'll be safe at all times?" Maverick asks, concerned.

I nod, forcing a smile. "I might be my father's daughter, but I'm not stupid enough to put myself in danger, and neither is he, despite all the situations he's found himself in. He raised me right. So, once I've played my part, I'm done. It will be up to Beau and whoever is clean to deal with."

Beau slides to the edge of his chair, clasping his hands together. "This is serious, Hayden. Those allegations, whether true or false—"

"Hey, she wouldn't have made them unless she was sure," Maverick interrupts, his jaw clenching.

"It might not turn out to be one of them. But my gut is rarely wrong, and evidence is evidence. With it being done this way, no one is directly accused or are tipped off so they can cover their tracks. And your boss could fire you over such a serious allegation."

"I've worked with Rob since I started full time. He's dedicated to his job. I can't see him being involved."

"But would you bet your life on it? Faith's life?" I ask, raising an eyebrow.

His jaw hardens. "No. No, I wouldn't."

"So you need to go along with this. It's the only way it will work," I tell him, my lips pulling down into a frown.

He gives me a short nod. "It can't be next weekend though. Come in the following Monday after we have our monthly meeting. That way, we are all there. Then set up the meeting for Friday the same week at nine. I know Walker is working the night shift then, so he'll have no other choice but to bring Colin and Rob in. It's also my night off, so they might ask me to come in. I'll make the excuse that I'm out for a meal with family. You can use the excuse that she wanted to meet near a crowded place. We have bars and clubs on that street. Liam is a genius for thinking of the double ploy."

"I planned it," I grit out. "And that's fine. I'll let Liam know." I stand up, brushing off my Ninja pyjamas. "I don't need to tell you to keep this to yourself and act normal."

He runs a hand across his face, still dazed by the news. "No."

"Oh, and I told Faith I came here because Clayton needed help with his…" I whistle, my gaze travelling to his crotch.

"Great."

TWENTY-FOUR

O UR FOUR DAYS AWAY HAVE come to an end. We had said goodbye to everyone after getting off at the coach station, thanking Beau and Faith for a great time away.

Before leaving for our trip to the Butterfly Village, we stopped off at Nightingale Care Home to go visit his father, who, luckily, is still doing okay.

I hadn't realised how eager Clayton was to see his dad. He had hidden the worry and stress easily from me; either that, or I had taken his mind off it. The minute we stepped into his father's room, his shoulders sagged with relief and a wide smile spread across his face, even though the worry was still there.

Yet, even with the reassurance his dad was okay, he left quiet and withdrawn. And he's been this way ever since I left him and his father to spend some quality time together. I can't help but worry that I was mistaken about his father's intentions when it came to me and Clayton.

His silence in the car has only made it worse. There's a chance he's sitting right there, running through ways to end this. Whatever 'this' is. And if his father had disapproved, I have no doubt in my mind that he will do whatever it takes to make him happy.

Because how can you say no to a dying man?

You can't.

And I wouldn't want him to. If roles were reversed… well, maybe not reversed. I've never really listened to my dad, but if it was my mum, I'd do exactly the same.

I want to voice my concern, but I don't want to come across as one of those girls that clung, and yet the girly part inside of me that I try to stow away, can't help but cling to him. I want him in a way I've never wanted anything else. Yet the rebellious side of me wants to say, 'fuck it, we don't need a man'.

I'm at war with myself.

Taking a deep breath, I decide to be straight with him. I can't be anyone but myself right now, and I never shy away from anything.

"Clayton, if you'd like to cancel this trip, I'm good with it."

He takes his eyes off the road for a second, his brows pulling together. "Why would you think I'd want that?"

"You don't seem overly joyed right now. In fact, you don't seem yourself at all."

His fingers tighten around the steering wheel. "I'm sorry."

"Is it your dad? Because I spoke to Amelia and she said he's doing okay, that there hasn't been a change in his health."

"I know. That isn't it. He seems to really like it there."

"So *why are you* being quiet? I'm not gonna lie, it's making me feel uncomfortable."

He blows out a breath. "That wasn't my intention. I'm sorry." He gives me another quick glance before continuing. "When you left the room, he pulled me up on how we were together. He guessed right away."

"He doesn't approve," I surmise.

"The opposite in fact," he explains, a smile pulling at the corner of his lips. "He thinks you'll be good for me."

I grin, relaxing somewhat. "Because I rock, right?"

He lets out a chuckle. "Yeah, that. Apparently, I'm uptight."

"Right about now I'd normally agree with you. You can be uptight. But, Clayton, you've been under a lot of pressure."

"I was young when my mum died, still at school. When she died, all I wanted to do was make her proud. I still do. So I made sure I passed all my exams, helped Dad as much as I could, since he was struggling after we lost her, and helped my sister with her school work. I dedicated my life to achieving my goals. I've never really had time to pause, time to unwind. Even when I took that year to travel, I was never relaxed. I didn't do what other lads were doing at my age. The only time I felt that kind of freedom was when I was racing. Being out on the track, it was only the road in front of me, everything else washed away."

"I can understand that. What I don't understand is your distance. Do you feel differently about me now that I'm potentially available to you? I know most men stop finding someone attractive when there's no longer secrecy or the chase."

He lets out a chuckle. "Only an idiot would find you unattractive."

I grit my teeth at him avoiding my question once again. It doesn't feel like he's being straight with me.

"Clayton," I bite out.

"Hayden," he breathes out, mocking me.

"Pull the car over," I snap, sitting straighter in my chair. I want answers, and if he won't give them to me, I'm walking. I won't spend the next two days with someone who doesn't seem to want me around.

We're out in the middle of nowhere, twenty minutes from Butterfly Village. I'm not actually sure what the town is called, I just know the name it's famously known for. It has one of the best butterfly gardens in England.

"I'm not pulling over."

"Pull the damn car over, right now, and tell me what the fuck is going on with you and why you're acting so bloody weird."

"Okay, okay," he yells, checking his mirror before pulling into the layby and driving onto a small dirt road until we're just out of sight.

"Now explain," I order, folding my arms across my chest.

He drops his head back on the headrest. "You're going to think it's ridiculous."

"Try me," I tell him, unclipping my belt so I can sit and face him.

"After getting to know your family, I'm really going to sound like a pussy."

I smack his arm. "I fucking loathe that saying. Pussies are a lot stronger. Not only does a baby the size of a melon come out of it, but it tends to take a good 'beating'. Dicks, on the other hand, only need the slightest tap and you act like you just took a round of bullets."

He forces out a laugh. "You got me there." He watches me for a moment, before continuing. "I like you, Hayden, more than just the great sex."

"Well, duh, I keep telling you I'm awesome. But I'm sensing another *but*."

"But Dad's words keep playing in my head. What if things progress between us, and down the line, things change? I change. His words held merit today, Hayden. When I'm with you, I do feel different; I do feel free and relaxed. You make my world pause. You make me see a whole new life. Your entire being is filled with life. You live it to the fullest and have no regrets.

"How am I supposed to know it's not a faze, that what draws me to you now won't disappear?"

"That's a lot of 'what ifs'," I tell him gently, ignoring the flutter in my stomach over his description of me.

His expression turns sombre. "I told you when we were at the cabins that I didn't want to see you hurt, and I meant it."

"Clayton, you can't live your life like that. Billions of people start a relationship not knowing if it's going to last or if it will end. But that's the joy of living life. We make our own choices, lead our own paths, and you need to start living yours. You shouldn't be asking yourself if you'll hurt me, or if your dad will disapprove, or if people will talk at work. You should be asking yourself if it's what you really want." I watch him for a moment, unblinking. "And I hate to break it to you, but it could be me that hurts you."

He smirks, unclipping his belt and pushing his chair back, making room. "Come here," he orders, tapping is thigh. I climb over the parking brake and straddle his thighs. "It sounds like you want a relationship with me."

It's my turn to smirk as I place my hands on either side of his neck. "Don't tell me this is the part where you ask me to be your girlfriend, because I warn you now, I'll tease you mercilessly."

Laughing, he shakes his head, his fingers digging into my hips. "Why don't we see how things go before I pass you a note with a 'tick yes or no to be my girlfriend'?"

"Very grown up of you," I tease, running my nose along his before kissing the corner of his mouth.

"At work, we need to keep it professional and quiet for a little while."

I bite my bottom lip, leaning back. That's a lot to ask. "I'm never professional, so it might raise a few questions if I start now."

"How about you do you, and I'll do me?" he offers, kissing the tip of my nose.

"How about I just do you," I offer, my voice low, raspy.

"Here?" he asks, his pupils dilating.

I scan our surroundings, considering it for a moment, but then I'm reminded of the mess I'd have to sit in until we reached the Travelodge, and change my mind.

"Let's hurry up to the Travelodge. I'd rather we had a bed."

He presses his lips against mine. "Since we've only managed to have sex twice in a bed, that sounds like a good idea."

"Let's go then."

CLAYTON PUSHES OPEN the door to our room, throwing the key and luggage inside the room.

I squeal with laughter as he lifts me up off my feet, bringing his lips to mine.

The door slams shut, the lock clicking into place as he continues into the room.

I massage my tongue against his as he deepens the kiss. With a groan, he drops me to the bed, causing me to bounce a little.

He follows, bending over me as he grabs the back of my neck, lifting my head towards him as he takes control of the kiss.

I moan into his mouth whilst reaching for the bottom of my hoody, gripping that and my shirt at the same time.

He sits up, helping me lift it over my head before reaching for his own jacket. I watch with rapt attention as he slides it off his shoulders, before unbuttoning his shirt, teasing me with glimpses of his abs. I squirm beneath him, my chest rising and falling as he shuffles back off the bed, keeping his heated gaze solely on me.

My tongue runs across the seam of my lip, my gaze drawn to his crotch as he unzips his jeans, before slowly pushing them down and pulling them off, dropping them on the end of the bed.

"Kiss me," I plead.

His pupils dilate, irises darkening as he kneels on the bed, bending over me, before thrusting his tongue into my mouth.

I roll my hips as he hungrily tears at my joggers, pushing them down my thighs. I push them the rest of the way off, kicking them somewhere across the room.

My body burns with need as I push him to the side, rolling on top of him, groaning at the feel of his nakedness pressed against mine.

"My turn," I tell him, lifting my sports bra over my head, leaving me in only my knickers. I lean down, swirling my tongue around his nipple before slowly licking my way down his body, over his abs. He groans, dropping his head back on the bed.

I moan when I reach the 'V', his muscles tightening as I grip his dick, slowly running my hand over his pulsing shaft.

A squeal passes through my lips when he grips me under the armpits, pulling me up his body before rolling us over, him on top.

"My turn," he rasps, licking my neck.

I arch my back, moaning when he hits the sensitive spot on my neck.

"You were on top last time," I remind him, tensing my thighs around him as I roll us again. This time, the bed isn't there to catch us.

I cry out when we land on the floor, yet Clayton only lets out a small groan before reaching for me again, gripping the back of my neck and pulling me towards him, taking my lips in a fiery kiss.

I grind myself on him, causing wetness to pool between my legs as I begin to pulse with need.

He clutches the straps of my knickers, tearing them from my body.

"Oh God," I moan, rubbing my clit against his hardness.

"Fuck!"

A whimper escapes me when he presses his thumb over my clit, rubbing in a circular motion.

"Condom," I breathe out, digging my fingers into his biceps.

"Jeans. On the edge of the bed," he rasps out, before proceeding to kiss down my chest. He takes my nipple into his mouth, leaving it tender when he reaches for the other.

I lift up a little, blindly patting my way across the bed until I feel the denim under my fingers. I pull the jeans down, searching his pockets for his wallet and pulling a condom from the stash he only topped up this morning.

Clear liquid spills from the top of his cock as I slowly roll the condom over his hardness.

I rise to my knees as he grabs his cock, pumping it once, twice, whilst pressing his thumb harder against my clit, driving me wild.

I moan, finding it hard to keep still as I lower myself over him, my pussy tightening around him.

"Oh God," I groan, placing my hands on his chest for balance.

It feels so good to have him inside of me; tingles shoot through my stomach.

"Fuck," he groans, gripping my hip with one hand, his attention on his dick sliding in and out of me as I thrust up and down.

The carpet burns my knees as I push myself down harder, speeding up my movements, my body chasing the orgasm I know is coming.

Clayton reaches up, kissing his way down my neck before biting the tops of my breasts. I moan through the pleasure as I arch my back, causing my chest to push out.

He licks over the bite mark, and my entire body shudders at the sensation, goose bumps breaking out all over my body.

I ground myself down harder, our skin slapping together in a mad frenzy.

The tips of my fingers dig into his chest as I cry out my orgasm, electricity shooting through my veins. Clayton follows, gripping me tighter as his body tenses, shuddering through his own orgasm.

Our sweat mingles together when I fall against his chest, both of us breathing hard.

I blow hair out of my face, resting my chin on his chest as I look up at him. "Can't we just spend the next two days in bed?" I moan, pressing a kiss to his pec.

He runs a hand down my hair, smiling. "And ruin tomorrow? No chance. It's Valentine's Day, and I have something planned that I'm hoping you'll enjoy."

I smile, kissing him once more before dropping my head on his shoulder, exhausted. "How can I say no to that?"

TWENTY-FIVE

THE MESSAGE STILL SAYS THE same thing, no matter how many times I read it. My stomach churns as I read it once more.

BEAU: Another break-in happened last night. A man in his eighties was severely beaten to death. His wife was found tied to the end of her bed, forced to watch. It's not confirmed, but they think she died of a heart attack just before the police got there. I know I had my reservations about this, but I'm in. All in.

My phone slips out of my hand as the door to our room opens.

Clayton steps through, a bag in one hand while the other pulls out his earphones. Sweat beads on his head and neck, soaking into his grey hoody.

He frowns when he looks up, seeing me on the bed. "Is everything okay?"

I nod, forcing a smile as I slide my phone under the bed. "Yeah. Did you enjoy your run?" I sniff, smelling the mouth-watering aroma of freshly cooked bacon. "My God, please tell me that whatever that is, it's mine."

He chuckles, sitting beside me on the bed as he kicks his trainers off. He pulls two foiled packets out and two plastic cups with lids, placing them on the bedside table.

"Sausage, bacon and egg sarnie," he explains, before passing me the drink. "And this is your hot chocolate. I don't want you snapping at me all day."

"I really could get used to this," I tell him, breathing in the aroma before placing it on the side. "What time is it?"

We hadn't gone to sleep until the early hours of the morning, and as much as I'd like to blame it on the great sex, it was because we had to get some work done.

"Just before noon. I let you lie in while I went for a run. I found this place next door and decided to grab some food before coming up."

"What *are* our plans for today?"

"It's a surprise. But that isn't until half one."

I smirk, raising my eyebrows. "Oh, yeah?"

"Yes. So, we have time to eat this and shower," he tells me, kissing the corner of my mouth.

My smile is wide as he kisses along my jaw. I love this side of him. "Is that all?"

He grabs my sandwich off my lap, chucking it onto the bedside table.

"I can think of one or two things we can do," he rasps, his voice low.

Laughter spills out of me when he swings my body up and over him.

Yeah, I could definitely get used to this.

HE BROUGHT ME to a pottery class. Pottery. Out of all the things I imagined, this was not on the list.

The class teacher had shown us how to use the equipment and gave us a quick run-down on what to do, yet I still have no clue. Movies make this look piss easy.

My clay spins out of control and splatters back into a clump for what feels like the tenth time.

I can't help but laugh. My competitive side wants to nail it, but the other part just wants this to be over. I hate sucking at something.

The lady next to me, who's disapproved of me from the second I walked in, glares at me.

"Shh, this is meant to be relaxing."

Stumped, I can only ignore her. Not even the background music is relaxing. It's actually annoying, especially the grating noise of what I assume is meant to be a bird tweeting. Instead, it sounds like a slaughterhouse.

It doesn't help that it's boring too. The only time I sit still is when I'm playing video games.

Although, I am getting plenty of entertainment out of the couple in front of us. They haven't stopped bickering since we walked in.

I lean to the side, glad Clayton moved his station closer to mine, and whisper, "They'll break up within a week."

Distracted, his clay begins to spin out of control, and he groans as his vase is destroyed.

"Huh?"

"Them," I tell him, jerking my head towards the couple.

He watches them for a moment before shaking his head. "I don't know. He looks smitten."

I draw back because it's clear he hasn't got a clue. "No. She's the dominant one in their relationship. He's only come along today to keep her happy, but by the looks of it, he's two minutes away from walking out. He looks miserable."

Clayton's lips twitch. "She looks like she's trying to keep them together."

"Thank you," the lady in question barks, turning around and sending me a glare.

"The girl had a point," the guy adds, giving up on his vase. Or urn. It was hard to tell.

I puff out my chest. "It's what I do. I'm good at reading people."

"Shush," the lady next to us hisses.

I narrow my eyes on her. "Can't you see they're having problems? Have a heart. It's Valentine's Day." I leave her with her mouth hanging open and turn back to the guy. "You really shouldn't let her tell you what to do."

"Who do you think you are? You don't know what you're talking about," she snaps.

"Hayden," Clayton warns, amusement in his voice.

"Actually, I do. Although you're a person who normally gets what she wants, you aren't always this bossy and controlling. You can be reasonable. I reckon he's done something you didn't like, even after you told him not to. Now he's trying to make it up to you, even though he doesn't feel like he's in the wrong. He loves you so much he's willing to put up with the snarky remarks and abuse, just to make you happy."

Her lips part, eyes widening. "How? Who are you?"

"Hayden," I tell her. "So, what did he do?"

The guy snorts, rolling his eyes. "I went to my mother's because she's been ill."

"James, your mother needs to let you go. She was unbearable before when it came to her *precious boy*. Now that we're living together, it's infuriating and just plain creepy. She acts like your girlfriend, not your mum."

"Louise," he breathes out sharply. "She was sick. She needed me."

"I cannot believe you started this," Clayton whispers.

I shrug, smirking. "Are you bored now, though?"

He loses his chuckle when our teacher, Claire, slowly steps over to us, frowning. "This programme will only work if you relax; feel the clay through your fingers, hear the music in your veins. Now, take a deep breath, let the music flow through you."

What a load of bullshit.

"I'd rather hear what she has to say," I tell her, arching my eyebrow.

Another couple in the room wince yet nod when Claire turns in their direction. "We kind of do too."

"This isn't that kind of class."

I smile wide at her frustration. "Take a seat, Karen, it's about to get interesting."

"Oh God," Clayton mumbles.

"It's Claire," she huffs.

"You know, she's right. It is getting interesting. Tell them about your mum, how she calls every night, how she told us we couldn't get married or have kids until she was ready and healthy. That woman has more wrong with her than a hypochondriac, and her main symptom is smothering," Louise confesses.

I point at Louise. "Maybe I was wrong about you." I cluck my tongue at James. "You really should cut the cord."

Louise slams her hand down on the pile of clay. "Exactly. He missed our anniversary because she happened to be sick. She knew we had plans to go away. And when I told him she was fine, that she was manipulating him, he wouldn't listen and went running to help her."

"She's my mum, Louise. I'm not going to stop seeing her because you think she's lying. I'm all she has," he crows. "And you aren't perfect either. I read those messages from Dean, the guy you work with."

I grin, bouncing in my seat as I turn to Clayton. "This is so good."

Chuckling, he shakes his head. "You are terrible."

Pride fills my chest. "Thanks."

"If you saw them, then you'd know I told him no, that I wasn't interested. But it's not too late to reconsider. I want a man, not a boy who still needs his mummy to give him permission."

"Guys, I really think we should relax now," Claire soothes, holding her hands up.

"No," Louise and James yell.

"Tell her how you feel, James," I goad. "Get it out."

He nods, his face flushed. "I've changed my entire life for you: swapped jobs, homes. How can you be this selfish?"

"You picked up rubbish because your mum told you to get a job close by, that if you got a job using your degree, it would take you away from her. You make more as a computer technician."

"You moan about everything. There hasn't been a time when we've gone out that you haven't complained about something or another. Look at us now.

It was your idea to come here today, and all you've done is complain about the smell, the music, and the fact we paid a fortune for it to be a load of crap."

"I have had a lot of positive feedback. If you would just listen and take a breath…" Claire argues, rocking back on her feet.

"This isn't a competition on who is the worst, James. This is about you and your mum."

"Technically, it started with your attitude," I remind her, being helpful.

"Not helping," Clayton grumbles, pretending to actually work on his clay.

I snort. "I think I've helped a lot, thank you."

"Yes. Yes, you have," James confirms. "Now I know how she really feels."

"Are you kidding me?" Louise yells in his face. "Don't you dare make out that you're innocent in all of this."

Throwing his hands up, he then slaps them down on his thighs. "You're making me choose between you and my mum."

"No, I'm not. I'm asking you to leave the nest, James. I love you, I do, but I'm sick of her being a third person in our relationship. Visit her, take her soup when she's actually sick, but my God, stop her from dictating every aspect of your life. She's holding you back, and one day, when she's dead and buried, you'll take a look around and realise you have no one because she's secluded you from living life."

"She said you'd do this," he blurts out, his hands clenching. "She even knew you'd cheat on me, said it the moment I told her about you."

"I've never cheated on you," she shouts, throwing a clump of clay at him, splattering it all over his T-shirt. "Are you even listening to yourself or hearing what I'm saying?"

"Please, take a deep—"

"Shut up!" James and Louise yell at Claire.

"You know what, I don't have to listen to this," Louise snaps, ripping her apron off. She grabs her bag, stopping in front of James. "We're over."

"Did not see that coming," I mumble, watching her storm out.

James sits there for a second, dumbfounded. Once it all hits him, he's up so fast he nearly trips over his own feet, catching himself on the station beside him.

"Apron," Claire yells at him.

He pauses, ripping it over his head before continuing to chase after Louise. "Louise! Wait! I'm sorry. We can get through this. I'll do anything. Please, Louise."

I glance down at the mess in front of me, sighing. "I guess it's safe to say I'm not an artist."

"Really?" the lady next to me snaps.

"What is your problem, or are you always this friendly?" I snap back.

"You've just broken up a relationship and you didn't even blink. Instead, you comment on your model," she tells me sharply. "Which, by the way, is terrible."

I can't argue with her there. It's just a heap of crap. However, who is she to comment?

"Puh-lease, they were bound to break up eventually. I just sped it along. And shouldn't you be glad that you don't have to listen to them argue anymore?"

Her scorching gaze has me chuckling, and when I turn to Clayton, his shoulders are shaking from silent laughter.

"What?"

"Your family were right about you. You cause chaos everywhere you go."

"I really do, don't I?"

A throat clears as Claire stands in front of our stations. She runs a hand over her apron, her neck flushed.

"I'm really sorry, but I'm going to have to ask you to leave."

"What, why?" I bellow. "I've done nothing wrong."

"You've sucked the peace and serenity out of this room."

"Come on, Hayden. Let's go," Clayton orders, struggling to keep his face straight.

"This is your fault. I was happy to stay in bed all day and have sex. But no, you had this big surprise," I grumble.

"Please leave!" Claire squeaks, sweat beading on her forehead.

"We're going," Clayton assures her, picking up my belongings from under my station.

One of the other couples stands up, the guy turning to us. "Hey, sorry to be rude, but could you recommend another place for us to go next that isn't so, um…"

"Dull? Boring?" I finish, smiling at the fear that flashes in his eyes when Claire turns to him.

"Yeah," he replies, shoulders sagging.

"There's a Bonza Bingo here. It's basically a nightclub that you play bingo in to win prizes."

"Ooh, I love bingo," his girlfriend gushes.

"And I hear there's a lot of great places to eat here," Clayton adds.

"Thanks, mate," he replies, reaching for his own stuff before following us out.

"Please tell me you have food on our plans today. I'm starving," I admit, pushing through the exit.

Clayton chuckles, wrapping his arm around my shoulders. "Yes, our reservation is for five."

"That's hours away," I whine. "It had better be good food."

He presses a kiss to the side of my head. "I did some research before coming here. Comic Con isn't the only reason I chose here. There's a food place close by that offers different types of ethnic food that I knew you'd love."

I lick my lips hungrily yet can't help but feel butterflies in my stomach at how sweet his actions are. "That is the nicest thing anyone has ever done for me. Can't we go now?"

He grins as he pulls me into his arms, pressing his warm lips against mine. "No, because right now, all I want to do is get you naked. You have no idea how hot it was to watch your hands try to smooth over that clay."

I squeeze my thighs together as I wrap my arms around his neck. "So what are you waiting for?"

TWENTY-SIX

CLAYTON

IT'S HARD TO KEEP A STRAIGHT face as I carry Hayden out of the restaurant. I thought I knew her brand of crazy, thought I had become adept to it more over the past week, but I was wrong.

"I'm telling you, I will do it," Hayden yells, making me chuckle as I let her down, pulling her away from the entrance.

"Hayden," I murmur, failing to keep the amusement out of my voice.

"Can you believe her? Who does she think she is calling me fat? That was my cake. Mine!"

"She was six," I remind her before finally letting it all out, bending at my knees, laughing uproariously. "You just threatened to make a meme out of a six-year-old because she took the last velvet cake."

I laugh harder, my sides hurting. She keeps on surprising me at every turn, and I love it. Love that she can do that. I never know what is going to spill out of those beautiful lips when she speaks.

"I'm not liking your tone." She sniffs, resting against a wall that runs along the small stony shore.

"You, you—I cannot believe you did that."

"Aren't you supposed to stand up for me? She kicked me fucking hard, Clayton," she snaps.

I fall to the bench beside me, my face aching while my sides hurt as laughter spills out of me.

How does she keep doing this to me?

"You told her it had vegetables in it."

Growling, she stomps her foot, sitting on the bench next to me, crossing her arms. "I can't believe you're laughing about this. I really wanted that damn cake. And who the hell were they to throw *me* out. *She* should have been the one to leave."

"Again, she was six," I remind her, chuckling when she pouts.

She watches me for a moment, biting her bottom lip. "Did I embarrass you? Not that I care. She had it coming. I mean, who does that? Who steals food?"

"Why would you think I'd be embarrassed?"

She shrugs, looking away. "Others are usually put off by my behaviour. Personally, I don't get it. I am who I am."

With a serious expression, I turn to her, taking her hand. "I don't get it either. There's nothing wrong with who you are. It's kind of refreshing."

"Good. Because the sex is pretty good."

"Pretty good, huh," I murmur, arching my eyebrow.

She sniffs, crossing her arms over her chest. "You have room for improvement."

She's such a liar, and she knows it.

"There's an ice cream store next to where we are staying. They don't shut until eight. We could go."

"That won't make up for the velvet cake but it's a start," she sighs, leaning into me. "I've had such a good day. Comic Con was the shit."

"I still can't believe you got them to let you try that super hero suit on."

She looks away, biting her bottom lip. "Yeah, it was cool."

I groan. "Hayden, what did you do?"

"I don't like the way you assume I've done something."

"I know you did," I state matter of fact.

Lifting her chin, she lets out a puff of air. "The guy didn't exactly let me. I may or may not have spilt something on that game he was playing on. He was distracted."

Getting up, I then pull her up from the bench, bending down to kiss her. "You really are a wild child."

"Born and raised," she proudly states, wrapping her arms around my neck.

Bending down, I kiss her again, pulling her body flush against mine. I will never get enough of her taste. She tastes sweet with a hint of chocolate.

"Let's go get your ice cream," I tell her when I pull away.

She blinks up at me. "With a brownie?"

Chuckling, I nod. "Always."

We begin our short walk back to the Travelodge. I made sure when I booked a room that everything was within walking distance, knowing Hayden would hate the exercise.

"I forgot to ask earlier because, stealing the suit and all, but what did the home want?"

Nightingales had called earlier about Dad's treatment plan, saying he needed antibiotics for his fever. I was worried, but my sister assured me she would keep me updated. Even so, I still felt guilty for not being there but when I called Dad, he chewed my ear off and told me under no circumstances was I to go back until I had showed Hayden I wasn't some pompous asshole.

"They just wanted to update me on Dad. He has a fever, so they've given him antibiotics."

"Why didn't you say anything? We should go back."

I pull her to stop outside the ice cream shop and take her in my arms, smiling. "I love that you care. I do. But he's fine," I assure her. "But, I do have a question; what did Dad mean when he told me to thank you?"

Laughing, she sags into me, a mischievous look in her eye. "I may or may not have sent him the picture of you up on stage with that drag queen, Luna, and the video I got of you squealing like a girl when the dog was chasing you."

"Your dad put steak in my pocket," I remind her, still not happy about it.

"But you didn't know that."

"Not until the beast ripped my coat apart. I thought I was going to die," I growl. "How the hell did your dad even do that?"

She shrugs, not even the slightest bit impressed that he managed to steal my coat unnoticed and fill the inside with steak. And I only have theories as to how he knew that dog would be there, and that it was addicted to steak.

"He has a gift. You never know what he will do."

"I guess I know where you get it from."

"Thank you," she states proudly, frowning when my phone rings. "Is it the home?"

Seeing my assistant's number, I grimace in apology to Hayden. "No, but I do need to get this. It's Clarke." I pull out a twenty from my pocket. "Why don't you go grab your sugar coma food while I take this."

She snatches it out of my hand with a fiery grin. "You don't need to tell me twice."

I shake my head as I answer my phone. "Clarke, everything okay?"

"Yes, but I just need to check something. Did you want the Larkin contract faxed through tonight?"

"Yes," I tell him, catching sight of Hayden through the shop window. I'm taken off guard to see her laughing and joking with an older lady, who has a dog in her bag. She's stroking the top of the dog's head, bending down and cooing at it.

"Clayton?"

"Yes, um, sorry. Go ahead and send it."

I end the call, and instead of going inside, I continue to watch her. Her smile lights up the room, and as she talks to the old lady in front of her, she does it with her entire body. She does it with soul.

I'll never get used to her. She's strong, stubborn and outspoken, and yet she's much more. Despite her behaviour at times, despite her strong will and the walls she has up, she's one of the kindest, most caring and selfless people I know.

Not even her fighting with six-year-olds could put me off her. I love that she speaks her mind, not caring what others think of her. Because she knows there is more to her and she only cares that she knows that. *I* know there's more to her. But I'll take her crazy if it means I get to have her because she's one of the best people to be around.

And each time I get a glimpse of what's underneath, I want her even more.

She gives the dog one last stroke before heading towards me, half eaten ice cream in hand.

"Everything okay?"

"Did you not get me one?" I muse.

Her mouth sensually closes around the spoon, sucking the mint ice cream into her mouth. "Nope. I did buy the old lady one inside though."

I look over her shoulder, seeing the woman smiling as she takes her order. "What, why?"

"Because she didn't have enough change."

I smile, glancing down at her. "You surprise me at every turn."

"I like to keep people on their toes," she tells me, leaning up to give me a spoonful of ice cream.

Knowing she doesn't give it away freely, I take it, the coldness sharp on my sensitive teeth.

Her pupils dilate as she steps closer, scanning my face. "Why are you looking at me like you want to eat me and not this yummy ice cream? I mean, I don't share with just anyone you know. You should enjoy it."

I snatch the tub from her, throwing it in the bin, and before she can protest, I press my lips against hers.

A vicious curse leaves her lips before I slide my tongue inside, massaging mine against hers. She moans, clinging to my jacket.

I feel her shiver under me as she pulls back, breathing heavily. "I'm not sure they'd appreciate the view." I glance to the side, noticing the old lady and a few members of staff staring out of the window, all smiling.

"Let's go," I tell her, my voice husky as I lead her into the Travelodge, pulling her into the lift.

She pulls at my jacket, kissing me passionately as I shove her against the side of the lift.

I unzip her coat before palming her waist, squeezing.

She lets out a groan when the doors open. I lift her up, smiling as she wraps her legs around my waist.

"God, I want you so bad," I growl, sliding the key card out my back pocket and into the door.

Shutting the door behind us, I walk her to the end of the bed, placing her on her feet. Within seconds, we're both reaching for each other's clothes.

I groan when I get another look at her in her black laced bra and briefs. Her toned body has my cock twitching.

Her hand runs over my bare chest and a tortured pleasure shoots through me. I won't last. Not with her. Not with her hands on me.

I gently lie her back on the bed, gripping her briefs and slowly slide them down her legs. "Take off your bra," I order.

She moans, reaching up to unclip it. When her gorgeous breasts are free, I eye them for a moment, moaning.

I cup her pussy, rubbing the palm of my hand over her clit. She arches, moaning low in her throat.

"Please," she rasps, rising her hips off the bed.

I smirk, bending down and kissing her pubic bone, licking down to her mould and over her clit.

She bucks, slapping her hands down on the sheets, gripping them. I continue to torture her, flicking the tip of my tongue over her clit as I pump a finger inside of her.

"I want you inside me," she growls, her breathing coming faster.

"Tonight, we are going slow."

"What?" she screeches before another moan escapes her.

I thrust another finger into her, forcing back a smirk at the sound of her moans. "I want you slow."

"I want it hard."

I thrust another finger up inside of her, pumping at a nice, steady pace. "You'll have what I give you."

I continue to pump my fingers in and out of her whilst sucking her clit into my mouth. She bucks, convulsing under me as she screams through her orgasm.

I kneel over her, pushing her up the bed before settling between her legs.

"Clayton," she groans, gripping my shoulders.

"I've got you," I tell her, leaning over to grab a condom off the side. I roll it on, loving the heated expression on her face as she watches me.

I lean down, kissing along her neck, breathing her in. "You smell good. Really good."

"Fuck me," she begs.

My cock presses against her wetness, sliding through her slick folds. I lean down, capturing her lips with mine, demanding access with my tongue. Her fingers dig into my shoulders harder and I growl, reaching down and lining my cock at her entrance before thrusting hard inside her.

"Clayton," she cries out.

Slowly, I rock in and out, watching as her face scrunches up in frustration. "Slow," I remind her, thrusting inside.

"Stop torturing me," she pleads, thrusting her hips up.

I lean down, sucking her nipple into my mouth before letting it go with a pop. I rise up, running a hand through her hair as I stare down at her. Her lips part, her lids lowering in a flutter.

"You drive me insane."

"You are driving me insane," she growls.

I smirk before leaning down, kissing her deeply. I feel like I'm burning from within, my entire body heating from having her.

Her muscles clench around my cock, and I moan, tensing above her. It's hard not to ram inside her hard and fast, but we've done that. I want to show her she means more to me than a quick fuck.

Her nails rake down my back and she knows what that does to me. I growl against her lips, speeding up my movements.

"You are torture," I tell her, my voice raspy.

"Ditto," she tells me, bringing my head down for another kiss.

My cock slides through her wetness with ease, throbbing inside of her.

I reach down between us, rubbing her clit in a slow, torturous circular motion.

"Oh God," she moans, squeezing her eyes shut.

When she opens them, she blinks up at me, her breathing laboured. I cup her jaw, locking my gaze with hers.

Her pupils dilate, her lips parting on a soft puff of air. "Clayton," she whispers.

I'm close, too close, and I want to make sure she comes first.

"Hayden."

Her eyes close as every muscle in her body tightens, her hips arching off the bed as a moan escapes her lips.

Feeling her tighten around my cock, my body trembles through my own orgasm. I shoot my load into the condom as I continue to ride out my orgasm.

I strum my thumb over her cheek and her lids flutter open and a flash of vulnerability passes through her.

I open my mouth—to say what, I don't know—but no words form.

"What?" she asks, her brows drawn together.

"Nothing," I lie, before getting up to depose of the condom.

Coming back in, she's still in the same position, looking relaxed and sated. A smug smile pulls at my lips as I get in beside her, pulling her into my arms.

"Okay, slow isn't so bad," she murmurs before yawning.

I run my hand down her back, stroking her soft skin. "It's really not."

"Thank you for an amazing couple of days."

I reach around, cupping her breast in my hand, squeezing the soft globe. "It's not over yet."

She begins to squirm, her lips parting as arches into my touch. "It's not?"

I grin, running my hand down her stomach, over her pubic bone. "Oh no, it's really not."

She laughs when I roll us so she's on top, her hair flowing down. "I guess I should do all the work this time."

My grin widens as I cup her backside, thrusting her wet pussy over my fully hard cock. "Yeah, I guess you should."

She leans down, kissing me and all I can think of is how lucky I am to have her. With past relationships, I got bored, not just in the bedroom, but in general. With Hayden, neither are going to be a problem.

And I won't change it for anything.

She's under my skin in the best way.

TWENTY-SEVEN

THE GREY SKY DARKENS ABOVE me as I stand outside the police station. Rain is inevitable and the wind is strong, promising us another day and night of bad weather.

I still have five minutes until the time Beau told me to head inside. He's going to make sure he's walking past when I arrive.

My phone beeps with a message. Leaning against the wall, away from the stairs leading up to the station, I slide it out of my black leather jacket, smiling at 'Hot Jerk Boss' popping up on my screen.

It was my first day back today, and although he went back last week, we still spent pretty much every night together at my place. However, last night, I didn't get to see him as he had to be up early today.

HOT JERK BOSS: I know you're already coming in earlier today to go over what you missed, but would it be wrong of me to ask you to come in earlier? I could order dinner to my office for us both.

The time on my phone says it's four in the afternoon, so his offer would save me going home for a few hours and being bored.

HAYDEN: Sounds tempting, but you in a suit, in your office, door locked… eating is not what will be on my mind.

It's a couple of minutes before he replies.

HOT JERK BOSS: Getting a hard on at work whilst you are in the middle of a boring conference meeting isn't as exciting as people make it out to be.

Laughing, I type out my reply, my fingers flying across the screen.

HAYDEN: Is Gillian from downstairs there?

Gillian is one of the researchers for the nature and wildlife magazine on the first floor. It's a different department to the station but still owned by the Cross family. There are times we cross paths with her on our floor, mostly when we've been short-staffed. Her curious nature scares other people in the building. It's like she knows what people are thinking or what they've done.

HOT JERK BOSS: Yes! How did you know? She's freaking me out. She's been staring at me for five minutes with a disgusted look upon her face.

HOT JERK BOSS: Please say you'll come and keep me company. I should be out of here in about an hour.

HAYDEN: I'll bring food. I've got something to do first, so I'll message you when I'm on my way.

When I see his smiley face emoji, I smile and slide my phone back into my pocket.

I have to get this done. My stomach is in knots because I'm worried I'm going to fuck this up. There are people relying on me, even if they don't know it, to get this done. I can't let them down. I can pull the wool over many people's eyes, but for some reason, that inkling of doubt keeps crawling up my spine, making me think they'll see right through this ploy.

Inhaling, I straighten my jacket before taking the first step up to the large building.

As I reach the wide oak double doors, I put on my game face, inhaling and exhaling quick breaths before pushing open the door and rushing to the front desk, pretending to be out of breath. I need them to take me seriously. If I'm calm and collected, I'm worried they'll make me wait. Although, this is only for the receptionist. When I go into that meeting, I'm going in headstrong.

"I need to speak to PC Rob Howard. It's about the break-ins that have been happening."

"Calm down, miss. Let me take your name," the older lady behind the desk asks.

"Please, this is important. I really need to see him."

"Hayden? What are you doing here?" Beau asks, repeating his rehearsed speech. "Is everything okay?"

I sag against the counter, blowing out a breath. "Beau, I really need to speak to Rob and the people who are working the break-ins. I have really important information."

"Let her through, Hayley," Beau orders gently.

"That's not protocol. She needs to be signed in," she argues.

"She's family. If she says it's important, it's important."

"Okay, but if anyone asks, I'll tell them you let her through," she tells him.

He gestures for me to go to the side door, where Hayley proceeds to buzz me in.

"Are they all here?" I whisper when I reach him, ducking my head so no one can read my lips.

He places a hand on the bottom of my back, guiding me down a hallway. "Yes."

He pushes open a door to what looks like a conference room. An oval table sits in the middle, surrounded by eight brown chairs, three of which are occupied by Rob and two others.

The eldest of the three sits forward, frowning at Beau and I. "Beau, this is a private meeting."

Rob looks up, stunned to see me for a minute, before his eyes widen. "Please tell me they didn't get to you?"

"You knew?" Beau grits out.

Rob winces. "You know Hayden; she wouldn't let it drop. I did warn her."

"We'll talk about it after," Beau warns him, before turning to the older gentlemen who first spoke. "This is Hayden Carter. She's my fiancé's cousin. Hayden has some important information about the break-ins that you need to hear."

"Take a seat. I'm detective Walker, this is PC Fisher, and from what I can see, you already know PC Howard."

Fisher stays quiet, watching, processing, but for someone in his mid-forties, he's probably used to doing that.

Rob still looks sick with worry, his eyes shadowed from lack of sleep. If one of them is guilty, they aren't showing their hand, which means they've been hiding this for longer than people realise. Someone who can be this cool and collected has had practice.

They most likely think they'll get away with it.

Beau pulls out a chair at the end of the table, and I take it, smiling at him as he sits down in the chair beside me.

"Hi," I greet, giving them a small wave. I try not to put on much of a show. Rob will see right through it, having met me before.

"What information do you have for us?" Fisher asks, paying more attention now.

"Before I reveal anything more, I'll need your cooperation."

They sit up straighter in their seats, expressions serious. Something tells me it has nothing to do with the seriousness of the situation, but the fact a girl has come in and told them what to do. The only ones who don't seem as fazed are Beau and Rob. Which is a good sign for Rob.

"If we can, we will," Walker practically forces out.

"I've been following the story, asking questions of potential witnesses—"

"I asked you not to do that," Rob snaps, frowning at me. "Look what happened to Christina."

"If she has something, let her speak. You can hash out your disagreements after. I, for one, would like to hear what she has to say. These burglaries need to end," Fisher comments, his jaw clenched when he looks at Rob.

Hmm, it seems those two aren't besties.

I clear my throat when it becomes tense. "A girl contacted me yesterday morning. She claims to have evidence that can provide proof with regards to the burglaries, although she wouldn't tell me of what or of whom, and that she could only talk to me. She feels like she's being watched, and that whoever these people are, they know she has information that could be a problem for them, so she doesn't feel safe to hand in the evidence herself.

"She's going to meet me on Friday at nine pm to hand it over."

"What's stopping them from getting to her before then?" Walker asks, rubbing a hand over his beard.

"She has gone into hiding and said she will contact me on a pay as you go phone so they can't trace her. And as of this morning, I got word out that I'm going to the old cattle market on Friday to collect evidence that will put a stop to these crimes."

"Why would you leak that?" Beau snaps. "You've put a target on your head and put yourself in danger, Hayden."

I grin, clasping my hands together on the table. "Because while I'm meeting her at another location in town, you guys can surround the cattle market and arrest whoever turns up."

"I think it should be one of us who goes," Rob declares, a little pale.

It's hard not to look at Beau, to see if he's thinking the same as me over Rob's comment. It's hard to tick him off the list when he reacts like that, yet it could just mean he's worried.

"She will only meet me, Rob. She made that clear," I tell him.

"That's not how this works," Fisher argues. "If she has evidence, she needs to come to us."

I push back my chair, letting them see my disappointment. "Then I'll tell her to meet me somewhere else and pray they don't hurt her before then, because I'm not putting her at risk. Too many people have been hurt because of this gang. It needs to be put to an end."

"Wait," Walker yells, placing his pen down. "I'll listen. I can get word out and have a team put together."

"But then you have a chance of them being tipped off," Beau muses, pretending to be in thought. "We should keep it as low key as possible."

"Are you saying we have a leak?" Walker accuses, his face turning red.

"No, but who here can honestly say that someone hasn't listened in on their conversations? It only takes one person to overhear and we are screwed."

"And what if more than one of them show up?" Rob asks, his attention on Beau and me.

"Call for help," I offer dryly. "I'm not doing this if she's going to be put at risk."

"How do we know this isn't a set up for the gang to get you alone? They've killed before, Hayden," Rob stresses.

"I'm not stupid. That was the first thing that popped into my head when she called. I looked her up on Facebook. She hasn't been active since she witnessed whatever she did that night. This is the real thing, and she's scared out of her mind. She's a good person, just finished college. I can't see someone like that being mixed up in a gang that is clearly trying to steal to make money. Can you?"

"And how do we know that what she has warrants an arrest or is even worth the manpower and time this will take?" Fisher asks, his gaze narrowed on me. "We could be working on real leads. Not some 'maybe' story."

I sit back down in my chair, arching my eyebrow at him. "She has video footage of who she assumes is the leader, and photos. I might not know what or who is on that video, but it's enough to scare the girl to death. She was genuinely petrified, telling me I couldn't trust anyone. She told me I couldn't tell the police because she felt even they couldn't protect her. She wanted me to take this to my boss."

"This is the break we need, even if it isn't conventional," Walker confesses.

"She didn't tell you any more?" Rob asks.

"No, and I didn't ask. I didn't want to risk scaring her away. Hell, she doesn't know I'm here today. I spent the whole night stewing over what I should do. I'm worried she won't turn up if she knew."

"What's her name?" Fisher asks, poising his pen over his paper.

"Look, I did this against her wishes. I'm not going to reveal her identity until I know for sure she's safe."

Walker sits forward, running a hand over his jaw. "So why *did* you come?"

"Because it was the right thing to do, and I know how hard Rob has been working to bring these people in. I knew I could trust him and Beau."

"That goes without saying, but I warned you not to look into this," Rob comments, frowning.

"If I had listened to you, you wouldn't have this evidence right now."

"We thank you for coming to us," Walker declares.

"I still think one of us should go with you, just to be safe," Rob stresses.

"No one will know where I am or when we are meeting. I'll be fine. It's in town and the place can get busy on weekends, you know that."

"I have that dinner with Faith and our parents on Friday night. I'll have to cancel again."

"My God, please don't. She made herself sick worrying over plans last week, don't stress her out even more."

"But—"

I give him a pointed look. "No buts."

Walker sits forward. "We will still need to bring in at least two other officers to cover the ground. I know you said no more people, but to cover that derelict building, we will need more men. We can also have the place completely locked down so no one can hide inside to blindside us."

Turning to Beau, I suck in my bottom lip. "What do you think?"

He reaches out to pat the top of my hand. "I think it's a good idea. This way, they can make sure everything is covered by an officer."

"If you think it's best, I suppose it will be okay."

"Is there anything else you can tell us?" Walker asks.

One of you is corrupt doesn't seem like the appropriate answer, so instead, I say, "Nope. That's everything."

"We will still need to speak to the witness," Rob explains softly, making me doubt his innocence once again.

"As soon as I know she will be safe, I'll bring her here. I'll explain who Beau is and that she's safe and can trust him."

"We will let you know once we have them in custody," Walker promises.

"Just keep one of us updated on Friday. If anything feels out of place, don't hesitate to call," Fisher offers.

"You can call me. I can pass anything on," Beau lies. "These guys will be busy and need their focus."

"I'm good with that."

"So, on Friday at nine, you'll go meet this witness and we will sort out everything on our end.

I puff out a breath, smiling. "Thank you. I'll be glad for it to be over."

"No, thank you for coming to us and not doing this alone. You did the right thing," Walker promises.

"Any time," I reply, pushing out of my chair. "I have to get going. I have work. Thank you for hearing me out."

"I'll walk you out," Beau offers, standing up.

I wave goodbye to the others before stepping out of the room, opening my mouth to curse whoever it is out.

But Beau grips my waist, pausing my words. "Don't say anything," he whispers from the corner of his mouth. We reach the door leading out, and he forces a smile to Hayley. "Buzz us out please, Hayley."

The door beeps and Beau places his hand on it, pushing it open.

The second we step outside, I take in a lungful of air. "That was intense."

"Yeah," he agrees wearily.

"I don't even know what to say. Each of them asked questions that could implicate them in one way or another."

"Agreed. I didn't get a better read on them either. Those questions would be something we would ask anyway, so nothing really stood out."

"Maybe I'm wrong," I add, yet I don't believe my words. One of them is guilty. I can feel it.

Beau runs a hand through his hair, blowing out a breath. "No, I don't think you are. I had my doubts before, you know I did, but after that meeting, I could feel it. I can't explain it."

"I'm sorry. I wish I had been wrong, if that helps."

"It's fucked up, that's for sure. Before you came, I looked over the timeline of the break-ins, and there isn't a pattern. Which is unusual as they're normally in one local area."

"What about the times you thought you had the gang's location?"

"Same. It didn't add up. Someone was definitely tipping them off. Some of the raids were planned only minutes before we left, which means someone had to have called or messaged them on the way."

"Who was there?" I ask, hopeful.

"That's the thing, we all were. Even I was sent out on that raid."

My lips part, ready to ask if he could access phone records during that time, but movement from behind Beau pulls my attention.

I duck my head, hiding my lips from him. "Rob is here."

I look up, forcing a smile as Rob strolls over. "Hey, Rob."

"Everything okay over here?" he asks, his brows pulled together.

"Yeah, I was just telling Beau to stop stressing about not being there. He's set on cancelling with Faith, which I don't think is wise."

Rob slaps Beau on the shoulder, gripping him. "Stop worrying, mate. We have her covered. I promise she will be safe."

Beau forces a smile. "Thanks, man."

"I'll leave you to it. I really do need to get going," I inform them, before giving Beau a pointed look. "I'll speak to you later."

He gives me a short nod. "Bye, Hayden."

"See you around, short stuff. And stay safe, yeah? You never know what they'll do to you if they find out what you've been up to," Rob warns.

A sense of foreboding crawls up my spine as I give him a tight smile.

"They'd regret trying. Us Carter's aren't known to be taken down easily."

I take a few steps backwards, giving them a salute before turning and heading towards my car.

For Rob's sake, he'd better be innocent.

My family would destroy him.

TWENTY-EIGHT

MY HEART HASN'T BEEN IN tonight's segment and it's showed in my work. I'm actually surprised we finished earlier than normal, as I read quarter to nine on my phone.

I had been distracted the whole night, waiting to receive a message off Beau or Liam. I hadn't heard from either since earlier on in the day, when Beau called to say they had set up.

My concern is probably unwarranted; we still have fifteen minutes until the initial meet is meant to take place. Yet Beau and I had hoped someone would show up early. We both want this finished; Beau more than me, since someone he considers a friend is a suspect.

It's taking a toll on him.

However, I know Beau will contact me if there's an update. And yet my stomach churns with an uneasy feeling, just like it has done all day.

I can't shake the feeling or sense of dread that I have somehow put Beau in danger. It's playing on mind, making me feel sick. Faith would never forgive me if anything happened to him. And she just found her happy. I don't want to be the reason it was taken away.

"Hayden?" Clayton barks, snapping his fingers in front of me.

I shake my thoughts away, coming out of my daze as I glance around the room at those watching me with concern.

I slap Clayton's hand away when he continues to snap his fingers and glare up at him. "What is your problem? And why are you clicking your fingers at me?"

He watches me for a moment, concern morphing over his expression before he masks it, tightening his features. "My office, now!" he barks, storming out of the studio.

Once he's gone, Chrissy steps forward, looking away from the door Clayton just exited through. "Are you okay, Hayden?"

I snort, waving her off. "He doesn't scare me."

Leana slides her chair over to me, grimacing. "I think she's referring to the fact you've not been yourself. Your body is here, but you aren't. I'm still shocked you agreed with what Josie's boyfriend said about her. He was really cruel and harsh. You normally rip a guy like that into shreds."

Thinking back, I can't remember a Josie, or much of our last caller. I had been too distracted by my phone and what was taking place.

I rub a hand over my face, letting out a weary sigh. "Fuck, I'm so sorry. I've got a really bad headache."

"Would you like me to go and talk to Mr. Cross for you, and explain? You can leave early then," Chrissy offers, her voice low, soft.

I force a smile. "No. But thank you. It makes him feel better when he gets to yell at me."

Their laughter sounds forced as worry creases their foreheads.

"I'll be fine," I assure them, giving them a short wave as I get up.

I exit the studio room, making my way down the corridor to Clayton's office, checking my phone once more.

Nothing. Again.

I don't want to worry. I know Beau can take care of himself. But I can't help it.

"There you are," Clayton announces, coming to a stop outside his office door. "What is up with you tonight?"

I pinch the bridge of my nose. "Are you asking as my boss or the guy I'm sleeping with?"

He looks up and down the corridor to check the coast is clear before gripping my wrist and pulling me into his office. He drags me over to his desk, leaning me against it before he takes a seat in his desk chair.

I wiggle my arse on the desk, sitting back, and begin to swing my legs.

"Now, why would it matter which part of me is asking? And since when was I just the guy you're sleeping with?"

"You're the one who wanted to keep it professional at work. So as my boss, I'll apologise for being distracted. I've had a headache."

"Do you need food, is that why you're being a bitch?"

"I'm not a bitch and I'm not hungry." And for the second time in my life, I'm not. My stomach is in knots.

"So, what is it?" he splutters, frowning at me. "I know I haven't done anything wrong."

"I've got a headache," I grit out, checking my phone.

He snatches it from my hand. "Answer me."

"Hey," I snap, reaching for it.

He shakes his head, placing it on the desk next to me before gripping my hands in his to stop me reaching for it. "Talk to me. Tell me what's going on. If you want what this is between us to end, just say so. I'm a big boy."

My brow furrows. "Why on earth would I want that? You're great in bed."

He guffaws. "Is that all I am to you?"

My shoulders drop and I duck my head a little. "No. You're more than that. I'm just tired and have a headache. I get cranky when I'm ill," I lie, not ready to tell him about the story until I know there is a story.

His eyes heat as he runs his palms up my thighs. "Do you want me to make it better?"

I smirk, scanning his office briefly as all the fantasies I've had about having him in here resurface. He's decorated since he took over. It's all grey and black with dark oak furniture.

I reach for his tie, pulling him towards me. His chair slides forward, bringing him closer.

"Don't tease me. You know I've been wanting you to fuck me on your desk," I breathe against his lips.

Grinning, he stands, pulling me to the edge of the desk, my core pressing against his hardness. My thighs clench as I wrap them around him.

"I'm not teasing," he rasps, pressing a kiss to my neck.

I tilt my head to the side, giving him more access, before gripping his blazer. "Then I won't stop you."

I feel him smile against my neck as I rock against him. He reaches for my jacket, sliding it off one shoulder as he pulls out my plain white T-shirt from my ripped jeans. I moan, squeezing my thighs around him.

A phone vibrates across the table, but I don't pull away, instead bringing his lips to mine as I slide part of his blazer off.

His tongue massages mine, leaving my brain frazzled. It's like all the feelings take over and turn my mind to mush. The only thing better than him kissing me, is him being inside of me.

Every nerve stands on end as I grip the hair at the nape of his neck, deepening the kiss.

When the vibrating starts up again, Clayton tries to pull away, but I pull him back, kissing him once more.

"Phone," he mumbles against my mouth, gripping my hips and rocking me against his hard on.

"Ignore it and keep doing what you're doing," I order.

The phone starts up again and Clayton pulls back slightly, grabbing a phone off the desk. Lost in my own mind, it takes me a few seconds to realise it's mine.

I go to reach for it, but he pulls back, reading the message.

I snatch the phone from him once he's distracted, unable to look at him as I click on the messages Beau has sent.

BEAU: I don't think they took the bait.

BEAU: We're going to stay on for a bit longer.

BEAU: No one is here. Maybe this lead is another dead end. The break-ins might just be gang related.

I look up at Clayton and watch his nostrils flare. His hands drop to his sides, forming clenched fists.

"Clayton?" I whisper, trying to form the words to explain.

"Please tell me that isn't what I think it is," he grits out.

"Clayton—"

He slams his hand on the back of his chair, pushing it into a filing cabinet. "Please fucking tell me that isn't about the burglaries," he growls, levelling me with a glowering look.

"I…" I pause, not knowing what to say. I hadn't expected him to be so furious or react like this. I knew he would be mad, yes, but not like this.

He takes a step back, running a hand through his hair. "It is," he affirms, snarling in disgust.

I stand, straightening my jacket and tucking my T-shirt back into my jeans. "It's fine. Beau is at a location ready to catch the cop who could be working with the gang. You don't have to worry. I did it. I might have actually put a stop to them."

"What?" he yells, spinning to face me. "How could you be so fucking stupid, Hayden?"

"Excuse me?" I grit out.

I can move past him being pissed, but his anger is something I won't stand for. He has no idea. He's overreacting.

"I told you, Hayden; I told you to leave this fucking story alone. Did nothing I said register with you? You had no business sticking your nose into this. It is not your job."

"Well tough shit. I wanted you to see what I was capable of. I wanted to prove to you that I could do this, and I have."

"What, by not following orders? Putting yourself in danger? For purposely doing something you knew you weren't allowed to? Is that what you're capable of?" he snaps, taking in a deep breath. "My God, Hayden, you could have been hurt or worse. Do you not see that?"

"No, I wanted to show you that I'm more than some advice host. I've done everything! Everything your father and this job has asked of me. I've earned this position. If your company won't sponsor a new blog, then I'll go rogue and do it myself. I'm sure someone else will see my potential and hire me."

"That is not the point and we both know it. Do you not care about your safety at all?" he roars. "People have died. A reporter died looking into this story."

"I was perfectly safe," I scream back. "I can do this."

"And what about Love Loop Live? Did you consider what this would do to the segment?"

"Is that all you fucking care about?" I snap, shoving away from the table and moving around the desk, my breathing laboured.

"No, and you know it isn't."

"No, I don't know it. I don't fucking care about any of it anymore. I work hours I'm not paid for to make sure it's all taken care of, earning just a little over minimum wage, while Tim on floor one has worked here for a shorter time and already has a sports column.

"So why should it be different for me, Clayton? Why? I like this job, but I don't love it. Your father told me every time I went to him with the proposal that he would look into it. And guess what, it never happened. I'm not even asking to do one or the other—I'm happy to do both and leave Nightingales—but no one will meet me halfway."

My nails cut into my palms as I stand there, clenching my hands.

"I'm not my father. And he is no longer your boss. I am. And I specifically asked you not to put yourself in harm's way."

"That isn't up to you," I scream, throwing my hands up. "I made the choice. Me. I made it. You could make one too. I had hoped when you took over that modern updates would be made."

"Now you're telling me how to run my company?" he grits out. "I'm the boss here, not you."

I shake my head, taking another step back. "No, because that isn't my place, just like yours isn't telling me what to do," I spit out, turning to leave.

"I am not finished talking to you!"

I spin around, my eyes squeezed into thin slits. "Well I am. I'm so fucking finished."

"You've still got emails to go through," he reminds me, his voice hard.

"And I'll do them. I just don't have to listen to you anymore. You've made your point very clear."

"Hayden—"

"No, I don't want to hear it. I'm going for some fresh air. I'll be back to finish my work after."

"Hayden," he breathes out, his shoulders sagging.

I stop with my hand on the door handle, ducking my head. I can't face him. Not without breaking down.

Maybe he was right about relationships not working in a workplace. Because right now, it's him I want to go to, him I want to tell about my shit day, yet he's the reason my night was shit.

"I just need five minutes," I explain, forcing my voice to remain calm, when inside I'm fuming.

"Don't leave. We need to talk about this," he pleads, his voice a mixture of anger and calm.

I pull open the door, taking a step out, but pause in the doorway, glancing over my shoulder.

"Clayton?"

"Yes?"

"Boss or not, if you ever yell at me like that again, I will knee you in the fucking balls."

I don't wait around for a reply, or another lecture for talking back at my 'boss'. I'm done.

I head down the corridor towards the staff lift that goes down to the back entrance, where the staff car park is.

"Hayden?" Leana yells, startling me.

After pressing the call button for the lift, I turn to face her. "Yeah?"

She takes a staggering step backwards, her jaw dropping. "Wow! Do you need an alibi, because I'll give you one, I swear."

"Huh?"

She stops fidgeting, tilting her head. "You look like you just murdered someone."

I force a laugh. "Yeah," I murmur, spotting the bag in her hand. "Is that mine?"

She jumps, looking down at the bag before handing it over. "Yes, you left it in the studio."

"Thanks, but I'll be back up in a minute. I need to finish going over messages and emails."

"You aren't going home? Me and Chrissy can do that."

"No, it's fine. There's a few things I really need to finish up anyway," I explain, stepping into the lift. "See you in five minutes."

She shoves her hands into her pockets, taking a step back.

I close my eyes as the door shuts; mine and Clayton's argument playing on a loop in my head.

Can't he see that what I'm doing is for good?

Bailey has designed me a kick ass website that's set to launch once I have Clayton's approval, since I added Cross Global as partner, which could link to Love Loop Live. The title for the blog is a work-in-progress, so it's Carter News until I can come up with something better.

I'd put weeks' worth of work into making sure it looked good for when I was ready to reveal it to him, and he didn't even give me chance to explain, let alone show him. Not that I had the opening to tell him.

Angrily, I push open the exit door, causing it to slam against the metal bar outside.

Rain splatters across my face when I step out.

"Hayden, I've been waiting for you," a familiar voice says, his tone low as he steps out of the shadows, uniform present.

My pulse races. "What are you doing here?" I ask, taking a step back.

His smile is taunting. "Because you asked me to come get you."

His sickly-sweet voice couldn't be any more fake. "It's you," I breathe, his lie rolling over me, causing a shiver of goose bumps to break out over my skin.

I spin around, ready to run back inside to safety, but he grabs me from behind, pulling me against his chest.

"Me!" he breathes low against my ear.

TWENTY-NINE

CLAYTON

S OMETIMES I NEED A LITTLE guidance, and today is that day. Hayden is a complicated woman. She's tough, fiery and speaks her mind, but she has never reacted this angrily before tonight.

I'm angry at myself for overreacting. I knew I was then, but I couldn't stop it spewing from my lips. I was just so goddamn mad at her for putting herself at risk.

But I'm madder at myself for making her believe she isn't worth it. I crushed her dream. Her dream. And I'm punishing myself for it now. That was never my intention.

She didn't think I was listening to her, but all I had done was listen. Her idea held merit, and I do believe it would be good for Cross Global.

The only person who can help with my dilemma is my dad.

I've just finished running through everything that happened between me and Hayden, and her proposal.

"So, what should I do, Dad?"

He lets out a wheezy cough. "Son, why are you telling me all of this?"

I pinch the bridge of my nose. I thought it would have been obvious to him. "I don't want to let you down or do something you wouldn't approve of," I explain.

"What do you think about it?" he asks, sounding tired.

"I think the girl I've come to care about just stormed out of my office because I yelled at her for putting her life at risk. Her proposal is a good one, brilliant in fact, and it would stop her chasing after dangerous stories if she got to do what she wanted. This article she wants to write, a reporter has already died looking into it."

I exhale a breath, falling back in my chair. It feels good to get it off my chest.

"I'm only going to say this once, so listen up, son." He clears his throat before continuing. "The business is yours now. Not mine. You don't need my permission to move forward on other projects. That said, I've been putting Hayden off since she first came to me with the proposal. I wanted you to be the one to launch it. You deserved to have something that was yours, something you helped build so you felt like you achieved Cross Global."

I grip my forehead, pinching the skin. "Jesus, I'm such a fucking idiot."

"Well, yes, but Hayden's not. In all my life I've never met anyone as complex as her. She fought her way through her job and even set fire to pervy Barry's car. I've got a recording saved in the office somewhere. She's a keeper. Now go tell her the good news and leave me alone. You won't have me to hold your hand forever, son."

The thought twists my stomach. "I know, Dad. I just want to make you proud."

"I am proud. Of both of my children. Now go, I want to finish playing checkers with Linny."

"Linny?" I squeak. "Isn't that the lady who streaks up and down the halls at least once a day?"

"She's clothed now, so go."

"Speak to you tomorrow. Night, Dad."

"Please do. I can't wait to hear how Hayden kicked your arse."

I laugh, ending the call. Getting up, I exit the office, running into Chrissy and Leana.

"Hey, have you seen Hayden?"

"No," Chrissy replies. "We were actually just coming to see if she was with you."

"Yeah, she went down in the lift about fifteen minutes ago and said she'd be back in five, but we've not seen her."

My brows draw together as I give them a nod. "Thank you. I'll go check outside."

I race down the hall, pressing the button for the lift, not wanting to miss her if I take the stairs. There's no way Hayden would take the stairs.

Seconds later, I'm stepping on, pressing the button to the ground floor.

All I have to do is explain why I was mad, tell her I'm sorry, and then tell her the good news. She can be reasonable.

Stepping into the empty lobby, I call out, "Hayden?" receiving no answer.

I push through the doors leading outside, shivering when the cold wind hits me, along with droplets of rain.

I duck my head, catching sight of Hayden's bag and phone left abandoned on the floor.

My breath hitches as I race over, picking it up off the floor.

"Hayden?" I yell, searching the car park for any signs of her. "Hayden!"

Her phone vibrates in my hand, and a sliver of fear has me answering. "Beau, what is going on? Is Hayden with you?"

"Clayton?" he asks, sounding confused.

"Yes, is Hayden with you?" I yell, my gut clenching as I take a look behind the bins.

"No, she's not with me. I thought she was with you."

I run a hand through my hair, spinning in a circle as I look around the car park. "We had an argument. She walked out for some fresh air about fifteen minutes ago. I came out to look for her and found her phone and bag on the floor. What is going on, Beau? Does this have anything to do with the story she was working on?"

"You knew?" he asks, surprised.

"That's what our argument was over. Where is she?" I plead, kicking a post.

"Where are you?" Beau asks in a tight voice.

"Outside work. I'm in the staff car park, which is at the back of the building," I tell him, taking a breath. "They've taken her, haven't they?"

"I'm not sure," he tells me, but I can hear the lie. "I'm on my way. Stay there."

"Should I call the police?"

"No! Whatever you do, do not trust any officer right now. I'm coming."

"What the fuck should I do then?" I roar, worried for her safety.

"Call her dad. I'll call Maverick. Tell him to meet you there," he orders, before ending the call.

"Mr Cross, is everything okay?"

I turn to face Chrissy, forcing a smile. "Could you get my coat from the back of the door in my office and tell security to meet me here?"

"Where's Hayden? Is everything okay?"

"Please!" I plead. "I'll explain everything after. I promise."

"Okay, I'll be right back."

I turn back to the car park, pulling her dad's contact up in her phone.

Please be okay. Please, Hayden, be okay.

"I DON'T KNOW WHO the fuck to call," Beau growls, pacing back and forth, phone in hand.

"Call anyone," I yell at him.

He glares up at me. "And tip them off that we know? No. I'm not putting her at risk."

"So what the fuck should I do?"

"Let me think," he snaps, closing his eyes. They fly open and he stares at me. "I'm going to call Leon. He was another officer brought in on the case last minute."

"What the fuck has happened to my daughter?" Max roars, slamming his car door. Rain soaks him as he moves towards us under the shelter.

Beau steps back, talking on the phone, leaving me to deal with an angry father. "One of you aren't there, Leon. Who is it? Who isn't there?"

Maverick and a guy called Liam are still in the back of his van, doing God knows what with the computer equipment stored there.

When he doesn't slow down as he approaches, I brace myself, ready for the shove he gives me.

"Stop," I snap, pushing him back.

"This is your fault. Don't think I don't know you wouldn't let her do the job she wanted. You let her fucking do this."

"No, I didn't," I growl. "I found out tonight, and I'm less happy than you are right now. This is what I was fucking scared of."

Beau curses, ending the call, and walks over to us. "What is fucking going on? Who has my daughter?"

"I don't know. They've got their hands full trying to detain the group of teenagers that showed up. He can't account for anyone missing, and everyone who is suspect isn't in his line of vision right now."

"You said that the cattle market was a ploy. If they knew, why would they send people there?" I ask, ducking further under the shelter when the rain begins to come down faster.

"I don't give a fuck what was a ploy or what wasn't. I give a fuck that my daughter isn't here right now," Max roars, his face paling as he struggles to catch his breath.

Beau launches through what has happened, what Hayden found out and about the night she went to him and Maverick. Another thing she hid from me.

Max turns to me, pointing at the building. "Check the CCTV footage. There has to be something on there," he declares, his voice cracking.

I grimace, shoving my hands in my pockets. "The lines were cut at quarter past eight."

His jaw clenches as he stares at Beau, a storm brewing in his eyes before he steps forward, knocking the wind out of him when he shoves him back.

"Why the fuck didn't any of you protect her? You should have been watching her."

"Max," I call out, trying to pull him back, but he shoves me away, breathing hard as his face reddens.

"Don't fucking touch me. How the fuck didn't you notice she was gone? And why the fuck are you here?"

"Are you listening to yourself?"

"Calm down," Beau warns, breaking us apart.

"He doesn't need to be here," Max snaps.

"Yes, I do," I burst out, clenching my hands.

"Calm down," Beau warns when Max takes a threatening step towards me.

"Calm down? Calm down? She's my fucking daughter and she's missing. I just had to lie to her fucking mother, so she didn't worry herself sick again. Don't tell me to calm the fuck down," he roars, letting the rain pour over him. "She didn't fight as a premi to get fucking murdered by some corrupt pig. So get out of my way and tell me something useful," he yells, before turning to me. "And get out of my face. She should have been safe here."

"Yes, she should have. And I'll blame myself for the rest of my life. I was the reason she came out for fresh air," I tell him vehemently, letting him see the guilt and pain it has caused me. "But respectfully, I'm not going anywhere. Not until Hayden tells me otherwise."

"You're her boss. She doesn't need a fucking paycheque right now."

"I'm more than her boss and you know it," I snap. "Now shut up and let's figure out where she is."

He snorts. "You're too old for her."

"I love her," I burst out, surprising myself. "And there's nothing you can do that will make me walk away, so don't even fucking try it."

'Max!" Maverick calls, jumping out the back of the van he and Liam have been working in. He wanted to check the surveillance videos from other buildings.

"You fucking knew," Max growls, his feet splashing up puddles as he races over, charging at his brother. He punches him the jaw, taking him to the ground.

"Max," Beau yells, trying to pull him off.

"Calm the fuck down," Maverick snaps, pushing him away and getting up.

Max follows, grinding his teeth together as he meets Maverick's unrelenting glare. "You fucking knew."

"Max, if I knew it was going to turn out like this, I would never have let her be involved," he explains, wiping blood off his lip. "I would have told you. I swear to you."

Max's temples pulse as he drops his hands to his sides, clenching his fists. "No, you should have told me anyway. You watched what I went through in that hospital when we almost lost Landon. You saw what it did to me. How could you think this would be okay? Why, Mav? Why?" he asks, staring daggers into his brother. "If I lose my daughter, I'll never forgive you. We will be done."

Maverick staggers back, looking utterly wounded, like he's just taken a knife to the stomach.

"Max, there was no way of talking her out of this. I tried," Beau explains gently, bracing himself.

Max's chin drops to his neck, his shoulders sagging. "I can't lose her. I can't. We can't. This will kill my wife. She's only just recovering from Landon's scare," he whispers brokenly.

"I'm so sorry," Maverick rasps, his watery eyes on his brother. "I'm truly sorry."

"Dad?" Liam and Landon call out, running over to us through the rain.

He startles, scrubbing the rain off his face before looking up at his sons. "What are you doing here?"

Landon shares a look with Liam before turning to his dad. "We aren't sure. We both felt like we needed to get to Hayden. We tried calling her, but she didn't answer, so we rang Mum, knowing Hayden goes to see her most Friday's after work, and Mum said you were coming to look at Hayden's car, but that she didn't believe you."

"You lied, didn't you?" Liam asks, looking distraught. "Something has happened to our sister."

Landon casts him a sharp look. "No, it hasn't. Don't talk daft."

Liam shakes his head, his eyes dropping. "Yes, it has. This is the same feeling Hayden and I got when you were in the hospital. We just knew."

"She's a fighter," I remind them, hating the dread in their expressions. It's like they've cast her off already.

"Why are you even here?" Landon barks, eyeing me with disgust.

Max's phone rings and we all turn to him, watching as his brows pull together while he looks down at his phone.

"Hello? Hayden? Where the fuck are you? Are you hurt?" he rushes out, moving under the shelter as he puts his phone on loudspeaker.

Beau races off to the back of the van, while Landon, Liam and Maverick step under the shelter, crowding the phone.

"Hayden, where are you?" Landon asks, but Max slaps his chest.

"Shut up, let her speak."

Hayden groans, and in the background, it sounds like rain is hitting a tin. "Dad, I really need a favour. I've been kidnapped and I need you to come and get me."

"I fucking know you've been kidnapped. I'm your dad; I know everything. Tell me something I don't know," he barks, yet the relief pours over his expression at the sound of her voice.

"In the boot of a car," she fires back. "I cannot believe you are having a go right now."

"Whose phone are you on?" Maverick asks, glancing at Max hesitantly.

She groans. "Please tell me the whole family isn't there."

"Hayden," Max growls.

"Alright, alright. I don't know whose phone this is. There were three or four of them. I pinched it out of a pocket when they were struggling to get me in the boot. Fuckers knocked me out."

"Are you okay?" I rush out, stepping closer to the phone.

"This is not happening," she moans.

"Of course you robbed it. I didn't raise a stupid girl. But lose the attitude, Hayden. I'm so pissed at you right now," her dad warns.

"Dad, don't make me regret choosing to memorise your number in case of an emergency. This is an emergency, and if anyone can get me out of this, it's you. I don't need you losing it on me now. You promised you'd always be there," she tells me him, her voice shaking a little. "And I don't want you attacking everyone around you because you're scared and being a drama queen."

He snorts, rolling his eyes at the phone. "I'm the only one keeping it together. Do you have any idea who took you, where they're taking you?"

"No, I… shit, they're slowing down," she whispers. "Dad, you need to tell Beau it's—"

"I'll have that, you bitch," a deep voice vibrates down the phone.

"Hayden," Max yells, his eyes wide.

She screams as a struggle is heard over the phone. "I'm going to kick your balls so fucking hard you'll be spitting them out," she yells, causing us all to wince.

It takes everything for me not to protect my own balls.

"She always goes for the balls," Liam rasps, his face a little green.

"Hello? Hayden? I swear to God, if you touch my daughter, I will hunt you fucking down," Max roars, right before the line goes dead. "Fuck!"

He goes to throw the phone but thinks better of it, screaming into the sky.

I link my fingers together, placing them on top of my head, my breath catching as I take a step back.

"Got her. I traced the phone and tracked the GPS," Liam, their family friend, announces, rushing over to us. "Let's go."

As we head for the cars, I throw Beau the keys to my car. "You drive."

"I've linked the signal to your phone," Liam calls out, opening the passenger side of the door to Max's car.

"I'm coming with you," Landon calls out to us.

Beau pauses before he gets in the car, looking down at his phone. "That son of a bitch."

THIRTY

MY HANDS SLIDE THROUGH THE mud and leaves as strong arms throw me roughly to the floor. A stick cuts along my cheek as I struggle to get a grip.

My head is still pounding from having something large and heavy whacked across the back of my skull.

I swing my leg out, hitting the tallest of the four in the shin when he goes to grab me.

"Get her up, Low," says the dark voice as its owner steps away from the back of the car.

Low hoists me up by my armpits, gripping me firmly in place when I struggle to get free.

"How could you do this?" I growl at Fisher, blinking raindrops from my eyes. "You're a cop."

He smirks, stepping closer. "It was quite simple really, and they made it so, so easy."

I don't recognise the man staring back at me. There's no resemblance to the man I met Monday in that conference room. None at all.

The way he stands, sure and cocky, no remorse or guilt for his actions or involvement. His expression is hard, contrast to the concern and worry he had worn in a perfect mask in that room. It was all lie.

All of it.

Even his eyes are pure hatred, the orbs holding nothing but darkness. It's eerie.

And as a torch of light shines on him, revealing just how dark this man is, everything begins to click into place.

He isn't just a corrupt officer leaking information. He's the brain behind the entire cooperation, down to every last burglary.

I feel stupid for missing it, for not coming to the assumption sooner. However, it's all making perfect sense to me right now; every detail I didn't read into. Each house that was robbed had something worth stealing. They knew exactly what house to hit. All because of the man standing before me.

It was him.

"It's you. All of this is you," I scream, when the reality of just what he has done hits me. All those poor souls, all those frightened men and women. "Why would you do this?"

I'm pulled back against a hard chest and my shoulders sink, yet a murderous rage is brewing inside of me.

"Ah, I wondered if you knew of my involvement. It was funny to watch and help the officers try to catch a man that doesn't exist."

I spit in his face, struggling to get out of the hold Low has on me.

Fisher grinds his teeth together, his expression boiling with fury as he steps forward, slapping me across the face.

The rain soothes the sting his handprint has left. "Why? Why would you do this?"

He wipes the spit off his nose and cheek before taking a menacing step towards me. I straighten my back, pressing my lips together, ready for whatever he's going to do.

"I've spent years of my life getting abused from those I swore to protect. I got spat on, hit, and dealt with low-lives, only for a majority to get off anyway," he snaps.

"And you don't see the irony?"

He ignores me, continuing with his rant. "The people I risked my life to help? They didn't care. I didn't get a thanks. Parents? They teach their children to be scared of us, which in turn, turned them against me, against us.

"The men I worked with or for? Pathetic excuses for men. And I did all of it for pennies. I lost everything because of this fucking job. Everything! My home when our pay was cut or our hours were dropped. My wife left when I started drinking to help cope with the difficult day. That's why I did it, Hayden. I want what I'm owed. It's been a long time coming."

"All I'm hearing is *wah, wah, wah,*" I snap, my gaze drifting over to the boy who is no older than twelve, shaking and wide-eyed. "You're using kids to do your dirty work."

His gaze also lands on the young boy, a sinister smirk pulling at his lips.

"They want money, which I provide. What more could they want? And with me in charge, it keeps them out of trouble."

Is he delusional?

"Can you hear yourself?" I snap, trying to pull my arms free. My gaze goes to the other guy around my age, who is covered in spider tattoos. "And you're happy to be used by an old dude who is throwing a tantrum because his poor life didn't go his—"

My lungs burn as I wheeze, the air knocked out of my chest from Fisher's punch to my stomach.

"Shut the fuck up, you mouthy little bitch," he snaps, stepping back.

My soaked hair sticks to my face as I lift my head to level him with a glare. "Fuck you," I croak out, panting.

Tattooed guy chuckles, ducking his head a little to meet my gaze. "We're here because we want to be. No fucker messes with us. We've run off three notorious gangs and have members begging to join us."

"And we've got pockets of cash, don't we, Kyle?" Low adds, growling low in my ear when I shove my shoulder into him.

"So do half of the population who get off their arse each morning and have a real job," I snap.

Low's grip on me tightens. "Please tell me I get to end her."

"Now, Low, you know it's your brother's initiation night. JJ must be the one to do it. And since he's already witnessed too much, you know the rule if he doesn't," Fisher reminds him, sending JJ a look that promises retribution if he doesn't do what's demanded of him.

My head whirls to the boy, who takes a step back, his eyes bulging with fear.

"He's just a boy," I argue, curling my lip in disgust.

"And tonight, he will become a man," Fisher explains.

My mind instantly goes to all the burglaries that had resulted in rape, and my stomach sinks.

I close my eyes, summoning a deep breath. I will die before I let that happen to me. My mum told me about Aunt Kayla and the trauma she lived through when I was a teenager. I had wondered why she was wary around men other than my dad and uncles. She lived through hell and it has stayed with her.

I can't do that.

If he's going to destroy a piece of my soul, there is no way I'm not going down fighting.

"He's just a boy, you sick bastard," I yell, kicking back at Low.

Fisher's lip curls. "You should have listened to Rob when he told you not to poke your nose in."

"They'll know it was you. Nothing you can do to me will make me keep quiet," I warn him, making sure I take in every detail of Kyle and JJ.

Fisher strides forward, grabbing my chin between his thumb and index finger in a bruising grip. "They'll never know I was here. I made sure of it. They'll be too busy trying to detain the group I sent as a distraction so I could slip away and slip back in easily."

I'm unsure whether he knows about our plan.

"Beau will know."

He forces a laugh, his eyes hardening. "You think I didn't know you two put on a show last Monday? The minute you said witness I knew you suspected a dirty cop. I made sure to get rid of any witnesses," he barks.

"The old lady."

He grins. "To be honest, none of us touched her. After I threatened her, I made sure the boys let her see they were watching her. It was luck that she had a heart attack."

"That's why you came to my work," I guess.

"Yes. I'll give it to you, you put on a good show. But I'm better. Let me guess, Beau is waiting at the other location for someone to show up?"

"Yes, so he'll know it's you when you leave here. Someone will have noticed by now that you aren't there."

"Ah, but you see, I made sure to reveal Rob's location at the cattle market to my friends. He will also struggle to explain his whereabouts."

"You arsehole," I scream, dread filling my stomach. "Beau will still know it's you. He isn't stupid. He'll figure it out."

"Maybe, maybe not. Accidents happen all the time in our line of work," he suggests, wiggling his eyebrows.

"And me?" I ask with a sharp bite.

His eyebrows bunch together. "You'll be dead. You'll be no concern after tonight," he tells me, his voice void of any kind of emotion. He turns to Kyle, nodding. "We need to burn the car."

Kyle nods, striding over to the back of the car. He pulls out a canister of petrol and douses the car.

"And me?" Low asks, gripping me tighter. I wince.

Stepping back, Fisher pulls a knife out of his belt, an evil glint in his eye. JJ's hands begin to shake as he slowly raises them, taking the knife from Fisher.

Ruffling the boy's hair, Fisher bends down to meet his gaze. "Are you going to make me and your brother proud tonight?"

"Yes, sir," JJ whispers.

"Good," Fisher grits out, standing up. "Make her suffer."

"You really are going to regret this," I warn, gritting my teeth.

"What, no, 'you can't do this', 'please help me'?" Fisher mocks.

My eyes narrow into slits, staring at him dead on. "No. I don't need to, because you'll be screaming those later. If I don't kill you, my dad or brothers will."

He chuckles, dismissing me, and turns to Kyle. "Get the other tank. We've got a job to do."

"C'mon, bro, let's get this done," Low barks, dragging me deeper into the forest, away from the petrol fumes.

"And don't think you won't regret this either," I yell, before screaming out when my hair is pulled back.

The trees blanket us in darkness, and it takes me a moment to get used to it.

JJ pulls a torch out of his pocket, shining it in front of us as the smell of smoke fills the night air.

Low throws me to the floor and I skid along the ground, grazing my knees and my palms. I dig my fingers into the ground, gripping dirt and stones in my hands before kneeling, ready to make a run for it.

My eyes roll to the back of my head when Low lands a solid kick to my stomach. "I don't think so," he warns me, rolling me onto my back, his blue eyes narrowed down on me.

"Low," JJ whispers, shining the light over me.

"Do it," Low snaps at his brother, crushing my hand into the ground.

I cry out, blinking past the pain as I throw the dirt in my hand up at him. He kicks me again, knocking my teeth together.

"I'm scared," JJ rasps.

"You don't have to do this, JJ," I declare, panting.

"He does," Low barks. "Do it, JJ. You know what will happen to you if you don't."

JJ falls to his knees beside me, his lips trembling as tears fall down his cheeks.

Each time I move, Low presses his booted foot down harder, causing the pain to intensify.

"I have a family," I rush out, staring at JJ. "I'm a triplet, the only girl."

"Shut up," he cries out.

"My mum, she... she loves me. She always wanted a daughter after being with my dad for so long. She was surprised when she also had two boys in there as well."

"Do it," Low yells, slapping his brother across the head.

A sob tears from his throat as he stares down at me, and I try one last time, forcing tears to my eyes. "I'm nine weeks pregnant. Please don't kill my baby too," I lie, having no shame.

"Low," he whispers, staring up at his brother helplessly.

Low kicks me once again. "She's fucking lying, brother. Don't be a fucking wimp and embarrass me now."

He drops the flashlight to the ground, bringing his palm to his eye socket and rubbing in circles.

"They'll kill me if I don't do this. They've done it before. I don't want to die," he whispers brokenly.

My heart clenches at his declaration, and the fear in his voice.

"Do it," I order, my voice firm. "Do it."

His hand trembles as he raises the knife, hovering it above my stomach. "I'm so sorry," he sobs out.

"So am I," I whisper, before moving quickly. I snatch the knife out of his hand with my free one.

I turn, driving the knife into Low's leg, my hand warming as blood spurts through my fingers. His expression is drawn in agony, his mouth open in shock as I pull the knife out. I bring my knees to my chest and kick out. JJ, who is sitting on the balls of his feet in shock, gets my boot to the face.

"You fucking bitch," Low roars, gripping my hair in his hands and yanking.

I scream, and in a jerk reaction, I plunge the knife into his other leg, just above his knee. I drop to the floor, shuffling backwards to move out of his way.

"Fuck," I whisper at the sight of blood.

He sways as he puts one foot forward, before falling to the ground, howling.

I always thought I could stomach defending myself, knowing it would be for the greater good. I mean, life without me would suck. Yet, stabbing someone isn't all it's cracked up to be.

"Low?" Kyle yells, and I hear him moving through the forest.

Crawling forwards, I reach for the torch, gripping it tight when it slips out of my hand. I flick it off, getting to my feet and wobbling my way into the forest.

As the footsteps grow closer, I begin to run, tripping and smacking into branches. I sashay to the left, slinking further into the darkness.

My feet catch on something and I trip, falling to the ground, my sore hand landing in a pile of stingers.

"Fuck," I whisper.

I lift myself off the ground, but when I hear movement close by, I drop back down, holding my breath.

To the side, a small flash of light from a phone can be seen.

"Fisher, you need to get back. She's gone. I am looking." He pauses mid-step, glancing around. "She stabbed him. Fucking stabbed him. No. He's knocked out."

He takes another step away, and I begin to relax, slowly rising to my knees. Twigs snap, echoing around the forest, and I grimace, holding my breath.

Fuck!

There's a stream close by, I can hear it. All I need to do is get there and follow it downstream, where I'll be able to find help.

Slowly, I tilt my head to the side, in Kyle's direction, hoping he hadn't heard me.

My hope is short-lived when I watch him swivel in my direction, turning on the torch on his phone.

It shines in my direction, and I hear him curse, moving towards me.

"Fuck," I grouch, blowing out a breath as I get to my feet and push off into a run, Kyle chasing me.

If he doesn't kill me, running fucking will.

Or I'll kill him for making me run.

THIRTY-ONE

MY LUNGS BURN AS I PUSH my legs harder, dodging trees and bushes. There's no clear path, no guide or trail to follow. And the deeper I push into the forest, the thicker the bushes, stingers and weeds get. The rain isn't my friend either. It's making the ground soggy and my clothes heavy. The only good thing about it is the relief I'm getting from it pouring over my heated body.

I slow into a jog before stopping completely, resting my palms against a tree as I duck my head, panting for air.

Glancing over my shoulder, I scan the area, checking for Kyle. I don't see him, but it doesn't mean he isn't there. He's fast, too fast. I only managed to escape by zigzagging my way through the forest, hoping by chance he would lose me. He did. But I know it won't be long until he catches up again.

They always do.

Sliding my back against the tree, I drop to my arse, resting. My eyes close as I take a deep breath in and exhale.

I'm not made for this. I warned my parents when they refused to write a letter to excuse my absence from P.E. that exercise would be the death of me.

I bet they regret calling me dramatic now.

I have never felt intense pain like I do right now in my legs. My thighs are screaming at me to stop, to put them out of their misery. I'm certain I have cramp in my vagina. I hurt all over.

Instinctively, I palm the side of my head, a hiss slipping through my lips at the surge of pain. When I pull away, my hand is covered in blood. It isn't the only thing bleeding. I must be covered all over with it, and I don't think all of it is mine. My favourite fucking shirt is not only dirty but splattered in Low's blood.

I'm never going to get this fucking out. And it isn't the season to go buy a new one.

I shoot up when the crunch and crack of snapping twigs echoes through the air. My eyes widen as a spot of light in the distance shines. It's Kyle, still shining the light from his phone.

I am done.

I'm done running.

As quietly as I can, I crawl around the tree, ducking out of sight when his figure becomes more solid.

He's close, but so is the stream. The whoosh of running water is my only hope. I only have to get to there and I'll be able to find my way back to a town. There's no way I'm going to die in the woods because I got fucking lost. That is not how my story is going to end.

"Where the fuck are you?" Kyle roars, and for a second, I think he's talking to me, but then he continues. "I'm not going down for this, for you. Yeah? Then where the fuck are you? Okay." He pauses, and I watch him drop the phone to his side, tilting his head back. "Fuck!"

My palms sting as I blindly feel around the ground for a weapon, careful not to make any noise.

I can't keep outrunning him. My soaked clothes are weighing me down, making it harder to move.

He doesn't even sound out of breath, whereas my heart is doing overtime, struggling to catch a breath.

I have to fight.

And as much as my dad is going to give me shit for putting myself at risk, he also taught me fight or flight. And right now, it's fight. All I have to do is injure him enough to slow him down.

Hell, if it wasn't raining, I'd climb a tree and hide out until my dad got here, but I'm not risking my neck over that whooped ass.

I inwardly groan at my choices of weapon. All I have around me that I could potentially use are sticks, branches, stones, and a shit load of ivy.

I force as many stones into my pockets as I can, which isn't many, since today, of all days, I decided to wear the tightest pair of fucking jeans I owned.

They couldn't have kidnapped me on a Simba pyjamas and hoody day?

I want to cheer when my fingers wrap around a thick branch, heavy, yet not so big I can't lift it up. It's the perfect size.

Slowly, I get to my feet, using the tree for support, before resting my back against the bark, listening to the sounds of Kyle's boots drawing closer.

"May the odds be in *my* favour, motha' fucka'," I whisper, barely audible.

It's his light that shines first, next to where I'm standing, so slowly, I raise the branch over my shoulder.

His footsteps get closer and I hold my breath, my heart raising as I steady my hands. Seconds later, his foot comes into view, crunching down on the leaves and twigs, and I swing the branch with as much force as I can muster, aiming for his face.

A squeak passes through my lips when I step out of hiding and see I only hit his chest.

He looks up, his eyes hard.

"How fucking tall are you?" I snap, swinging the branch again.

He sees it coming this time, catching it in his hand while his other snaps out, gripping around my neck like a vice.

"You silly fucking cunt," he growls, throwing the branch away.

"Can't breathe," I rasp, my toes trying to find purchase on the ground.

This is not how I saw this playing out. Not one single bit.

"I'm going to snap your fucking neck," he spits, baring his teeth. "That was my cousin you fucking stabbed tonight."

"Y-you say t-that like I'm s-supposed to c-care," I stutter, fighting for another breath.

I shoot him a venomous look when his grip tightens. Lifting my arms, I slap my palms as hard as I can over his ears, stunning him. He howls, and when he loosens his grip, I use his distraction to my advantage by kicking him in the balls.

I grunt in pain as I drop to my arse on the cold, wet ground.

"You fucking slag," he shrieks, falling to his knees.

"Don't say I didn't warn you," I gasp out, breathing hard.

I use the balls of my feet to push back, twisting my body to the side to try and force myself up. I feel weak, my legs like jelly.

He continues to choke behind me yet still manages to snatch my ankle tight, dragging me towards him. I claw at the ground, forcing myself to move forward, but to no avail.

Screaming out, I reach for the stones in my pocket, lobbing them at him one after the other as I kick out.

I'm tiring. My entire body is. Yet it's all I can do. The adrenaline pumping through my body is giving me no choice but to kick out, even if every kick feels like hitting rock.

Frustration pours through me when he continues to overpower me, crawling over my body like he has every God given right. My hips twist side to side as he straddles the bottom of my legs, blocking me from using them.

"Get the fuck off me, you little bitch," I shrill, slapping at him with no direction. I hit anywhere I can reach, not stopping.

"It's nothing personal," he sneers, punching me in the gut.

"Oh, this is so fucking personal. And you have no idea what hell you've just rained down on yourself," I scream, sitting up long enough to grab his face, digging my nails into skin.

Spasms rock his body as I dig my thumbs into his eye sockets, using enough pressure to cause pain yet not enough that I have to deal with eyeball goo and blood on my thumb for the rest of my life.

A bloodcurdling scream tears from his throat as he pulls back, dropping to the ground on his side.

"I'm going to rip your insides from your body with my bare hands," he roars, so loud it echoes through the trees.

I kick him the rest of the way off me before rolling to my hands and knees and standing on shaky legs. I bend over, looking down at him curled into a fetal position, and scoff.

"You should have done your homework before coming after me, but then that would mean actually doing work," I snap, bending down to pick up his forgotten phone.

I race off into the darkness, pulling the flashlight out of my pocket when I get far enough away to turn it on.

Stopping for a moment, I quickly dial Dad's number before continuing to run parallel to the stream.

"Not a good time," Dad snaps in greeting.

"Dad, it's me again," I pant. "Are you close?"

"Are you dying? Why do you sound like you're dying?" he asks, his tone going high.

"What?" Liam yells.

"I'm running," I grouch. "That's why."

"Didn't I tell you to listen to me? Didn't I?" he gloats.

"Dad, what's happening?" Liam yells.

"I told you to stay in shape," Dad finishes.

"Are you fucking kidding me right now, Dad? And there's nothing wrong with my body. It's a fucking hot body and I don't feel the need to torture it."

"Just saying. Let this be a lesson to you."

"I didn't ask to be kidnapped," I sputter, ducking under a branch.

"Well, you sound like you're dying. How did you get free? You are free, right?"

I grin, stepping past a rock. "I stabbed one in the leg, twice, knocked another out, and just clawed the eyes out of another."

"I'm proud, baby girl. Please tell me it was this Fisher guy who you stabbed."

"She stabbed a guy?" Liam squeaks, sounding closer to the phone. "Why does she have all the fun?"

"No, it wasn't. I don't know where he is, Dad. And it won't be long until Kyle comes after me again. Fucker is tall."

"Where are you?"

The low battery warning rings in my ear, and I groan. "Dad, the battery is going to die any second. I'm heading downstream—"

A hand smacks into my windpipe, knocking me off my feet and to the floor. I inhale sharply, staring up at the trees and night sky, stunned.

"Hayden? Hayden?" I hear Dad yell from the phone next to me on the ground.

My hand rests on my throat as I gasp for air, struggling to focus on the figure looming above me.

When Fisher comes into focus, stamping his foot over the phone, I glare, gritting my teeth together. "Are you fucking kidding me?"

Pure anger radiates from him as he watches me in annoyance. "You've been more trouble than it's worth. I guess I'll have to end you myself."

The kick to my side has me rolling over. It feels like sharp blades stabbing into my lungs.

I blow leaves and dirt out of my mouth before tilting my head to the side and narrowing my eyes at Fisher. "You should never have sent a man to do a woman's job."

"That's not the—"

"Kung fu, mother fucker," I rasp, kicking my leg out as hard as I can, aiming for his groin. I hit my target perfectly.

A cry escapes my lips at the pain shooting up my leg. I don't wait for him to recover or pick up the torch or phone. I push up, shakily taking a step, then another, before pushing into a run, my entire body feeling like jelly.

I know it won't keep him down for long. Men like him always manage to find a way back up.

My dad will come.

He always does.

THIRTY-TWO

CLAYTON

THE DARK SKY RUMBLES WITH thunder above us, the lightening illuminating the top of the trees. Rain comes down in sheets, making it hard for us to see past the headlights.

If this isn't a bad omen, I don't know what is.

Leaves and fallen twigs scatter across the road and car as the wind pushes them around and out of the forest.

It's crazy, and Hayden, my wild card, who I have come to know and love, is out in it, having God knows what done to her.

Images, none of which are good, are running through my mind. I need to get to her. Not knowing if she's okay is killing me, and for the first time in my life, I feel a rage inside of me that I have never felt before.

I might be an uptight guy when it comes to work, but I never get angry. I'm not one of those guys who finds joy in pounding on another guy. Right now, it's all I can think about. I want to wrap my hands around the neck of the guy who is responsible for all of this.

She might be feisty, but she's small. There's only so much she can take, not only to her body, but to Hayden as a person. Even the strongest can break.

A message from Walker pops up on Beau's phone.

I lean forward, replaying the message to Beau, who is driving. "They've found Rob. He was tied up not far from the cattle market. Apparently, they planned to go back to untie him once they had the go ahead from Fisher. I guess the kids are already talking."

"Fuck!" Beau growls, sagging back against his seat. He grips the steering wheel, his knuckles turning white. "It was so he wouldn't have an alibi for his whereabouts. Fisher made sure all the evidence would point to Rob."

His phone rings, cutting the rest of what he was going to say off. I swipe my finger across the phone to answer when I see it's Max.

"Do you have her?" I rush out, leaning forward in my seat.

"We're here. There's a burnt-out car not far from where the last phone signal was. Liam has called your boss to bring others here. They're on their way."

"What about Hayden?" I growl, tapping my foot relentlessly on the mat of the car. "Is she okay?"

"Don't take that tone with me, fancy pants. I'm going to find her. She's *my* daughter. Which is how she managed to get a phone and call me. She's heading downstream, whatever fucking direction that is," he explains, sounding out of breath.

"Stop the car!" I blurt out, unclipping my belt.

Beau hesitates. "We're nearly there."

"What's pretty boy crying over now? Hayden hates sissies, you know," Max interrupts.

"She's going downstream," I yell, stressed because none of them seem to be as strung up as me about this. Hayden is in danger. "Stop the car, now, Beau. I'm going to head into the woods from this end. We'll have more chance of finding her."

"Shit! He's right. Pull over," Landon barks.

Beau pulls over to the side of the road, clicking on his hazards. "Quick, I'm going to carry on and meet Liam and the others."

We jump out of the car, into the pouring rain, and race across the road, taking a leap up the wall made of stones, branches and wire.

My fingers slip on the rock above me, and I lose my footing. Hanging on by one hand, I struggle to keep a grip until a hand wraps around my wrist, pulling me up.

"Cheers."

He grunts, not looking impressed. "You really should start working out. Hayden is always getting herself into crazy situations."

"I do!" I snap, pushing off the ground and into a run, holding my phone out with the torch on.

"And a word of warning," he yells, wiping rain from his face. "You hurt her and survive what she will do to you, me and Liam will come for you."

"Got it," I hiss, before mumbling, "Loud and clear."

After sprinting for a good five minutes through the heavy rain, we come to a stop.

"We could be looking in the wrong direction," Landon snaps before cupping his hands around his mouth and yelling, "Hayden!"

"Shush," I order, holding my index finger up when he goes to moan at me again. "Listen!"

The sound of gushing water echoes in the air, letting us know we are close. With recent floods, the stream that was there was probably deep enough to swim in and is no doubt flowing too fast for Hayden to cross it.

My gaze locks with Landon's when the wind carries the sound of a tortured scream. We both barrel towards the sound, our feet picking up dirt as we fly through the trees.

The sound of the stream gets louder, the water angrily flowing downstream when we shoot through a small clearing.

Up ahead, Hayden comes into view, and a smile pulls at the corner of my lips. So much relief pours through me that I slow a little, taking in the moment, glad she's okay.

She's really okay.

I hadn't allowed myself to let all the fear in. I locked it in a box and closed it away, knowing that if I let it in, I wouldn't be able to think straight.

My smile drops the second a man steps into view, stepping closer to Hayden. My heart catches in my throat when she sways, looking weak and tired.

"I'll get you for this," she screams, clawing at his face when he grabs her.

"Hayden!" I yell, swallowing down the fear.

His reply is drowned out by the thunder rumbling in the sky, the sound bouncing off the trees. I push myself harder, keeping in line with Landon as we race to get her.

When the guy—who I assume is Fisher—grabs her around the neck and begins to walk her backwards, so she's at the edge of the raging water, terror sucks the air from my lungs.

"No, no, no," I repeat when I realise we aren't going to reach her in time. "Hayden!"

Just as we're metres away, Max comes speeding through the trees, using the distraction of me calling out to her to tackle Fisher to the ground.

My heart shudders in relief, until my gaze lands back on Hayden. Her eyes widen as she realises she's going to fall, her arms flailing in the air.

"No!" I scream, not knowing how far that fall goes.

"Hayden," Landon roars.

Without thinking, Landon and I both follow, jumping over the edge and into the water. Icy cold needles stab me all over as I surface, gasping for breath.

"Fuck," I curse, feeling my muscles tighten.

I tread water, searching for Hayden when I can't see her. Hayden can swim. I know she can. Yet she's nowhere to be found.

"Where is she?" I ask a pale-faced Landon, who has just come up for air.

He's just about to duck back under when something catches his attention. "There!" he yells, pointing a little further down the stream.

I draw in a long breath when I see the sight of her, face down, unmoving in the water and somehow snagged on a fallen tree.

The water slams against my back as I freeze. I can't lose her. I just got her.

"No," Landon chokes out before swimming his way over to her.

I push forward, kicking my feet with gusto as I swim over to her. I turn her around as Landon works on freeing her.

"Please, God, no," I pant, blinking rain out of my eyes.

I rest her head against my shoulder, and a whimper escapes my lips when I see one side of her face is smeared in blood. It's not even her only injury. Bruises are forming on her neck, clearly outlining the hand that must have wrapped around her throat in a vice-like grip, yet she came crashing through those trees, exhaustion tearing at her with every stride, and still she held her ground when that fucker caught up with her. Her palms are scraped raw, yet dirt and blood are caked beneath her nails, evidence she clawed at someone. I can see she fought back, and she fought well.

"We can't risk trying to go back upstream to the others. The current is too strong," Landon explains, helping me keep her head above water when it begins to rise.

"Can you get up there?" I yell, jerking my head towards the wall of rock, mud and roots from bushes and trees.

"Landon," Liam yells, skidding to a stop above us.

I cover Hayden, protecting her from the stones and dirt that break off, falling over us.

Leaning back, I wipe the hair off her face, giving her a little shake. "Wake up. Please, wake up."

"She's not fucking sleeping," Landon snaps, pulling at some ivy wound around some branches.

"Holy fuck!" Beau curses, coming to a stop next to Liam.

"Help her," I plead, coughing when a gush water splashes over us and into my face.

"Liam, get down on your stomach and lean over the edge. I'll hold onto your legs so you can reach down. Grab Landon first," Beau orders.

"No, get Hayden. I don't know if she's breathing," I argue, kissing her temple.

"Oh God," Liam moans, staring down at her from his position on his stomach. He looks pale, his chin trembling.

"We need the help to get her up. She's unconscious," Beau snaps, gripping Liam's ankles.

I grip onto a load of ivy and branches, keeping us close to the side as Landon climbs up with Liam's help. There is no way I'm willing to risk the water sweeping us away. It feels like it's angry at us, punishing us as it tears its way downstream.

"Hold her up," Liam strains out, his face red.

I heave her up over my head as much as I can. "You got her?"

"Got her," Liam wheezes, dragging her up with Landon's help.

I drop my chin to my chest, inhaling and exhaling deep breaths.

She's safe.

I'm not going to lose her.

"C'mon, man," Liam yells, reaching down to me.

I grasp his wrist as he grabs mine. "Thanks."

"Don't look so surprised," he rasps out, heaving me up. "I didn't want her to skin me alive because I left you to swim with the fishes. And she has a thing for kneeing guys in the balls when they piss her off."

I fall to my stomach when I reach the top, my heart stopping at the sight of Landon doing compressions.

"Come on, Hayden," he shouts, pushing his hands down on her chest.

"No, no, no," I hiss, crawling over to her, running my hand over her hair.

Her body is too small for the force he is using. With each jerk of her body, my heart lurches.

"No," Max croaks, swaying next to the man responsible for all this, his broken gaze on his daughter.

Fisher splutters out a laugh before spitting blood to the ground. "Got the bitch."

My heels rise from the ground, ready to tear into the callous human being, but the animalistic sound that tears from Max's chest, stops me.

I've never seen rage like it. Hayden warned me her dad could get mad when one of them were hurt, but nothing could have prepared me for the sight before me. His face morphs into something I don't recognise as he turns to Fisher, his jaw clenched.

He headbutts him, screaming in his face. "I'm going to tear you apart."

Hayden flinches beneath me, and I glance down, my heart racing before the most beautiful sound ever reaches me.

She lifts her head, coughing as water spills out of her mouth.

"Thank God. Thank God," I breathe out, my shoulders shaking as a low groaning sound bubbles from my throat. "Thank you."

I pepper kisses all over her face, my eyes filling with tears as Landon falls on his arse beside her, his knees drawn to his chest.

"Max, he's unconscious," the older Liam drawls, striding over to us.

"I thought I told you to stay with the others," Beau growls, his brows pinching together.

"The police have them. They've called social services to come sit with the boy. Turns out, the brother has custody of him. He's shook up."

"Is the ambulance here?"

"No, I've called it. I told them to meet us on the road, in case Hayden was hurt. Is she okay?" he asks, stepping closer, his expression drawn tight as he glances down at Hayden.

"She died," Liam, her brother, croaks. "You all need to stop fucking dying."

"We should get her to the road. They won't be able to get here," he explains.

I run my hands over her hair, tears streaming from my eyes. "Hayden, I'm here. I'm here. It's okay," I assure her.

Max skids to his knees next to me, gently running his palm down her cheek. "You're okay. You're okay," he chants, staring down at her.

"Stop being a pussy," she rasps, her voice husky as she squeezes my hand.

"I told you she doesn't like sissies," he reminds me, wiping the tears from his cheeks.

"Dad," she whispers hoarsely.

"It's okay. We can toughen him up if you decide to keep him."

"I'm not going anywhere," I growl, glaring at him.

He arches is eyebrows at me, his lips twitching in amusement. "If I wanted you gone, you'd be gone. The only reason I haven't is because she can hold a grudge. And as mad as she'll get at me, she'll miss me more. No one should be deprived of my company," he says, his attention returning to Hayden. A few quiet seconds pass before he adds, "She loves me more than she loves you."

Hayden makes a noise in the back of her throat. "Make him stop," she croaks.

Gently lifting her badly bruised hand in his, he presses a kiss to the top. "You need to stop doing this to me. Why can't you get knocked up like normal girls?" he argues, kissing her forehead.

"Dad…"

"Yes, baby?"

"When I get some energy, can you remind me to slap you?"

He bumps his forehead against hers, smiling wide. "There's my girl."

Someone approaching snags my attention, and I look up, lips parting when Maverick steps out of the shadows, dragging an unconscious guy by the hand.

"Found this one trying to escape," he announces, before sucking in a breath at the sight of his niece, his eyes filling with pain.

I help Hayden when she tries to sit up, letting her rest against my chest.

"So you beat him?" Beau asks, arching an eyebrow. "My paperwork is going to last me weeks."

He shrugs, letting go of the guy's wrist. It thumps to the ground. "He pissed me off by going after my niece." He looks to Max, his expression downcast. "And I had to show someone how sorry I was."

Max looks over at Hayden, who's teeth begin to chatter. He takes his coat off, wrapping it around her shoulders.

"Let's get her to the ambulance," Max announces. "And Maverick?"

"Yeah?"

"I'm sorry. I was just—I was…"

"Trust me, I get it."

"I'll get Fisher," Beau declares.

"No you fucking won't," Max snaps. "As much as I'd love to carry my daughter out of here, I want to make sure that fucker isn't going anywhere."

"Max, his hands are tied up," Beau reminds him. "And handcuffed."

"Is that ivy?" Landon asks, squinting.

Max puffs his chest out, nodding. "Fucker won't think of messing with me or mine again."

"I'll run back for the car and meet you on the road," Liam tells us, turning to younger Liam, who still looks lost. "You want to come?"

"I'm not leaving Hayden," he tells him, his voice low.

I pick Hayden up and cradle her in my arms, and her eyes flutter open. "Yay," she cheers weakly. "I don't have to walk."

THIRTY-THREE

HAYDEN

THE FLASHING BLUE LIGHTS FROM the ambulance are causing my head to spin. I shove the paramedic's hand away when he goes to shine the light in my eyes again.

"Let me check you over," he argues, lifting his hand again.

"Get that out of my face," I snap.

"Miss, please…"

"I'm fine," I croak, looking over his shoulder. "How is he tied to the tree?"

We had arrived at the road at the same time as the paramedics. Instead of lying back on the gurney, I opted to sit in the doorway, wanting to assess my surroundings. I'm still struggling to relax, my body on high alert.

"Ignore that," Clayton whispers, wrapping the foiled blanket tighter around me.

"Why does Dad have a stick?"

The paramedic shakily turns to look. "I thought they took that off him," he whispers.

Clayton shakes his head at me. "I'd say your dad is protecting his cub, but he's not guarding Fisher to protect him. He's making sure no other corrupt cop lets him free or mistakes him for a good guy."

"It was just him," I announce, resting my head against his shoulder. "He's the only cop involved, the one in charge. It was all him."

"It's okay," he soothes, rubbing his hand down my arm.

"No, it's not," I tell him. People lost their lives or are suffering with PTSD because of his choices. All out of anger and greed."

"Tonight could have ended differently," Clayton whispers when the paramedic climbs into the back of the ambulance, mumbling about grabbing a sedative for Dad.

I tilt my head up, narrowing my eyes. "Now is not the time to say I told you so. I'm tired and can't form appropriate comebacks."

"I'm not saying that to you," he assures me, his irises darkening. "I was so fucking scared, Hayden. So fucking scared I had lost you. I had gone outside to apologise to you, and to tell you the good news, and you were gone. I'm a lot of things, Hayden. I can be difficult and moody, but one thing I never considered myself to be is a romantic." He takes a deep breath while my heart pounds against my ribcage, waiting for him to continue. "I love you. I know it's too soon, and I know it's crazy, but that's how you make me feel. Crazy. In the time I've known you, I've been a party planner, a homeless guy, a stranger, a charity case, a stripper, and God knows what else," he tells me, making me grimace.

"I panic when I'm put on the spot like that. And in all fairness, I couldn't help my cousin's neighbour believing me about you being a stripper. You are hot," I rush out.

He kisses me, shutting me up as laughter shines in his eyes for a moment. "Let me finish," he says, exasperated.

Rolling my eyes sends a wave of dizziness through me, so I close them briefly whilst taking a deep breath.

"You've introduced me as a lot of things, but never your boyfriend."

I blink up at him. "Is this where you pass me the note?"

He groans. "Hayden, I'm trying to tell you that I want to be with you. No secrets. No hiding. No waiting. I love you and want us to be together."

"Sorry, but I really wanted the note," I tell him, pouting.

"Then I'll give you the note. But if you were to have it now, what would your answer be?"

I give him a dopey smile. "I'd totally tick yes."

"You're a pain in the arse."

I lean up, pressing my lips to his, sighing at the warmth coming from him. I never wanted to admit it, but I loved him too. It wasn't fear that he could break me that held me back, because I knew deep down in my heart, I'd make him hurt worse. My fear had been to love someone who didn't love me back or couldn't love me because of who I am.

But Clayton, he had seen me at my whacky worst and my crazy best and still loved me. He never put me down for being who I am. He's what my mum is to Dad. He didn't try to change me, he rode along with me.

And someone who could survive four days with my family was worth keeping.

"I love you too. Maybe. Kind of."

He laughs against my lips, pressing a kiss to them before pulling back. "I'll take the 'I love you'."

"Now, what was this good news?"

"It's about your job," he tells me, sitting back a little.

"If you're going to fire me, do it tomorrow," I tell him, closing my eyes at the pain shooting through me.

"No. I'm not going to fire you," he mutters.

"Do you two always argue?" Liam asks, lifting his head up from his knees. "Because I'm exhausted just listening to you."

"Why didn't you leave with Uncle Liam?" I ask him.

He arches an eyebrow, giving me an 'are you serious' look. "We aren't leaving you."

"I'm fine," I groan, even though I know it's pointless. And if this was one of them, I wouldn't leave either.

"Yeah? Wait till you look in a mirror," he snaps. "You aren't fine."

I groan, squeezing Clayton's hand. "Tell me about my job."

"I need to confess something first. I've never disapproved of your proposal. I actually wanted to kick myself for not coming up with it myself."

"Really?"

"Yes," he confirms, giving me a small smirk. "But you know how you're always calling me a jerk?"

"That's who 'Hot Jerk Boss' is in your phone," Liam declares, earning a groan from Landon.

"Will you shut up and let him speak. And we will talk about you snooping later," I snap, narrowing my eyes on him.

He audibly swallows, glancing at Landon, who shakes his head. "She's totally going to kick your arse. And she's stabbed someone now. She'll have the stomach for it."

I whine. "I'm not a serial killer."

Liam grins. "It was badass."

"Anyway," Clayton interrupts, glaring at Liam. "I already told you how I felt about my dad and how I didn't want to let him down. I thought that because he said no, he wouldn't approve."

"He did?" I guess, groaning at the sharp pain in my ribs when I move.

He wraps the sheet around me tighter. "He did. He was waiting for me to approve it. I came to tell you congratulations and that I was sorry for yelling at you."

"You fucking yelled at her?" Landon growls.

"I'm sorry," Clayton declares, lowering his head.

"I'm not made of glass," I tell him. "It will take more than you getting pissed to hurt me."

"Police are here for Fisher," Landon announces, standing up.

I force myself off the back of the ambulance and Clayton tries to pick me back up. "No, I need to go to him."

"You need to rest," he stresses. "You've still not let the paramedic finish looking you over."

"That's because I'm fine."

"No, you aren't," all three tell me.

"Why do you have stones in your pocket?" Clayton murmurs.

"Why are you feeling her arse?" Liam grits out.

"I had to improvise," I explain, blinking up at him. "Please, there's something I really need to say to him."

"Fine," Clayton agrees, letting me lean against him as I lumber my way over to where Dad is guarding Fisher.

"Hayden," Dad warns, blocking me from reaching Fisher.

"Dad, I just need to say something."

He closes his eyes, letting out a breath before leaning in. "Just don't hit him. The police frown upon it," he warns me, eyeing the cop trying to cut Fisher free, before stepping back, swinging the branch up to rest on his shoulders.

I give Dad a curt nod and he steps aside. I walk over to Fisher, bending down, a wide smile on my face. Seeing him bruised and bleeding gives me warm fuzzies.

"What the fuck do you want?"

"I've been dying to say something to you."

"What?" he snarls, rearing back.

I grin wider, letting him see how smug I am. "Gotcha!"

He struggles against his binds, screaming. "You little fucking bitch. You'll regret this. You'll fucking regret it."

I laugh, the gesture burning my lungs, but I do it, wanting to show him he hasn't won. "No. I told you *you'd* regret this. I warned you. Now you'll never get a chance to hurt another person again. I. Got. You."

"I'm innocent," he states, raising his head.

"And I'm an angel," I snap.

Dad bends down next to Fisher, his hands resting between his thighs. He grins, patting Fisher's head, causing him to struggle harder. "You shouldn't have fucked with a Carter."

"Because now you'll be fucked all over," Landon grits out. "In prison."

"Who are you?" Fisher shouts at me, his face red.

"Someone you really shouldn't have messed with," I tell him, wiggling my fingers when the other two cops heave him to his feet. "Bye, motherfucker."

I stagger back when Rob appears out of nowhere, charging at Fisher. "How could you do this?" he yells, taking a swing at him.

Dad winces. "That's got to hurt."

"Dad?"

"Yes, baby."

"Did you call Mum?" I ask, my vision blurring a little.

He tenses, drawing in a sharp breath. "She's going to fucking kill me."

"Why didn't you come to me?" Rob barks out, storming over to us.

"Hey," Landon snaps, shoving him back a little.

I grimace. "I couldn't. You know I couldn't. I never believed it was you. But could I put another life on it? No! Beau didn't think it was you either."

"You should have come to me," he argues, scanning me from head to toe, guilt flashing in his eyes.

"You would have done the same," I whisper.

"It's all over. We have them all," he informs me.

Reality hits me like a train, and I sway on my feet. "It's over? It's really—"

"Hayden!" is roared in my ears before my world turns black.

I WAKE UP TO the brutal sound of my mum shrieking. I open my eyes, watching as she slaps Dad's chest over and over again, tears streaming down her face.

"How could you leave without telling me, Max? She's my daughter."

"I'm sorry. So fucking sorry," he tells her.

"Hey," Maverick whispers, pulling my attention away from my mum and dad.

I glance around, surprised to find only Maverick in here. "Where?" I croak, my throat dry.

"We're at the hospital. You passed out. Everything's fine and you can go home once the two-hour observation is up."

"The others?"

"Everyone is out in the waiting area, but Clayton and your brothers have gone to get a hot drink."

"You okay?" I whisper when his face drops.

"He's mad at me. He blames me and he has every right to. I kept it from him as revenge for getting my son arrested."

"You didn't know this would happen. It's not your fault," I murmur, squeezing his hand.

He forces a smile, yet the sadness is there, bright and open for everyone to see. "I've been through hell and back with my brothers. Our childhood was not like yours until we lived with our granddad. I've done all I can to make sure they have everything they need to thrive, to survive, to live. I failed to protect them during a time when they really needed me to, and I've worked my hardest to make up for that. But I let him down. He nearly lost Landon, and tonight, he nearly lost you. I failed him. Again. Failed him in a way he will never be able to forgive."

"He will. He loves you."

Maverick's eyes mist over. "When you have kids, you'll understand. He loves you more. And as much as I regret my choice, I'm proud of how you fought tonight. Just… please, don't do it again. We need you to be okay."

I startle at Dad's booming voice. "Damn straight she won't be doing it again."

I smirk at Maverick. "Yeah, Dad said I can get pregnant."

Dad chokes on a breath, wheezing when he glances up at me. "It was a stressful moment. I didn't mean it."

I shrug. "You said it now. You can't take it back."

Maverick gets up, leaning over to kiss my forehead as Mum rushes to the other side of me. "I'll give these some room and go wait in the waiting area."

"I'm sorry, Mav," Dad chokes out, his eyes glassing over.

Maverick stops in front of him. "You were right. I should have told you."

"No, I, um…" He stares at Mum, gulping. "I overreacted. Kind of. I mean, she's my daughter. I had a right to get mad."

Maverick stops Dad, pulling him in for a hug. "Forgive me."

"Dude, I'm a married man," Dad yells, forcing a laugh when Maverick turns red at all the eyes watching on.

"Love you too, dickhead."

"Honey, you need to stop doing these things. It's not good for my health," Mum stresses, kissing the good side of my head.

"I'm sorry, Mum."

"You didn't say sorry to me," Dad grumbles.

"Leave her alone, Max. Can't you see she's injured?"

"See it? The entire fucking hospital can see it," he booms.

"Dad," I groan, wincing at the pounding in my head.

Mum bursts out crying, and I shake my head. "Mum, I'm fine."

"I can't keep going through this. I'll never make it without you. Without any of my kids."

"What about me?" Dad argues, sitting up.

"Mum?" I call out, smiling.

"I can't. I can't lose you. Any of you," she wails, clutching my hand.

"And me, right?" Dad asks, his voice getting a little louder. He looks utterly dejected.

"I'm fine, Mum. I promise. And it's not something I plan on ever going through again. Running through rain, in a forest when it's pitch black, is not as easy as it looks. Movies fucking lie. I have a whole new view on horror movies now. I understand why those fuckers die or get found," I rant, my sore legs reminding of the hell I went through. "Running! Running gets them fucking killed."

"Oh, baby," Mum cries.

"And I'm hungry. Really hungry," I declare, resting back on my pillow. "I've not eaten all night."

Mum looks out of the room, searching for someone. "Let me go ask a doctor if you can eat." She gets up, leaning down to kiss me. "I love you."

"Love you too, Mum."

Dad rests his elbows on the bed. "She meant me too, right?"

I chuckle at his downcast expression. "Dad, I love you too."

"I know you do. But, girl, hear me when I say this, don't do this shit again. You're small, and you're mighty, but you're not invincible. Tonight could have gone seriously wrong, and call me selfish, but I'd rather you die old, in bed, and not over something that isn't your fight."

"Dad, you don't mean that," I remind him, giving him a pointed look. He always told us to fight for what we believed in, even if it was to save the lives of ants.

"No. Yes. No." He shakes his head, groaning. "What you did was brave, yes, but, girl, it was dangerous. You could have come to any one of us for help."

"I know," I whisper, flashes of images running through my head of the knife JJ held.

"I'm pissed at you for not coming to me, but I understand your need to do this alone. I'm just so fucking glad you're okay. If anything ever happened to you, I'd never forgive myself."

"I'm sorry, Dad."

"Is this a bad time?" Clayton asks, stepping through the curtain.

"Yes," Dad answers.

I smile. "No."

He heads over to the space where Mum was just standing, dropping a drink on the cabinet next to the bed.

Dad leans down, kissing my head. "I'll go see what's taking your mum so long."

"You're going to get food, aren't you?"

He grins. "I burnt off my daily calories chasing after you through the woods. What did you expect? I'm a growing man."

I chuckle. "You don't count calories."

"I don't need to. I just know," he tells me, turning to leave.

"Wait," I call out. "I stabbed a guy. Will I be arrested?"

Dad frowns, walking back over to me and grabbing my hand. "No. It was self-defence. And even if it wasn't, those fuckers have enough on their hands explaining a dirty cop." Sighing, he gives my hand a squeeze. "And if it were me, I would have stabbed him in the chest. You kind of dropped the ball there."

"Really?" Clayton mutters dryly.

"Are the police here?"

"They are. They need to ask a few questions, but Beau has got them to come back later in the day for a full statement."

I nod, coughing. "Thanks for coming to save me."

"I promised you I'd always be there, didn't I?"

I grin. "You really did."

He looks over at Clayton. "If you hurt her——"

"And I survive what she does to me, you'll come after me. I know," Clayton finishes. "I've been told that a lot tonight."

Dad shakes his head. "Don't fuck it up then," he warns him, before glancing down at me. "Are you sure about him?"

I smile, knowing this is coming from the sensible side of my dad. "I am, Dad. Now go get me some food."

"Do all of your family have violent tendencies?" Clayton asks when Dad leaves.

"Yes. I told you, we're all crazy."

"How are you feeling?"

"Sore, but good. As soon as my aunt turns up with my clothes, I'm going home. I want to put on my Captain America pyjamas and go to sleep. In *my* bed."

"Yeah, about that… I'll be staying with you. Your mum is outside now, ordering your brothers to go make up your old room at hers."

I groan, closing my eyes. "She isn't?"

He chuckles, lifting the blanket higher up my chest. "She is. And I don't want to get in her bad books by demanding that I'll be the one staying with you."

"Chicken," I tease.

His eyebrows shoot to his hairline. "Nope. Clever. I watched your dad tie a man to a tree today using ivy and rope from the back of Liam's car. I'm never going to underestimate him again."

"I still can't believe you came for me," I admit, feeling sleepy.

"I'll always come for you," he replies, pressing his lips to mine. "I have something for you."

"Please tell me it's chocolate cake with sprinkles."

Laughing, he shakes his head before reaching into his back pocket and pulling out a piece of paper and a pen. "I need you to answer."

I take the note and pen, laughter spilling from my lips.

WILL YOU BE MY GIRLFRIEND?

TICK YES

TICK NO

"I don't know," I mumble, frowning down at the paper. "This seems like a big commitment."

"Hayden," he growls, leaning down a little.

Laughter spills out of me as I tick the 'yes' box. "It's yes. Always yes."

And it would be. If I have learned anything from tonight, it's that life is too short. I have to grab on to life while I can, and I want to do that with Clayton by my side, for as long as he wants me.

This chapter of our lives may have ended, but for us as a couple, it's just the beginning.

And I can't wait to find out what our next adventure will bring.

EPILOGUE

MADDOX

MADISON STRIDES INTO THE KITCHEN, helping herself to the food in my cupboards. She pulls out bag of Doritos before leaning back against the counter.

"You really need to let us do something about your neighbours."

I grunt, tying up my trainers. "Do you think I haven't tried? Nothing phases them. The council aren't doing anything. I really don't want to turn to drastic measures, but with the way they've been, I'm gonna have to."

"Did you turn their water blue yet?"

Grinning at my kind yet devious sister, I nod. "Yes. I broke in a few months ago and made sure to clog all their drains with crap, hoping the smell would drive them out."

She picks up a dirty sock off the side, throwing it to the floor. "You really need to hire someone to come and clean this place at least once a week."

"Lily helped, but now that arsehole monopolizes her time."

"He's her husband," she explains, grinning.

"And I'm her best friend."

The music next door gets louder, and I groan, my head pounding. It has been like this all night and most of the morning.

"Why don't we cut their electric?"

"I will tonight if they haven't passed out blind drunk. Though I'm worried the electrical company have someone watching the place."

Laughing, she steps away from the counter, grabbing her jacket. "How many times have you done it?"

I grin. "Too many. But it's fun to watch them lose it."

"What about just going around with Dad and having a word?"

"Because I went around with Landon and that word turned into a brawl in the street. We were lucky one of the neighbours witnessed it, as they tried to place the blame on us."

"Wait, wasn't that when you suspected one of them of stealing your tools?"

"I know it was one of them."

"You've been putting up with this for nearly year. You look shattered, Maddox."

"Well, their time is up because I'm done waiting for the council to find a place they haven't already been removed from."

We walk down the hallway and I stop near the door, grabbing my keys off the hook Mum bought me when I finished doing the house up.

"Uncle Max needs an outlet. You should set him on them," she tells me as she waits for me to lock up.

Laughter spills out of me. "Is he still calling Hayden every five minutes to make sure she took her birth control?"

"Yes," she admits, laughing. "She's dreading today."

Today we're going to a party Clayton is throwing in celebration of Hayden's new job and success. It has been two weeks since she was kidnapped, and in that time, her life has changed. People had read her story, and she's now all people can talk about.

Next door's son, who not long ago turned eighteen, skids his car up the curb, over my drive and onto his. He parks carelessly over their driveaway, which is filled with upturned cobble and dirt.

"Is he even old enough to drive?"

"Yes, but I don't think the little bastard has a licence, and I'm pretty sure the car is stolen. Not one of them work."

"Yo, you got a problem, mate?" the guy yells, glaring over the hood of his car.

"I'm staring at it," I tell him, grinning.

He looks behind him like the dickhead he is before turning back to us, his gaze running over Madison.

"Want to come party?"

"With you?" she squeaks.

He flashes his yellow, crooked teeth when he smiles at her. "I can show you a good time."

"With you?" she repeats.

"Yo, you dumb?"

"If I were to go with you, yes. Yes, I would be," she explains, wiggling her fingers at him as she laughs. "Toddle along."

"Kayne, where's my beer?" a woman yells from the front door, a beer can in hand. She's in her forties and wearing a short black tank top with a pair of leggings that flash off her podgy belly.

Us forgotten, Kayne grabs a bag from the backseat before running up to his mum.

Madison whistles through her teeth. "Lovely family."

"Come on, we don't want to miss the fun when Clayton and Hayden share the news that they've moved in together."

"They're going to announce that?" she asks, confused when we reach my car.

"No, I am. But it's for their own good."

I don't hear her reply as I stop short next to the passenger side of my truck. A car pulls into the drive across the road, a house my uncle had bought but has stayed empty until now. I had finished the repairs a month ago, and I was surprised when he didn't sell it on.

Sheer black hair is the first thing I notice, before a woman with a banging body steps out, her back to us as she stares up at the house.

She's wearing navy blue trousers and a blue nurse's top, the trousers fitting snug across her round arse.

"Fuck me!"

Madison nudges me. "You don't have a chance."

I glare down at her. "Of course I fucking do. I'm a fucking catch. There isn't anyone I can't get into bed."

"You won't."

"Watch me. I'll go over there, beg her to look at my wounds, and she'll be naked within minutes."

A snort of disgust and amusement comes from her. "You worry me sometimes. You don't even have an injury."

I wink, smirking. "I won't need one once I turn the charm on."

"You're shit out of luck. Your charm won't work on her."

I rear back, my pride wounded. "Why do you need to be so negative? Of course she'll want me."

"*She's* pregnant," Madison reveals, grinning.

My head swivels back to the woman. She's standing near the boot of her car, her hand rubbing the bottom of her back. I lower my gaze to her perfectly round stomach, my shoulders sagging in defeat.

"Fucking hell."

Slapping me on the shoulder, Madison laughs. "It sucks to be you."

She's beautiful, stunning, and if she hadn't turned around, I would never have guessed she was pregnant.

Yet she is, and I have two rules. You don't mess with pregnant or taken women. I don't mind kids, but they scare me. Sunday scares me and I'm her favourite uncle.

It isn't just that though. I have heard so many women bringing men in and out of their child's life. Their children grow attached, and then *boom*! They break up and that child is left confused, wondering why the person they had come to love and look up to has gone. I'd never do that to a child. I never want to be that man.

I've felt this way ever since a young girl, maybe nine or ten, showed up at the lot, asking for a member of staff who worked for me. Her broken plea for him to see her was hard to witness. He wasn't nasty about it, but he wasn't nice either when he said she needed to go home, that he and her mum were no longer an item after five years of being with each other.

So yeah, that's why I stay away from pregnant or single mums.

I shudder when her forest green eyes snap my way. Her smile drops for a second, before she composes herself, raising her arm to wave.

"Yep, you don't have a chance. Even if she was single."

I give the woman a chin lift before pushing Madison into the truck. "You know me, I don't do anything other than one-night stands anyway."

"She's pretty," Madison comments.

She's wrong. She isn't pretty. She is stunning. But that doesn't matter. I never fuck with women who have kids.

"Want to hit the drive-through?" I ask, changing the subject as I reverse down my drive.

"Yes, I'm starving. Hope already messaged to say Max and the triplets are already on the food."

I force a smile at the woman standing next to her boot, still watching us, her rich black hair blowing around her.

Yep, whoever she's with is one lucky fucker.

AUTHOR'S NOTE

I really hope you guys enjoyed Hayden's story as much as I did writing it. You can't begin to imagine how relieved and excited I am to have her story published. And her cover? WOW. Nothing short of amazing. I'm absolutely besotted with it. Cassy at Pink Ink Designs is incredible.

If you enjoyed her story, please, please leave a review on the platform you bought it from. It helps not only authors but encourages other readers to read the series.

To those who continue to love and support this series, THANK YOU. It means a lot to me that you guys enjoy this kind of crazy. Your messages over this series make me laugh to no end. It's an overwhelming moment when I get to see the book through your eyes. It's why I love reading your reviews. Never hesitate to reach out.

As you might have guessed, Maddox is next. It's also the next book I am writing, which I am excited to get started on for you all.

I know some of you are wondering when the next Take a Chance book will be released. I'm hoping to get to the next one soon.

If you would like to keep up to date with my WIP, then you are welcome to join my readers group of Facebook: Lisa's Luscious Readers.

Lastly, as always, I want to thank my editor, Stephanie. YOU ARE AMAZING, my little midget. Thank you for giving me the inspiration to deliver Hayden the way she was meant to be portrayed. You helped bring life to a character who is nearly as crazy as you are. Thank you for being awesome.

Lurves you.

ABOUT THE AUTHOR

Lisa Helen Gray is Amazon's best-selling author of the Forgotten Series and the Carter Brothers series.

She loves hanging out, but most of all, curling up with a good book or watching movies. When she's not being a mum, she's a writer and a blogger.

She loves writing romance novels with a HEA and has a thing for alpha males.

I mean, who doesn't!

Just an ordinary girl surrounded by extraordinary books.

OTHER BOOKS BY LISA HELEN GRAY

A Carter Brother Series
Malik – Book One
Mason – Book Two
Myles – Book Three
Evan Book 3.5
Max – Book Four
Maverick – Book Five

A Next Generation Carter Brother Novel
Faith – Book One
Aiden – Book Two
Landon – Book Three
(Read Soul of my Soul next)
Hayden – out now

Take A Chance
Soul of my Soul

I Wish
If I could I'd Wish it all Away
Wishing For A Happily Ever After

Forgotten Series
Better Left Forgotten – Book One
Obsession – Book Two
Forgiven – Book Three

Whithall University
Foul Play – Book One
Game Over – Book Two
Almost Three – Book Three

Kingsley Academy

Wrong Crowd – Book One

Crowd of Lies – Book Two

Printed in Great Britain
by Amazon

80389139R00185